NORTHANGER ABBEY

Jane Austen
After the portrait by Cassandra

NORTHANGER ABBEY

Jane Austen

Second Edition

edited by
Claire Grogan

broadview literary texts

National Library of Canada Cataloguing in Publication Data

Austen Jane, 1775-1817
    Northanger Abbey

2nd ed.
(Broadview literary texts)
Includes bibliographical references.
ISBN 1-55111-479-8

I. Grogan, Claire, 1961-   II. Title   III. Series
PR4034.N7 2002   823'.7   C2002-900673-2

Broadview Press Ltd. is an independent, international publishing house, incorporated in 1985.

North America:
P.O. BOX 1243, Peterborough, Ontario, Canada K9J 7H5
3576 California Road, Orchard Park, NY 14127
TEL: (705) 743-8990; FAX (705) 743-8353;
E-MAIL: customerservice@broadviewpress.com

United Kingdom:
Thomas Lyster Ltd.,
Unit 9, Ormskirk Industrial Park
Old Boundary Way, Burscough Road.,
Ormskirk, Lancashire L39 2YW
TEL: (01695) 575112; FAX: (01695) 570120; E-MAIL: books@tlyster.co.uk

Australia:
St. Clair Press, P.O. BOX 287, Rozelle, NSW 2039
TEL: (02) 818-1942; FAX: (02) 418-1923

www.broadviewpress.com

Broadview Press is grateful to Professor L.W. Conolly for advice on editorial matters for the Broadview Literary Texts series.

Broadview Press gratefully acknowledges the financial support of the Ministry of Canadian Heritage through the Book Publishing Industry Development Program.

PRINTED IN CANADA

Contents

Introduction

Northanger Abbey was written and rewritten by Jane Austen over a period of at least twenty years and has since been read and re-read by innumerable others. Not surprisingly it has precipitated a wide range of critical response, both favourable and unfavourable, utilizing almost every conceivable interpretive methodology or strategy. In the novel *Small World* (1984), David Lodge's character Morris Zapp self-aggrandizingly professes to have written the definitive word on Austen:

> I think I can say in all modesty I was *the* Jane Austen man. I wrote five books on Jane Austen, every one of which was trying to establish what her novels meant – and, naturally, to prove that no one had properly understood what they meant before. ... the aim ... was to be utterly exhaustive, to examine the novels from every conceivable angle – historical, biographical, rhetorical, mythical, structural, Freudian, Jungian, Marxist, existentialist, Christian, allegorical, ethical, phenomenological, archetypal, you name it. So that when each commentary was written, there would be *nothing further to say* about the novel in question. (24)

Despite Zapp's confident assertion readers continue to interpret *Northanger Abbey* in a myriad of ways. The aim of this edition is to contextualize *Northanger Abbey* within the political, social and economic concerns of its time to enable the modern reader to better appreciate the comic and political nuances of this Austen novel.

Austen's discussions of novel reading, novel readers, and the nature of the novel, make *Northanger Abbey* the most overtly literary of her works. *Northanger Abbey* centres on the heroine Catherine Morland's development as a reader in the broadest sense. Catherine becomes an adept reader not only of texts but also of people and of situations. But it is not only Catherine who learns about the importance of reading and a judicious choice of reading material since the novel is also an exercise in reading for the reader. Our challenge lies not only in Austen's numerous references to, quotations from, and parodies of other fictional and non-fictional works, but also in the challenge of interpretation itself – the fluidity of language and meaning. Austen demands a sophisticated level of reading on the reader's part to untangle the novel's complex intertextual web and interpret the authorial comments about genres and writers.

Austen's continual play with social and fictional conventions in her novel means that our work as reader parallels that of the heroine herself. As Catherine reads herself in relation to other people, other texts, and other situations so the modern reader must also situate herself in relation to other works, other genres, and other critics' readings. Reading is shown to be a complicated but enjoyable act for all readers of and within the novel.

The Novel's History

According to Cassandra Austen's memorandum, the first manuscript draft of *Northanger Abbey*, entitled "Susan," "was written about the years [17]98 & [17]99." In 1803 Jane Austen sold her manuscript for ten pounds to the publisher Crosby who advertised it in their *Flowers of Literature*: "in the Press, *Susan*; a novel, in 2 vols." For unknown reasons however, "Susan" was never published. It was not until April 1809 that Austen, under the pseudonym Mrs. Ashton Dennis, wrote to Crosby to determine the situation.[1] She acknowledged herself "the Authoress" and enquired why it had never "appeared in print." She even offered to provide another copy should the press have mislaid the original. Her determination to see her work published is apparent in the concluding remark that "should no notice be taken of this address, I shall feel myself at liberty to secure the publication of my work by applying elsewhere." Critics Eileen Morris and Margaret Kirkham deem Austen's pseudonym ("I am, Gentlemen, etc, etc., M.A.D.") most appropriate for venting her spleen about the printing house's delays.[2]

Austen received an abrupt reply that left her in no doubt that if she attempted to publish elsewhere Crosby would take "proceedings to stop the sale." Her only recourse was to repurchase "the MS. ... for the [ten pounds] paid for it." This curt exchange prompted Austen to set "Susan" aside and concentrate on revising "Elinor and Marianne" – a work she published with another publisher and her own money as *Sense and Sensibility* in 1812. It was not until 1816, soon after the publication of *Emma*, that the requisite ten pounds were sent to Crosby and Austen regained her manuscript. She renamed it "Catherine" (prompted perhaps by the publication of the anonymous novel *Susan* in 1809) and wrote a short advertisement to prepare it for publication. This time, however, Austen herself delayed publication. She explains in a letter to her niece Fanny Knight (13 March 1817) that "Miss Catherine is put upon the shelve [sic] for the present, and I do not know that she will ever come out."[3] In fact, "Catherine" remained on the shelf until after Austen's death in July 1817. Only then did her brother Henry, although Cassandra was the executrix, arrange for its posthumous publication as *Northanger Abbey*.

Henry included his sister's advertisement for the 1816 manuscript "Catherine" when he published it as *Northanger Abbey*. The advertisement is a curious piece in which Jane Austen notes that "thirteen years have passed since it was finished, many more since it was begun." Although she does not explain the publishers' behaviour in buying yet not publishing her manuscript, she draws the reader's attention to it. Austen reasons that "some observation is necessary upon those parts of the work which thirteen years have made comparatively obsolete," specifically "places, manners, books, and opinions." In reality Austen's descriptions of place were as accurate in 1816 as they had been in 1803 and apart from the fact Mr. James King was now Master of Ceremonies of the Upper rooms and not the Lower rooms all other observations of Bath life are correct.

Manners well might have changed between the late 1790s and 1816 since English society was undergoing immense social and political upheaval. Rapid industrialisation led to a dramatic increase in urban populations, and the burgeoning middle class promoted booming trade and subsequent demands for luxury goods, publications, and improved living standards. There were also undoubtedly changes in fashion, but Austen's comments about social conduct remain pertinent since she targets general types or characteristics.

Even the many "books" referred to or referenced in *Northanger Abbey* were still understandable and often widely read in 1816. Neither Radcliffe's Gothic novels nor the many Gothic elements would have confused the 1816 reader, as other parodies (Eaton Stannard Barett's *The Heroine*, 1813, Thomas Love Peacock's *Nightmare Abbey*, 1818) were favourably received and many later works employed Gothic elements (Mary Shelley's *Frankenstein*, 1818, Maturin's *Melmoth the Wanderer*, 1820).

Most critics hypothesize that it was Austen's "opinions" that accounted for the publishing delay in 1803 and for Austen's fears that her work was outdated by 1816. Austen certainly does use *Northanger Abbey* to raise issues central to the early revolutionary period (1789-1800) − those of individual rights and responsibilities, intellectual capabilities, the merging of the middle class's values and money with the aristocracy's land and status, morality and education − but while the public were less sympathetic towards any pro-revolutionary ideas in 1816 these revolutionary concerns continued to influence and shape nineteenth-century English society.

The critic Park Honan suggests that Crosby withheld "Susan" from publication because of a conflict of interest.[4] Crosby had not only published Ann Radcliffe's *The Mysteries of Udolpho* (1794) but advertised it as the "most approved Modern Novel." His company not only had a vested interest in maintaining Radcliffe's reputation but had also publicly defended modern fiction from its many detractors. Honan argues that publishing Austen's parody of Gothic and Sentimental fiction would have undermined Crosby's position. This surmise does not, however, satisfactorily explain why the manuscript was initially purchased and advertised.

Margaret Kirkham suggests that Crosby's delay in publishing *Northanger Abbey* had more to do with Austen's support of feminist views, the outspoken "sparkle of intelligence" with which she endows her heroines, and also the outspoken defence of the genre of the novel within her work. Kirkham argues that Austen's concern about "comparatively ... obsolete ... opinions" indicates an awareness that what was pertinent to the feminist debate of the

1790s was largely inappropriate because it was unacceptable by 1816.[5] Anti-revolutionary sentiment had largely quashed feminist activity in England by the early 1800s, and people were increasingly intolerant of any agitation for women's rights or assertions of intellectual or economic independence. Indeed, many still felt it was improper for women to publish or enter public discussions and especially those of a political bent. The posthumous two-volume set of *Northanger Abbey* and *Persuasion* (1818) was the first of Austen's works to be publicly accredited to her since she is named in the Biographical Notice.

However, despite public disapproval of women writers Austen's inclusion of her defence of novels and women novelists suggests that she felt it was pertinent to the 1816 reader.

Austen's concern that "Catherine" reflects social, political, and economic opinions which are too outspoken for the 1816 readership indicates that the historical moment is important. Obviously, if, as some critics argue, her works are apolitical and ahistorical the passage of time would be irrelevant. It is relevant, however, because *Northanger Abbey* includes many references (albeit of a subtle or broad nature) to Austen's society's economic, social, and political situation.

The horrors and riots associated with the revolutionary turmoil in France profoundly affected people across the British Channel. Events happening less than fifty miles away were viewed and discussed with increasing alarm throughout the 1790s. Napoleon Buonaparte's expansionist policy in the early 1800s kept the British Isles under threat of invasion. Numerous passages and phrases in *Northanger Abbey* indicate how the French Revolution and its aftermath affected English society. The Austen family experienced the atrocities of the French Revolution when the Comte de Feuillide, the husband of Jane's favourite cousin Eliza, returned to Paris in 1794. His attempts to defend his friend, the Marquis de Marboeuf, against spurious charges levelled by the revolutionary tribune led to his being guillotined in February. It was this cousin Eliza who later married Jane's brother Henry in December 1797.

The immediacy of the French Revolution meant that many nineteenth-century readers had personal experience of civic disturbance. Events such as the Gordon Riots of 1780 saw an assembly of sixty thousand people in St. George's Fields end in violence. Such expressions of public discontent and government-sanctioned repression continued to occur throughout the early 1800s. One notorious occurrence was an open-air meeting on political reform in St. Peter's Fields, Manchester (1819), which became known as the Peterloo Massacre because eleven people were killed and over four hundred injured. Consequently the famous scene in *Northanger Abbey* in which Catherine's and Eleanor Tilney's misunderstanding prompts a discussion about riots would probably have been read quite differently by nineteenth-century readers than by twentieth-century readers.

Civic disturbance was brought even closer to the Austen household when the same cousin Eliza witnessed a riot in London, June 1792, shortly before visiting Steventon. Her alarm is palpable as she recounts:

> The noise of the populace, the drawn swords & pointed bayonets of the guards, the fragments of brick and mortar thrown on every side, one of which nearly killed my Coachman, the firing at one end of the street which was already begun, altogether in short alarmed me so much that I really have not been well since. The confusion continued all that day & night & the following day, & for these eight & forty hours, I have seen nothing but large parties of soldiers parading up & down this street ... my apprehensions have been that they would set fire to the houses that they were bent on demolishing.[6]

This event bears an uncanny resemblance to the story Henry Tilney invents to laugh away Eleanor's and Catherine's fears because of their misunderstanding. Eleanor misinterprets Catherine's description of a new Gothic publication as "something very shocking indeed [to] soon come out in London" as a reference to an impending riot. Henry, as wise male mentor, clears up this misunderstanding. However his humorous exaggeration of the threatened riot mirrors the real one of Eliza's letter. Henry describes how Eleanor

pictured to herself a mob of three thousand men assembling in St. George's Fields; the Bank attacked, the Tower
threatened, the streets of London flowing with blood, a detachment of the 12th Light Dragoons, (the hopes of the
nation), called up from Northampton to quell the insurgents, and the gallant Capt. Frederick Tilney, in the moment of charging at the head of his troop, knocked off his
horse by a brickbat from an upper window. (127)

Henry's speech is a reworking of the information in Eliza's letter:
a fictional reworking of factual material. His concluding condescending remark that "the fears of the sister have added to the
weakness of the woman" only highlights the difference of interpretation. Although the fictional incident was not in fact based on
an incident of an actual riot, personal experience suggests that it
might easily have been.

As a member of the established order Henry, in his reading of
the "riot" for Eleanor and Catherine, down plays civic disturbance although its existence was all too real for the average person. Henry inflicts his own interpretation onto Eleanor's and
Catherine's misunderstanding to impose a sense of order.

Eleanor's instinctive panic, from an otherwise very restrained
and controlled young lady, indicates how frightened people were
of civic unrest. Since news of such disturbances was often garbled
and intermingled with gossip one had to read carefully to distinguish fact from fiction. While the misunderstanding is clearly
explained to Henry's satisfaction, I expect Austen anticipated some
of her readers would read events differently.

Austen uses fact as fiction in a work traditionally seen as the
development of a young girl's ability to differentiate between fact
and fiction. In so doing Austen shakes our ability to interpret
things in a single, straightforward manner – to differentiate clearly between fact and fiction.

Austen's numerous comments about reading, writing, and
publishing reflect the increased censorship and acts of repression
of the 1790s and early 1800s.[7] The most outspoken gesture is her
defence of the novel at the end of chapter five. The plot is halted
while the narrator defends the novel and women novelists from all

manner of critics. "Let us not desert one another," she pleads with other women writers as she rejects society's assumptions of female inferiority, and defends the novel against its detractors:

> We are an injured body. Although our productions have afforded more extensive and unaffected pleasure than those of any other literary corporation in the world, no species of composition has been so much decried. From pride, ignorance, or fashion, our foes are almost as many as our readers. (59)

Many women novelists portray heroines who mock or abstain from novel-reading (Hervey *Louisa* 1:38-39, Williams *Julia* 2:48) or who read novels with disastrous consequences (Opie *Adeline Mowbray* 1:55, Hays *Memoirs of Emma Courtney* 1:25, Wollstonecraft *The Wrongs of Woman* 1:89).

Such open disparagement reflects the widespread condemnation of novels and novel reading in the late eighteenth century. Educational treatises and conduct books argued that such reading was a gross mismanagement of time which led to the muddling of fiction for reality and overindulged the female reader's sensibility and sense of self importance.

Typical criticisms by educationalists such as John Bennett (*Letters to a Young Lady* 1789) describe novels as "profligate and improper books" which provide "that fatal poison to virtue" (1: 144), while James Fordyce, in his extremely popular *Sermons To Young Women*, terms novels "an infernal brood of futility and lewdness" and "considers "the general run of novels as utterly unfit [for the female reader] as they paint ... loose and luscious ... scenes of pleasure and passion altogether improper for you to behold, even in the mind's eye" (1: 149). He asserts that "she who can bear to peruse [novels] must be in her soul a prostitute, let her reputation in life be what it will" (1: 148-49).

Many women writers also decry the genre. Hannah More notes that "Novels, which chiefly used to be dangerous in one respect, are now become mischievous in a thousand [because] they are continually shifting their ground, and enlarging their sphere" (*Strictures* 1: 32). Austen is not alone in opposing such criticisms, but as Anna Laetitia Barbauld notes in her *Introduction to the British Novelists* (1810) "a collection of novels has a better chance of giving pleasure than of commanding respect" (1:1).

Many women writers limited themselves to a very moderate support of the genre; polemicist and novelist Mary Hays argued that while "the indiscriminate perusal of romances and novels" is unsatisfactory because "the generality of works of this kind are frivolous, if not pernicious ... there are ... many exceptions" (*Letters and Essays* 90). Charlotte Smith is more pointed in her preface to *Letters of A Solitary Wanderer*: "A young woman who is so weak as to become in imagination the Heroine of a Novel, would have been a foolish, frivolous, and affected character, though she had never heard of a circulating library" (1: vi-vii). Thus Austen's decision to leave her strident defence in chapter five of *Northanger Abbey* over the many years of its curious publishing history attests to her own intense support and determination to raise the perception and status of women novelists.

Austen's observations indicate a clear awareness of the publishing world, market trends, and biases in a patriarchal society for "while the abilities of the nine-hundredth abridger of the History of England, or of the man who collects and publishes in a volume some dozen lines of Milton, Pope, and Prior ... are eulogized by a thousand pens, – there seems almost a general wish of decrying the capacity and undervaluing the labour of the novelist" (59).

Whether one agrees that Austen's "opinions" date the novel her Advertisement continues to pique the reader's curiosity about *Northanger Abbey*'s unusual publishing history and about the politics of writing and publishing for women writers of fiction. Perhaps Austen read the political situation of 1816 astutely enough to employ appropriately veiled allusions to contemporary events to avoid personal recriminations and yet include an advertisement that prepares the careful reader for these allusions.

Henry Austen read and assessed the political and publishing climate in 1818 in such a way that the novel, once he prefixed his Biographical Notice, would not bring calumny upon his sister's head and reputation (as William Godwin had on Mary Wollstonecraft with his frank *Memoirs* in 1798). In his Biographical Notice Henry details Jane's "uneventful" life, stresses her meek, submissive manner, her domesticity and overwhelming Christian piety. The Biographical Notice itself has been interpreted either straight-forwardly as an avowal of Jane's unconscious art or sceptically as a sign of Henry's anxiety about the public response in light of the Wollstonecraft controversy and post-revolutionary conservative attitudes about female intellect and appropriate feminine behaviour.

Clearly the prefatory material alters our interpretation and expectation both of the novel and of Jane Austen herself. In an appropriately ironic twist, the issue of reading and interpretation is raised even before we begin the novel. Henry's stressing of his sister's Christian meekness and piety makes it easier for the reader to dismiss either Catherine Morland's or the narrative voice's "sparkle of intelligence." Indeed, Whately's 1821 review commends her above all as "a good Christian writer" and one wonders how much Henry's Biographical Notice coloured this assessment. (See Appendix E.) Henry attempts to down-play the novel's tongue-in-cheek tone and prompt a literal, non-political reading in order to make it a reaffirmation of social mores and feminine propriety. However, the undercurrents throughout the novel defy any such attempts to silence or contain them.

The framing paraphernalia around the novel is not limited to the Biographical Notice and Austen's Advertisement. Originally designed as a two-volume work, set in two locations, Bath and Northanger, *Northanger Abbey* was finally published as half of a four-volume set with *Persuasion*. Both works were published together by Murray in December 1817 (1818 on the title-page) as a run of 1,750 four-volume copies. Despite the limited critical response 1,409 copies sold at £1.4.0. within a year. (See Appendix E.) In fact "this four-volume dual published on very inexpensive paper and sold on commission earned £518.6.5, more than any earlier Austen novel, even though the last 283 copies had to be remaindered at 3s. 1d each."[8] The titles of the earlier manuscript versions, "Susan" and "Catherine" respectively, stress the importance of the young heroine and her entrance into society. However, the eventual title of *Northanger Abbey* (it is not clear whether this was Jane's or Henry's choice) shifts the focus from the female protagonist to a symbol of patriarchal power – the abbey, a brick and mortar edifice. This shift in focus from a young woman to a place perhaps accounts for some readers' difficulties with the novel's uneven narrative voice and its uneasy mixture of parody and imitation of Gothic and sentimental fiction. Highlighting the abbey ties the work to the patriarchal concerns of birth, inheritance, and social standing – motivating forces for General Tilney and the Thorpes and yet very secondary for Catherine herself. Emphasis on the abbey rather than on Catherine's person and her development unbalances the work for many readers and misdirects them. Repositioning Catherine's experiences and education as the centrepiece links both volumes more coherently since Catherine learns how to read people both at Bath and during her residence at Northanger. In both places Catherine learns to recognize, if not always deal successfully with, a variety of types of people. Catherine is introduced to the modern individual through such characters as General Tilney, John and Isabella Thorpe (to a lesser degree Mrs. Allen), since they are all characterized by their mercenary obsessions, whether for clothes, horses, carriages, or the latest gardening gadgetry.

The Importance of Reading to Jane Austen

Jane Austen's novels, letters, and journals testify that she and her family were avid readers, especially and unashamedly, of novels. When asked in December 1789 to subscribe to a new circulating library, Austen scoffed at the proprietor's reassurance that it would include more than just novels: "She might have spared this pretension to *our* family, who are great Novel-readers and not ashamed of being so."[9] *Northanger Abbey* is obviously a novel strongly influenced by fictional and non fictional works. Austen refers to, or parodies, works by Frances Burney, William Cowper, Maria Edgeworth, William Gilpin, Thomas Gray, Elizabeth Hervey, Samuel Johnson, Matthew Lewis, Alexander Pope, Ann Radcliffe, Samuel Richardson, William Shakespeare, Charlotte Smith and Helen Maria Williams. As her most overtly literary work *Northanger Abbey* is a novel about other novels, their influence, and their readers. Austen uses Catherine to draw upon most of the conventions of fiction of the late eighteenth century. She repeatedly calls upon the reader's knowledge of other fictional works to highlight the fact that she is herself writing a novel –.one that defies easy categorisation as a parody, a novel of manners, a didactic novel, a sentimental fiction, or a *Bildungsroman*.

Although the heroine Catherine is preoccupied by her reading of Radcliffe's *Mysteries of Udolpho*, any reader well versed in the Gothic quickly perceives that Austen borrows more liberally from Radcliffe's *Sicilian Romance* (1790) and her *Romance of the Forest* (1791). Henry's fanciful story about Dorothy and the secret door behind the arras, told as he drives Catherine to Northanger, is derivative of *The Romance of the Forest*. (see Appendix C.1.) Likewise Catherine's refusal to be daunted in her surmises about the General's ill-treatment of his wife echoes Radcliffe's *Sicilian Romance* in which the wife is imprisoned for fifteen years after a supposititious funeral. (See footnote 1, p. 189.)

Austen both parodies and compliments other writers, their chosen subject matter, and their writing styles. She does not dismiss any one genre totally (except perhaps the magazines) although she satirizes their weaknesses. She obviously enjoys reading and teases her readers with subtle allusions throughout *Northanger Abbey*. Austen makes reading an enjoyable and challenging process to illustrate that very few things can be read in a single, straightforward manner – every thing has more than one meaning. Whether we read an incident as typical of the Gothic, the sentimental, or burlesque depends upon our perspective and our background knowledge – knowledge we are continually acquiring and using to reassess and reread the evidence before us in much the same way as Catherine herself does. The plurality of meaning recurs throughout and destabilizes our ability to interpret confidently words or actions. The novel's closing sentence draws attention to the fluidity of language and interpretation: "I leave it to be settled by whomsoever it may concern, whether the tendency of this work be altogether to recommend parental tyranny, or reward filial disobedience." Austen indicates how the reader's desires, sense of impartiality or even reading competence are all tenuous. Since meaning seems dangerously dependent at times on what one wishes it to mean, Austen teaches both Catherine and the reader to resist allowing desires to determine meaning.

The most influential works of non fiction in *Northanger Abbey* are those by William Gilpin. Henry Austen observed in his Biographical Notice that "she was enamoured of Gilpin and the Picturesque." Gilpin's formative influence on Austen is evident throughout *Northanger Abbey* as she reproduces many of his comments on art, the picturesque, the ruins and abbeys of Britain, and incorporates Gilpin's phrases, definitions, and the concept of artistic organisation in Henry Tilney's lecture on Beechen Cliff. (See Appendix C.2.) Austen values Gilpin's ability to teach his readers to appreciate nature by portraying it to them in terms of pictures and to appreciate art by making them look at nature as though they were artists.

How Austen's Characters Read

In a novel about reading how and what the characters read is of great importance. Five main conversations about reading centre on the Gothic novel and indicate that Austen expects her readers to learn from the characters' different responses. It is not just a question of which books characters read, but how each reading colours their understanding of other people and situations.

We learn in the opening pages that Catherine "never could learn or understand anything before she was taught" (38). She has to experience things to gain knowledge and insight. This is in stark contrast to the proposed paragon of Hannah More's educational *Essays* (1777) where we discover that the perfect young lady learns without studying: "it is not uncommon to find a lady, who, though she does not know a rule of syntax, scarcely ever violates one; and who constructs every sentence she utters, with more propriety than many a learned dunce" (57). Catherine is neither a heroine from the sentimental or Gothic novel nor even from the contemporary conduct book for she is neither innately all knowing nor perfect. Unlike the sentimental heroines whose traits are described in Appendix C.3, Catherine Morland has living, middle-class parents, numerous friendly siblings, is unskilled in art and music, exhibits limited interest in animals, writing or reading poetry, has no scheming guardian or step parent to thwart her desires, undergoes only a mock abduction at the hands of John

Thorpe and makes a very humble and uneventful début in Bath. Catherine is, however, eager for experience which she initially finds in books. As a heroine in training she dutifully learns the stock phrases and expressions although unlike Isabella Thorpe she never actually uses them. However, Catherine does use literature to understand people or new situations since it broadens her field of knowledge. She believes that the poets are correct in stating that love is indeed blind, as evidenced by Isabella's declaration that Catherine's brother James is handsome (131). However, when James surprises Catherine in Bath she presumes he is visiting her and the Allens. She has no need of literature to understand her brother's motive because a visit is within the realm of her experience. Similarly she does not read life as though it were a romance while she is in Bath. She automatically presumes that the woman at Henry Tilney's side in the Pump-room is his sister and not her rival. Unlike Isabella who pines as a lover should (albeit only for a few hours!), falls in love at first sight (Isabella's self damning declaration "so it always is with me ... − the first moment I beheld him − my heart was irrecoverably gone." [131]), Catherine maintains her appetite, sleeps solidly, and shows no signs of wasting away in silence.

Catherine is an avid reader of the Gothic while at Bath, specifically Radcliffe's *Mysteries of Udolpho*, and prefers reading to much of the socializing that initially occurs. However, her grip on reality is shaken when the opportunity to visit a real castle (Blaise) or an abbey arises. What she has only read about promises to become a reality − fiction threatens to become fact. Conversely and with much hilarity, her reality in turn becomes a fiction. Catherine, with Henry's encouragement, likens her trip to Northanger Abbey to one in a novel in which she is the heroine, the centre of attention, to whom adventures occur. Life is too good to be true and thus becomes a type of fiction or fantasy − what she has only read about. Problems arise at Northanger because she has more experience of novel reading than life and so she interprets events and people's actions according to the novels she has read. As she enters *Northanger Abbey* her primary concern is for the welfare of her straw bonnet since she does not want to be caught unprepared as the heroine Emily was in Radcliffe's *Mysteries of Udolpho*. This does not make her a quixotic character like those in Charlotte Lennox's *Female Quixote* (1752) or Charlotte Smith's *Ethelinde* (1789) because Catherine does not want novels to be her reality. Catherine's inexperience simply leaves her unprepared to deal with everyday things. Unlike her truly quixotic predecessors, Catherine develops her reading skills through the novel. Her experiences in Bath and at Northanger Abbey ultimately make her a better reader of texts, landscapes, people, and situations.

Isabella Thorpe acts as a counterpoint to Catherine. Isabella's reading, like much of her behaviour, is shallow and superficial. She is a poor reader of books and gains most of her literary insight from her friend Miss Andrews. She is adept at assuming the heroine's role because she uses fiction to create the reality she desires. She pragmatically uses fiction to hide her purposeful manoeuvres. Her reading is not escapism so much as opportunism. Fiction provides a means for articulating her ambitions. It is left ambiguous whether fiction creates her ambitious nature or is merely an avenue for its expression. Austen expects her reader to see through Isabella's character and recognize her audacious planning and cunning. She is a product of the education system that Wollstonecraft so despises in her *Vindication of the Rights of Woman* (1792) in which "the cultivation of the understanding is always subordinate to the acquirement of some corporeal accomplishment" (23), and in which "sensibility is nurtured at the expense of understanding" (82). Isabella uses fiction to justify her status as lover but she does not perceive life as a novel. She is not misled; she merely oversteps herself when she flirts with someone equally manipulative and purposeful. Frederick Tilney gets the upper hand because he is male and society condones his behaviour rather than hers. The double standard is applied since Frederick is backed by money, gender, and status. Frederick, unlike James, correctly reads Isabella. He shamelessly plays games and uses his personal charms to entertain himself.

Isabella's brother John Thorpe is a boorish, inattentive reader whose crude nature is made apparent by his preference for Matthew Lewis's *The Monk*. He is an inattentive and tasteless rattle. Like Isabella, John repeats what he has heard about books rather than hazard his own reading. His one venture ends in the embarrassing blunder when he disagrees with Catherine's suggestion that he might enjoy *The Mysteries of Udolpho*: "Not I, faith! No, if I read any, it shall be Mrs. Radcliff's" (71).

Both Henry and Eleanor Tilney are competent, attentive readers who enjoy fiction and non fiction. As a male Henry controls most situations by directing the conversation, although he is obviously more benevolent than Frederick, John, or General Tilney. Eleanor reads in accordance with accepted educational treatises since she exhibits little independent thought or action and is well aware of her dependent position. She is very much a puppet in the patriarchal system. In this respect Eleanor is an isolated, sad creature who epitomizes the ideal dutiful daughter figure. She has learnt to read her father's moods accurately in order to avoid problems. Although her brother Henry makes her life more bearable Eleanor conforms to society's dictates. She is a much more perceptive reader than her selfish father, General Tilney, whose greed ironically makes him misread the facts. He is too self absorbed and self-interested to read carefully or verify his sources. Despite his age and experience he proves a very poor reader when he believes Catherine to be an heiress. He reads Catherine into the scenario that best suits him. Ironically General Tilney, the Gothic villain, the patriarchal tyrant, a representative of the established order, reads Catherine as though she were the heroine of a romance. His desire to find riches and beauty for his son make him fall prey to the delusional qualities of novels. He, like Catherine, temporarily slips into thinking that life is a novel.

The Modern Reader and *Northanger Abbey*

That Jane Austen has proved to be "a critic's novelist *par excellence*"[10] and that *Northanger Abbey* has prompted a wide range of sophisticated and intriguing readings is evidenced by the extensive bibliography in Graham Handley's *Jane Austen* (1992) which details readings of it as a Gothic burlesque, as a Sentimental parody, as a *Bildungsroman*, as an anti-Jacobin text, as notable for its feminist sympathies, for its overriding economic preoccupation, and for its socio-historical commentary.[11]

It is, of course, wholly unlikely that a definitive reading will ever exist or that the process of reading will ever stop. The fictional

Morris Zapp himself concludes that such a project "couldn't succeed because it isn't possible, and it isn't possible because of the nature of language itself, in which meaning is constantly being transferred from one signifier to another and can never be absolutely possessed" (*Small World*, 24).

Northanger Abbey will continue to be read and interpreted by future generations because Austen prefers a rich ambiguity to simplistic definition. *Northanger Abbey* is a text about reading, reading novels, reading people and reading situations, directed by Austen at both the heroine and her readers. Anxieties about being misread prompted Austen to defend herself both in the novel and in her Advertisement, while Henry Austen's anxieties prompted him to characterize his sister in his Biographical Notice as an exemplary Christian. In the novel itself Jane Austen repeatedly foils the reader's expectations by mixing genres and voices so that *Northanger Abbey* does not fit easily into any preconceived literary category, whether Gothic, Gothic parody, burlesque, or novel of Manners but moves among them all. We appear to have anchored our reading strategy and deciphered the text one moment only to be forced a page later into a reassessment of our reading. For Austen, life, like her novel, is a continual process of reading and rereading.

Notes

1 See Appendix A.
2 Eileen Morris, "Jane Austen's Hidden Message to a Publisher," *Persuasions*, 16, 4 (Dec 1982): 16-17; Margaret Kirkham, *Jane Austen, Feminism and Fiction* (Sussex: Harvester Press, 1983) 71.
3 *Jane Austen's Letters to her Sister Cassandra and Others*, ed., R.W. Chapman (Oxford: Clarendon Press) 484.
4 Park Honan, *Jane Austen: Her Life* (New York: St. Martin's, 1987) 384.
5 Margaret Kirkham, *Jane Austen, Feminism and Fiction*, 66-73.
6 R.A. Austen-Leigh, *Austen Papers 1704-1856* (London, 1870-71) 146. See Appendix B.
7 The year 1794 witnessed the Treason Trials of several English-Jacobin writers, the suspension of Habeas Corpus, and the passing of the Treasonable Practices Act. Newspaper Publication acts to monitor and control potentially criminal and seditious writings were passed in 1792, 1795, 1798 and 1799. The years 1795 and 1799 also saw acts against Combinations and 1799 saw the suppression of the Corresponding Society.

8   Jan Fergus, *Jane Austen: A Literary Life* (New York: St. Martin's, 1991) 37.

9   *Jane Austen's Letters to Her Sister Cassandra and Others*, 38.

10 B.C. Southam, *Jane Austen*, ed. Ian Scott-Kilvert. Writers and Their Work Series 241 (Essex: Longman, 1975) 3.

11 Graham Handley, *Jane Austen* (London: Bristol Classical Press, 1992).

A Note on the Text

Jane Austen's manuscript of *Northanger Abbey* does not survive. The sole authority is the first edition which was posthumously published.[1] Although the proofs were obviously not corrected by Austen the edition contains few detectable errors. The text in this present edition adopts the emendations noted by R.W. Chapman in his *Oxford Illustrated Jane Austen* (1923), revised by Mary Lascelles in 1965, 1969.

This edition retains first-edition spelling.

I should like to thank the Senate Research Committee of Bishop's University for financial assistance. In preparing the second edition I have benefited from the comments and insights of many readers, particularly Shelley King, Betty Hoddinott and Brigitte Brauch-Velhorn. Special thanks to Peter Sabor for his judicious input and continued willingness to share his extensive knowledge of Austen, and to Graham Hoddinott for help in piecing Catherine's travel itinerary together.

My thanks to Barbara Conolly and Don LePan at Broadview for their continued professional help.

---

[1] Only a trimmed title-page of "Susan" in Austen's hand survives at the Pierpont Morgan library.

Jane Austen: A Brief Chronology

1775 Jane Austen born at Steventon (16 Dec)

1785 attends the Abbey school in Reading with Cassandra

1786 both leave Abbey school (Dec)

1793 writes last item of *Juvenilia* (3 June); visits Butler-Harrison cousins in Southampton with Cassandra

1794 M. de Feuillide guillotined in Paris (22 Feb); possibly writes *Lady Susan* this year

1795 first draft of "Elinor and Marianne"

1796 starts *First Impressions*

1797 finishes *First Impressions* (Aug); rejected by Cadell (1 Nov); reworks "Elinor and Marianne" into *Sense and Sensibility* (Nov); visits the Leigh-Perrots in Bath; marriage of Henry and Eliza de Feuillide (31 Dec)

1798 begins "Susan"; leaves Godmersham for Steventon

1799 arrives in Bath and stays at 13 Queen St with mother, Edward and Elizabeth (17 May); returns to Steventon (30 June); probably finishes "Susan"

1800 George Austen retires as Rector of Steventon (Dec)

1801 Austens leave Steventon for Bath; lease 4 Sydney Place, Bath, and then leave for a holiday in the West country; Henry resigns commission in Oxfordshire Militia and sets up as a banker and Army agent in London; James Austen and family move to Steventon (May)

1802 revises "Susan"; Harris Bigg-Wither proposes (2 Dec)

1803 "Susan" sold to the publisher Crosby of London for £10

1804 probably writes *The Watsons*; Mrs Austen seriously ill during the spring; Austens move to 3 Green Park Buildings East, Bath

1805 George Austen dies (21 Jan); move to 25 Gay Street, Bath

1806 take lodgings in Trim Street, Bath (29 Jan); leave Bath for Adelstrop (2 Jul)

1807 Austens move into house in Castle Square, Southampton

1809   attempts to secure publication of "Susan"; moves into Chawton Cottage with Cassandra and mother

1810   *Sense and Sensibility* accepted for publication

1811   *Sense and Sensibility* published anonymously (30 Oct); reworks "First Impressions" into *Pride and Prejudice*

1812   sells copyright of *Pride and Prejudice* to Egerton

1813   *Pride and Prejudice* appears anonymously (28 Jan); Eliza de Feuillide dies (25 Apr)

1814   commences *Emma* (21 Jan); *Mansfield Park* published (9 May)

1815   *Emma* finished (29 Mar); begins *Persuasion* (8 Aug); *Emma* published (Dec)

1816   unwell (spring); Henry buys back "Susan," which Austen revises and renames "Catherine"; Henry's bank fails (15 Mar); first draft of *Persuasion* finished (18 Jul); *Persuasion* completed (6 Aug); Henry ordained, becomes curate of Chawton (Dec)

1817   starts *Sanditon* (27 Jan); makes her will (27 Apr); Cassandra accompanies her to Winchester, where they lodge at 8 College St. (24 May); dies in early morning (18 Jul); Henry arranges publication of *Northanger Abbey* and *Persuasion*; *Northanger Abbey* and *Persuasion* published together with Henry's "Biographical Notice" (Dec)

NORTHANGER ABBEY:

AND

PERSUASION.

BY THE AUTHOR OF " PRIDE AND PREJUDICE,"
" MANSFIELD-PARK," &c.

⸺⬥⸺

WITH A BIOGRAPHICAL NOTICE OF THE
AUTHOR.

▬▬▬

IN FOUR VOLUMES.

VOL. I.

▬▬▬

LONDON:

JOHN MURRAY, ALBEMARLE-STREET.

1818.

Title-Page, 1818 Edition

Biographical Notice of the Author[1]

The following pages are the production of a pen which has already contributed in no small degree to the entertainment of the public. And when the public, which has not been insensible to the merits of "Sense and Sensibility," "Pride and Prejudice," "Mansfield Park," and "Emma," shall be informed that the hand which guided the pen is now mouldering in the grave, perhaps a brief account of Jane Austen will be read with a kindlier sentiment than simple curiosity.

Short and easy will be the task of the mere biographer. A life of usefulness, literature, and religion, was not by any means a life of event. To those who lament their irreparable loss, it is consolatory to think that, as she never deserved disapprobation, so, in the circle of her family and friends, she never met reproof; that her wishes were not only reasonable, but gratified; and that to the little disappointments incidental to human life was never added, even for a moment, an abatement of good-will from any who knew her.

Jane Austen was born on the 16th of December, 1775, at Steventon, in the county of Hampshire. Her father was Rector of that parish upwards of forty years. There he resided, in the conscientious and unassisted discharge of his ministerial duties, until he was turned of seventy years. Then he retired with his wife, our authoress, and her sister to Bath, for the remainder of his life, a period of about four years. Being not only a profound scholar, but possessing a most exquisite taste in every species of literature, it is not wonderful that his daughter Jane should, at a very early age, have become sensible to the charms of style, and enthusiastic in

---

1   The *Biographical Notice of the Author* by Henry Austen prefaced the posthumous four-volume set *Northanger Abbey* and *Persuasion* (1818); a slightly altered version, entitled "Memoir of Miss Austen," dated October 1832, prefaced Bentley's edition of *Sense and Sensibility* (1833).

   Henry Thomas Austen (1771-1850), soldier, banker and clergyman, the fourth son of George Austen, was Jane Austen's favourite brother and acted for her in publishing matters.

the cultivation of her own language. On the death of her father she removed, with her mother and sister, for a short time, to Southampton, and finally, in 1809, to the pleasant village of Chawton, in the same county. From this place she sent into the world those novels, which by many have been placed on the same shelf as the works of a D'Arblay and an Edgeworth. Some of these novels had been the gradual performances of her previous life. For though in composition she was equally rapid and correct, yet an invincible distrust of her own judgement induced her to withhold her works from the public, till time and many perusals had satisfied her that the charm of recent composition was dissolved. The natural constitution, the regular habits, the quiet and happy occupations of our authoress, seemed to promise a long succession of amusement to the public, and a gradual increase of reputation to herself. But the symptoms of a decay, deep and incurable, began to shew themselves in the commencement of 1816. Her decline was at first deceitfully slow; and until the spring of this present year, those who knew their happiness to be involved in her existence could not endure to despair. But in the month of May, 1817, it was found advisable that she should be removed to Winchester for the benefit of constant medical aid, which none even then dared to hope would be permanently beneficial. She supported, during two months, all the varying pain, irksomeness, and tedium, attendant on decaying nature, with more than resignation, with a truly elastic cheerfulness. She retained her faculties, her memory, her fancy, her temper, and her affections, warm, clear, and unimpaired, to the last. Neither her love of God, nor of her fellow creatures flagged for a moment. She made a point of receiving the sacrament before excessive bodily weakness might have rendered her perception unequal to her wishes. She wrote whilst she could hold a pen, and with a pencil when a pen was become too laborious. The day preceding her death she composed some stanzas replete with fancy and vigour. Her last voluntary speech conveyed her thanks to her medical attendant; and to the final question asked of her, purporting to know her wants, she replied, "I want nothing but death."

She expired shortly after, on Friday the 18th of July, 1817, in the arms of her sister, who, as well as the relator of these events, feels too surely that they shall never look upon her like again.

Jane Austen was buried on the 24th of July, 1817, in the cathedral church of Winchester, which, in the whole catalogue of its mighty dead, does not contain the ashes of a brighter genius or a sincerer Christian.

Of personal attractions she possessed a considerable share. Her stature was that of true elegance. It could not have been increased without exceeding the middle height. Her carriage and deportment were quiet, yet graceful. Her features were separately good. Their assemblage produced an unrivalled expression of that cheerfulness, sensibility, and benevolence, which were her real characteristics. Her complexion was of the finest texture. It might with truth be said, that her eloquent blood spoke through her modest cheek. Her voice was extremely sweet. She delivered herself with fluency and precision. Indeed she was formed for elegant and rational society, excelling in conversation as much as in composition. In the present age it is hazardous to mention accomplishments. Our authoress would, probably, have been inferior to few in such acquirements, had she not been so superior to most in higher things. She had not only an excellent taste for drawing, but, in her earlier days, evinced great power of hand in the management of the pencil. Her own musical attainments she held very cheap. Twenty years ago they would have been thought more of, and twenty years hence many a parent will expect their daughters to be applauded for meaner performances. She was fond of dancing, and excelled in it. It remains now to add a few observations on that which her friends deemed more important, on those endowments which sweetened every hour of their lives.

If there be an opinion current in the world, that perfect placidity of temper is not reconcileable [sic] to the most lively imagination, and the keenest relish for wit, such an opinion will be rejected for ever by those who have had the happiness of knowing the authoress of the following works. Though the frailties, foibles, and follies of others could not escape her immediate detection, yet even on their vices did she never trust herself to comment with unkindness. The affectation of candour is not uncommon; but she had no affectation. Faultless herself, as nearly as human nature can be, she always sought, in the faults of others, something to excuse, to forgive or to forget. Where extenuation was impossible, she had a sure refuge in silence. She never uttered either a hasty, a silly, or a severe expression. In short, her temper was as polished as her wit. Nor were her manners inferior to her temper. They were of the happiest kind. No one could be often in her company without feeling a strong desire of obtaining her friendship, and cherishing a hope of having obtained it. She was tranquil without reserve or stiffness; and communicative without intrusion or self-sufficiency. She became an authoress entirely from taste and inclination. Neither the hope of fame nor profit mixed with her early motives. Most of her works, as before observed, were composed many years previous to their publication. It was with extreme difficulty that her friends, whose partiality she suspected whilst she honoured their judgement, could prevail on her to publish her first work. Nay, so persuaded was she that its sale would not repay the expense of publication, that she actually made a reserve from her very moderate income to meet the expected loss. She could scarcely believe what she termed her great good fortune when "Sense and Sensibility" produced a clear profit of about £150. Few so gifted were so truly unpretending. She regarded the above sum as a prodigious recompense for that which had cost her nothing. Her readers, perhaps, will wonder that such a work produced so little at a time when some authors have received more guineas than they have written lines. The works of our authoress, however, may live as long as those which have burst on the world with more éclat. But the public has not been unjust; and our authoress was far from thinking it so. Most gratifying to her was the applause which from time to time reached her ears from those who were competent to discriminate. Still, in spite of such applause, so much did she shrink from notoriety, that no accumulation of fame would have induced her, had she lived, to affix her name to any productions of her pen. In the bosom of her own family she talked of them freely, thankful for praise, open to remark, and submissive to criticism. But in public she turned away from any allusion to the character of an authoress. She read aloud with very great taste and effect. Her own works, probably, were never heard to so much advantage as from her own mouth; for she partook largely in all the best gifts of the comic muse. She was a warm and judicious admirer of landscape, both in nature and on canvass. At a very early age she was enamoured of Gilpin on the Picturesque;[1] and she seldom changed her opinions either on books or men.

Her reading was very extensive in history and belles lettres; and her memory extremely tenacious. Her favourite moral writers were Johnson in prose, and Cowper in verse. It is difficult to say at what age she was not intimately acquainted with the merits and defects of the best essays and novels in the English language. Richardson's power of creating, and preserving the consistency of his characters, as particularly exemplified in "Sir Charles Grandison," gratified the natural discrimination of her mind, whilst her taste secured her from the errors of his prolix style and tedious narrative. She did not rank any work of Fielding quite so high. Without the slightest affectation she recoiled from every thing gross. Neither nature, wit, nor humour, could make her amends for so very low a scale of morals.

Her power of inventing characters seems to have been intuitive, and almost unlimited. She drew from nature; but, whatever may have been surmised to the contrary, never from individuals.

The style of her familiar correspondence was in all respects the same as that of her novels. Every thing came finished from her pen; for on all subjects she had ideas as clear as her expressions were well chosen. It is not hazarding too much to say that she never dispatched a note or letter unworthy of publication.

One trait only remains to be touched on. It makes all others unimportant. She was thoroughly religious and devout; fearful of giving offence to God, and incapable of feeling it towards any fellow creature. On serious subjects she was well-instructed, both by reading and meditation, and her opinions accorded strictly with those of our Established Church.

London, Dec. 13, 1817.

---

1   William Gilpin, author of numerous works about the picturesque. Most specifically *Three Essays: on Picturesque Beauty; on Picturesque Travel; and on Sketching Landscape: to which is added a poem, on Landscape Painting* (London, 1792) and *Observations, Relative to Picturesque Beauty on the Mountains and Lakes of Cumberland and Westmoreland* (London, 1786). See Appendix C.2.

Since concluding the above remarks, the writer of them has been put in possession of some extracts from the private correspondence of the authoress. They are few and short; but are submitted to the public without apology, as being more truly descriptive of her temper, taste, feelings, and principles than any thing which the pen of a biographer can produce.

The first extract is a playful defence of herself from a mock charge of having pilfered the manuscripts of a young relation.

"What should I do, my dearest E. with your manly, vigorous sketches, so full of life and spirit? How could I possibly join them on to a little bit of ivory, two inches wide, on which I work with a brush so fine as to produce little effect after much labour?"[1]

The remaining extracts are from various parts of a letter written a few weeks before her death.

"My attendant is encouraging, and talks of making me quite well. I live chiefly on the sofa, but am allowed to walk from one room to the other. I have been out once in a sedan-chair, and am to repeat it, and be promoted to a wheel-chair as the weather serves. On this subject I will only say further that my dearest sister, my tender, watchful, indefatigable nurse, has not been made ill by her exertions. As to what I owe to her, and to the anxious affection of all my beloved family on this occasion, I can only cry over it, and pray to God to bless them more and more."[2]

She next touches with just and gentle animadversion on a subject of domestic disappointment. Of this the particulars do not concern the public. Yet in justice to her characteristic sweetness and resignation, the concluding observation of our authoress thereon must not be suppressed.

"But I am getting too near complaint. It has been the appointment of God, however secondary causes may have operated."

---

1   Cf. *Letters*, 468–69, 16 December 1816, to James Edward Austen. This was misquoted in the original.

2   The original has not been found although Chapman dates it the end of May 1817 (*Letters*, 497).

The following and final extract will prove the facility with which she could correct every impatient thought, and turn from complaint to cheerfulness.

"You will find Captain – a very respectable, well-meaning man, without much manner, his wife and sister all good humour and obligingness, and I hope (since the fashion allows it) with rather longer petticoats than last year."

London, Dec. 20, 1817.

ADVERTISEMENT

BY THE AUTHORESS TO

NORTHANGER ABBEY

This little work was finished in the year 1803, and intended for immediate publication. It was disposed of to a bookseller, it was even advertised, and why the business proceeded no farther, the author has never been able to learn. That any bookseller should think it worth while to purchase what he did not think it worth while to publish seems extraordinary. But with this, neither the author nor the public have any other concern than as some observation is necessary upon those parts of the work which thirteen years have made comparatively obsolete. The public are entreated to bear in mind that thirteen years have passed since it was finished, many more since it was begun, and that during that period, places, manners, books, and opinions have undergone considerable changes.

CHAPTER I

No one who had ever seen Catherine Morland in her infancy, would have supposed her born to be an heroine. Her situation in life, the character of her father and mother, her own person and disposition, were all equally against her. Her father was a clergyman, without being neglected, or poor, and a very respectable man, though his name was Richard[1] – and he had never been handsome. He had a considerable independence, besides two good livings – and he was not in the least addicted to locking up his daughters.[2] Her mother was a woman of useful plain sense, with a good temper, and, what is more remarkable, with a good constitution. She had three sons before Catherine was born; and instead of dying in bringing the latter into the world, as anybody might expect, she still lived on – lived to have six children more – to see them growing up around her, and to enjoy excellent health herself. A family of ten children will be always called a fine family, where there are heads and arms and legs enough for the number; but the Morlands had little other right to the word, for they were in general very plain, and Catherine, for many years of her life, as plain as any. She had a thin awkward figure, a sallow skin without colour, dark lank hair, and strong features; – so much for her person; – and not less unpropitious for heroism seemed her mind. She was fond of all boy's plays, and greatly preferred cricket not merely to dolls, but to the more heroic enjoyments of infancy, nursing a

---

1   A family joke. Cf. Jane Austen's letter to Cassandra, 15 September 1796: "Mr Richard Harvey's match is put off till he has got a Better Christian name, of which he has great hopes." Perhaps an ironic reference to the recalcitrant publisher Richard Crosby. Joan Klingel Ray suggests that the name Richard is part of Austen's anti-gothic parody since "it is well nigh impossible to find a Richard in the very Gothic fiction Austen was satirizing" (142).

2   Allusion to novels such as Samuel Richardson's *Clarissa* (1747-8) and Henry Fielding's *Tom Jones* (1749).

dormouse, feeding a canary-bird, or watering a rose-bush. Indeed she had no taste for a garden; and if she gathered flowers at all, it was chiefly for the pleasure of mischief — at least so it was conjectured from her always preferring those which she was forbidden to take. — Such were her propensities — her abilities were quite as extraordinary. She never could learn or understand anything before she was taught; and sometimes not even then, for she was often inattentive, and occasionally stupid. Her mother was three months in teaching her only to repeat the "Beggar's Petition";[1] and after all, her next sister, Sally, could say it better than she did. Not that Catherine was always stupid, — by no means; she learnt the fable of "The Hare and Many Friends,"[2] as quickly as any girl in England. Her mother wished her to learn music; and Catherine was sure she should like it, for she was very fond of tinkling the keys of the old forlorn spinnet; so, at eight years old she began. She learnt a year, and could not bear it; — and Mrs. Morland, who did not insist on her daughters being accomplished in spite of incapacity or distaste, allowed her to leave off. The day which dismissed the music-master was one of the happiest of Catherine's life. Her taste for drawing was not superior; though whenever she could obtain the outside of a letter[3] from her mother, or seize upon any other odd piece of paper, she did what she could in that way, by drawing houses and trees, hens and chickens, all very much like one another. — Writing and accounts she was taught by her father; French by her mother: her proficiency in either was not remarkable, and she shirked her lessons in both whenever she

---

1   Cf. "The Beggar's Petition" in *Poems on Several Occasions* (Wolverhampton, 1769) by the Revd. Thomas Moss. This was an exceptionally sentimental "standing dish" used for elocution lessons and often learnt by rote. Catherine's inability to memorize such a tawdry piece indicates her refreshingly independent spirit.

2   Cf. John Gay's *Fables* (1727). The hare's plight in the "Hare and Many Friends." who makes quick and ready friends of many animals whom all fail to help when the dangerous pack of hounds appear, foreshadows Catherine's own predicament. This was the most popular of Gay's fables and one in which the author's aligning himself with the deserted hare prompted Pope to write "Gay dies unpensioned with a hundred friends."

3   Since envelopes were not used the address was written on one side of the letter.

could. What a strange, unaccountable character! – for with all these symptoms of profligacy at ten years old, she had neither a bad heart nor a bad temper; was seldom stubborn, scarcely ever quarrelsome, and very kind to the little ones, with few interruptions of tyranny; she was moreover noisy and wild, hated confinement and cleanliness, and loved nothing so well in the world as rolling down the green slope at the back of the house.[1]

Such was Catherine Morland at ten. At fifteen, appearances were mending; she began to curl her hair and long for balls; her complexion improved; her features were softened by plumpness and colour, her eyes gained more animation, and her figure more consequence. Her love of dirt gave way to an inclination for finery, and she grew clean as she grew smart; she had now the pleasure of sometimes hearing her father and mother remark on her personal improvement. "Catherine grows quite a good-looking girl, – she is almost pretty to day," were words which caught her ears now and then; and how welcome were the sounds! To look *almost* pretty is an acquisition of higher delight to a girl who has been looking plain the first fifteen years of her life, than a beauty from her cradle can ever receive.

Mrs Morland was a very good woman, and wished to see her children everything they ought to be; but her time was so much occupied in lying-in and teaching the little ones, that her elder daughters were inevitably left to shift for themselves; and it was not very wonderful that Catherine, who had by nature nothing heroic about her, should prefer cricket, base ball, riding on horseback, and running about the country at the age of fourteen, to books – or at least books of information – for, provided that nothing like useful knowledge could be gained from them, pro-

---

1 Cf. Locke's *Some Thoughts Concerning Education* (1693): "Another thing that is of great advantage to every one's health, but especially children's, is, to be much in the *open air*, and very little as may be by the fire, even in winter. ... And altho' greater regard be to be had to Beauty in the daughters, yet I will take the liberty to say, that the more they are in the *air*, without prejudice to their faces, the stronger and healthier they will be; and the nearer they come to the hardships of their brothers in their education, the greater advantage will they receive from it all the remaining part of their lives" (Sect. 9.10-11).

vided they were all story and no reflection, she had never any objection to books at all. But from fifteen to seventeen she was in training for a heroine; she read all such works as heroines must read to supply their memories with those quotations which are so serviceable and so soothing in the vicissitudes of their eventful lives.

From Pope,[1] she learnt to censure those who

> "bear about the mockery of woe."

From Gray,[2] that

> "Many a flower is born to blush unseen,
> "And waste its fragrance on the desert air."

From Thompson,[3] that

> — "It is a delightful task
> "To teach the young idea how to shoot."

And from Shakspeare [sic][4] she gained a great store of information — amongst the rest, that

> — "Trifles light as air,
> "Are, to the jealous, confirmation strong,
> "As proofs of Holy Writ."

That

> "The poor beetle, which we tread upon,
> "In corporal sufferance feels a pang as great
> "As when a giant dies."

---

1 "Elegy to the Memory of an Unfortunate Lady" (1717).
2 Misquote from Thomas Gray's *Elegy in a Country Churchyard* (1751).
3 *The Seasons*, "Spring" (1728).
4 Shakespeare: *Othello* III.iii. 322 (misquoted); *Measure for Measure* III.i.79 (misquoted); *Twelfth Night* II.iv.117.

And that a young woman in love always looks

- "like Patience on a monument
"Smiling at Grief."

So far her improvement was sufficient – and in many other points she came on exceedingly well; for though she could not write sonnets, she brought herself to read them; and though there seemed no chance of her throwing a whole party into raptures by a prelude on the pianoforte, of her own composition, she could listen to other people's performance with very little fatigue. Her greatest deficiency was in the pencil – she had no notion of drawing – not enough even to attempt a sketch of her lover's profile, that she might be detected in the design.[1] There she fell miserably short of the true heroic height. At present she did not know her own poverty, for she had no lover to pourtray. She had reached the age of seventeen, without having seen one amiable youth who could call forth her sensibility; without having inspired one real passion, and without having excited even any admiration but what was very moderate and very transient. This was strange indeed! But strange things may be generally accounted for if their cause be fairly searched out. There was not one lord in the neighbourhood; no – not even a baronet. There was not one family among their acquaintance who had reared and supported a boy accidentally found at their door – not one young man whose origin was unknown. Her father had no ward, and the squire of the parish no children.

But when a young lady is to be a heroine, the perverseness of forty surrounding families cannot prevent her. Something must and will happen to throw a hero in her way.

Mr Allen, who owned the chief of the property about Fullerton, the village in Wiltshire where the Morlands lived, was ordered to Bath for the benefit of a gouty constitution; – and his lady, a good-humoured woman, fond of Miss Morland, and probably aware that if adventures will not befall a young lady in her own

---

1   As a mock heroine Catherine lacks the artistic skills that characterize the majority of sentimental heroines. See Appendix C.3.

village, she must seek them abroad, invited her to go with them. Mr and Mrs Morland were all compliance, and Catherine all happiness.

CHAPTER 2

In addition to what has been already said of Catherine Morland's personal and mental endowments, when about to be launched into all the difficulties and dangers of a six weeks' residence in Bath, it may be stated, for the reader's more certain information, lest the following pages should otherwise fail of giving any idea of what her character is meant to be; that her heart was affectionate, her disposition cheerful and open, without conceit or affectation of any kind – her manners just removed from the awkwardness and shyness of a girl; her person pleasing, and, when in good looks, pretty – and her mind about as ignorant and uninformed as the female mind at seventeen usually is.

When the hour of departure drew near, the maternal anxiety of Mrs Morland will be naturally supposed to be most severe. A thousand alarming presentiments of evil to her beloved Catherine from this terrific separation must oppress her heart with sadness, and drown her in tears for the last day or two of their being together; and advice of the most important and applicable nature must of course flow from her wise lips in their parting conference in her closet. Cautions against the violence of such noblemen and baronets as delight in forcing young ladies away to some remote farm-house, must, at such a moment, relieve the fulness of her heart. Who would not think so? But Mrs Morland knew so little of lords and baronets, that she entertained no notion of their general mischievousness, and was wholly unsuspicious of danger to her daughter from their machinations. Her cautions were confined to the following points. "I beg, Catherine, you will always wrap yourself up very warm about the throat, when you come from the rooms at night; and I wish you would try to keep some account of the money you spend; – I will give you this little book on purpose."

Sally, or rather Sarah, (for what young lady of common gentility will reach the age of sixteen without altering her name as far as she can?)[1] must from situation be at this time the intimate friend and confidante of her sister. It is remarkable, however, that she neither insisted on Catherine's writing by every post, nor exacted her promise of transmitting the character of every new acquaintance, nor a detail of every interesting conversation that Bath might produce. Every thing indeed relative to this important journey was done, on the part of the Morlands, with a degree of moderation and composure, which seemed rather consistent with the common feelings of common life, than with the refined susceptibilities, the tender emotions which the first separation of a heroine from her family ought always to excite. Her father, instead of giving her an unlimited order on his banker, or even putting an hundred pounds bank-bill into her hands, gave her only ten guineas, and promised her more when she wanted it.

Under these unpromising auspices, the parting took place, and the journey began. It was performed with suitable quietness and uneventful safety. Neither robbers nor tempests befriended them, nor one lucky overturn to introduce them to the hero. Nothing more alarming occurred than a fear, on Mrs Allen's side, of having once left her clogs behind her at an inn, and that fortunately proved to be groundless.

They arrived at Bath. Catherine was all eager delight; – her eyes were here, there, everywhere, as they approached its fine and striking environs, and afterwards drove through those streets which conducted them to the hotel. She was come to be happy, and she felt happy already.

---

1 Changing names was commonplace both in Austen's life and in the fiction she read. Austen's cousin Elizabeth was known as Betsy until her sixteenth year when she changed her name to the more fashionable and ladylike diminutive of her name Eliza in 1777. Amongst the fictional examples is Eaton Stannard Barrett's *The Heroine* (1813), in which Cherry Wilkinson adopts the name Cheribina de Willoughby. Austen read *The Heroine* in March 1814, telling Cassandra that she "was very much amused by it. I wonder James did not like it better. It diverted me exceedingly" (Le Faye, *Jane Austen's Letters* 255). And in what Mrs. Morland terms a "very clever essay" in *The Mirror*, which she hopes will cure Catherine's moping over her expulsion from the Abbey, Mr. Homespun refers to his newly fashionable daughter Elizabeth, who "is offended if we call her Betty." See current footnote 1 p. 231.

They were soon settled in comfortable lodgings in Pulteney-street.

It is now expedient to give some description of Mrs Allen, that the reader may be able to judge, in what manner her actions will hereafter tend to promote the general distress of the work, and how she will, probably, contribute to reduce poor Catherine to all the desperate wretchedness of which a last volume is capable – whether by her imprudence, vulgarity, or jealousy – whether by intercepting her letters, ruining her character, or turning her out of doors.

Mrs Allen was one of that numerous class of females, whose society can raise no other emotion than surprise at there being any men in the world who could like them well enough to marry them. She had neither beauty, genius, accomplishment, nor manner. The air of a gentlewoman, a great deal of quiet, inactive good temper, and a trifling turn of mind, were all that could account for her being the choice of a sensible, intelligent man like Mr Allen. In one respect she was admirably fitted to introduce a young lady into public, being as fond of going every where and seeing every thing herself as any young lady could be. Dress was her passion. She had a most harmless delight in being fine; and our heroine's entrée into life could not take place till after three or four days had been spent in learning what was mostly worn, and her chaperon was provided with a dress of the newest fashion. Catherine too made some purchases herself, and when all these matters were arranged, the important evening came which was to usher her into the Upper Rooms.[1] Her hair was cut and dressed by the best hand, her clothes put on with care, and both Mrs Allen and her maid declared she looked quite as she should do. With such encouragement, Catherine hoped at least to pass uncensured through the crowd. As for admiration, it was always very welcome when it came, but she did not depend on it.

Mrs Allen was so long in dressing, that they did not enter the ball-room till late. The season was full, the room crowded, and the

---

1   The Upper Rooms, opened in 1771, were a separate building north of the Lower Rooms and on a higher elevation. During the season four balls were held each week in these Rooms. All Austen's details of Bath social life are accurate. See Appendix F.

two ladies squeezed in as well as they could. As for Mr Allen, he repaired directly to the card-room, and left them to enjoy a mob by themselves. With more care for the safety of her new gown than for the comfort of her protegée, Mrs Allen made her way through the throng of men by the door, as swiftly as the necessary caution would allow; Catherine, however, kept close at her side, and linked her arm too firmly within her friend's to be torn asunder by any common effort of a struggling assembly. But to her utter amazement she found that to proceed along the room was by no means the way to disengage themselves from the crowd; it seemed rather to increase as they went on, whereas she had imagined that when once fairly within the door, they should easily find seats and be able to watch the dances with perfect convenience. But this was far from being the case, and though by unwearied diligence they gained even the top of the room, their situation was just the same; they saw nothing of the dancers but the high feathers of some of the ladies. Still they moved on – something better was yet in view; and by a continued exertion of strength and ingenuity they found themselves at last in the passage behind the highest bench. Here there was something less of crowd than below; and hence Miss Morland had a comprehensive view of all the company beneath her, and of all the dangers of her late passage through them. It was a splendid sight, and she began, for the first time that evening, to feel herself at a ball: she longed to dance, but she had not an acquaintance in the room. Mrs Allen did all that she could do in such a case by saying very placidly, every now and then, "I wish you could dance, my dear, – I wish you could get a partner." For some time her young friend felt obliged to her for these wishes; but they were repeated so often, and proved so totally ineffectual, that Catherine grew tired at last, and would thank her no more.

They were not long able, however, to enjoy the repose of the eminence they had so laboriously gained. – Every body was shortly in motion for tea, and they must squeeze out like the rest. Catherine began to feel something of disappointment – she was tired of being continually pressed against by people, the generality of whose faces possessed nothing to interest, and with all of whom she was so wholly unacquainted, that she could not relieve the irksomeness of imprisonment by the exchange of a syllable with any of her fellow captives; and when at last arrived in the tea-room, she felt yet more the awkwardness of having no party to join, no acquaintance to claim, no gentleman to assist them. – They saw nothing of Mr Allen; and after looking about them in vain for a more eligible situation, were obliged to sit down at the end of a table, at which a large party were already placed, without having any thing to do there, or any body to speak to, except each other.

Mrs Allen congratulated herself, as soon as they were seated, on having preserved her gown from injury. "It would have been very shocking to have it torn," said she, "would not it? – It is such a delicate muslin. – For my part I have not seen any thing I like so well in the whole room, I assure you."

"How uncomfortable it is," whispered Catherine, "not to have a single acquaintance here!"

"Yes, my dear," replied Mrs Allen, with perfect serenity, "it is very uncomfortable indeed."

"What shall we do? – The gentlemen and ladies at this table look as if they wondered why we came here – we seem forcing ourselves into their party."

"Aye, so we do. – That is very disagreeable. I wish we had a large acquaintance here."

"I wish we had *any*; – it would be somebody to go to."

"Very true, my dear; and if we knew anybody we would join them directly. The Skinners were here last year – I wish they were here now."

"Had not we better go away as it is? – Here are no tea things for us, you see."

"No more there are, indeed. How very provoking! But I think we had better sit still, for one gets so tumbled in such a crowd! How is my head,[1] my dear? – Somebody gave me a push that has hurt it, I am afraid."

"No, indeed, it looks very nice. – But, dear Mrs Allen, are you sure there is nobody you know in all this multitude of people? I think you *must* know somebody."

"I don't, upon my word – I wish I did. I wish I had a large ac-quaintance here with all my heart, and then I should get you a

---

1 An arrangement of pomaded hair dressed with gauze and ribbon.

partner. I should be so glad to have you dance. There goes a strange-looking woman! What an odd gown she has got on! – How old fashioned it is! Look at the back."

After some time they received an offer of tea from one of their neighbours; it was thankfully accepted, and this introduced a light conversation with the gentleman who offered it, which was the only time that anybody spoke to them during the evening, till they were discovered and joined by Mr Allen when the dance was over.

"Well, Miss Morland," said he, directly, "I hope you have had an agreeable ball."

"Very agreeable indeed," she replied, vainly endeavouring to hide a great yawn.

"I wish she had been able to dance," said his wife, "I wish we could have got a partner for her. – I have been saying how glad I should be if the Skinners were here this winter instead of last; or if the Parrys had come, as they talked of once, she might have danced with George Parry. I am so sorry she has not had a partner!"

"We shall do better another evening I hope," was Mr Allen's consolation.

The company began to disperse when the dancing was over – enough to leave space for the remainder to walk about in some comfort; and now was the time for a heroine, who had not yet played a very distinguished part in the events of the evening, to be noticed and admired. Every five minutes, by removing some of the crowd, gave greater openings for her charms. She was now seen by many young men who had not been near her before. Not one, however, started with rapturous wonder on beholding her, no whisper of eager inquiry ran round the room, nor was she once called a divinity by anybody. Yet Catherine was in very good looks, and had the company only seen her three years before, they would *now* have thought her exceedingly handsome.

She *was* looked at, however, and with some admiration; for, in her own hearing, two gentlemen pronounced her to be a pretty girl. Such words had their due effect; she immediately thought the evening pleasanter than she had found it before – her humble vanity was contented – she felt more obliged to the two young men for this simple praise than a true quality heroine would have been for fifteen sonnets in celebration of her charms, and went to her chair in good humour with everybody, and perfectly satisfied with her share of public attention.

CHAPTER 3

Every morning now brought its regular duties; – shops were to be visited; some new part of the town to be looked at; and the Pump-room[1] to be attended, where they paraded up and down for an hour, looking at everybody and speaking to no one. The wish of a numerous acquaintance in Bath was still uppermost with Mrs Allen, and she repeated it after every fresh proof, which every morning brought, of her knowing nobody at all.

They made their appearance in the Lower Rooms; and here fortune was more favourable to our heroine. The master of the ceremonies[2] introduced to her a very gentlemanlike young man as a partner; – his name was Tilney. He seemed to be about four or five and twenty, was rather tall, had a pleasing countenance, a very intelligent and lively eye, and, if not quite handsome, was very near it. His address was good, and Catherine felt herself in high luck. There was little leisure for speaking while they danced; but when they were seated at tea, she found him as agreeable as she had already given him credit for being. He talked with fluency and spirit – and there was an archness and pleasantry in his manner which interested, though it was hardly understood by her. After chatting some time on such matters as naturally arose from the objects around them, he suddenly addressed her with – "I have hitherto been very remiss, madam, in the proper attentions of a partner here; I have not yet asked you how long you have been in Bath; whether you were ever here before; whether you have been at the Upper Rooms, the theatre, and the concert; and how you like the place altogether. I have been very negligent – but are

---

1 See Appendix F.
2 Mr James King (mentioned by name in Chapter Three) was Master of Ceremonies in the Lower Rooms from 1785-1805 when he became M.C. of the Upper Rooms.

you now at leisure to satisfy me in these particulars? If you are I will begin directly."

"You need not give yourself that trouble, sir."

"No trouble I assure you, madam." Then forming his features into a set smile, and affectedly softening his voice, he added, with a simpering air, "Have you been long in Bath, madam?"

"About a week, sir," replied Catherine, trying not to laugh.

"Really!" with affected astonishment.

"Why should you be surprized, sir?"

"Why, indeed!" said he, in his natural tone – "but some emotion must appear to be raised by your reply, and surprize is more easily assumed, and not less reasonable than any other. – Now let us go on. Were you never here before, madam?"

"Never, sir."

"Indeed! Have you yet honoured the Upper Rooms?"

"Yes, sir, I was there last Monday."

"Have you been to the theatre?"

"Yes, sir, I was at the play on Tuesday."

"To the concert?"

"Yes, sir, on Wednesday."

"And are you altogether pleased with Bath?"

"Yes – I like it very well."

"Now I must give one smirk, and then we may be rational again."

Catherine turned away her head, not knowing whether she might venture to laugh.

"I see what you think of me," said he gravely – "I shall make but a poor figure in your journal tomorrow."

"My journal!"

"Yes, I know exactly what you will say: Friday, went to the Lower Rooms; wore my sprigged muslin robe with blue trimmings – plain black shoes – appeared to much advantage; but was strangely harassed by a queer, half-witted man, who would make me dance with him, and distressed me by his nonsense."

"Indeed I shall say no such thing."

"Shall I tell you what you ought to say?"

"If you please."

"I danced with a very agreeable young man, introduced by Mr

King; had a great deal of conversation with him – seems a most extraordinary genius – hope I may know more of him. *That*, madam, is what I *wish* you to say."

"But, perhaps, I keep no journal."

"Perhaps you are not sitting in this room, and I am not sitting by you. These are points in which a doubt is equally possible. Not keep a journal! How are your absent cousins to understand the tenour of your life in Bath without one? How are the civilities and compliments of every day to be related as they ought to be, unless noted down every evening in a journal? How are your various dresses to be remembered, and the particular state of your complexion, and curl of your hair to be described in all their diversities, without having constant recourse to a journal? – My dear madam, I am not so ignorant of young ladies' ways as you wish to believe me; it is this delightful habit of journalizing which largely contributes to form the easy style of writing for which ladies are so generally celebrated. Every body allows that the talent of writing agreeable letters is peculiarly female. Nature may have done something, but I am sure it must be essentially assisted by the practice of keeping a journal."

"I have sometimes thought," said Catherine, doubtingly, "whether ladies do write so much better letters than gentlemen! That is – I should not think the superiority was always on our side."

"As far as I have had opportunity of judging, it appears to me that the usual style of letter-writing among women is faultless, except in three particulars."

"And what are they?"

"A general deficiency of subject, a total inattention to stops, and a very frequent ignorance of grammar."

"Upon my word! I need not have been afraid of disclaiming the compliment. You do not think too highly of us in that way."

"I should no more lay it down as a general rule that women write better letters than men, than that they sing better duets, or draw better landscapes. In every power, of which taste is the foundation, excellence is pretty fairly divided between the sexes."

They were interrupted by Mrs Allen: – "My dear Catherine," said she, "do take this pin out of my sleeve; I am afraid it has torn a hole already; I shall be quite sorry if it has, for this is a favourite gown, though it cost but nine shillings a yard."

"That is exactly what I should have guessed it, madam," said Mr Tilney, looking at the muslin.[1]

"Do you understand muslins, sir?"

"Particularly well; I always buy my own cravats, and am allowed to be an excellent judge; and my sister has often trusted me in the choice of a gown. I bought one for her the other day, and it was pronounced to be a prodigious bargain by every lady who saw it. I gave but five shillings a yard for it, and a true Indian muslin."

Mrs Allen was quite struck by his genius. "Men commonly take so little notice of those things," said she: "I can never get Mr Allen to know one of my gowns from another. You must be a great comfort to your sister, sir."

"I hope I am, madam."

"And pray, sir, what do you think of Miss Morland's gown?"

"It is very pretty, madam," said he, gravely examining it; "but I do not think it will wash well; I am afraid it will fray."

"How can you," said Catherine, laughing, "be so —" she had almost said strange.

"I am quite of your opinion, sir," replied Mrs Allen; "and so I told Miss Morland when she bought it."

"But then you know, madam, muslin always turns to some account or other; Miss Morland will get enough out of it for a handkerchief, or a cap, or a cloak. — Muslin can never be said to be wasted. I have heard my sister say so forty times, when she has been extravagant in buying more than she wanted, or careless in cutting it to pieces."

"Bath is a charming place, sir; there are so many good shops here. We are sadly off in the country; not but what we have very good shops in Salisbury, but it is so far to go; — eight miles is a long way; Mr Allen says it is nine, measured nine; but I am sure it

---

1   Since muslin, a delicately woven cotton fabric, could cost as much as thirty-six shillings a yard, Mrs. Allen's material is relatively inexpensive. Henry, with his curiously feminine interest in the price of women's clothing, seems to have accurately located the place of Mrs. Allen's muslin on the consumer scale: somewhere between conspicuous consumption and a downright bargain.

cannot be more than eight; and it is such a fag – I come back tired to death. Now here one can step out of doors and get a thing in five minutes."

Mr Tilney was polite enough to seem interested in what she said; and she kept him on the subject of muslins till the dancing recommenced. Catherine feared, as she listened to their discourse, that he indulged himself a little too much with the foibles of others. – "What are you thinking of so earnestly?" said he, as they walked back to the ball-room; – "not of your partner, I hope, for, by that shake of the head, your meditations are not satisfactory."

Catherine coloured, and said, "I was not thinking of any thing."

"That is artful and deep, to be sure; but I had rather be told at once that you will not tell me."

"Well then, I will not."

"Thank you; for now we shall soon be acquainted, as I am authorized to tease you on this subject whenever we meet, and nothing in the world advances intimacy so much."

They danced again; and, when the assembly closed, parted, on the lady's side at least, with a strong inclination for continuing the acquaintance. Whether she thought of him so much, while she drank her warm wine and water, and prepared herself for bed, as to dream of him when there, cannot be ascertained; but I hope it was no more than in a slight slumber, or a morning doze at most; for if it be true, as a celebrated writer has maintained, that no young lady can be justified in falling in love before the gentleman's love is declared,[1] it must be very improper that a young lady should dream of a gentleman before the gentleman is first known to have dreamt of her. How proper Mr Tilney might be as a dreamer or a lover had not yet perhaps entered Mr Allen's head, but that he was not objectionable as a common acquaintance for his young charge he was on inquiry satisfied; for he had early in

---

1   Austen's footnote: "Vide a letter from Mr Richardson, No.97. vol. ii, *Rambler.*" "This is the only allusion that Austen references in the novel. It is to an essay publicly attributed to Samuel Richardson for the first time in 1803. Austen may have been eager to use her novel, originally scheduled to be published in 1803, to give this new attribution additional weight. Henry's *Biographical Notice* also singles out Richardson for particular mention (see p. 33 above and footnote 1, p. 64 below).

the evening taken pains to know who her partner was, and had been assured of Mr Tilney's being a clergyman, and of a very respectable family in Gloucestershire.

CHAPTER 4

With more than usual eagerness did Catherine hasten to the Pump-room the next day, secure within herself of seeing Mr Tilney there before the morning were over, and ready to meet him with a smile: – but no smile was demanded – Mr Tilney did not appear. Every creature in Bath, except himself, was to be seen in the room at different periods of the fashionable hours; crowds of people were every moment passing in and out, up the steps and down; people whom nobody cared about, and nobody wanted to see; and he only was absent. "What a delightful place Bath is," said Mrs Allen, as they sat down near the great clock,[1] after parading the room till they were tired; "and how pleasant it would be if we had any acquaintance here."

This sentiment had been uttered so often in vain, that Mrs Allen had no particular reason to hope it would be followed with more advantage now; but we are told to "despair of nothing we would attain," as "unwearied diligence our point would gain;"[2] and the unwearied diligence with which she had every day wished for the same thing was at length to have its just reward, for hardly had she been seated ten minutes before a lady of about her own age, who was sitting by her, and had been looking at her attentively for several minutes, addressed her with great complaisance in these words: – "I think, madam, I cannot be mistaken; it is a long time since I had the pleasure of seeing you, but is not your name Allen?" This question answered, as it readily was, the stranger pronounced her's to be Thorpe; and Mrs Allen immediately rec-

---

1 The famous Tompion clock was a prominent feature of the Pump-room.
2 Cf. Thomas Dyche's *A Guide to the English Tongue* (1707) which included lines for children to copy out and learn by rote. Austen alludes to one of Dyche's two-line copy-texts when Mrs Allen comments "we are told to 'despair of nothing we would attain,' as 'unwearied diligence our point would gain.'" Jan Fergus (*Jane Austen: A Literary Life* 1991), p. 37, notes there were over a hundred eighteenth-century editions of Dyche's work.

ognized the features of a former schoolfellow and intimate, whom she had seen only once since their respective marriages, and that many years ago. Their joy on this meeting was very great, as well it might, since they had been contented to know nothing of each other for the last fifteen years. Compliments on good looks now passed; and, after observing how time had slipped away since they were last together, how little they had thought of meeting in Bath, and what a pleasure it was to see an old friend, they proceeded to make inquiries and give intelligence as to their families, sisters, and cousins, talking both together, far more ready to give than to receive information, and each hearing very little of what the other said. Mrs Thorpe, however, had one great advantage as a talker, over Mrs Allen, in a family of children; and when she expatiated on the talents of her sons, and the beauty of her daughters, – when she related their different situations and views, – that John was at Oxford, Edward at Merchant Taylors,[1] and William at sea, – and all of them more beloved and respected in their different station than any other three beings ever were, Mrs Allen had no similar information to give, no similar triumphs to press on the unwilling and unbelieving ear of her friend, and was forced to sit and appear to listen to all these maternal effusions, consoling herself, however, with the discovery, which her keen eye soon made, that the lace on Mrs Thorpe's pelisse was not half so handsome as that on her own.

"Here come my dear girls," cried Mrs Thorpe, pointing at three smart looking females, who, arm in arm, were then moving towards her. "My dear Mrs Allen, I long to introduce them; they will be so delighted to see you: the tallest is Isabella, my eldest; is not she a fine young woman? The others are very much admired too, but I believe Isabella is the handsomest."

The Miss Thorpes were introduced; and Miss Morland, who had been for a short time forgotten, was introduced likewise. The name seemed to strike them all; and, after speaking to her with great civility, the eldest young lady observed aloud to the rest, "How excessively like her brother Miss Morland is!"

---

1   Merchant Taylors' school was established by the London merchant's Guilds to provide accessible schooling for their children.

"The very picture of him indeed!" cried the mother – and "I should have known her any where for his sister!" was repeated by them all, two or three times over. For a moment Catherine was surprized; but Mrs Thorpe and her daughters had scarcely begun the history of their acquaintance with Mr James Morland, before she remembered that her eldest brother had lately formed an intimacy with a young man of his own college, of the name of Thorpe; and that he had spent the last week of the Christmas vacation with his family, near London.

The whole being explained, many obliging things were said by the Miss Thorpes of their wish of being better acquainted with her; of being considered as already friends, through the friendship of their brothers, &c. which Catherine heard with pleasure, and answered with all the pretty expressions she could command; and, as the first proof of amity, she was soon invited to accept an arm of the eldest Miss Thorpe, and take a turn with her about the room. Catherine was delighted with this extension of her Bath acquaintance, and almost forgot Mr Tilney while she talked to Miss Thorpe. Friendship is certainly the finest balm for the pangs of disappointed love.

Their conversation turned upon those subjects, of which the free discussion has generally much to do in perfecting a sudden intimacy between two young ladies; such as dress, balls, flirtations, and quizzes.[1] Miss Thorpe, however, being four years older than Miss Morland, and at least four years better informed, had a very decided advantage in discussing such points; she could compare the balls of Bath with those of Tunbridge; its fashions with the fashions of London; could rectify the opinions of her new friend in many articles of tasteful attire; could discover a flirtation between any gentleman and lady who only smiled on each other; and point out a quiz through the thickness of a crowd. These powers received due admiration from Catherine, to whom they were entirely new; and the respect which they naturally inspired might have been too great for familiarity, had not the easy gaiety of Miss Thorpe's manners, and her frequent expressions of delight on this acquaintance with her, softened down every feeling of awe, and left nothing but

---

1   Odd looking persons or things, objects of ridicule.

tender affection. Their increasing attachment was not to be satisfied with half a dozen turns in the Pump-room, but required, when they all quitted it together, that Miss Thorpe should accompany Miss Morland to the very door of Mr Allen's house; and that they should there part with a most affectionate and lengthened shake of hands, after learning, to their mutual relief, that they should see each other across the theatre at night, and say their prayers in the same chapel the next morning. Catherine then ran directly up stairs, and watched Miss Thorpe's progress down the street from the drawing-room window; admired the graceful spirit of her walk, the fashionable air of her figure and dress; and felt grateful, as well she might, for the chance which had procured her such a friend.

Mrs Thorpe was a widow, and not a very rich one; she was a good-humoured, well-meaning woman, and a very indulgent mother. Her eldest daughter had great personal beauty, and the younger ones, by pretending to be as handsome as their sister, imitating her air, and dressing in the same style, did very well.

This brief account of the family is intended to supersede the necessity of a long and minute detail from Mrs Thorpe herself, of her past adventures and sufferings, which might otherwise be expected to occupy the three or four following chapters; in which the worthlessness of lords and attornies might be set forth, and conversations, which had passed twenty years before, be minutely repeated.

CHAPTER 5

Catherine was not so much engaged at the theatre that evening, in returning the nods and smiles of Miss Thorpe, though they certainly claimed much of her leisure, as to forget to look with an inquiring eye for Mr Tilney in every box which her eye could reach; but she looked in vain. Mr Tilney was no fonder of the play than the Pump-room. She hoped to be more fortunate the next day; and when her wishes for fine weather were answered by seeing a beautiful morning, she hardly felt a doubt of it; for a fine Sunday in Bath empties every house of its inhabitants, and all the world appears on such an occasion to walk about and tell their acquaintance what a charming day it is.

As soon as divine service was over, the Thorpes and Allens eagerly joined each other; and after staying long enough in the Pump-room to discover that the crowd was insupportable, and that there was not a genteel face to be seen, which everybody discovers every Sunday throughout the season, they hastened away to the Crescent,[1] to breathe the fresh air of better company. Here Catherine and Isabella, arm in arm, again tasted the sweets of friendship in an unreserved conversation; – they talked much, and with much enjoyment; but again was Catherine disappointed in her hope of re-seeing her partner. He was no where to be met with; every search for him was equally unsuccessful, in morning lounges or evening assemblies; neither at the upper nor lower rooms, at dressed or undressed balls, was he perceivable; nor among the walkers, the horsemen, or the curricle-drivers of the morning. His name was not in the Pump-room book, and curiosity could do no more. He must be gone from Bath. Yet he had not mentioned that his stay would be so short! This sort of mysteriousness, which is always so becoming in a hero, threw a fresh grace in Catherine's imagination around his person and manners, and increased her anxiety to know more of him. From the Thorpes she could learn nothing, for they had been only two days in Bath before they met with Mrs Allen. It was a subject, however, in which she often indulged with her fair friend, from whom she received every possible encouragement to continue to think of him; and his impression on her fancy was not suffered therefore to weaken. Isabella was very sure that he must be a charming young man; and was equally sure that he must have been delighted with her dear Catherine, and would therefore shortly return. She liked him the better for being a clergyman, "for she must confess herself very partial to the profession;" and something like a sigh escaped her as she said it. Perhaps Catherine was wrong in not demanding the cause of that gentle emotion – but she was not experienced enough in the finesse of love, or the duties of friendship, to know when delicate raillery was properly called for, or when a confidence should be forced.

Mrs Allen was now quite happy – quite satisfied with Bath.

1 The promenade in Bath. See Appendix F.

She had found some acquaintance, had been so lucky too as to find in them the family of a most worthy old friend; and, as the completion of good fortune, had found these friends by no means so expensively dressed as herself. Her daily expressions were no longer, "I wish we had some acquaintance in Bath!" They were changed into, – "How glad I am we have met with Mrs Thorpe!" – and she was as eager in promoting the intercourse of the two families, as her young charge and Isabella themselves could be; never satisfied with the day unless she spent the chief of it by the side of Mrs Thorpe, in what they called conversation, but in which there was scarcely ever any exchange of opinion, and not often any resemblance of subject, for Mrs Thorpe talked chiefly of her children, and Mrs Allen of her gowns.

The progress of the friendship between Catherine and Isabella was quick as its beginning had been warm, and they passed so rapidly through every gradation of increasing tenderness, that there was shortly no fresh proof of it to be given to their friends or themselves. They called each other by their Christian name, were always arm in arm when they walked, pinned up each other's train for the dance, and were not to be divided in the set; and if a rainy morning deprived them of other enjoyments, they were still resolute in meeting in defiance of wet and dirt, and shut themselves up, to read novels together. Yes, novels; – for I will not adopt that ungenerous and impolitic custom so common with novel writers, of degrading by their contemptuous censure the very performances, to the number of which they are themselves adding[1] – joining with their greatest enemies in bestowing the harshest epithets on such works, and scarcely ever permitting them to be read by their own heroine, who, if she accidentally

---

[1] Female writers such as Hannah More, Elizabeth Hamilton and Jane West. For example Maria Edgeworth writes in her Advertisement to *Belinda* (1801): "The following work is offered to the public as a *Moral Tale* – the author not wishing to acknowledge a Novel. Were all novels like those of Madame de Crousay, Mrs Inchbald, Miss Burney, or Dr Moore, she would adopt the name of novel with delight. But so much folly, error, and vice are disseminated in books classed under this denomination, that it is hoped the wish to assume another title will be attributed to feelings that are laudable and not fastidious."

take up a novel, is sure to turn over its insipid pages with disgust. Alas! If the heroine of one novel be not patronized by the heroine of another, from whom can she expect protection and regard? I cannot approve of it. Let us leave it to the Reviewers to abuse such effusions of fancy at their leisure, and over every new novel to talk in threadbare strains of the trash with which the press now groans. Let us not desert one another; we are an injured body.[1] Although our productions have afforded more extensive and unaffected pleasure than those of any other literary corporation in the world, no species of composition has been so much decried. From pride, ignorance, or fashion, our foes are almost as many as our readers. And while the abilities of the nine-hundredth abridger of the History of England,[2] or of the man who collects and publishes in a volume some dozen lines of Milton, Pope, and Prior, with a paper from the Spectator, and a chapter from Sterne, are eulogized by a thousand pens, – there seems almost a general wish of decrying the capacity and undervaluing the labour of the novelist, and of slighting the performances which have only genius, wit, and taste to recommend them. "I am no novel reader – I seldom look into novels – Do not imagine that I often read novels – It is really very

---

1   Many novelists portray heroines who mock novel-reading and refuse to read novels (Hervey *Louisa* 1:38-39, Williams *Julia* 2:48) or depict heroines who read novels with disastrous consequences (Opie *Adeline Mowbray* 1:55, Hays *Memoirs of Emma Courtney* 1:25, Wollstonecraft *The Wrongs of Woman* 1:89).

2   Cf. Goldsmith's *History of England* (1771); an *Abridgement* was published in 1774. Goldsmith's *History of England* was a textbook at her father's Steventon school and the Austen family copy, still in the possession of descendants today, was read and heavily annotated by Jane, probably during her early teens. Jane was a vehement defender of the Stuarts, from Mary Queen of Scots onwards, and the pages of volumes three and four are peppered with her exclamations of praise for them and condemnation of their enemies. ... Other marginalia in Goldsmith show that in her teens Austen was staunchly anti-Whig and anti-Republican" (W. Austen Leigh, *Jane Austen: A Family Record* 55). Austen's own miniature burlesque *History of England* (1791), a witty parody of Goldsmith's much longer *Abridgement*, indicates her delight in parodying tedious historians and denouncing them in favour of her own "partial, prejudiced" work "with ... very few dates" by an "ignorant Historian" (*Minor Works* 6.139).

well for a novel." – Such is the common cant. – "And what are you reading, Miss —?" "Oh! it is only a novel!" replies the young lady; while she lays down her book with affected indifference, or momentary shame. – "It is only Cecilia, or Camilla, or Belinda;"[1] or, in short, only some work in which the greatest powers of the mind are displayed, in which the most thorough knowledge of human nature, the happiest delineation of its varieties, the liveliest effusions of wit and humour, are conveyed to the world in the best chosen language. Now, had the same young lady been engaged with a volume of the Spectator, instead of such a work, how proudly would she have produced the book, and told its name; though the chances must be against her being occupied by any part of that voluminous publication, of which either the matter or manner would not disgust a young person of taste: the substance of its papers so often consisting in the statement of improbable circumstances, unnatural characters, and topics of conversation, which no longer concern any one living; and their language, too, frequently so coarse as to give no very favourable idea of the age that could endure it.

CHAPTER 6

The following conversation, which took place between the two friends in the Pump-room one morning, after an acquaintance of eight or nine days, is given as a specimen of their very warm attachment, and of the delicacy, discretion, originality of thought, and literary taste which marked the reasonableness of that attachment.

They met by appointment; and as Isabella had arrived nearly five minutes before her friend, her first address naturally was – "My dearest creature, what can have made you so late? I have been waiting for you at least this age!"

---

1   *Cecilia* (1782) and *Camilla* (1796) by Frances Burney; *Belinda* (1801) by Maria Edgeworth. The name "Miss J. Austen, Steventon" appears in the list of over a thousand subscribers prefixed to *Camilla*. Other subscribers include Miss Berry, Mrs Elizabeth Carter, Miss Edgeworth, Mrs Hamilton, Mrs E. Hervey, Mrs Hannah More, Miss Thrale and Mrs Piozzi.

"Have you, indeed! – I am very sorry for it; but really I thought I was in very good time. It is but just one. I hope you have not been here long?"

"Oh! these ten ages at least. I am sure I have been here this half hour. But now, let us go and sit down at the other end of the room, and enjoy ourselves. I have an hundred things to say to you. In the first place, I was so afraid it would rain this morning, just as I wanted to set off; it looked very showery, and that would have thrown me into agonies! Do you know, I saw the prettiest hat you can imagine, in a shop window in Milsom-street[1] just now – very like yours, only with coquelicot[2] ribbons instead of green; I quite longed for it. But, my dearest Catherine, what have you been doing with yourself all this morning? – Have you gone on with Udolpho?"

"Yes, I have been reading it ever since I woke; and I am got to the black veil."[3]

"Are you, indeed? How delightful! Oh! I would not tell you what is behind the black veil for the world! Are not you wild to know?"

"Oh! Yes, quite; what can it be? – But do not tell me – I would not be told upon any account. I know it must be a skeleton, I am sure it is Laurentina's skeleton.[4] Oh! I am delighted with the book! I should like to spend my whole life in reading it. I assure you, if it had not been to meet you, I would not have come

---

1   Milsom St, Bath St. and Bond St. were the three main shopping thoroughfares at Bath. R.S. Neale cites a 19th century description of Milsom Street: "The street is elegant and imposing ... all is bustle and gaiety: numerous dashing equipages passing and re-passing and then gracing the doors of the tradesmen. The shops are tastefully laid out; capacious and elegant; ... in short Milsom Street ... afford[s] to the utmost extent everything towards supplying the real or imaginary wants of the visitors" (qtd in Vredenburgh). See Appendix F.

2   Brilliant red, poppy-red.

3   Cf. Ann Radcliffe's *Mysteries of Udolpho*. In vol.II. ch.6, the heroine faints upon lifting a black veil covering a large picture. Only in the antepenultimate chapter does the reader discover that the veil covers a wax figure dressed in a shroud and disfigured by worms and not the skeleton of the Lady Laurentini. See Appendix C.1.

4   Mme Laurentini not Laurentina.

away from it for all the world."

"Dear creature! How much I am obliged to you; and when you have finished Udolpho, we will read the Italian[1] together; and I have made out a list of ten or twelve more of the same kind for you."

"Have you, indeed! How glad I am! – What are they all?"

"I will read you their names directly; here they are, in my pocket-book. Castle of Wolfenbach, Clermont, Mysterious Warnings, Necromancer of the Black Forest, Midnight Bell, Orphan of the Rhine, and Horrid Mysteries.[2] Those will last us some time."

"Yes, pretty well; but are they all horrid, are you sure they are all horrid?"

"Yes, quite sure; for a particular friend of mine, a Miss Andrews, a sweet girl, one of the sweetest creatures in the world, has read every one of them. I wish you knew Miss Andrews, you would be delighted with her. She is netting herself the sweetest cloak you can conceive. I think her as beautiful as an angel, and I am so vexed with the men for not admiring her! – I scold them all amazingly about it."

"Scold them! Do you scold them for not admiring her?"

"Yes, that I do. There is nothing I would not do for those who are really my friends. I have no notion of loving people by halves;

---

1   Ann Radcliffe's *The Italian: or the Confessional of the Black Penitent* (1797).
2   All genuine Gothic works:

    Eliza Parsons, *Castle of Wolfenbach* 1793.
    Regina Maria Roche, *Clermont* 1798.
    The Necromancer: or the Tale of the Black Forest. Trans. from the
      German of Lawrence Flammenberg by Peter Teuthold. 1794.
    [Francis Lathom], *The Midnight Bell* 1798.
    Eleanor Sleath, *The Orphan of the Rhine* 1798.
    Peter Will, *Horrid Mysteries* From the German of the Marquis of
      Grosse. (1796).

All but *The Midnight Bell* (which Jane Austen's father borrowed from the library) were Minerva Press productions. See Michael Sadleir "The Northanger Novels," *English Association Phamphlet* No. 68 (1927).

it is not my nature. My attachments are always excessively strong. I told Capt. Hunt at one of our assemblies this winter, that if he was to tease me all night, I would not dance with him, unless he would allow Miss Andrews to be as beautiful as an angel. The men think us incapable of real friendship, you know, and I am determined to shew them the difference. Now, if I were to hear anybody speak slightingly of you, I should fire up in a moment: – but that is not at all likely, for *you* are just the kind of girl to be a great favourite with the men."

"Oh! dear," cried Catherine, colouring. "how can you say so?"

"I know you very well; you have so much animation, which is exactly what Miss Andrews wants, for I must confess there is something amazingly insipid about her. Oh! I must tell you, that just after we parted yesterday, I saw a young man looking at you so earnestly – I am sure he is in love with you." Catherine coloured, and disclaimed again. Isabella laughed. "It is very true, upon my honour, but I see how it is; you are indifferent to every body's admiration, except that of one gentleman, who shall be nameless. Nay, I cannot blame you – (speaking more seriously) – your feelings are easily understood. Where the heart is really attached, I know very well how little one can be pleased with the attention of any body else. Every thing is so insipid, so uninteresting, that does not relate to the beloved object![1] I can perfectly comprehend your feelings."

"But you should not persuade me that I think so very much about Mr Tilney, for perhaps I may never see him again."

"Not see him again! My dearest creature, do not talk of it. I am sure you would be miserable if you thought so."

"No, indeed, I should not. I do not pretend to say that I was not very much pleased with him; but while I have Udolpho to read, I feel as if nobody could make me miserable. Oh! the dreadful black veil! My dear Isabella, I am sure there must be Laurentina's skeleton behind it."

"It is so odd to me, that you should never have read Udolpho before; but I suppose Mrs Morland objects to novels."

---

1   Variant of Shakespeare's *Twelfth Night* (ii.iv).

"No, she does not. She very often reads Sir Charles Grandison[1] herself; but new books do not fall in our way."

"Sir Charles Grandison! That is an amazing horrid book, is it not? – I remember Miss Andrews could not get through the first volume."

"It is not like Udolpho at all; but yet I think it is very entertaining."

"Do you indeed! – you surprize me; I thought it had not been readable. But, my dearest Catherine, have you settled what to wear on your head to-night? I am determined at all events to be dressed exactly like you. The men take notice of *that* sometimes you know."[2]

"But it does not signify if they do;" said Catherine, very innocently.

"Signify! Oh, heavens! I make it a rule never to mind what they say. They are very often amazingly impertinent if you do not treat them with spirit, and make them keep their distance."

"Are they? – Well, I never observed *that*. They always behave very well to me."

"Oh! they give themselves such airs. They are the most conceited creatures in the world, and think themselves of so much importance! – By the bye, though I have thought of it a hundred times, I have always forgot to ask you what is your favourite complexion in a man. Do you like them best dark or fair?"

"I hardly know. I never much thought about it. Something

---

1 Samuel Richardson's *Sir Charles Grandison* (1753-4). In this second allusion to Samuel Richardson's *Sir Charles Grandison*, Catherine informs us that the sensible Mrs. Morland often reads this particular work which is in stark contrast to the vacuous Isabella, who has never opened it and whose supposedly bookish friend Miss Andrews "could not get through the first volume." Austen was adapting *Sir Charles Grandison* as a miniature play at about the same time as she was writing *Northanger Abbey*. Her knowledge of Richardson's novel, according to her nephew, was unsurpassed: "Every circumstance narrated in *Sir Charles Grandison*, all that was ever said or done in the cedar parlour, was familiar to her; and the wedding days of Lady L. and Lady G. were as well remembered as if they had been living friends" (J.E. Austen-Leigh *Memoir of Jane Austen* 89). See also page 52 footnote 1 above.

2 Clearly Isabella has read current sentimental fiction in which female friends often dress alike to attract attention.

between both, I think. Brown – not fair, and not very dark."

"Very well, Catherine. That is exactly he. I have not forgot your description of Mr Tilney; – 'a brown skin, with dark eyes, and rather dark hair.' – Well, my taste is different. I prefer light eyes, and as to complexion – do you know – I like a sallow better than any other. You must not betray me, if you should ever meet with one of your acquaintance answering that description."

"Betray you! – What do you mean?"

"Nay, do not distress me. I believe I have said too much. Let us drop the subject."

Catherine, in some amazement, complied; and after remaining a few moments silent, was on the point of reverting to what interested her at that time rather more than any thing else in the world, Laurentina's skeleton; when her friend prevented her, by saying, – "For Heaven's sake! let us move away from this end of the room. Do you know, there are two odious young men who have been staring at me this half hour. They really put me quite out of countenance. Let us go and look at the arrivals. They will hardly follow us there."

Away they walked to the book; and while Isabella examined the names, it was Catherine's employment to watch the proceedings of these alarming young men.

"They are not coming this way, are they? I hope they are not so impertinent as to follow us. Pray let me know if they are coming. I am determined I will not look up."

In a few moments Catherine, with unaffected pleasure, assured her that she need not be longer uneasy, as the gentlemen had just left the Pump-room.

"And which way are they gone?" said Isabella, turning hastily round. "One was a very good-looking young man."

"They went towards the churchyard."

"Well, I am amazingly glad I have got rid of them! And now, what say you to going to Edgar's Buildings[1] with me, and looking at my new hat? You said you should like to see it."

Catherine readily agreed. "Only," she added, "perhaps we may overtake the two young men."

---

1   See Appendix F.

"Oh! Never mind that. If we make haste, we shall pass by them presently, and I am dying to shew you my hat."

"But if we only wait a few minutes, there will be no danger of our seeing them at all."

"I shall not pay them any such compliment, I assure you. I have no notion of treating men with such respect. *That* is the way to spoil them."

Catherine had nothing to oppose against such reasoning; and therefore, to shew the independence of Miss Thorpe, and her resolution of humbling the sex, they set off immediately as fast as they could walk, in pursuit of the two young men.

CHAPTER 7

Half a minute conducted them through the Pump-yard to the archway, opposite Union-passage; but here they were stopped. Every body acquainted with Bath may remember the difficulties of crossing Cheap-street[1] at this point; it is indeed a street of so impertinent a nature, so unfortunately connected with the great London and Oxford roads, and the principal inn of the city, that a day never passes in which parties of ladies, however important their business, whether in quest of pastry, millinery, or even (as in the present case) of young men, are not detained on one side or other by carriages, horsemen, or carts. This evil had been felt and lamented, at least three times a day, by Isabella since her residence in Bath; and she was now fated to feel and lament it once more, for at the very moment of coming opposite to Union-passage, and within view of the two gentlemen who were proceeding through the crowds, and threading the gutters of that interesting alley, they were prevented crossing by the approach of a gig,[2] driven along on bad pavement by a most knowing-looking coachman with all the vehemence that could most fitly endanger the lives of himself, his companion, and his horse.

"Oh, these odious gigs!" said Isabella, looking up, "how I detest them." But this detestation, though so just, was of short duration,

---

1 See Appendix F.
2 See Appendix J.4.

for she looked again and exclaimed, "Delightful! Mr Morland and my brother!"

"Good heaven! 'tis James!" was uttered at the same moment by Catherine; and, on catching the young men's eyes, the horse was immediately checked with a violence which almost threw him on his haunches, and the servant having now scampered up, the gentlemen jumped out, and the equipage was delivered to his care.

Catherine, by whom this meeting was wholly unexpected, received her brother with the liveliest pleasure; and he, being of a very amiable disposition, and sincerely attached to her, gave every proof on his side of equal satisfaction, which he could have leisure to do, while the bright eyes of Miss Thorpe were incessantly challenging his notice; and to her his devoirs were speedily paid, with a mixture of joy and embarrassment which might have informed Catherine, had she been more expert in the developement of other people's feelings, and less simply engrossed by her own, that her brother thought her friend quite as pretty as she could do herself.

John Thorpe, who in the mean time had been giving orders about the horses, soon joined them, and from him she directly received the amends which were her due; for while he slightly and carelessly touched the hand of Isabella, on her he bestowed a whole scrape[1] and half a short bow. He was a stout young man of middling height, who, with a plain face and ungraceful form, seemed fearful of being too handsome unless he wore the dress of a groom, and too much like a gentleman unless he were easy where he ought to be civil, and impudent where he might be allowed to be easy. He took out his watch: "How long do you think we have been running it from Tetbury,[2] Miss Morland?"

"I do not know the distance." Her brother told her that it was twenty-three miles.

"*Three*-and-twenty!" cried Thorpe; "five-and-twenty if it is an inch." Morland remonstrated, pleaded the authority of road-books, innkeepers, and milestones; but his friend disregarded them all; he had a surer test of distance. "I know it must be five-and-

---

1   A scrape refers to the drawing back of the foot when bowing; it seems to imply awkwardness or rusticity in John Thorpe.
2   See Appendix H.

twenty," said he, "by the time we have been doing it. It is now half after one; we drove out of the inn-yard at Tetbury as the town-clock struck eleven; and I defy any man in England to make my horse go less than ten miles an hour in harness; that makes it exactly twenty-five."

"You have lost an hour," said Morland; "it was only ten o'clock when we came from Tetbury."

"Ten o'clock! it was eleven, upon my soul! I counted every stroke. This brother of yours would persuade me out of my senses, Miss Morland; do but look at my horse; did you ever see an animal so made for speed in your life?" (The servant had just mounted the carriage and was driving off.) "Such true blood! Three hours and a half indeed coming only three-and-twenty miles! look at that creature, and suppose it possible if you can."

"He *does* look very hot, to be sure."

"Hot! he had not turned a hair till we came to Walcot Church:[1] but look at his forehead;[2] look at his loins; only see how he moves; that horse *cannot* go less than ten miles an hour: tie his legs and he will get on. What do you think of my gig, Miss Morland? a neat one, is not it? Well hung; town built; I have not had it a month. It was built for a Christ-church[3] man, a friend of mine, a very good sort of fellow; he ran it a few weeks, till, I believe, it was convenient to have done with it. I happened just then to be looking out for some light thing of the kind, though I had pretty well determined on a curricle too;[4] but I chanced to meet him on Magdalen

---

1   Thorpe is characteristically exaggerating his horse's physical prowess since Walcot Church, although a separate ecclesiastical district, was located in north Bath! See Appendix F. Austen's parents were married at this church on 26 April 1764 and her father was buried there on 26 January 1805.

2   That part of the horse which is in front of the rider.

3   Oxford University is comprised of thirty-six independent, self-contained and self-governing colleges. Christchurch was founded by Cardinal Wolsey in 1525. After Wolsey's fall it was taken over by Henry VIII who refounded it in 1546.

4   Both gigs and curricles were light open carriages, but since curricles were normally drawn by two horses and gigs by one, curricles were faster, more expensive, and more prestigious. Despite John Thorpe's constant boasting, his choice of vehicle indicates that he in fact has very limited financial resources since he buys a gig, second hand from a fellow

Bridge, as he was driving into Oxford, last term: 'Ah! Thorpe,' says he, 'do you happen to want such a little thing as this? it is a capital one of the kind, but I am cursed tired of it.' 'Oh! d——,' said I, 'I am your man; what do you ask?' And how much do you think he did, Miss Morland?"

"I am sure I cannot guess at all."

"Curricle-hung you see; seat, trunk, sword-case, splashing-board, lamps, silver moulding, all you see complete; the iron-work as good as new, or better. He asked fifty guineas; I closed with him directly, threw down the money, and the carriage was mine."

"And I am sure," said Catherine, "I know so little of such things that I cannot judge whether it was cheap or dear."

"Neither one nor t'other; I might have got it for less I dare say; but I hate haggling, and poor Freeman wanted cash."

"That was very good-natured of you," said Catherine, quite pleased.

"Oh! d— it, when one has the means of doing a kind thing by a friend, I hate to be pitiful."

An inquiry now took place into the intended movements of the young ladies; and, on finding whither they were going, it was decided that the gentlemen should accompany them to Edgar's Buildings, and pay their respects to Mrs Thorpe. James and Isabella led the way; and so well satisfied was the latter with her lot, so contentedly was she endeavouring to ensure a pleasant walk to him who brought the double recommendation of being her brother's friend, and her friend's brother, so pure and uncoquettish were her feelings, that, though they overtook and passed the two offending young men in Milsom-street, she was so far from seeking to attract their notice, that she looked back at them only three times.

John Thorpe kept of course with Catherine, and, after a few minutes' silence, renewed the conversation about his gig – "You will find, however, Miss Morland, it would be reckoned a cheap thing by some people, for I might have sold it for ten guineas

---

student. He boasts that the accoutrements make it is as good as new and as good as a curricle. The fifty guineas he pays for the gig indicates that it was neither the prestigious bargain he boasts of nor over priced since Felton lists a standard Chair-Back Gig at £57.5.6. See William Felton *Treatise on Carriages* (London, 1794) and Appendix J. 3 and J. 4..

more the next day; Jackson, of Oriel,[1] bid me sixty at once; Morland was with me at the time."

"Yes," said Morland, who overheard this; "but you forget that your horse was included."

"My horse! oh, d— it! I would not sell my horse for a hundred. Are you fond of an open carriage, Miss Morland?"

"Yes, very; I have hardly ever an opportunity of being in one; but I am particularly fond of it."

"I am glad of it; I will drive you out in mine every day."

"Thank you," said Catherine, in some distress, from a doubt of the propriety of accepting such an offer.

"I will drive you up Lansdown Hill[2] to-morrow."

"Thank you; but will not your horse want rest?"

"Rest! he has only come three-and-twenty miles today; all nonsense; nothing ruins horses so much as rest; nothing knocks them up so soon. No, no; I shall exercise mine at the average of four hours every day while I am here."

"Shall you indeed!" said Catherine very seriously, "that will be forty miles a day."

"Forty! aye, fifty, for what I care. Well, I will drive you up Lansdown to-morrow; mind, I am engaged."

"How delightful that will be!" cried Isabella, turning round: "my dearest Catherine, I quite envy you; but I am afraid, brother, you will not have room for a third."

"A third indeed! no, no; I did not come to Bath to drive my sisters about; that would be a good joke, faith! Morland must take care of you."

This brought on a dialogue of civilities between the other two; but Catherine heard neither the particulars nor the result. Her companion's discourse now sunk from its hitherto animated pitch, to nothing more than a short decisive sentence of praise or condemnation on the face of every woman they met; and Catherine, after listening and agreeing as long as she could, with all the civility and deference of the youthful female mind, fearful of hazarding an opin-

---

1 Founded in 1326, by King Edward II, as the House of the Blessed Mary the Virgin in Oxford but commonly known as Oriel.

2 See Appendix G.

ion of its own in opposition to that of a self-assured man, especially where the beauty of her own sex is concerned, ventured at length to vary the subject by a question which had been long uppermost in her thoughts; it was, "Have you ever read Udolpho, Mr Thorpe?"

"Udolpho! Oh, Lord! not I; I never read novels; I have something else to do."

Catherine, humbled and ashamed, was going to apologize for her question, but he prevented her by saying, "Novels are all so full of nonsense and stuff; there has not been a tolerably decent one come out since Tom Jones, except The Monk;[1] I read that t'other day; but as for all the others, they are the stupidest things in creation."

"I think you must like Udolpho, if you were to read it; it is so very interesting."

"Not I, faith! No, if I read any, it shall be Mrs Radcliff's; her novels are amusing enough; they are worth reading; some fun and nature in *them*."

"Udolpho was written by Mrs Radcliff," said Catherine, with some hesitation, from the fear of mortifying him.

"No sure; was it? Aye, I remember, so it was; I was thinking of that other stupid book, written by that woman they make such a fuss about, she who married the French emigrant."

"I suppose you mean Camilla?"

"Yes, that's the book; such unnatural stuff! – An old man playing at see-saw, I took up the first volume once and looked it over, but I soon found it would not do; indeed I guessed what sort of stuff it must be before I saw it: as soon as I heard she had married an emigrant, I was sure I should never be able to get through it."

"I have never read it."

"You had no loss I assure you; it is the horridest nonsense you can imagine; there is nothing in the world in it but an old man's playing at see-saw and learning Latin;[2] upon my soul there is not."

---

1 Henry Fielding, *Tom Jones* (1749), Matthew Gregory Lewis, *The Monk* (1796).

2 In Burney's *Camilla* (1. ch 3-4) the ridiculous Sir Hugh Tyrold both plays see-saw with his nephews and nieces and attempts to repair his classical education by employing a tutor. The see-saw game has dramatic consequences since the niece Eugenia is crippled by a fall from it and

This critique, the justness of which was unfortunately lost on poor Catherine, brought them to the door of Mrs Thorpe's lodgings, and the feelings of the discerning and unprejudiced reader of Camilla gave way to the feelings of the dutiful and affectionate son, as they met Mrs Thorpe, who had descried them from above, in the passage. "Ah, mother! how do you do?" said he, giving her a hearty shake of the hand: "where did you get that quiz of a hat, it makes you look like an old witch? Here is Morland and I come to stay a few days with you, so you must look out for a couple of good beds some where near." And this address seemed to satisfy all the fondest wishes of the mother's heart, for she received him with the most delighted and exulting affection. On his two younger sisters he then bestowed an equal portion of his fraternal tenderness, for he asked each of them how they did, and observed that they both looked very ugly.

These manners did not please Catherine; but he was James's friend and Isabella's brother; and her judgment was further bought off by Isabella's assuring her, when they withdrew to see the new hat, that John thought her the most charming girl in the world, and by John's engaging her before they parted to dance with him that evening. Had she been older or vainer, such attacks might have done little; but, where youth and diffidence are united, it requires uncommon steadiness of reason to resist the attraction of being called the most charming girl in the world, and of being so very early engaged as a partner; and the consequence was, that, when the two Morlands, after sitting an hour with the Thorpes, set off to walk together to Mr Allen's, and James, as the door was closed on them, said, "Well, Catherine, how do you like my friend Thorpe?" instead of answering, as she probably would have done, had there been no friendship and no flattery in the case, "I do not like him at all;" she directly replied, "I like him very much; he seems very agreeable."

"He is as good-natured a fellow as ever lived; a little of a rattle;

---

subsequently replaces the heroine Camilla as heiress to Sir Tyrold's fortune. These incidents occur very early in the novel (less than half way through the first of five volumes) and indicate John Thorpe's poor reading stamina.

but that will recommend him to your sex I believe: and how do you like the rest of the family?"

"Very, very much indeed: Isabella particularly."

"I am very glad to hear you say so; she is just the kind of young woman I could wish to see you attached to; she has so much good sense, and is so thoroughly unaffected and amiable; I always wanted you to know her; and she seems very fond of you. She said the highest things in your praise that could possibly be; and the praise of such a girl as Miss Thorpe even you, Catherine," taking her hand with affection, "may be proud of."

"Indeed I am," she replied; "I love her exceedingly, and am delighted to find that you like her too. You hardly mentioned any thing of her, when you wrote to me after your visit there."

"Because I thought I should soon see you myself. I hope you will be a great deal together while you are in Bath. She is a most amiable girl; such a superior understanding! How fond all the family are of her; she is evidently the general favourite; and how much she must be admired in such a place as this — is not she?"

"Yes, very much indeed, I fancy; Mr Allen thinks her the prettiest girl in Bath."

"I dare say he does; and I do not know any man who is a better judge of beauty than Mr Allen. I need not ask you whether you are happy here, my dear Catherine; with such a companion and friend as Isabella Thorpe, it would be impossible for you to be otherwise; and the Allens, I am sure are very kind to you?"

"Yes, very kind; I never was so happy before; and now you are come it will be more delightful than ever; how good it is of you to come so far on purpose to see *me*."

James accepted this tribute of gratitude, and qualified his conscience for accepting it too, by saying with perfect sincerity, "Indeed, Catherine, I love you dearly."

Inquiries and communications concerning brothers and sisters, the situation of some, the growth of the rest, and other family matters now passed between them, and continued, with only one small digression on James's part, in praise of Miss Thorpe, till they reached Pulteney-street, where he was welcomed with great kindness by Mr and Mrs Allen, invited by the former to dine with them, and summoned by the latter to guess the price and weigh the merits of a new muff and tippet. A pre-engagement in Edgar's Buildings prevented his accepting the invitation of one friend, and obliged him to hurry away as soon as he had satisfied the demands of the other. The time of the two parties uniting in the Octagon Room[1] being correctly adjusted, Catherine was then left to the luxury of a raised, restless, and frightened imagination over. the pages of Udolpho, lost from all worldly concerns of dressing and dinner, incapable of soothing Mrs Allen's fears on the delay of an expected dress-maker, and having only one minute in sixty to bestow even on the reflection of her own felicity, in being already engaged for the evening.

CHAPTER 8

In spite of Udolpho and the dress-maker, however, the party from Pulteney-street reached the Upper-rooms in very good time. The Thorpes and James Morland were there only two minutes before them; and Isabella having gone through the usual ceremonial of meeting her friend with the most smiling and affectionate haste, of admiring the set of her gown, and envying the curl of her hair, they followed their chaperons, arm in arm, into the ballroom, whispering to each other whenever a thought occurred, and supplying the place of many ideas by a squeeze of the hand or a smile of affection.

The dancing began within a few minutes after they were seated; and James, who had been engaged quite as long as his sister, was very importunate with Isabella to stand up; but John was gone into the card-room to speak to a friend, and nothing, she declared, should induce her to join the set before her dear Catherine could join it too: "I assure you," said she, "I would not stand up without your dear sister for all the world; for if I did we should certainly be separated the whole evening." Catherine accepted this kindness with gratitude, and they continued as they were for three minutes longer, when Isabella, who had been talking to James on the other side of her, turned again to his sister and whispered, "My dear creature, I am afraid I must leave you, your brother is so amazingly

---

1   A meeting place in Bath. See Appendix F.

impatient to begin; I know you will not mind my going away, and I dare say John will be back in a moment, and then you may easily find me out." Catherine, though a little disappointed, had too much good-nature to make any opposition, and the others rising up, Isabella had only time to press her friend's hand and say, "Good-bye, my dear love," before they hurried off. The younger Miss Thorpes being also dancing, Catherine was left to the mercy of Mrs Thorpe and Mrs Allen, between whom she now remained. She could not help being vexed at the non-appearance of Mr Thorpe, for she not only longed to be dancing, but was likewise aware that, as the real dignity of her situation could not be known, she was sharing with the scores of other young ladies still sitting down all the discredit of wanting a partner. To be disgraced in the eye of the world, to wear the appearance of infamy while her heart is all purity, her actions all innocence, and the misconduct of another the true source of her debasement, is one of those circumstances which peculiarly belong to the heroine's life, and her fortitude under it what particularly dignifies her character. Catherine had fortitude too; she suffered, but no murmur passed her lips.

From this state of humiliation, she was roused, at the end of ten minutes, to a pleasanter feeling, by seeing, not Mr Thorpe, but Mr Tilney, within three yards of the place where they sat; he seemed to be moving that way, but he did not see her, and therefore the smile and the blush, which his sudden reappearance raised in Catherine, passed away without sullying her heroic importance. He looked as handsome and as lively as ever, and was talking with interest to a fashionable and pleasing-looking young woman, who leant on his arm, and whom Catherine immediately guessed to be his sister; thus unthinkingly throwing away a fair opportunity of considering him lost to her for ever, by being married already. But guided only by what was simple and probable, it had never entered her head that Mr Tilney could be married; he had not behaved, he had not talked, like the married men to whom she had been used; he had never mentioned a wife, and he had acknowledged a sister. From these circumstances sprang the instant conclusion of his sister's now being by his side; and therefore, instead of turning of a deathlike paleness, and falling in a fit on Mrs Allen's bosom, Catherine sat erect, in the perfect use of her senses, and with cheeks only a little redder than usual.

Mr Tilney and his companion, who continued, though slowly, to approach, were immediately preceded by a lady, an acquaintance of Mrs Thorpe; and this lady stopping to speak to her, they, as belonging to her, stopped likewise, and Catherine, catching Mr Tilney's eye, instantly received from him the smiling tribute of recognition. She returned it with pleasure, and then advancing still nearer, he spoke both to her and Mrs Allen, by whom he was very civilly acknowledged. "I am very happy to see you again, sir, indeed; I was afraid you had left Bath." He thanked her for her fears, and said that he had quitted it for a week, on the very morning after his having had the pleasure of seeing her.

"Well, sir, and I dare say you are not sorry to be back again, for it is just the place for young people – and indeed for every body else too. I tell Mr Allen, when he talks of being sick of it, that I am sure he should not complain, for it is so very agreeable a place, that it is much better to be here than at home at this dull time of year. I tell him he is quite in luck to be sent here for his health."

"And I hope, madam, that Mr Allen will be obliged to like the place, from finding it of service to him."

"Thank you, sir. I have no doubt that he will. – A neighbour of ours, Dr Skinner, was here for his health last winter, and came away quite stout."

"That circumstance must give great encouragement."

"Yes, sir – and Dr Skinner and his family were here three months; so I tell Mr Allen he must not be in a hurry to get away."

Here they were interrupted by a request from Mrs Thorpe to Mrs Allen, that she would move a little to accommodate Mrs Hughes and Miss Tilney with seats, as they had agreed to join their party. This was accordingly done, Mr Tilney still continuing standing before them; and after a few minutes consideration, he asked Catherine to dance with him. This compliment, delightful as it was, produced severe mortification to the lady; and in giving her denial, she expressed her sorrow on the occasion so very much as if she really felt it, that had Thorpe, who joined her just afterwards, been half a minute earlier, he might have thought her sufferings rather too acute. The very easy manner in which he then told her that he had kept her waiting, did not by any means reconcile her more to her lot; nor did the particulars which he entered into while they were standing up, of the horses and dogs of the friend whom he had just left, and of a proposed exchange of terriers between them, interest her so much as to prevent her looking very often towards that part of the room where she had left Mr Tilney. Of her dear Isabella, to whom she particularly longed to point out that gentleman, she could see nothing. They were in different sets. She was separated from all her party, and away from all her acquaintance; – one mortification succeeded another, and from the whole she deduced this useful lesson, that to go previously engaged to a ball, does not necessarily increase either the dignity or enjoyment of a young lady. From such a moralizing strain as this, she was suddenly roused by a touch on the shoulder, and turning round, perceived Mrs Hughes directly behind her, attended by Miss Tilney and a gentleman. "I beg your pardon, Miss Morland," said she, "for this liberty, – but I cannot anyhow get to Miss Thorpe, and Mrs Thorpe said she was sure you would not have the least objection to letting in this young lady by you." Mrs Hughes could not have applied to any creature in the room more happy to oblige her than Catherine. The young ladies were introduced to each other, Miss Tilney expressing a proper sense of such goodness, Miss Morland with the real delicacy of a generous mind making light of the obligation; and Mrs Hughes, satisfied with having so respectably settled her young charge, returned to her party.

Miss Tilney had a good figure, a pretty face, and a very agreeable countenance; and her air, though it had not all the decided pretension, the resolute stilishness of Miss Thorpe's, had more real elegance. Her manners shewed good sense and good breeding; they were neither shy, nor affectedly open; and she seemed capable of being young, attractive, and at a ball, without wanting to fix the attention of every man near her, and without exaggerated feelings of extatic delight or inconceivable vexation on every little trifling occurrence. Catherine, interested at once by her appearance and her relationship to Mr Tilney, was desirous of being acquainted with her, and readily talked therefore whenever she could think of any thing to say, and had courage and leisure for saying it. But the hindrance thrown in the way of a very speedy intimacy, by the frequent want of one or more of these requisites, prevented their doing more than going through the first rudiments of an acquaintance, by informing themselves how well the other liked Bath, how much she admired its buildings and surrounding country, whether she drew, or played or sang, and whether she was fond of riding on horseback.

The two dances were scarcely concluded before Catherine found her arm gently seized by her faithful Isabella, who in great spirits exclaimed – "At last I have got you. My dearest creature, I have been looking for you this hour. What could induce you to come into this set, when you knew I was in the other? I have been quite wretched without you."

"My dear Isabella, how was it possible for me to get at you? I could not even see where you were."

"So I told your brother all the time – but he would not believe me. Do go and see for her, Mr Morland, said I – but all in vain – he would not stir an inch. Was not it so, Mr Morland? But you men are all so immoderately lazy! I have been scolding him to such a degree, my dear Catherine, you would be quite amazed. – You know I never stand upon ceremony with such people."

"Look at that young lady with the white beads round her head," whispered Catherine, detaching her friend from James – "It is Mr Tilney's sister."

"Oh! heavens! You don't say so! Let me look at her this moment. What a delightful girl! I never saw any thing half so beautiful! But where is her all-conquering brother? Is he in the room? Point him out to me this instant, if he is. I die to see him. Mr Morland, you are not to listen. We are not talking about you."

"But what is all this whispering about? What is going on?"

"There now, I knew how it would be. You men have such restless curiosity! Talk of the curiosity of women, indeed! – 'tis nothing. But be satisfied, for you are not to know any thing at all of the matter."

"And is that likely to satisfy me, do you think?"

"Well, I declare I never knew any thing like you. What can it signify to you, what we are talking of. Perhaps we are talking about you, therefore I would advise you not to listen, or you may happen to hear something not very agreeable."

In this common-place chatter, which lasted some time, the original subject seemed entirely forgotten; and though Catherine was very well pleased to have it dropped for a while, she could not avoid a little suspicion at the total suspension of all Isabella's impatient desire to see Mr Tilney. When the orchestra struck up a fresh dance, James would have led his fair partner away, but she resisted. "I tell you, Mr Morland," she cried, "I would not do such a thing for all the world. How can you be so teasing; only conceive, my dear Catherine, what your brother wants me to do. He wants me to dance with him again, though I tell him that it is a most improper thing, and entirely against the rules. It would make us the talk of the place, if we were not to change partners."

"Upon my honour," said James, "in these public assemblies, it is as often done as not."

"Nonsense, how can you say so? But when you men have a point to carry, you never stick at anything. My sweet Catherine, do support me; persuade your brother how impossible it is. Tell him, that it would quite shock you to see me do such a thing; now would not it?"

"No, not at all; but if you think it wrong, you had much better change."

"There," cried Isabella, "you hear what your sister says, and yet you will not mind her. Well, remember that it is not my fault, if we set all the old ladies in Bath in a bustle. Come along, my dearest Catherine, for heaven's sake, and stand by me." And off they went, to regain their former place. John Thorpe, in the meanwhile, had walked away; and Catherine, ever willing to give Mr Tilney an opportunity of repeating the agreeable request which had already flattered her once, made her way to Mrs Allen and Mrs Thorpe as fast as she could, in the hope of finding him still with them – a hope which, when it proved to be fruitless, she felt to have been highly unreasonable. "Well, my dear," said Mrs Thorpe, impatient for praise of her son, "I hope you have had an agreeable partner."

"Very agreeable, madam."

"I am glad of it. John has charming spirits, has not he?"

"Did you meet Mr Tilney, my dear?" said Mrs Allen.

"No, where is he?"

"He was with us just now, and said he was so tired of loung-ing about, that he was resolved to go and dance; so I thought perhaps he would ask you, if he met with you."

"Where can he be?" said Catherine, looking round; but she had not looked round long before she saw him leading a young lady to the dance.

"Ah! he has got a partner; I wish he had asked *you*," said Mrs Allen; and after a short silence, she added, "he is a very agreeable young man."

"Indeed he is, Mrs Allen," said Mrs Thorpe, smiling compla-cently; "I must say it, though I *am* his mother, that there is not a more agreeable young man in the world."

This inapplicable answer might have been too much for the comprehension of many; but it did not puzzle Mrs Allen, for after only a moment's consideration, she said, in a whisper to Cather-ine, "I dare say she thought I was speaking of her son."

Catherine was disappointed and vexed. She seemed to have missed by so little the very object she had had in view; and this persuasion did not incline her to a very gracious reply, when John Thorpe came up to her soon afterwards, and said, "Well, Miss Mor-land, I suppose you and I are to stand up and jig it together again."

"Oh, no; I am much obliged to you, our two dances are over; and, besides, I am tired, and do not mean to dance any more."

"Do not you? – then let us walk about and quiz people.[1] Come along with me, and I will show you the four greatest quizzers in the room; my two younger sisters and their partners. I have been laughing at them this half hour."

Again Catherine excused herself; and at last he walked off to quiz his sisters by himself. The rest of the evening she found very dull; Mr Tilney was drawn away from their party at tea, to attend that of his partner; Miss Tilney, though belonging to it, did not sit near her, and James and Isabella were so much engaged in convers-ing together, that the latter had no leisure to bestow more on her friend than one smile, one squeeze, and one "dearest Catherine."

---

[1] R. W. Chapman (*The Novels of Jane Austen*) points out that *quizzers* in the next sentence should perhaps be *quizzes*, since John Thorpe regards his sisters as *objects* of ridicule.

CHAPTER 9

The progress of Catherine's unhappiness from the events of the evening, was as follows. It appeared first in a general dissatisfaction with every body about her, while she remained in the rooms, which speedily brought on considerable weariness and a violent desire to go home. This, on arriving in Pulteney-street, took the direction of extraordinary hunger, and when that was appeased, changed into an earnest longing to be in bed; such was the extreme point of her distress; for when there she immediately fell into a sound sleep which lasted nine hours, and from which she awoke perfectly revived, in excellent spirits, with fresh hopes and fresh schemes. The first wish of her heart was to improve her acquaintance with Miss Tilney, and almost her first resolution, to seek her for that purpose, in the Pump-room at noon. In the Pump-room, one so newly arrived in Bath must be met with, and that building she had already found so favourable for the discovery of female excellence, and the completion of female intimacy, so admirably adapted for secret discourses and unlimited confidence, that she was most reasonably encouraged to expect another friend from within its walls. Her plan for the morning thus settled, she sat quietly down to her book after breakfast, resolving to remain in the same place and the same employment till the clock struck one; and from habitude very little incommoded by the remarks and ejaculations of Mrs Allen, whose vacancy of mind and incapacity for thinking were such, that as she never talked a great deal, so she could never be entirely silent; and, therefore, while she sat at her work, if she lost her needle or broke her thread, if she heard a carriage in the street, or saw a speck upon her gown, she must observe it aloud, whether there were any one at leisure to answer her or not. At about half past twelve, a remarkably loud rap drew her in haste to the window, and scarcely had she time to inform Catherine of there being two open carriages at the door, in the first only a servant, her brother driving Miss Thorpe in the second, before John Thorpe came running upstairs, calling out, "Well, Miss Morland, here I am. Have you been waiting long? We could not come before; the old devil of a coachmaker was such an eternity finding out a thing fit to be got into, and now it is ten thousand to one, but they break down before we are out of the street. How do you do, Mrs Allen? A famous ball last night, was not it? Come, Miss Morland, be quick, for the others are in a confounded hurry to be off. They want to get their tumble over."

"What do you mean?" said Catherine, "where are you all going to?" "Going to? why, you have not forgot our engagement! Did not we agree together to take a drive this morning? What a head you have! We are going up Claverton Down."

"Something was said about it, I remember," said Catherine, looking at Mrs Allen for her opinion; "but really I did not expect you."

"Not expect me! that's a good one! And what a dust you would have made, if I had not come."

Catherine's silent appeal to her friend, meanwhile, was entirely thrown away, for Mrs Allen, not being at all in the habit of conveying any expression herself by a look, was not aware of its being ever intended by anybody else; and Catherine, whose desire of seeing Miss Tilney again could at that moment bear a short delay in favour of a drive, and who thought there could be no impropriety in her going with Mr Thorpe, as Isabella was going at the same time with James, was therefore obliged to speak plainer. "Well, ma'am, what do you say to it? Can you spare me for an hour or two? shall I go?"

"Do just as you please, my dear," replied Mrs Allen, with the most placid indifference. Catherine took the advice, and ran off to get ready. In a very few minutes she re-appeared, having scarcely allowed the two others time enough to get through a few short sentences in her praise, after Thorpe had procured Mrs Allen's admiration of his gig; and then receiving her friend's parting good wishes, they both hurried downstairs. "My dearest creature," cried Isabella, to whom the duty of friendship immediately called her before she could get into the carriage, "you have been at least three hours getting ready. I was afraid you were ill. What a delightful ball we had last night. I have a thousand things to say to you; but make haste and get in, for I long to be off."

Catherine followed her orders and turned away, but not too soon to hear her friend exclaim aloud to James, "What a sweet girl she is! I quite doat on her."

"You will not be frightened, Miss Morland," said Thorpe, as he handed her in, "if my horse should dance about a little at first setting off. He will, most likely, give a plunge or two, and perhaps take the rest[1] for a minute; but he will soon know his master. He is full of spirits, playful as can be, but there is no vice in him."

Catherine did not think the portrait a very inviting one, but it was too late to retreat, and she was too young to own herself frightened; so, resigning herself to her fate, and trusting to the animal's boasted knowledge of its owner, she sat peaceably down, and saw Thorpe sit down by her. Every thing being then arranged, the servant who stood at the horse's head was bid in an important voice "to let him go," and off they went in the quietest manner imaginable, without a plunge or a caper, or any thing like one. Catherine, delighted at so happy an escape, spoke her pleasure aloud with grateful surprize; and her companion immediately made the matter perfectly simple by assuring her that it was entirely owing to the peculiarly judicious manner in which he had then held the reins, and the singular discernment and dexterity with which he had directed his whip. Catherine, though she could not help wondering that with such perfect command of his horse, he should think it necessary to alarm her with a relation of its tricks, congratulated herself sincerely on being under the care of so excellent a coachman; and perceiving that the animal continued to go on in the same quiet manner, without shewing the smallest propensity towards any unpleasant vivacity, and (considering its inevitable pace was ten miles an hour) by no means alarmingly fast, gave herself up to all the enjoyment of air and exercise of the most invigorating kind, in a fine mild day of February, with the consciousness of safety. A silence of several minutes succeeded their first short dialogue; – it was broken by Thorpe's saying very abruptly, "Old Allen is as rich as a Jew – is not he?"

Catherine did not understand him – and he repeated his question, adding in explanation, "Old Allen, the man you are with."

"Oh! Mr Allen, you mean. Yes, I believe, he is very rich."

"And no children at all?"

"No – not any."

---

1   React to being checked.

"A famous thing for his next heirs. He is *your* godfather, is not he?"

"My godfather! – no."

"But you are always very much with them."

"Yes, very much."

"Aye, that is what I meant. He seems a good kind of old fellow enough, and has lived very well in his time, I dare say; he is not gouty for nothing. Does he drink his bottle a-day now?"

"His bottle a-day! no. Why should you think of such a thing? He is a very temperate man, and you could not fancy him in liquor last night?"

"Lord help you! – You women are always thinking of men's being in liquor. Why, you do not suppose a man is overset by a bottle? I am sure of *this* – that if every body was to drink their bottle a- day, there would not be half the disorders in the world there are now. It would be a famous good thing for us all."

"I cannot believe it."

"Oh! lord, it would be the saving of thousands. There is not the hundredth part of the wine consumed in this kingdom, that there ought to be. Our foggy climate wants help."

"And yet I have heard that there is a great deal of wine drunk in Oxford."

"Oxford! There is no drinking at Oxford now, I assure you. Nobody drinks there. You would hardly meet with a man who goes beyond his four pints at the utmost. Now, for instance, it was reckoned a remarkable thing, at the last party in my rooms, that upon an average we cleared about five pints a head. It was looked upon as something out of the common way. *Mine* is famous good stuff, to be sure. You would not often meet with any thing like it in Oxford – and that may account for it. But this will just give you a notion of the general rate of drinking there."

"Yes, it does give a notion," said Catherine warmly, "and that is, that you all drink a great deal more wine than I thought you did. However, I am sure James does not drink so much."

This declaration brought on a loud and overpowering reply, of which no part was very distinct, except the frequent exclamations, amounting almost to oaths, which adorned it, and Catherine was left, when it ended, with rather a strengthened belief of there being a great deal of wine drank in Oxford, and the same happy conviction of her brother's comparative sobriety.

Thorpe's ideas then all reverted to the merits of his own equipage, and she was called on to admire the spirit and freedom with which his horse moved along, and the ease which his paces, as well as the excellence of the springs, gave the motion of the carriage. She followed him in all his admiration as well as she could. To go before, or beyond him was impossible. His knowledge and her ignorance of the subject, his rapidity of expression, and her diffidence of herself put that out of her power; she could strike out nothing new in commendation, but she readily echoed whatever he chose to assert, and it was finally settled between them without any difficulty, that his equipage was altogether the most complete of its kind in England, his carriage the neatest, his horse the best goer, and himself the best coachman. – "You do not really think, Mr Thorpe," said Catherine, venturing after some time to consider the matter as entirely decided, and to offer some little variation on the subject, "that James's gig will break down?"

"Break down! Oh! lord! Did you ever see such a little tittuppy[1] thing in your life? There is not a sound piece of iron about it. The wheels have been fairly worn out these ten years at least – and as for the body! Upon my soul, you might shake it to pieces yourself with a touch. It is the most devilish little rickety business I ever beheld! – Thank God! we have got a better. I would not be bound to go two miles in it for fifty thousand pounds."

"Good heavens!" cried Catherine, quite frightened, "then pray let us turn back; they will certainly meet with an accident if we go on. Do let us turn back, Mr Thorpe; stop and speak to my brother, and tell him how very unsafe it is."

"Unsafe! Oh, lord! what is there in that? they will only get a roll if it does break down; and there is plenty of dirt, it will be excellent falling. Oh, curse it! the carriage is safe enough, if a man knows how to drive it; a thing of that sort in good hands will last above twenty years after it is fairly worn out. Lord bless you! I would undertake for five pounds to drive it to York and back again, without losing a nail."

---

1 Unsteady, shaky.

Catherine listened with astonishment; she knew not how to reconcile two such very different accounts of the same thing; for she had not been brought up to understand the propensities of a rattle, nor to know to how many idle assertions and impudent falsehoods the excess of vanity will lead. Her own family were plain matter-of-fact people, who seldom aimed at wit of any kind; her father, at the utmost, being contented with a pun, and her mother with a proverb; they were not in the habit therefore of telling lies to increase their importance, or of asserting at one moment what they would contradict the next. She reflected on the affair for some time in much perplexity, and was more than once on the point of requesting from Mr Thorpe a clearer insight into his real opinion on the subject; but she checked herself, because it appeared to her that he did not excel in giving those clearer insights, in making those things plain which he had before made ambiguous; and, joining to this, the consideration, that he would not really suffer his sister and his friend to be exposed to a danger from which he might easily preserve them, she concluded at last, that he must know the carriage to be in fact perfectly safe, and therefore would alarm herself no longer. By him the whole matter seemed entirely forgotten; and all the rest of his conversation, or rather talk, began and ended with himself and his own concerns. He told her of horses which he had bought for a trifle and sold for incredible sums; of racing matches, in which his judgment had infallibly foretold the winner; of shooting parties, in which he had killed more birds (though without having one good shot) than all his companions together; and described to her some famous day's sport, with the fox-hounds, in which his foresight and skill in directing the dogs had repaired the mistakes of the most experienced huntsman, and in which the boldness of his riding, though it had never endangered his own life for a moment, had been constantly leading others into difficulties, which he calmly concluded had broken the necks of many.

Little as Catherine was in the habit of judging for herself, and unfixed as were her general notions of what men ought to be, she could not entirely repress a doubt, while she bore with the effusions of his endless conceit, of his being altogether completely agreeable. It was a bold surmise, for he was Isabella's brother;

and she had been assured by James, that his manners would recommend him to all her sex; but in spite of this, the extreme weariness of his company, which crept over her before they had been out an hour, and which continued unceasingly to increase till they stopped in Pulteney-street again, induced her, in some small degree, to resist such high authority, and to distrust his powers of giving universal pleasure.

When they arrived at Mrs Allen's door, the astonishment of Isabella was hardly to be expressed, on finding that it was too late in the day for them to attend her friend into the house: – "Past three o'clock!" it was inconceivable, incredible, impossible! and she would neither believe her own watch, nor her brother's, nor the servant's; she would believe no assurance of it founded on reason or reality, till Morland produced his watch, and ascertained the fact; to have doubted a moment longer *then*, would have been equally inconceivable, incredible, and impossible; and she could only protest, over and over again, that no two hours and a half had ever gone off so swiftly before, as Catherine was called on to confirm; Catherine could not tell a falsehood even to please Isabella; but the latter was spared the misery of her friend's dissenting voice, by not waiting for her answer. Her own feelings entirely engrossed her; her wretchedness was most acute on finding herself obliged to go directly home. – It was ages since she had had a moment's conversation with her dearest Catherine; and, though she had such thousands of things to say to her, it appeared as if they were never to be together again; so, with smiles of most exquisite misery, and the laughing eye of utter despondency, she bade her friend adieu and went on.

Catherine found Mrs Allen just returned from all the busy idleness of the morning, and was immediately greeted with, "Well, my dear, here you are;" a truth which she had no greater inclination than power to dispute; "and I hope you have had a pleasant airing?"

"Yes, ma'am, I thank you; we could not have had a nicer day."

"So Mrs Thorpe said; she was vastly pleased at your all going."

"You have seen Mrs Thorpe, then?"

"Yes, I went to the Pump-room as soon as you were gone, and there I met her, and we had a great deal of talk together. She says there was hardly any veal to be got at market this morning, it is so uncommonly scarce."

"Did you see any body else of our acquaintance?"

"Yes; we agreed to take a turn in the Crescent, and there we met Mrs Hughes, and Mr and Miss Tilney walking with her."

"Did you indeed? and did they speak to you?"

"Yes, we walked along the Crescent together for half an hour. They seem very agreeable people. Miss Tilney was in a very pretty spotted muslin, and I fancy, by what I can learn, that she always dresses very handsomely. Mrs Hughes talked to me a great deal about the family."

"And what did she tell you of them?"

"Oh! a vast deal indeed; she hardly talked of any thing else."

"Did she tell you what part of Gloucestershire they come from?"

"Yes, she did; but I cannot recollect now. But they are very good kind of people, and very rich. Mrs Tilney was a Miss Drummond, and she and Mrs Hughes were schoolfellows; and Miss Drummond had a very large fortune; and, when she married, her father gave her twenty thousand pounds, and five hundred to buy wedding-clothes. Mrs Hughes saw all the clothes after they came from the warehouse."

"And are Mr and Mrs Tilney in Bath?"

"Yes, I fancy they are, but I am not quite certain. Upon recollection, however, I have a notion they are both dead; at least the mother is; yes, I am sure Mrs Tilney is dead, because Mrs Hughes told me there was a very beautiful set of pearls that Mr Drummond gave his daughter on her wedding-day and that Miss Tilney has got now, for they were put by for her when her mother died."

"And is Mr Tilney, my partner, the only son?"

"I cannot be quite positive about that, my dear; I have some idea he is; but, however, he is a very fine young man Mrs Hughes says, and likely to do very well."

Catherine inquired no further; she had heard enough to feel that Mrs Allen had no real intelligence to give, and that she was most particularly unfortunate herself in having missed such a meeting with both brother and sister. Could she have foreseen such a circumstance, nothing should have persuaded her to go out with the others; and, as it was, she could only lament her ill-luck, and think over what she had lost, till it was clear to her, that the drive had by no means been very pleasant and that John Thorpe himself was quite disagreeable.

CHAPTER 10

The Allens, Thorpes, and Morlands all met in the evening at the theatre; and, as Catherine and Isabella sat together, there was then an opportunity for the latter to utter some few of the many thousand things which had been collecting within her for communication, in the immeasurable length of time which had divided them. – "Oh, heavens! my beloved Catherine, have I got you at last?" was her address on Catherine's entering the box and sitting by her. "Now, Mr Morland," for he was close to her on the other side, "I shall not speak another word to you all the rest of the evening; so I charge you not to expect it. My sweetest Catherine, how have you been this long age? but I need not ask you, for you look delightfully. You really have done your hair in a more heavenly style than ever: you mischievous creature, do you want to attract every body? I assure you, my brother is quite in love with you already; and as for Mr Tilney – but *that* is a settled thing – even *your* modesty cannot doubt his attachment now; his coming back to Bath makes it too plain. Oh! what would not I give to see him! I really am quite wild with impatience. My mother says he is the most delightful young man in the world; she saw him this morning you know: you must introduce him to me. Is he in the house now? – Look about for heaven's sake! I assure you, I can hardly exist till I see him."

"No," said Catherine, "he is not here; I cannot see him any where."

"Oh, horrid! am I never to be acquainted with him? How do you like my gown? I think it does not look amiss; the sleeves were entirely my own thought. Do you know I get so immoderately sick of Bath; your brother and I were agreeing this morning that, though it is vastly well to be here for a few weeks, we would not live here for millions. We soon found out that our tastes were exactly alike in preferring the country to every other place; really, our opinions were so exactly the same, it was quite ridiculous!

There was not a single point in which we differed; I would not have had you by for the world; you are such a sly thing, I am sure you would have made some droll remark or other about it."

"No, indeed I should not."

"Oh, yes you would indeed; I know you better than you know yourself. You would have told us that we seemed born for each other, or some nonsense of that kind, which would have distressed me beyond conception; my cheeks would have been as red as your roses; I would not have had you by for the world."

"Indeed you do me injustice; I would not have made so improper a remark upon any account; and besides, I am sure it would never have entered my head."

Isabella smiled incredulously, and talked the rest of the evening to James.

Catherine's resolution of endeavouring to meet Miss Tilney again continued in full force the next morning; and till the usual moment of going to the Pump-room, she felt some alarm from the dread of a second prevention. But nothing of that kind occurred, no visitors appeared to delay them, and they all three set off in good time for the Pump-room, where the ordinary course of events and conversation took place; Mr Allen, after drinking his glass of water, joined some gentlemen to talk over the politics of the day and compare the accounts of their newspapers; and the ladies walked about together, noticing every new face, and almost every new bonnet in the room. The female part of the Thorpe family, attended by James Morland, appeared among the crowd in less than a quarter of an hour, and Catherine immediately took her usual place by the side of her friend. James, who was now in constant attendance, maintained a similar position, and separating themselves from the rest of their party, they walked in that manner for some time, till Catherine began to doubt the happiness of a situation which confining her entirely to her friend and brother, gave her very little share in the notice of either. They were always engaged in some sentimental discussion or lively dispute, but their sentiment was conveyed in such whispering voices, and their vivacity attended with so much laughter, that though Catherine's supporting opinion was not unfrequently called for by one or the other, she was never able to give any, from not having heard a word of the subject. At length however she was empowered to disengage herself from her friend, by the avowed necessity of speaking to Miss Tilney, whom she most joyfully saw just entering the room with Mrs Hughes, and whom she instantly joined, with a firmer determination to be acquainted, than she might have had courage to command, had she not been urged by the disappointment of the day before. Miss Tilney met her with great civility, returned her advances with equal good will, and they continued talking together as long as both parties remained in the room: and though in all probability not an observation was made, nor an expression used by either which had not been made and used some thousands of times before, under that roof, in every Bath season, yet the merit of their being spoken with simplicity and truth, and without personal conceit, might be something uncommon. –

"How well your brother dances!" was an artless exclamation of Catherine's towards the close of their conversation, which at once surprized and amused her companion.

"Henry!" she replied with a smile. "Yes, he does dance very well."

"He must have thought it very odd to hear me say I was engaged the other evening, when he saw me sitting down. But I really had been engaged the whole day to Mr Thorpe." Miss Tilney could only bow. "You cannot think," added Catherine after a moment's silence, "how surprized I was to see him again. I felt so sure of his being quite gone away."

"When Henry had the pleasure of seeing you before, he was in Bath but for a couple of days. He came only to engage lodgings for us."[1]

"*That* never occurred to me; and of course, not seeing him any where, I thought he must be gone. Was not the young lady he danced with on Monday a Miss Smith?"

"Yes, an acquaintance of Mrs Hughes."

---

1   The lodgings Henry engages are in the fashionable Milsom Street, a prestigious central location which satisfies both General Tilney's need to publicly display his wealth and status – since addresses of new arrivals in Bath were published in the Pump room – and his consumerist tendencies since Milsom Street was a central shopping thoroughfare in Bath. See footnote 1, p. 61 above and Appendix F.

"I dare say she was very glad to dance. Do you think her pretty?"

"Not very."

"He never comes to the Pump-room, I suppose?"

"Yes, sometimes; but he has rid out this morning with my father."

Mrs Hughes now joined them, and asked Miss Tilney if she was ready to go. "I hope I shall have the pleasure of seeing you again soon," said Catherine. "Shall you be at the cotillion ball tomorrow?"

"Perhaps we – Yes, I think we certainly shall."

"I am glad of it, for we shall all be there." – This civility was duly returned; and they parted – on Miss Tilney's side with some knowledge of her new acquaintance's feelings, and on Catherine's, without the smallest consciousness of having explained them.

She went home very happy. The morning had answered all her hopes, and the evening of the following day was now the object of expectation, the future good. What gown and what head-dress she should wear on the occasion became her chief concern. She cannot be justified in it. Dress is at all times a frivolous distinction, and excessive solicitude about it often destroys its own aim. Catherine knew all this very well; her great aunt had read her a lecture on the subject only the Christmas before; and yet she lay awake ten minutes on Wednesday night debating between her spotted and her tamboured[1] muslin, and nothing but the shortness of the time prevented her buying a new one for the evening. This would have been an error in judgment, great though not uncommon, from which one of the other sex rather than her own, a brother rather than a great aunt, might have warned her, for man only can be aware of the insensibility of man towards a new gown. It would be mortifying to the feelings of many ladies, could they be made to understand how little the heart of man is affected by what is costly or new in their attire; how little it is biased by the texture of their muslin, and how unsusceptible of peculiar tenderness towards the spotted, the sprigged, the mull, or the jackonet.[2] Woman is fine

---

1 Embroidery worked on a tambour frame; usually a rich gold and silver.
2 Mull is a thin variety of plain, soft muslin. Jaconet is a heavier, stouter, cotton fabric.

for her own satisfaction alone. No man will admire her the more, no woman will like her the better for it. Neatness and fashion are enough for the former, and a something of shabbiness or impropriety will be most endearing to the latter. – But not one of these grave reflections troubled the tranquillity of Catherine.

She entered the rooms on Thursday evening with feelings very different from what had attended her thither the Monday before. She had then been exulting in her engagement to Thorpe, and was now chiefly anxious to avoid his sight, lest he should engage her again; for though she could not, dared not expect that Mr Tilney should ask her a third time to dance, her wishes, hopes, and plans all centred in nothing less. Every young lady may feel for my heroine in this critical moment, for every young lady has at some time or other known the same agitation. All have been, or at least all have believed themselves to be, in danger from the pursuit of some one whom they wished to avoid; and all have been anxious for the attentions of some one whom they wished to please. As soon as they were joined by the Thorpes, Catherine's agony began; she fidgetted about if John Thorpe came towards her, hid herself as much as possible from his view, and when he spoke to her pretended not to hear him. The cotillions were over, the country-dancing beginning, and she saw nothing of the Tilneys. "Do not be frightened, my dear Catherine," whispered Isabella, "but I am really going to dance with your brother again. I declare positively it is quite shocking. I tell him he ought to be ashamed of himself, but you and John must keep us in countenance. Make haste, my dear creature, and come to us. John is just walked off, but he will be back in a moment."

Catherine had neither time nor inclination to answer. The others walked away, John Thorpe was still in view, and she gave herself up for lost. That she might not appear, however, to observe or expect him, she kept her eyes intently fixed on her fan; and a self-condemnation for her folly, in supposing that among such a crowd they should even meet with the Tilneys in any reasonable time, had just passed through her mind, when she suddenly found herself addressed and again solicited to dance, by Mr Tilney himself. With what sparkling eyes and ready motion she granted his request, and with how pleasing a flutter of heart she went with him to the set, may be easily imagined. To escape, and, as she believed, so narrowly escape John Thorpe, and to be asked, so immediately on his joining her, asked by Mr Tilney, as if he had sought her on purpose! – it did not appear to her that life could supply any greater felicity.

Scarcely had they worked themselves into the quiet possession of a place, however, when her attention was claimed by John Thorpe, who stood behind her. "Heyday, Miss Morland!" said he, "what is the meaning of this? – I thought you and I were to dance together."

"I wonder you should think so, for you never asked me." "That is a good one, by Jove! – I asked you as soon as I came into the room, and I was just going to ask you again, but when I turned round, you were gone! – this is a cursed shabby trick! I only came for the sake of dancing with *you*, and I firmly believe you were engaged to me ever since Monday. Yes; I remember, I asked you while you were waiting in the lobby for your cloak. And here have I been telling all my acquaintance that I was going to dance with the prettiest girl in the room; and when they see you standing up with somebody else, they will quiz me famously."

"Oh, no; they will never think of *me*, after such a description as that."

"By heavens, if they do not, I will kick them out of the room for blockheads. What chap have you there?" Catherine satisfied his curiosity. "Tilney," he repeated, "Hum – I do not know him. A good figure of a man; well put together. Does he want a horse? – Here is a friend of mine, Sam Fletcher, has got one to sell that would suit anybody. A famous clever animal for the road – only forty guineas. I had fifty minds to buy it myself, for it is one of my maxims always to buy a good horse when I meet with one; but it would not answer my purpose, it would not do for the field. I would give any money for a real good hunter. I have three now, the best that ever were back'd. I would not take eight hundred guineas for them. Fletcher and I mean to get a house in Leicestershire, against the next season. It is so d— uncomfortable, living at an inn."

This was the last sentence by which he could weary Catherine's attention, for he was just then born off by the resistless pressure of a long string of passing ladies. Her partner now drew near, and said, "That gentleman would have put me out of patience, had he staid with you half a minute longer. He has no business to withdraw the attention of my partner from me. We have entered into a contract of mutual agreeableness for the space of an evening, and all our agreeableness belongs solely to each other for that time. Nobody can fasten themselves on the notice of one, without injuring the rights of the other. I consider a country-dance as an emblem of marriage. Fidelity and complaisance are the principal duties of both; and those men who do not chuse to dance or marry themselves, have no business with the partners or wives of their neighbours."

"But they are such very different things! –"

"– That you think they cannot be compared together."

"To be sure not. People that marry can never part, but must go and keep house together. People that dance, only stand opposite each other in a long room for half an hour."

"And such is your definition of matrimony and dancing. Taken in that light certainly, their resemblance is not striking; but I think I could place them in such a view. – You will allow, that in both, man has the advantage of choice, woman only the power of refusal; that in both, it is an engagement between man and woman, formed for the advantage of each; and that when once entered into, they belong exclusively to each other till the moment of its dissolution; that it is their duty, each to endeavour to give the other no cause for wishing that he or she had bestowed themselves elsewhere, and their best interest to keep their own imaginations from wandering towards the perfections of their neighbours, or fancying that they should have been better off with anyone else. You will allow all this?"

"Yes, to be sure, as you state it, all this sounds very well; but still they are so very different. – I cannot look upon them at all in the same light, nor think the same duties belong to them."

"In one respect, there certainly is a difference. In marriage, the man is supposed to provide for the support of the woman; the woman to make the home agreeable to the man; he is to purvey, and she is to smile. But in dancing, their duties are exactly changed; the agreeableness, the compliance are expected from him, while she furnishes the fan and the lavender water. *That,* I suppose, was the difference of duties which struck you, as rendering the conditions incapable of comparison."

"No, indeed, I never thought of that."

"Then I am quite at a loss. One thing, however, I must observe. This disposition on your side is rather alarming. You totally disallow any similarity in the obligations; and may I not thence infer, that your notions of the duties of the dancing state are not so strict as your partner might wish? Have I not reason to fear, that if the gentleman who spoke to you just now were to return, or if any other gentleman were to address you, there would be nothing to restrain you from conversing with him as long as you chose?"

"Mr Thorpe is such a very particular friend of my brother's, that if he talks to me, I must talk to him again; but there are hardly three young men in the room besides him, that I have any acquaintance with."

"And is that to be my only security? alas, alas!"

"Nay, I am sure you cannot have a better; for if I do not know any body, it is impossible for me to talk to them; and, besides, I do not *want* to talk to any body."

"Now you have given me a security worth having; and I shall proceed with courage. Do you find Bath as agreeable as when I had the honour of making the inquiry before?"

"Yes, quite – more so, indeed."

"More so! – Take care, or you will forget to be tired of it at the proper time. – You ought to be tired at the end of six weeks."

"I do not think I should be tired, if I were to stay here six months."

"Bath, compared with London, has little variety, and so every body finds out every year. 'For six weeks, I allow Bath is pleasant enough; but beyond *that,* it is the most tiresome place in the world.' You would be told so by people of all descriptions, who come regularly every winter, lengthen their six weeks into ten or twelve, and go away at last because they can afford to stay no longer."

"Well, other people must judge for themselves, and those who go to London may think nothing of Bath. But I, who live in a small retired village in the country, can never find greater sameness in such a place as this, than in my own home; for here are a variety of amusements, a variety of things to be seen and done all day long, which I can know nothing of there."

"You are not fond of the country."

"Yes, I am. I have always lived there, and always been very happy. But certainly there is much more sameness in a country life than in a Bath life. One day in the country is exactly like another."

"But then you spend your time so much more rationally in the country."

"Do I?"

"Do you not?"

"I do not believe there is much difference."

"Here you are in pursuit only of amusement all day long."

"And so I am at home – only I do not find so much of it. I walk about here, and so I do there; – but here I see a variety of people in every street, and there I can only go and call on Mrs Allen."

Mr Tilney was very much amused. "Only go and call on Mrs Allen!" he repeated. "What a picture of intellectual poverty! However, when you sink into this abyss again, you will have more to say. You will be able to talk of Bath, and of all that you did here."

"Oh! yes. I shall never be in want of something to talk of again to Mrs Allen, or any body else. I really believe I shall always be talking of Bath, when I am at home again – I *do* like it so very much. If I could but have papa and mamma, and the rest of them here, I suppose I should be too happy! James's coming (my eldest brother) is quite delightful – and especially as it turns out, that the very family we are just got so intimate with, are his intimate friends already. Oh! who can ever be tired of Bath?"

"Not those who bring such fresh feelings of every sort to it, as you do. But papas and mammas, and brothers and intimate friends are a good deal gone by, to most of the frequenters of Bath – and the honest relish of balls and plays, and every-day sights, is past with them."

Here their conversation closed; the demands of the dance becoming now too importunate for a divided attention.

Soon after their reaching the bottom of the set, Catherine perceived herself to be earnestly regarded by a gentleman who stood among the lookers-on, immediately behind her partner. He was a very handsome man, of a commanding aspect, past the bloom, but not past the vigour of life; and with his eye still directed towards her, she saw him presently address Mr Tilney in a familiar whisper. Confused by his notice, and blushing from the fear of its being excited by something wrong in her appearance, she turned away her head. But while she did so, the gentleman retreated, and her partner, coming nearer, said, "I see that you guess what I have just been asked. That gentleman knows your name, and you have a right to know his. It is General Tilney, my father."

Catherine's answer was only "Oh!" – but it was an "Oh!" expressing every thing needful; attention to his words, and perfect reliance on their truth. With real interest and strong admiration did her eye now follow the General, as he moved through the crowd, and "How handsome a family they are!" was her secret remark.

In chatting with Miss Tilney before the evening concluded, a new source of felicity arose to her. She had never taken a country walk since her arrival in Bath. Miss Tilney, to whom all the commonly-frequented environs were familiar, spoke of them in terms which made her all eagerness to know them too; and on her openly fearing that she might find nobody to go with her, it was proposed by the brother and sister that they should join in a walk, some morning or other. "I shall like it," she cried, "beyond any thing in the world; and do not let us put it off – let us go tomorrow." This was readily agreed to, with only a proviso of Miss Tilney's, that it did not rain, which Catherine was sure it would not. At twelve o'clock, they were to call for her in Pulteney-street – and – "remember – twelve o'clock," was her parting speech to her new friend. Of her other, her older, her more established friend, Isabella, of whose fidelity and worth she had enjoyed a fortnight's experience, she scarcely saw any thing during the evening. Yet, though longing to make her acquainted with her happiness, she cheerfully submitted to the wish of Mr Allen, which took them rather early away, and her spirits danced within her, as she danced in her chair all the way home.

The morrow brought a very sober looking morning; the sun making only a few efforts to appear; and Catherine augured from it, every thing most favourable to her wishes. A bright morning so early in the year, she allowed, would generally turn to rain, but a cloudy one foretold improvement as the day advanced. She applied to Mr Allen for confirmation of her hopes, but Mr Allen, not having his own skies and barometer about him, declined giving any absolute promise of sunshine. She applied to Mrs Allen, and Mrs Allen's opinion was more positive. "She had no doubt in the world of its being a very fine day, if the clouds would only go off, and the sun keep out."

At about eleven o'clock, however, a few specks of small rain upon the windows caught Catherine's watchful eye, and "Oh! dear, I do believe it will be wet," broke from her in a most desponding tone.

"I thought how it would be," said Mrs Allen.

"No walk for me to-day," sighed Catherine; – "but perhaps it may come to nothing, or it may hold up before twelve."

"Perhaps it may, but then, my dear, it will be so dirty."

"Oh! that will not signify; I never mind dirt."

"No," replied her friend very placidly, "I know you never mind dirt."

After a short pause, "It comes on faster and faster!" said Catherine, as she stood watching at a window.

"So it does indeed. If it keeps raining, the streets will be very wet."

"There are four umbrellas up already. How I hate the sight of an umbrella!"

"They are disagreeable things to carry. I would much rather take a chair at any time."

"It was such a nice looking morning! I felt so convinced it would be dry!"

"Any body would have thought so indeed. There will be very few people in the Pump-room, if it rains all the morning. I hope Mr Allen will put on his great coat when he goes, but I dare say he will not, for he had rather do any thing in the world than walk out in a great coat; I wonder he should dislike it, it must be so comfortable."

The rain continued – fast, though not heavy. Catherine went every five minutes to the clock, threatening on each return that, if it still kept on raining another five minutes, she would give up the matter as hopeless. The clock struck twelve, and it still rained.

– "You will not be able to go, my dear."

"I do not quite despair yet. I shall not give it up till a quarter after twelve. This is just the time of day for it to clear up, and I do think it looks a little lighter. There, it is twenty minutes after twelve, and now I *shall* give it up entirely.

Oh! that we had such weather here as they had at Udolpho, or at least in Tuscany and the south of France! – the night that poor St Aubin died![1] – such beautiful weather!"

At half past twelve, when Catherine's anxious attention to the weather was over and she could no longer claim any merit from its amendment, the sky began voluntarily to clear. A gleam of sunshine took her quite by surprize; she looked round; the clouds were parting, and she instantly returned to the window to watch over and encourage the happy appearance. Ten minutes more made it certain that a bright afternoon would succeed, and justified the opinion of Mrs Allen, who had "always thought it would clear up."

But whether Catherine might still expect her friends, whether there had not been too much rain for Miss Tilney to venture, must yet be a question.

It was too dirty for Mrs Allen to accompany her husband to the Pump-room; he accordingly set off by himself, and Catherine had barely watched him down the street, when her notice was claimed by the approach of the same two open carriages, containing the same three people that had surprized her so much a few mornings back.

"Isabella, my brother, and Mr Thorpe, I declare! They are coming for me perhaps – but I shall not go – I cannot go indeed, for you know Miss Tilney may still call." Mrs Allen agreed to it. John

---

1   St Aubert (not Aubin), the heroine's father, dies in the late afternoon (*Mysteries of Udolpho* vol 1, ch. 7).

Thorpe was soon with them, and his voice was with them yet sooner, for on the stairs he was calling out to Miss Morland to be quick. "Make haste! make haste!" as he threw open the door – "put on your hat this moment – there is no time to be lost – we are going to Bristol. – How d'ye do, Mrs Allen?"

"To Bristol! Is not that a great way off? – But, however, I cannot go with you today, because I am engaged; I expect some friends every moment." This was of course vehemently talked down as no reason at all; Mrs Allen was called on to second him, and the two others walked in, to give their assistance. "My sweetest Catherine, is not this delightful? We shall have a most heavenly drive. You are to thank your brother and me for the scheme; it darted into our heads at breakfast-time, I verily believe at the same instant; and we should have been off two hours ago if it had not been for this detestable rain. But it does not signify, the nights are moonlight, and we shall do delightfully. Oh! I am in such extasies at the thoughts of a little country air and quiet! – so much better than going to the Lower Rooms. We shall drive directly to Clifton and dine there; and, as soon as dinner is over, if there is time for it, go on to Kingsweston."

"I doubt our being able to do so much," said Morland.

"You croaking fellow!" cried Thorpe, "we shall be able to do ten times more. Kingsweston! aye, and Blaize Castle too, and any thing else we can hear of; but here is your sister says she will not go."

"Blaize Castle!" cried Catherine; "what is that?"

"The finest place in England – worth going fifty miles at any time to see."

"What, is it really a castle, an old castle?"

"The oldest in the kingdom."[1]

---

1   Thorpe either lies or is ignorant of the fact that Blaize Castle was actually a sham built in 1766 for Thomas Farr, a Bristol sugar-merchant. Farr hoped to embellish the view from the windows of his house, and provide a hill-top platform for viewing. The sham, for which he paid £3,000, consists of a large circular room with three small towers around it, castellated and pierced by cruciform arrow-slits. The extensive picturesque gardens were laid out by (Humphrey) Henry Repton and the buildings by John Nash. See Maggie Lane, *Jane Austen Society Collected Reports 1976-1985*, Jane Austen Society: Great Britain, 1989, 316.

"But is it like what one reads of?"

"Exactly – the very same."

"But now really – are there towers and long galleries?"

"By dozens."

"Then I should like to see it; but I cannot – I cannot go."

"Not go! – my beloved creature, what do you mean?"

"I cannot go, because" – (looking down as she spoke, fearful of Isabella's smile) "I expect Miss Tilney and her brother to call on me to take a country walk. They promised to come at twelve, only it rained; but now, as it is so fine, I dare say they will be here soon."

"Not they indeed," cried Thorpe; "for, as we turned into Broad street, I saw them – does he not drive a phaeton with bright chestnuts?"[1]

"I do not know indeed."

"Yes, I know he does; I saw him. You are talking of the man you danced with last night, are not you?"

"Yes."

"Well, I saw him at that moment turn up the Lansdown Road, – driving a smart-looking girl."

"Did you indeed?"

"Did upon my soul; knew him again directly, and he seemed to have got some very pretty cattle too."

"It is very odd! but I suppose they thought it would be too dirty for a walk."

"And well they might, for I never saw so much dirt in my life. Walk! you could no more walk than you could fly! it has not been so dirty the whole winter; it is ancle-deep every where."

Isabella corroborated it: – "My dearest Catherine, you cannot form an idea of the dirt; come, you must go; you cannot refuse going now."

"I should like to see the castle; but may we go all over it? may we go up every staircase, and into every suite of rooms?"

"Yes, yes, every hole and corner."

"But then, – if they should only be gone out for an hour till it is drier, and call by and bye?"

"Make yourself easy, there is no danger of that, for I heard

---

1   See Appendix J.2.

Tilney hallooing to a man who was just passing by on horseback, that they were going as far as Wick Rocks."

"Then I will. Shall I go, Mrs Allen?"

"Just as you please, my dear."

"Mrs Allen, you must persuade her to go," was the general cry. Mrs Allen was not inattentive to it: – "Well, my dear," said she, "suppose you go." – And in two minutes they were off.

Catherine's feelings, as she got into the carriage, were in a very unsettled state; divided between regret for the loss of one great pleasure, and the hope of soon enjoying another, almost its equal in degree, however unlike in kind. She could not think the Tilneys had acted quite well by her, in so readily giving up their engagement, without sending her any message of excuse. It was now but an hour later than the time fixed on for the beginning of their walk; and, in spite of what she had heard of the prodigious accumulation of dirt in the course of that hour, she could not from her own observation help thinking, that they might have gone with very little inconvenience. To feel herself slighted by them was very painful. On the other hand, the delight of exploring an edifice like Udolpho, as her fancy represented Blaize Castle to be, was such a counterpoise of good, as might console her for almost any thing.

They passed briskly down Pulteney-street, and through Laura-place, without the exchange of many words. Thorpe talked to his horse, and she meditated, by turns, on broken promises and broken arches, phaetons and false hangings, Tilneys and trap-doors. As they entered Argyle-buildings, however, she was roused by this address from her companion, "Who is that girl who looked at you so hard as she went by?"

"Who? – where?"

"On the right-hand pavement – she must be almost out of sight now." Catherine looked round and saw Miss Tilney leaning on her brother's arm, walking slowly down the street. She saw them both looking back at her. "Stop, stop, Mr Thorpe," she impatiently cried, "it is Miss Tilney; it is indeed. – How could you tell me they were gone? – Stop, stop, I will get out this moment and go to them." But to what purpose did she speak? – Thorpe only lashed his horse into a brisker trot; the Tilneys, who had soon ceased to look after her, were in a moment out of sight round the corner of Laura-place, and in another moment she was herself whisked into the Market-place. Still, however, and during the length of another street, she intreated him to stop. "Pray, pray stop, Mr Thorpe. – I cannot go on. – I will not go on. – I must go back to Miss Tilney." But Mr Thorpe only laughed, smacked his whip, encouraged his horse, made odd noises, and drove on; and Catherine, angry and vexed as she was, having no power of getting away, was obliged to give up the point and submit.[1] Her reproaches, however, were not spared. "How could you deceive me so, Mr Thorpe? – how could you say, that you saw them driving up the Lansdown-road? – I would not have had it happen so for the world. – They must think it so strange; so rude of me! to go by them, too, without saying a word! You do not know how vexed I am – I shall have no pleasure at Clifton, nor in any thing else. I had rather, ten thousand times rather get out now, and walk back to them. How could you say you saw them driving out in a phaeton?" Thorpe defended himself very stoutly, declared he had never seen two men so much alike in his life, and would hardly give up the point of its having been Tilney himself.

Their drive, even when this subject was over, was not likely to be very agreeable. Catherine's complaisance was no longer what it had been in their former airing. She listened reluctantly, and her replies were short. Blaize Castle remained her only comfort; towards *that*, she still looked at intervals with pleasure; though rather than be disappointed of the promised walk, and especially rather than be thought ill of by the Tilneys, she would willingly have given up all the happiness which its walls could supply – the happiness of a progress through a long suite of lofty rooms, exhibiting the remains of magnificent furniture, though now for many years deserted – the happiness of being stopped in their way along narrow, winding vaults, by a low, grated door; or even of having their lamp, their only lamp, extinguished by a sudden gust of wind, and of being left in total darkness. In the meanwhile, they proceeded on their journey without any mischance; and were within view of the town of Keynsham, when a halloo from Mor-

---

1   This episode parodies the common abduction of heroines by rakish villains in sentimental fiction. See Amy Smith "Julia's and Louisa's" (38).

land, who was behind them, made his friend pull up, to know what was the matter. The others then came close enough for conversation, and Morland said, "We had better go back, Thorpe; it is too late to go on to-day; your sister thinks so as well as I. We have been exactly an hour coming from Pulteney-street, very little more than seven miles; and, I suppose, we have at least eight more to go. It will never do. We set out a great deal too late. We had much better put it off till another day, and turn round."

"It is all one to me," replied Thorpe rather angrily; and instantly turning his horse, they were on their way back to Bath.

"If your brother had not got such a d— beast to drive," said he soon afterwards, "we might have done it very well. My horse would have trotted to Clifton within the hour, if left to himself, and I have almost broke my arm with pulling him in to that cursed broken-winded jade's pace. Morland is a fool for not keeping a horse and gig of his own."

"No, he is not," said Catherine warmly, "for I am sure he could not afford it."

"And why cannot he afford it?"

"Because he has not money enough."

"And whose fault is that?"

"Nobody's, that I know of." Thorpe then said something in the loud, incoherent way to which he had often recourse, about its being a d— thing to be miserly; and that if people who rolled in money could not afford things, he did not know who could; which Catherine did not even endeavour to understand. Disappointed of what was to have been the consolation for her first disappointment, she was less and less disposed either to be agreeable herself, or to find her companion so; and they returned to Pulteney-street without her speaking twenty words.

As she entered the house, the footman told her that a gentleman and lady had called and inquired for her a few minutes after her setting off; that, when he told them she was gone out with Mr Thorpe, the lady had asked whether any message had been left for her; and on his saying no, had felt for a card, but said she had none about her, and went away. Pondering over these heart-rending tidings, Catherine walked slowly upstairs. At the head of them she was met by Mr Allen, who, on hearing the reason of their speedy return, said, "I am glad your brother had so much sense; I am glad you are come back. It was a strange, wild scheme."

They all spent the evening together at Thorpe's. Catherine was disturbed and out of spirits; but Isabella seemed to find a pool of commerce,[1] in the fate of which she shared, by private partnership with Morland, a very good equivalent for the quiet and country air of an inn at Clifton. Her satisfaction, too, in not being at the Lower Rooms, was spoken more than once. "How I pity the poor creatures that are going there! How glad I am that I am not amongst them! I wonder whether it will be a full ball or not! They have not begun dancing yet. I would not be there for all the world. It is so delightful to have an evening now and then to oneself. I dare say it will not be a very good ball. I know the Mitchells will not be there. I am sure I pity every body that is. But I dare say, Mr Morland, you long to be at it, do not you? I am sure you do. Well, pray do not let anybody here be a restraint on you. I dare say we could do very well without you; but you men think yourselves of such consequence."

Catherine could almost have accused Isabella of being wanting in tenderness towards herself and her sorrows; so very little did they appear to dwell on her mind, and so very inadequate was the comfort she offered. "Do not be so dull, my dearest creature," she whispered. "You will quite break my heart. It was amazingly shocking to be sure; but the Tilneys were entirely to blame. Why were not they more punctual? It was dirty, indeed, but what did that signify? I am sure John and I should not have minded it. I never mind going through any thing, where a friend is concerned; that is my disposition, and John is just the same; he has amazing strong feelings. Good heavens! what a delightful hand you have got! Kings, I vow! I never was so happy in my life! I would fifty times rather you should have them than myself."

---

1 A popular card-game usually played for small stakes in which exchange or barter is the chief feature. Each player places a stake and then, in succession, exchanges one of his/her three cards for another card until someone refuses. At such time the player with the best hand wins. A game involving barter is singularly appropriate enjoyment for Isabella, who is adept at exchanging one lover for another for explicitly commercial reasons.

And now I may dismiss my heroine to the sleepless couch, which is the true heroine's portion; to a pillow strewed with thorns and wet with tears. And lucky may she think herself, if she get another good night's rest in the course of the next three months.

CHAPTER 12

"Mrs Allen," said Catherine the next morning, "will there be any harm in my calling on Miss Tilney to-day? I shall not be easy till I have explained every thing."

"Go by all means, my dear; only put on a white gown; Miss Tilney always wears white."

Catherine cheerfully complied; and being properly equipped, was more impatient than ever to be at the Pump-room, that she might inform herself of General Tilney's lodgings, for though she believed they were in Milsom-street,[1] she was not certain of the house, and Mrs Allen's wavering convictions only made it more doubtful. To Milsom Street she was directed; and having made herself perfect in the number, hastened away with eager steps and a beating heart to pay her visit, explain her conduct, and be forgiven; tripping lightly through the church-yard, and resolutely turning away her eyes, that she might not be obliged to see her beloved Isabella and her dear family, who, she had reason to believe, were in a shop hard by. She reached the house without any impediment, looked at the number, knocked at the door, and inquired for Miss Tilney. The man believed Miss Tilney to be at home, but was not quite certain. Would she be pleased to send up her name? She gave her card. In a few minutes the servant returned, and with a look which did not quite confirm his words, said he had been mistaken, for that Miss Tilney was walked out. Catherine, with a blush of mortification, left the house. She felt almost persuaded that Miss Tilney was at home, and too much offended to admit her; and as she retired down the street, could not withhold one glance at the drawing-room windows, in expectation of seeing her there, but no one appeared at them. At the bottom of the street, however, she looked back again, and then,

---

1   See footnote 1, p. 91 and Appendix F.

not at a window, but issuing from the door, she saw Miss Tilney herself. She was followed by a gentleman, whom Catherine believed to be her father, and they turned up towards Edgar's-buildings. Catherine, in deep mortification, proceeded on her way. She could almost be angry herself at such angry incivility; but she checked the resentful sensation; she remembered her own ignorance. She knew not how such an offence as her's might be classed by the laws of worldly politeness, to what a degree of unforgivingness it might with propriety lead, nor to what rigours of rudeness in return it might justly make her amenable.

Dejected and humbled, she had even some thoughts of not going with the others to the theatre that night; but it must be confessed that they were not of long continuance: for she soon recollected, in the first place, that she was without any excuse for staying at home; and, in the second, that it was a play she wanted very much to see. To the theatre accordingly they all went; no Tilneys appeared to plague or please her; she feared that, amongst the many perfections of the family, a fondness for plays was not to be ranked; but perhaps it was because they were habituated to the finer performances of the London stage, which she knew, on Isabella's authority, rendered everything else of the kind "quite horrid." She was not deceived in her own expectation of pleasure; the comedy so well suspended her care, that no one, observing her during the first four acts, would have supposed she had any wretchedness about her. On the beginning of the fifth, however, the sudden view of Mr Henry Tilney and his father, joining a party in the opposite box, recalled her to anxiety and distress. The stage could no longer excite genuine merriment – no longer keep her whole attention. Every other look upon an average was directed towards the opposite box; and, for the space of two entire scenes, did she thus watch Henry Tilney, without being once able to catch his eye. No longer could he be suspected of indifference for a play; his notice was never withdrawn from the stage during two whole scenes. At length, however, he did look towards her, and he bowed – but such a bow! no smile, no continued observance attended it; his eyes were immediately returned to their former direction. Catherine was restlessly miserable; she could almost have run round to the box in which he sat, and forced him to hear her explanation. Feelings rather natural than heroic possessed her; instead of considering her own dignity injured by this ready condemnation – instead of proudly resolving, in conscious innocence, to shew her resentment towards him who could harbour a doubt of it, to leave to him all the trouble of seeking an explanation, and to enlighten him on the past only by avoiding his sight, or flirting with somebody else, she took to herself all the shame of misconduct, or at least of its appearance, and was only eager for an opportunity of explaining its cause.

The play concluded – the curtain fell – Henry Tilney was no longer to be seen where he had hitherto sat, but his father remained, and perhaps he might be now coming round to their box. She was right; in a few minutes he appeared, and, making his way through the then thinning rows, spoke with like calm politeness to Mrs Allen and her friend. – Not with such calmness was he answered by the latter: "Oh! Mr Tilney, I have been quite wild to speak to you, and make my apologies. You must have thought me so rude; but indeed it was not my own fault, – was it, Mrs Allen? Did not they tell me that Mr Tilney and his sister were gone out in a phaeton together? and then what could I do? But I had ten thousand times rather have been with you; now had not I, Mrs Allen?"

"My dear, you tumble my gown," was Mrs Allen's reply.

Her assurance, however, standing sole as it did, was not thrown away; it brought a more cordial, more natural smile into his countenance, and he replied in a tone which retained only a little affected reserve: – "We were much obliged to you at any rate for wishing us a pleasant walk after our passing you in Argyle-street: you were so kind as to look back on purpose."

"But indeed I did not wish you a pleasant walk; I never thought of such a thing; but I begged Mr Thorpe so earnestly to stop; I called out to him as soon as ever I saw you; now, Mrs Allen, did not – Oh! You were not there; but indeed I did; and, if Mr Thorpe would only have stopped, I would have jumped out and run after you."

Is there a Henry in the world who could be insensible to such a declaration? Henry Tilney at least was not. With a yet sweeter smile, he said every thing that need be said of his sister's concern, regret, and dependence on Catherine's honour. – "Oh! do not say Miss Tilney was not angry," cried Catherine, "because I know she was; for she would not see me this morning when I called; I saw her walk out of the house the next minute after my leaving it; I was hurt, but I was not affronted. Perhaps you did not know I had been there."

"I was not within at the time; but I heard of it from Eleanor, and she has been wishing ever since to see you, to explain the reason of such incivility; but perhaps I can do it as well. It was nothing more than that my father – they were just preparing to walk out, and he being hurried for time, and not caring to have it put off, made a point of her being denied. That was all, I do assure you. She was very much vexed, and meant to make her apology as soon as possible."

Catherine's mind was greatly eased by this information, yet a something of solicitude remained, from which sprang the following question, thoroughly artless in itself, though rather distressing to the gentleman: – "But, Mr Tilney, why were *you* less generous than your sister? If she felt such confidence in my good intentions, and could suppose it to be only a mistake, why should *you* be so ready to take offence?"

"Me! – I take offence!"

"Nay, I am sure by your look, when you came into the box, you were angry."

"I angry! I could have no right."

"Well, nobody would have thought you had no right who saw your face." He replied by asking her to make room for him, and talking of the play.

He remained with them some time, and was only too agreeable for Catherine to be contented when he went away. Before they parted, however, it was agreed that the projected walk should be taken as soon as possible; and, setting aside the misery of his quitting their box, she was, upon the whole, left one of the happiest creatures in the world.

While talking to each other, she had observed with some surprize, that John Thorpe, who was never in the same part of the house for ten minutes together, was engaged in conversation with General Tilney; and she felt something more than surprize, when she thought she could perceive herself the object of their attention and discourse. What could they have to say of her? She feared General Tilney did not like her appearance: she found it was implied in his preventing her admittance to his daughter, rather than postpone his own walk a few minutes. "How came Mr Thorpe to know your father?" was her anxious inquiry, as she pointed them out to her companion. He knew nothing about it; but his father, like every military man, had a very large acquaintance.

When the entertainment was over, Thorpe came to assist them in getting out. Catherine was the immediate object of his gallantry; and, while they waited in the lobby for a chair, he prevented the inquiry which had travelled from her heart almost to the tip of her tongue, by asking, in a consequential manner, whether she had seen him talking with General Tilney: — "He is a fine old fellow, upon my soul! — stout, active — looks as young as his son. I have a great regard for him, I assure you: a gentleman-like, good sort of fellow as ever lived."

"But how came you to know him?"

"Know him! — There are few people much about town that I do not know. I have met him for ever at the Bedford;[1] and I knew his face again to-day the moment he came into the billiard-room. One of the best players we have, by the bye; and we had a little touch together, though I was almost afraid of him at first: the odds were five to four against me; and, if I had not made one of the cleanest strokes that perhaps ever was made in this world — I took his ball exactly — but I could not make you understand it without a table; — however, I *did* beat him. A very fine fellow; as rich as a Jew. I should like to dine with him; I dare say he gives famous dinners. But what do you think we have been talking of? — you. Yes, by heavens! — and the general thinks you the finest girl in Bath."

"Oh! nonsense! how can you say so?"

"And what do you think I said?" (lowering his voice) "Well done, General, said I, I am quite of your mind."

Here Catherine, who was much less gratified by his admira-

---

1   The Bedford Coffee house near Covent Garden, London, was a regular haunt of David Garrick, William Collins, Henry Fielding, Alexander Pope, David Brinsley Sheridan, and Horace Walpole.

tion than by General Tilney's, was not sorry to be called away by Mr Allen. Thorpe, however, would see her to her chair, and, till she entered it, continued the same kind of delicate flattery, in spite of her entreating him to have done.

That General Tilney, instead of disliking, should admire her, was very delightful; and she joyfully thought, that there was not one of the family whom she need now fear to meet. – The evening had done more, much more, for her, than could have been expected.

CHAPTER 13

Monday, Tuesday, Wednesday, Thursday, Friday and Saturday have now passed in review before the reader;[1] the events of each day, its hopes and fears, mortifications and pleasures have been separately stated, and the pangs of Sunday only now remain to be described, and close the week. The Clifton scheme had been deferred, not relinquished, and on the afternoon's Crescent of this day, it was brought forward again. In a private consultation between Isabella and James, the former of whom had particularly set her heart upon going, and the latter no less anxiously placed his upon pleasing her, it was agreed that, provided the weather were fair, the party should take place on the following morning; and they were to set off very early, in order to be at home in good time. The affair thus determined, and Thorpe's approbation secured, Catherine only remained to be apprized of it. She had left them for a few minutes to speak to Miss Tilney. In that interval the plan was completed, and as soon as she came again, her agreement was demanded; but instead of the gay acquiescence expected by Isabella, Catherine looked grave, was very sorry, but could not go. The engagement which ought to have kept her from joining in the former attempt, would make it impossible for her to accompany them now. She had that moment settled with Miss Tilney to take their proposed walk to-morrow; it was quite determined, and she would not, upon any account, retract. But that she *must* and *should* retract, was

---

1   While Austen enjoyed and admired both Samuel Richardson and Frances Burney she was not above gently satirizing their protagonists' copious correspondence and journal entries.

instantly the eager cry of both the Thorpes; they must go to Clifton to-morrow, they would not go without her, it would be nothing to put off a mere walk for one day longer, and they would not hear of a refusal. Catherine was distressed, but not subdued. "Do not urge me, Isabella. I am engaged to Miss Tilney. I cannot go." This availed nothing. The same arguments assailed her again; she must go, she should go, and they would not hear of a refusal. "It would be so easy to tell Miss Tilney that you had just been reminded of a prior engagement, and must only beg to put off the walk till Tuesday."

"No, it would not be easy. I could not do it. There has been no prior engagement." But Isabella became only more and more urgent; calling on her in the most affectionate manner; addressing her by the most endearing names. She was sure her dearest, sweetest Catherine would not seriously refuse such a trifling request to a friend who loved her so dearly. She knew her beloved Catherine to have so feeling a heart, so sweet a temper, to be so easily persuaded by those she loved. But all in vain; Catherine felt herself to be in the right, and though pained by such tender, such flattering supplication, could not allow it to influence her. Isabella then tried another method. She reproached her with having more affection for Miss Tilney, though she had known her so little a while, than for her best and oldest friends; with being grown cold and indifferent, in short, towards herself. "I cannot help being jealous, Catherine, when I see myself slighted for strangers, I, who love you so excessively! When once my affections are placed, it is not in the power of any thing to change them. But I believe my feelings are stronger than any body's; I am sure they are too strong for my own peace; and to see myself supplanted in your friendship by strangers, does cut me to the quick, I own. These Tilneys seem to swallow up every thing else."

Catherine thought this reproach equally strange and unkind. Was it the part of a friend thus to expose her feelings to the notice of others? Isabella appeared to her ungenerous and selfish, regardless of every thing but her own gratification. These painful ideas crossed her mind, though she said nothing. Isabella, in the meanwhile, had applied her handkerchief to her eyes; and Morland, miserable at such a sight, could not help saying, "Nay, Catherine.

I think you cannot stand out any longer now. The sacrifice is not much; and to oblige such a friend – I shall think you quite unkind, if you still refuse."

This was the first time of her brother's openly siding against her, and anxious to avoid his displeasure, she proposed a compromise. If they would only put off their scheme till Tuesday, which they might easily do, as it depended only on themselves, she could go with them, and every body might then be satisfied. But "No, no, no!" was the immediate answer; "that could not be, for Thorpe did not know that he might not go to town on Tuesday." Catherine was sorry, but could do no more; and a short silence ensued, which was broken by Isabella, who in a voice of cold resentment said, "Very well, then there is an end of the party. If Catherine does not go, I cannot. I cannot be the only woman. I would not, upon any account in the world, do so improper a thing."

"Catherine, you must go," said James.

"But why cannot Mr Thorpe drive one of his other sisters? I dare say either of them would like to go."

"Thank ye," cried Thorpe, "but I did not come to Bath to drive my sisters about, and look like a fool. No, if you do not go, d— me if I do. I only go for the sake of driving you."

"That is a compliment which gives me no pleasure." But her words were lost on Thorpe, who had turned abruptly away.

The three others still continued together, walking in a most uncomfortable manner to poor Catherine; sometimes not a word was said, sometimes she was again attacked with supplications or reproaches, and her arm was still linked within Isabella's, though their hearts were at war. At one moment she was softened, at another irritated; always distressed, but always steady.

"I did not think you had been so obstinate, Catherine," said James; "you were not used to be so hard to persuade; you once were the kindest, best-tempered of my sisters."

"I hope I am not less so now," she replied, very feelingly; "but indeed I cannot go. If I am wrong, I am doing what I believe to be right."

"I suspect," said Isabella, in a low voice, "there is no great struggle."

Catherine's heart swelled; she drew away her arm, and Isabella made no opposition. Thus passed a long ten minutes, till they were again joined by Thorpe, who coming to them with a gayer look, said, "Well, I have settled the matter, and now we may all go tomorrow with a safe conscience. I have been to Miss Tilney, and made your excuses."

"You have not!" cried Catherine.

"I have, upon my soul. Left her this moment. Told her you had sent me to say that, having just recollected a prior engagement of going to Clifton with us to-morrow, you could not have the pleasure of walking with her till Tuesday. She said very well, Tuesday was just as convenient to her; so there is an end of all our difficulties. – A pretty good thought of mine – hey?"

Isabella's countenance was once more all smiles and good humour, and James too looked happy again.

"A most heavenly thought indeed! Now, my sweet Catherine, all our distresses are over; you are honourably acquitted, and we shall have a most delightful party."

"This will not do," said Catherine; "I cannot submit to this. I must run after Miss Tilney directly and set her right."

Isabella, however, caught hold of one hand; Thorpe of the other; and remonstrances poured in from all three. Even James was quite angry. When every thing was settled, when Miss Tilney herself said that Tuesday would suit her as well, it was quite ridiculous, quite absurd to make any further objection.

"I do not care. Mr Thorpe had no business to invent any such message. If I had thought it right to put it off, I could have spoken to Miss Tilney myself. This is only doing it in a ruder way; and how do I know that Mr Thorpe has – he may be mistaken again perhaps; he led me into one act of rudeness by his mistake on Friday. Let me go, Mr Thorpe; Isabella, do not hold me."

Thorpe told her it would be in vain to go after the Tilneys; they were turning the corner into Brock-street, when he had overtaken them, and were at home by this time.

"Then I will go after them," said Catherine; "wherever they are I will go after them. It does not signify talking. If I could not be persuaded into doing what I thought wrong, I never will be tricked into it." And with these words she broke away and hurried off. Thorpe would have darted after her, but Morland withheld him. "Let her go, let her go, if she will go."

She is as obstinate as —"

Thorpe never finished the simile, for it could hardly have been a proper one.

Away walked Catherine in great agitation, as fast as the crowd would permit her, fearful of being pursued, yet determined to persevere. As she walked, she reflected on what had passed. It was painful to her to disappoint and displease them, particularly to displease her brother; but she could not repent her resistance. Setting her own inclination apart, to have failed a second time in her engagement to Miss Tilney, to have retracted a promise voluntarily made only five minutes before, and on a false pretence too, must have been wrong. She had not been withstanding them on selfish principles alone, she had not consulted merely her own gratification; *that* might have been ensured in some degree by the excursion itself, by seeing Blaize Castle; no, she had attended to what was due to others, and to her own character in their opinion.

Her conviction of being right however was not enough to restore her composure, till she had spoken to Miss Tilney she could not be at ease; and quickening her pace when she got clear of the Crescent, she almost ran over the remaining ground till she gained the top of Milsom-street. So rapid had been her movements, that in spite of the Tilneys' advantage in the outset, they were but just turning into their lodgings as she came within view of them; and the servant still remaining at the open door, she used only the ceremony of saying that she must speak with Miss Tilney that moment, and hurrying by him proceeded upstairs. Then, opening the first door before her, which happened to be the right, she immediately found herself in the drawing-room with General Tilney, his son, and daughter. Her explanation, defective only in being — from her irritation of nerves and shortness of breath — no explanation at all, was instantly given. "I am come in a great hurry — It was all a mistake — I never promised to go — I told them from the first I could not go. — I ran away in a great hurry to explain it. — I did not care what you thought of me. — I would not stay for the servant."

The business, however, though not perfectly elucidated by this speech, soon ceased to be a puzzle. Catherine found that John Thorpe *had* given the message; and Miss Tilney had no scruple in owning herself greatly surprized by it. But whether her brother had still exceeded her in resentment, Catherine, though she instinctively addressed herself as much to one as to the other in her vindication, had no means of knowing. Whatever might have been felt before her arrival, her eager declarations immediately made every look and sentence as friendly as she could desire.

The affair thus happily settled, she was introduced by Miss Tilney to her father, and received by him with such ready, such solicitous politeness as recalled Thorpe's information to her mind, and made her think with pleasure that he might be sometimes depended on. To such anxious attention was the general's civility carried, that not aware of her extraordinary swiftness in entering the house, he was quite angry with the servant whose neglect had reduced her to open the door of the apartment herself. "What did William mean by it? He should make a point of inquiring into the matter." And if Catherine had not most warmly asserted his innocence, it seemed likely that William would lose the favour of his master forever, if not his place, by her rapidity.

After sitting with them a quarter of an hour, she rose to take leave, and was then most agreeably surprised by General Tilney's asking her if she would do his daughter the honour of dining and spending the rest of the day with her. Miss Tilney added her own wishes. Catherine was greatly obliged; but it was quite out of her power. Mr and Mrs Allen would expect her back every moment. The general declared he could say no more; the claims of Mr and Mrs Allen were not to be superseded; but on some other day he trusted, when longer notice could be given, they would not refuse to spare her to her friend. "Oh, no; Catherine was sure they would not have the least objection, and she should have great pleasure in coming." The general attended her himself to the street-door, saying every thing gallant as they went downstairs, admiring the elasticity of her walk, which corresponded exactly with the spirit of her dancing, and making her one of the most graceful bows she had ever beheld, when they parted.

Catherine, delighted by all that had passed, proceeded gaily to Pulteney-street; walking, as she concluded, with great elasticity, though she had never thought of it before. She reached home without seeing any thing more of the offended party; and now that she had been triumphant throughout, had carried her point and was secure of her walk, she began (as the flutter of her spirits subsided) to doubt whether she had been perfectly right. A sacrifice was always noble; and if she had given way to their entreaties, she should have been spared the distressing idea of a friend displeased, a brother angry, and a scheme of great happiness to both destroyed, perhaps through her means. To ease her mind, and ascertain by the opinion of an unprejudiced person what her own conduct had really been, she took occasion to mention before Mr Allen the half-settled scheme of her brother and the Thorpes for the following day. Mr Allen caught at it directly. "Well," said he, "and do you think of going too?"

"No; I had just engaged myself to walk with Miss Tilney before they told me of it; and therefore you know I could not go with them, could I?"

"No, certainly not; and I am glad you do not think of it. These schemes are not at all the thing. Young men and women driving about the country in open carriages! Now and then it is very well; but going to inns and public places together! It is not right; and I wonder Mrs Thorpe should allow it. I am glad you do not think of going; I am sure Mrs Morland would not be pleased. Mrs Allen, are not you of my way of thinking? Do not you think these kind of projects objectionable?"

"Yes, very much so indeed. Open carriages are nasty things. A clean gown is not five minutes wear in them. You are splashed getting in and getting out; and the wind takes your hair and your bonnet in every direction. I hate an open carriage myself."

"I know you do; but that is not the question. Do not you think it has an odd appearance, if young ladies are frequently driven about in them by young men, to whom they are not even related?"

"Yes, my dear, a very odd appearance indeed. I cannot bear to see it."

"Dear madam," cried Catherine, "then why did not you tell

me so before? I am sure if I had known it to be improper, I would not have gone with Mr Thorpe at all; but I always hoped you would tell me, if you thought I was doing wrong."

"And so I should, my dear, you may depend on it; for as I told Mrs Morland at parting, I would always do the best for you in my power. But one must not be over particular. Young people *will* be young people, as your good mother says herself. You know I wanted you, when we first came, not to buy that sprigged muslin, but you would. Young people do not like to be always thwarted."

"But this was something of real consequence; and I do not think you would have found me hard to persuade."

"As far as it has gone hitherto, there is no harm done," said Mr Allen; "and I would only advise you, my dear, not to go out with Mr Thorpe any more."

"That is just what I was going to say," added his wife.

Catherine, relieved for herself, felt uneasy for Isabella; and after a moment's thought, asked Mr Allen whether it would not be both proper and kind in her to write to Miss Thorpe, and explain the indecorum of which she must be as insensible as herself; for she considered that Isabella might otherwise perhaps be going to Clifton the next day, in spite of what had passed. Mr Allen, however discouraged her from doing any such thing. "You had better leave her alone, my dear, she is old enough to know what she is about; and if not, has a mother to advise her. Mrs Thorpe is too indulgent beyond a doubt; but however you had better not interfere. She and your brother chuse to go, and you will be only getting ill-will."

Catherine submitted; and though sorry to think that Isabella should be doing wrong, felt greatly relieved by Mr Allen's approbation of her own conduct, and truly rejoiced to be preserved by his advice from the danger of falling into such an error herself. Her escape from being one of the party to Clifton was now an escape indeed; for what would the Tilneys have thought of her, if she had broken her promise to them in order to do what was wrong in itself? if she had been guilty of one breach of propriety, only to enable her to be guilty of another?

CHAPTER 14

The next morning was fair, and Catherine almost expected another attack from the assembled party. With Mr Allen to support her, she felt no dread of the event: but she would gladly be spared a contest, where victory itself was painful; and was heartily rejoiced therefore at neither seeing nor hearing anything of them. The Tilneys called for her at the appointed time; and no new difficulty arising, no sudden recollection, no unexpected summons, no impertinent intrusion to disconcert their measures, my heroine was most unnaturally able to fulfil her engagement, though it was made with the hero himself. They determined on walking round Beechen Cliff,[1] that noble hill, whose beautiful verdure and hanging coppice render it so striking an object from almost every opening in Bath.

"I never look at it," said Catherine, as they walked along the side of the river, "without thinking of the south of France."

"You have been abroad then?" said Henry, a little surprized.

"Oh! no, I only mean what I have read about. It always puts me in mind of the country that Emily and her father travelled through, in the 'Mysteries of Udolpho.' But you never read novels, I dare say?"

"Why not?"

"Because they are not clever enough for you – gentlemen read better books."

"The person, be it gentleman or lady, who has not pleasure in a good novel, must be intolerably stupid. I have read all Mrs Radcliffe's works, and most of them with great pleasure. The Mysteries of Udolpho, when I had once begun it, I could not lay down again; – I remember finishing it in two days – my hair standing on end the whole time."

"Yes," added Miss Tilney, "and I remember that you undertook to read it aloud to me, and that when I was called away for only five minutes to answer a note, instead of waiting for me, you took the volume into the Hermitage-walk, and I was obliged to stay till you had finished it."

---

1   See Appendix F.

"Thank you, Eleanor; – a most honourable testimony. You see, Miss Morland, the injustice of your suspicions. Here was I, in my eagerness to get on, refusing to wait only five minutes for my sister; breaking the promise I had made of reading it aloud, and keeping her in suspense at a most interesting part, by running away with the volume, which, you are to observe, was her own, particularly her own. I am proud when I reflect on it, and I think it must establish me in your good opinion."

"I am very glad to hear it indeed, and now I shall never be ashamed of liking Udolpho myself. But I really thought before, young men despised novels amazingly."

"It is *amazingly*; it may well suggest *amazement* if they do – for they read nearly as many as women. I myself have read hundreds and hundreds. Do not imagine that you can cope with me in a knowledge of Julias and Louisas. If we proceed to particulars, and engage in the never-ceasing inquiry of 'Have you read this?' and 'Have you read that?' I shall soon leave you as far behind me as – what shall I say? – I want an appropriate simile; – as far as your friend Emily herself left poor Valancourt[1] when she went with her aunt into Italy. Consider how many years I have had the start of you. I had entered on my studies at Oxford, while you were a good little girl working your sampler at home!"[2]

"Not very good I am afraid. But now really do not you think Udolpho the nicest book in the world?"

"The nicest; – by which I suppose you mean the neatest. That must depend upon the binding."

"Henry," said Miss Tilney, "you are very impertinent. Miss Morland, he is treating you exactly as he does his sister. He is for ever finding fault with me, for some incorrectness of language, and now he is taking the same liberty with you. The word 'nicest,' as you used it, did not suit him; and you had better change it as soon as you can, or we shall be overpowered with Johnson and

---

1   The heroine Emily's beloved in Ann Radcliffe's *The Mysteries of Udolpho* from whom she is separated for the majority of the novel.

2   Amy Smith notes that "between 1760 and 1798, there were at least 19 novels published in London with either the name Julia or Louisa in a featured position in the title" which is ample testament to Henry's knowledge of contemporary fiction (43).

Blair[1] all the rest of the way."

"I am sure," cried Catherine, "I did not mean to say any thing wrong; but it *is* a nice book, and why should not I call it so?"

"Very true," said Henry, "and this is a very nice day, and we are taking a very nice walk, and you are two very nice young ladies. Oh! it is a very nice word indeed! – it does for every thing. Originally perhaps it was applied only to express neatness, propriety, delicacy, or refinement; people were nice in their dress, in their sentiments, or their choice. But now every commendation on every subject is comprised in that one word."

"While, in fact," cried his sister, "it ought only to be applied to you, without any commendation at all. You are more nice than wise. Come, Miss Morland, let us leave him to meditate over our faults in the utmost propriety of diction, while we praise Udolpho in whatever terms we like best. It is a most interesting work. You are fond of that kind of reading?"

"To say the truth, I do not much like any other."

"Indeed!"

"That is, I can read poetry and plays, and things of that sort, and do not dislike travels. But history, real solemn history, I cannot be interested in. Can you?"[2]

"Yes, I am fond of history."

"I wish I were too. I read it a little as a duty, but it tells me nothing that does not either vex or weary me. The quarrels of popes and kings, with wars or pestilences, in every page; the men all so good for nothing, and hardly any women at all it is very tiresome: and yet I often think it odd that it should be so dull, for a great deal of it must be invention. The speeches that are put into the heroes' mouths, their thoughts and designs the chief of all this must be invention, and invention is what delights me in other books."

---

1   Samuel Johnson's *Dictionary* (1755) and Hugh Blair's *Lectures on Rhetoric and Belles Lettres* (1783).

2   Cf. Mary Wollstonecraft's *Vindication of the Rights of Woman* (1792): "Unable to grasp any thing great, is it surprising that [females] find the reading of history a very dry task, and disquisitions addressed to the understanding intolerably tedious, and almost unintelligible? Thus are they necessarily dependant on the novelist for amusement" (Ch. 13 Sect. ii).

"Historians, you think," said Miss Tilney, "are not happy in their flights of fancy. They display imagination without raising interest. I am fond of history and am very well contented to take the false with the true. In the principal facts they have sources of intelligence in former histories and records, which may be as much depended on, I conclude, as any thing that does not actually pass under one's own observation: and as for the little embellishments you speak of, they are embellishments, and I like them as such. If a speech be well drawn up, I read it with pleasure, by whomsoever it may be made – and probably with much greater, if the production of Mr Hume or Mr Robertson,[1] than if the genuine words of Caractacus, Agricola, or Alfred the Great."

"You are fond of history! – and so are Mr Allen and my father; and I have two brothers who do not dislike it. So many instances within my small circle of friends is remarkable! At this rate, I shall not pity the writers of history any longer. If people like to read their books, it is all very well, but to be at so much trouble in filling great volumes, which, as I used to think, nobody would willingly ever look into, to be labouring only for the torment of little boys and girls, always struck me as a hard fate; and though I know it is all very right and necessary, I have often wondered at the person's courage that could sit down on purpose to do it."

"That little boys and girls should be tormented," said Henry, "is what no one at all acquainted with human nature in a civilized state can deny; but in behalf of our most distinguished historians, I must observe, that they might well be offended at being supposed to have no higher aim; and that by their method and style, they are perfectly well qualified to torment readers of the most advanced reason and mature time of life. I use the verb 'to torment', as I observed to be your own method, instead of 'to instruct', supposing them to be now admitted as synonimous."

"You think me foolish to call instruction a torment, but if you had been as much used as myself to hear poor little children first learning their letters and then learning to spell, if you had ever seen how stupid they can be for a whole morning together, and

---

1   David Hume's *History of England* (1754-62), William Robertson's *History of Scotland* (1759).

how tired my poor mother is at the end of it, as I am in the habit of seeing almost every day of my life at home, you would allow that to *torment* and to *instruct* might sometimes be used as synonimous words."

"Very probably. But historians are not accountable for the difficulty of learning to read; and even you yourself, who do not altogether seem particularly friendly to very severe, very intense application, may perhaps be brought to acknowledge that it is very well worth while to be tormented for two or three years of one's life, for the sake of being able to read all the rest of it. Consider − if reading had not been taught, Mrs Radcliffe would have written in vain − or perhaps might not have written at all."

Catherine assented − and a very warm panegyric from her on that lady's merits, closed the subject. − The Tilneys were soon engaged in another on which she had nothing to say. They were viewing the country with the eyes of persons accustomed to drawing, and decided on its capability of being formed into pictures, with all the eagerness of real taste. Here Catherine was quite lost. She knew nothing of drawing − nothing of taste: − and she listened to them with an attention which brought her little profit, for they talked in phrases which conveyed scarcely any idea to her. The little which she could understand however appeared to contradict the very few notions she had entertained on the matter before. It seemed as if a good view were no longer to be taken from the top of an high hill, and that a clear blue sky was no longer a proof of a fine day. She was heartily ashamed of her ignorance. A misplaced shame. Where people wish to attach, they should always be ignorant. To come with a well-informed mind is to come with an inability of administering to the vanity of others, which a sensible person would always wish to avoid. A woman especially, if she have the misfortune of knowing any thing, should conceal it as well as she can.[1]

---

[1] Cf. Lady Mary Wortley Montague's letter to her daughter Lady Bute about the education of her granddaughter: "The second caution to be given her (and which is most absolutely necessary) is to conceal whatever learning she attains, with as much solicitude as she would hide crookedness or lameness" (*Letters* January 1753, 237).

The advantages of natural folly in a beautiful girl have been already set forth by the capital pen of a sister author;[1] – and to her treatment of the subject I will only add in justice to men, that though to the larger and more trifling part of the sex, imbecility in females is a great enhancement of their personal charms, there is a portion of them too reasonable and too well informed themselves to desire any thing more in woman than ignorance. But Catherine did not know her own advantages – did not know that a good-looking girl, with an affectionate heart and a very ignorant mind, cannot fail of attracting a clever young man, unless circumstances are particularly untoward. In the present instance, she confessed and lamented her want of knowledge; declared that she would give any thing in the world to be able to draw; and a lecture on the picturesque immediately followed, in which his instructions were so clear that she soon began to see beauty in every thing admired by him, and her attention was so earnest, that he became perfectly satisfied of her having a great deal of natural taste. He talked of fore-grounds, distances, and second distances – side-screens and perspectives – lights and shades;[2] – and Catherine was so hopeful a scholar, that when they gained the top of Beechen Cliff,[3] she voluntarily rejected the whole city of Bath, as unworthy to make part of a landscape. Delighted with her progress, and fearful of wearying her with too much wisdom at once, Henry suffered the subject to decline, and by an easy transition from a piece of rocky fragment and the withered oak which he had placed near its summit, to oaks in general, to forests, the inclosure of them, waste lands, crown lands and government, he shortly found himself arrived at politics; and from politics, it was an easy step to silence. The general pause which succeeded his short dis-

---

1   The beautiful girl Indiana Lynmere in Frances Burney's *Camilla*.

2   See William Gilpin's *Three Essays: on Picturesque Beauty* ... (1792) for Austen's main source in which Gilpin describes foregrounds (68-70, 81), lights and shades (42, 75). See *Observations, Relating Chiefly to Picturesque beauty, on Several parts of England, particularly the Mountains and Lakes of Cumberland and Westmoreland* (1786) for discussion of side-screens (1.2. 145-52), foregrounds (1.8.103-06), lights and shades (1.1.81-91). See Appendix C.2.

3   See Appendix F.

quisition on the state of the nation, was put an end to by Catherine, who, in rather a solemn tone of voice, uttered these words, "I have heard that something very shocking indeed, will soon come out in London."

Miss Tilney, to whom this was chiefly addressed, was startled, and hastily replied, "Indeed! – and of what nature?"

"That I do not know, nor who is the author. I have only heard that it is to be more horrible than any thing we have met with yet."[1]

"Good heaven! – Where could you hear of such a thing?"

"A particular friend of mine had an account of it in a letter from London yesterday. It is to be uncommonly dreadful. I shall expect murder and every thing of the kind."

"You speak with astonishing composure! But I hope your friend's accounts have been exaggerated; – and if such a design is known beforehand, proper measures will undoubtedly be taken by government to prevent its coming to effect."

"Government," said Henry, endeavouring not to smile, "neither desires nor dares to interfere in such matters. There must be murder; and government cares not how much."

The ladies stared. He laughed, and added, "Come, shall I make you understand each other, or leave you to puzzle out an explanation as you can? No – I will be noble. I will prove myself a man, no less by the generosity of my soul than the clearness of my head. I have no patience with such of my sex as disdain to let themselves sometimes down to the comprehension of yours. Perhaps the abilities of women are neither sound nor acute – neither vigorous nor keen. Perhaps they may want observation, discernment, judgment, fire, genius, and wit."

"Miss Morland, do not mind what he says; – but have the goodness to satisfy me as to this dreadful riot."

"Riot! – what riot?"

"My dear Eleanor, the riot is only in your own brain. The confusion there is scandalous. Miss Morland has been talking of noth-

---

1   Reference to both the Gordon Riots of 1780 and recent civil unrest of the 1790s. See Francis Warren Roberts *Jane Austen and the French Revolution* (1979).

ing more dreadful than a new publication which is shortly to come out, in three duodecimo volumes, two hundred and seventy-six pages in each, with a frontispiece to the first, of two tombstones and a lantern – do you understand? – And you, Miss Morland – my stupid sister has mistaken all your clearest expressions. You talked of expected horrors in London – and instead of instantly conceiving, as any rational creature would have done, that such words could relate only to a circulating library, she immediately pictured to herself a mob of three thousand men assembling in St George's Fields, the Bank attacked, the Tower threatened, the streets of London flowing with blood, a detachment of the 12th Light Dragoons, (the hopes of the nation), called up from Northampton to quell the insurgents, and the gallant Capt. Frederick Tilney, in the moment of charging at the head of his troop, knocked off his horse by a brickbat from an upper window. Forgive her stupidity. The fears of the sister have added to the weakness of the woman; but she is by no means a simpleton in general."[1]

Catherine looked grave. "And now, Henry," said Miss Tilney, "that you have made us understand each other, you may as well make Miss Morland understand yourself – unless you mean to have her think you intolerably rude to your sister, and a great brute in your opinion of women in general. Miss Morland is not used to your odd ways."

"I shall be most happy to make her better acquainted with them."

"No doubt; – but that is no explanation of the present."

"What am I to do?"

"You know what you ought to do. Clear your character handsomely before her. Tell her that you think very highly of the understanding of women."

"Miss Morland, I think very highly of the understanding of all the women in the world – especially of those – whoever they may be – with whom I happen to be in company."

"That is not enough. Be more serious."

"Miss Morland, no one can think more highly of the understanding of women than I do. In my opinion, nature has given

---

1   See Appendix B.

them so much, that they never find it necessary to use more than half."

"We shall get nothing more serious from him now, Miss Morland. He is not in a sober mood. But I do assure you that he must be entirely misunderstood, if he can ever appear to say an unjust thing of any woman at all, or an unkind one of me."

It was no effort to Catherine to believe that Henry Tilney could never be wrong. His manner might sometimes surprise, but his meaning must always be just: — and what she did not understand, she was almost as ready to admire, as what she did. The whole walk was delightful, and though it ended too soon, its conclusion was delightful too; — her friends attended her into the house, and Miss Tilney, before they parted, addressing herself with respectful form, as much to Mrs Allen as to Catherine, petitioned for the pleasure of her company to dinner on the day after the next. No difficulty was made on Mrs Allen's side — and the only difficulty on Catherine's was in concealing the excess of her pleasure.

The morning had passed away so charmingly as to banish all her friendship and natural affection; for no thought of Isabella or James had crossed her during their walk. When the Tilneys were gone, she became amiable again, but she was amiable for some time to little effect; Mrs Allen had no intelligence to give that could relieve her anxiety, she had heard nothing of any of them. Towards the end of the morning, however, Catherine, having occasion for some indispensable yard of ribbon which must be bought without a moment's delay, walked out into the town, and in Bond Street overtook the second Miss Thorpe, as she was loitering towards Edgar's Buildings between two of the sweetest girls in the world, who had been her dear friends all the morning. From her, she soon learned that the party to Clifton had taken place. "They set off at eight this morning," said Miss Anne, "and I am sure I do not envy them their drive. I think you and I are very well off to be out of the scrape. — It must be the dullest thing in the world, for there is not a soul at Clifton at this time of year. Belle went with your brother, and John drove Maria."

Catherine spoke the pleasure she really felt on hearing this part of the arrangement.

"Oh! yes," rejoined the other, "Maria is gone. She was quite wild to go. She thought it would be something very fine. I cannot say I admire her taste; and for my part I was determined from the first not to go, if they pressed me ever so much."

Catherine, a little doubtful of this, could not help answering, "I wish you could have gone too. It is a pity you could not all go."

"Thank you; but it is quite a matter of indifference to me. Indeed, I would not have gone on any account, I was saying so to Emily and Sophia[1] when you overtook us."

Catherine was still unconvinced; but glad that Anne should have the friendship of an Emily and a Sophia to console her, she bade her adieu without much uneasiness, and returned home, pleased that the party had not been prevented by her refusing to join it, and very heartily wishing that it might be too pleasant to allow either James or Isabella to resent her resistance any longer.

CHAPTER 15

Early the next day, a note from Isabella, speaking peace and tenderness in every line, and entreating the immediate presence of her friend on a matter of the utmost importance, hastened Catherine, in the happiest state of confidence and curiosity, to Edgar's Buildings. – The two youngest Miss Thorpes were by themselves in the parlour; and, on Anne's quitting it to call her sister, Catherine took the opportunity of asking the other for some particulars of their yesterday's party. Maria desired no greater pleasure than to speak of it; and Catherine immediately learnt that it had been altogether the most delightful scheme in the world; that nobody could imagine how charming it had been, and that it had been more delightful than any body could conceive. Such was the information of the first five minutes; the second unfolded thus much in detail, – that they had driven directly to the York Hotel, ate some soup, and bespoke an early dinner, walked down to the Pump-room, tasted the water, and laid out some shillings in purses

---

1   Chapman (*The Novels*) points out that it is a mark of Anne Thorpe's vulgarity that she should so readily address the friends of the morning by their Christian names.

and spars;[1] thence adjourned to eat ice at a pastry-cook's, and hurrying back to the Hotel, swallowed their dinner in haste, to prevent being in the dark; and then had a delightful drive back, only the moon was not up, and it rained a little, and Mr Morland's horse was so tired he could hardly get it along.

Catherine listened with heartfelt satisfaction. It appeared that Blaize Castle had never been thought of; and, as for all the rest, there was nothing to regret for half an instant. – Maria's intelligence concluded with a tender effusion of pity for her sister Anne, whom she represented as insupportably cross, from being excluded the party.

"She will never forgive me, I am sure; but, you know, how could I help it? John would have me go, for he vowed he would not drive her, because she had such thick ancles. I dare say she will not be in good humour again this month; but I am determined I will not be cross; it is not a little matter that puts me out of temper."

Isabella now entered the room with so eager a step, and a look of such happy importance, as engaged all her friend's notice. Maria was without ceremony sent away, and Isabella, embracing Catherine, thus began: – "Yes, my dear Catherine, it is so indeed; your penetration has not deceived you. – Oh! that arch eye of yours! – It sees through every thing."

Catherine replied only by a look of wondering ignorance.

"Nay, my beloved, sweetest friend," continued the other, "compose yourself. I am amazingly agitated, as you perceive. Let us sit down and talk in comfort. Well, and so you guessed it the moment you had my note? – Sly creature! – Oh! my dear Catherine, you alone who know my heart can judge of my present happiness. Your brother is the most charming of men. I only wish I were more worthy of him. – But what will your excellent father and mother say? – Oh! heavens! when I think of them I am so agitated!"

Catherine's understanding began to awake: an idea of the truth suddenly darted into her mind; and, with the natural blush of so new an emotion, she cried out, "Good heaven! – my dear Isabella,

---

1   Any bright, non-metallic mineral. Probably ornaments made of crystalline material.

what do you mean? Can you – can you really be in love with James?"

This bold surmise, however, she soon learnt comprehended but half the fact. The anxious affection, which she was accused of having continually watched in Isabella's every look and action, had, in the course of their yesterday's party, received the delightful confession of an equal love. Her heart and faith were alike engaged to James. – Never had Catherine listened to any thing so full of interest, wonder, and joy. Her brother and her friend engaged! – New to such circumstances, the importance of it appeared unspeakably great, and she contemplated it as one of those grand events, of which the ordinary course of life can hardly afford a return. The strength of her feelings she could not express; the nature of them, however, contented her friend. The happiness of having such a sister was their first effusion, and the fair ladies mingled in embraces and tears of joy.

Delighting, however, as Catherine sincerely did in the prospect of the connection, it must be acknowledged that Isabella far surpassed her in tender anticipations. – "You will be so infinitely dearer to me, my Catherine, than either Anne or Maria: I feel that I shall be so much more attached to my dear Morland's family than to my own."

This was a pitch of friendship beyond Catherine.

"You are so like your dear brother," continued Isabella, "that I quite doated on you the first moment I saw you. But so it always is with me; the first moment settles every thing. The very first day that Morland came to us last Christmas – the very first moment I beheld him – my heart was irrecoverably gone. I remember I wore my yellow gown, with my hair done up in braids; and when I came into the drawing-room, and John introduced him, I thought I never saw any body so handsome before."

Here Catherine secretly acknowledged the power of love; for, though exceedingly fond of her brother, and partial to all his endowments, she had never in her life thought him handsome.

"I remember too, Miss Andrews drank tea with us that evening, and wore her puce-coloured sarsenet;[1] and she looked so

---

1   A very fine soft silk.

heavenly, that I thought your brother must certainly fall in love with her; I could not sleep a wink all right for thinking of it. Oh! Catherine, the many sleepless nights I have had on your brother's account! – I would not have you suffer half what I have done! I am grown wretchedly thin I know; but I will not pain you by describing my anxiety; you have seen enough of it. I feel that I have betrayed myself perpetually; – so unguarded in speaking of my partiality for the church! – But my secret I was always sure would be safe with *you*."

Catherine felt that nothing could have been safer; but ashamed of an ignorance little expected, she dared no longer contest the point, nor refuse to have been as full of arch penetration and affectionate sympathy as Isabella chose to consider her. Her brother she found was preparing to set off with all speed to Fullerton, to make known his situation and ask consent; and here was a source of some real agitation to the mind of Isabella. Catherine endeavoured to persuade her, as she was herself persuaded, that her father and mother would never oppose their son's wishes. – "It is impossible," said she, "for parents to be more kind, or more desirous of their children's happiness; I have no doubt of their consenting immediately."

"Morland says exactly the same," replied Isabella; "and yet I dare not expect it; my fortune will be so small; they never can consent to it. Your brother, who might marry any body!"

Here Catherine again discerned the force of love.

"Indeed, Isabella, you are too humble. – The difference of fortune can be nothing to signify."

"Oh! my sweet Catherine, in *your* generous heart I know it would signify nothing; but we must not expect such disinterestedness in many. As for myself, I am sure I only wish our situations were reversed. Had I the command of millions, were I mistress of the whole world, your brother would be my only choice."

This charming sentiment, recommended as much by sense as novelty, gave Catherine a most pleasing remembrance of all the heroines of her acquaintance; and she thought her friend never looked more lovely than in uttering the grand idea. – "I am sure they will consent," was her frequent declaration; "I am sure they will be delighted with you."

"For my own part," said Isabella, "my wishes are so moderate, that the smallest income in nature would be enough for me. Where people are really attached, poverty itself is wealth: grandeur I detest: I would not settle in London for the universe. A cottage in some retired village would be extasy. There are some charming little villas about Richmond."

"Richmond!" cried Catherine. – "You must settle near Fullerton. You must be near us."

"I am sure I shall be miserable if we do not. If I can but be near *you*, I shall be satisfied. But this is idle talking! I will not allow myself to think of such things, till we have your father's answer. Morland says that by sending it to-night to Salisbury, we may have it to-morrow. – To-morrow? – I know I shall never have courage to open the letter. I know it will be the death of me."

A reverie succeeded this conviction – and when Isabella spoke again, it was to resolve on the quality of her wedding-gown.

Their conference was put an end to by the anxious young lover himself, who came to breathe his parting sigh before he set off for Wiltshire. Catherine wished to congratulate him, but knew not what to say, and her eloquence was only in her eyes. From them however the eight parts of speech[1] shone out most expressively, and James could combine them with ease. Impatient for the realization of all that he hoped at home, his adieus were not long; and they would have been yet shorter, had he not been frequently detained by the urgent entreaties of his fair one that he would go. Twice was he called almost from the door by her eagerness to have him gone. "Indeed, Morland, I must drive you away. Consider how far you have to ride. I cannot bear to see you linger so. For Heaven's sake, waste no more time. There, go, go – I insist on it."

The two friends, with hearts now more united than ever, were inseparable for the day; and in schemes of sisterly happiness the hours flew along. Mrs Thorpe and her son, who were acquainted with every thing, and who seemed only to want Mr Morland's consent, to consider Isabella's engagement as the most fortunate circumstance imaginable for their family, were allowed to join their counsels, and add their quota of significant looks and

---

1   Cf. Hugh Blair's *Lectures on Rhetoric and Belles Lettres* (1783), Lecture VIII.

mysterious expressions to fill up the measure of curiosity to be raised in the unprivileged younger sisters. To Catherine's simple feelings, this odd sort of reserve seemed neither kindly meant, nor consistently supported; and its unkindness she would hardly have forborne pointing out, had its inconsistency been less their friend; – but Anne and Maria soon set her heart at ease by the sagacity of their "I know what;" and the evening was spent in a sort of war of wit, a display of family ingenuity; on one side in the mystery of an affected secret, on the other of undefined discovery, all equally acute.

Catherine was with her friend again the next day, endeavouring to support her spirits, and while away the many tedious hours before the delivery of the letters; a needful exertion, for as the time of reasonable expectation drew near, Isabella became more and more desponding, and before the letter arrived, had worked herself into a state of real distress. But when it did come, where could distress be found? "I have had no difficulty in gaining the consent of my kind parents, and am promised that every thing in their power shall be done to forward my happiness," were the first three lines, and in one moment all was joyful security. The brightest glow was instantly spread over Isabella's features, all care and anxiety seemed removed, her spirits became almost too high for controul, and she called herself without scruple the happiest of mortals.

Mrs Thorpe, with tears of joy, embraced her daughter, her son, her visitor, and could have embraced half the inhabitants of Bath with satisfaction. Her heart was overflowing with tenderness. It was "dear John," and "dear Catherine" at every word; – "dear Anne and dear Maria" must immediately be made sharers in their felicity; and two "dears" at once before the name of Isabella were not more than that beloved child had now well earned. John himself was no skulker in joy. He not only bestowed on Mr Morland the high commendation of being one of the finest fellows in the world, but swore off many sentences in his praise.

The letter, whence sprang all this felicity, was short, containing little more than this assurance of success; and every particular was deferred till James could write again. But for particulars Isabella could well afford to wait. The needful was comprised in Mr Morland's promise; his honour was pledged to make every thing easy; and by what means their income was to be formed, whether landed property were to be resigned, or funded money made over, was a matter in which her disinterested spirit took no concern. She knew enough to feel secure of an honourable and speedy establishment, and her imagination took a rapid flight over its attendant felicities. She saw herself at the end of a few weeks, the gaze and admiration of every new acquaintance at Fullerton, the envy of every valued old friend in Putney, with a carriage at her command, a new name on her tickets,[1] and a brilliant exhibition of hoop rings on her finger.

When the contents of the letter were ascertained, John Thorpe, who had only waited its arrival to begin his journey to London, prepared to set off. "Well, Miss Morland," said he, on finding her alone in the parlour, "I am come to bid you good bye." Catherine wished him a good journey. Without appearing to hear her, he walked to the window, fidgetted about, hummed a tune, and seemed wholly self-occupied.

"Shall not you be late at Devizes?" said Catherine. He made no answer; but after a minute's silence burst out with, "A famous good thing this marrying scheme, upon my soul! A clever fancy of Morland's and Belle's. What do you think of it, Miss Morland? *I* say it is no bad notion."

"I am sure I think it a very good one."

"Do you? – That's honest, by heavens! I am glad you are no enemy to matrimony, however. Did you ever hear the old song 'Going to one wedding brings on another?'[2] I say, you will come to Belle's wedding, I hope."

"Yes; I have promised your sister to be with her, if possible."

"And then you know" – twisting himself about and forcing a foolish laugh – "I say, then you know, we may try the truth of this same old song."

"May we? – but I never sing. Well, I wish you a good journey. I dine with Miss Tilney today, and must now be going home."

---

1   Visiting cards.
2   Proverbial. Cf. John Gay's *Wife of Bath* (1713) Act I: "One wedding, the Proverb says, begets another."

"Nay, but there is no such confounded hurry. – Who knows when we may be together again? – Not but that I shall be down again by the end of a fortnight, and a devilish long fortnight it will appear to me."

"Then why do you stay away so long?" replied Catherine – finding that he waited for an answer.

"That is kind of you, however – kind and good-natured. – I shall not forget it in a hurry. But you have more good-nature and all that, than any body living, I believe. A monstrous deal of good-nature, and it is not only good-nature, but you have so much, so much of every thing; and then you have such – upon my soul, I do not know any body like you."

"Oh! dear, there are a great many people like me, I dare say, only a great deal better. Good morning to you."

"But I say, Miss Morland, I shall come and pay my respects at Fullerton before it is long, if not disagreeable."

"Pray do. – My father and mother will be very glad to see you."

"And I hope – I hope, Miss Morland, *you* will not be sorry to see me."

"Oh! dear, not at all. There are very few people I am sorry to see. Company is always cheerful."

"That is just my way of thinking. Give me but a little cheerful company, let me only have the company of the people I love, let me only be where I like and with whom I like, and the devil take the rest, say I. – And I am heartily glad to hear you say the same. But I have a notion, Miss Morland, you and I think pretty much alike upon most matters."

"Perhaps we may; but it is more than I ever thought of. And as to *most matters*, to say the truth, there are not many that I know my own mind about."

"By Jove, no more do I. It is not my way to bother my brains with what does not concern me. My notion of things is simple enough. Let me only have the girl I like, say I, with a comfortable house over my head, and what care I for all the rest? Fortune is nothing. I am sure of a good income of my own; and if she had not a penny, why, so much the better."

"Very true. I think like you there. If there is a good fortune on one side, there can be no occasion for any on the other. No matter which has it, so that there is enough. I hate the idea of one great fortune looking out for another. And to marry for money I think the wickedest thing in existence. Good day. We shall be very glad to see you at Fullerton, whenever it is convenient." And away she went. It was not in the power of all his gallantry to detain her longer. With such news to communicate, and such a visit to prepare for, her departure was not to be delayed by any thing in his nature to urge; and she hurried away, leaving him to the undivided consciousness of his own happy address, and her explicit encouragement.

The agitation which she had herself experienced on first learning her brother's engagement, made her expect to raise no inconsiderable emotion in Mr and Mrs Allen, by the communication of the wonderful event. How great was her disappointment! The important affair, which many words of preparation ushered in, had been foreseen by them both ever since her brother's arrival; and all that they felt on the occasion was comprehended in a wish for the young people's happiness, with a remark, on the gentleman's side, in favour of Isabella's beauty, and on the lady's, of her great good luck. It was to Catherine the most surprizing insensibility. The disclosure however of the great secret of James's going to Fullerton the day before, did raise some emotion in Mrs Allen. She could not listen to that with perfect calmness; but repeatedly regretted the necessity of its concealment, wished she could have known his intention, wished she could have seen him before he went, as she should certainly have troubled him with her best regards to his father and mother, and her kind compliments to all the Skinners.

[*In the original edition the first volume ended here.*]

CHAPTER 16

Catherine's expectations of pleasure from her visit in Milsom-street were so very high, that disappointment was inevitable; and accordingly, though she was most politely received by General Tilney, and kindly welcomed by his daughter, though Henry was at home, and no one else of the party, she found, on her return, without spending many hours in the examination of her feelings, that she had gone to her appointment preparing for happiness which it had not afforded. Instead of finding herself improved in acquaintance with Miss Tilney, from the intercourse of the day, she seemed hardly so intimate with her as before; instead of seeing Henry Tilney to greater advantage than ever, in the ease of a family party, he had never said so little, nor been so little agreeable; and, in spite of their father's great civilities to her – in spite of his thanks, invitations, and compliments – it had been a release to get away from him. It puzzled her to account for all this. It could not be General Tilney's fault. That he was perfectly agreeable and good-natured, and altogether a very charming man, did not admit of a doubt, for he was tall and handsome, and Henry's father. *He* could not be accountable for his children's want of spirits, or for her want of enjoyment in his company. The former she hoped at last might have been accidental, and the latter she could only attribute to her own stupidity. Isabella, on hearing the particulars of the visit, gave a different explanation: "It was all pride, pride, insufferable haughtiness and pride! She had long suspected the family to be very high, and this made it certain. Such insolence of behaviour as Miss Tilney's she had never heard of in her life! Not to do the honours of her house with common good-breeding! – To behave to her guest with such superciliousness! – Hardly even to speak to her!"

"But it was not so bad as that, Isabella; there was no superciliousness; she was very civil."

"Oh! don't defend her! And then the brother, he, who had appeared so attached to you! Good heavens! well, some people's feelings are incomprehensible. And so he hardly looked once at you the whole day?"

"I do not say so; but he did not seem in good spirits."

"How contemptible! Of all things in the world inconstancy is my aversion. Let me entreat you never to think of him again, my dear Catherine; indeed he is unworthy of you."

"Unworthy! I do not suppose he ever thinks of me."

"That is exactly what I say; he never thinks of you. – Such fickleness! Oh! how different to your brother and to mine! I really believe John has the most constant heart."

"But as for General Tilney, I assure you it would be impossible for any body to behave to me with greater civility and attention; it seemed to be his only care to entertain and make me happy."

"Oh! I know no harm of him; I do not suspect him of pride. I believe he is a very gentleman-like man. John thinks very well of him, and John's judgment –"

"Well, I shall see how they behave to me this evening; we shall meet them at the rooms."

"And must I go?"

"Do not you intend it? I thought it was all settled."

"Nay, since you make such a point of it, I can refuse you nothing. But do not insist upon my being very agreeable, for my heart, you know, will be some forty miles off. And as for dancing, do not mention it I beg; *that* is quite out of the question. Charles Hodges will plague me to death, I dare say; but I shall cut him very short. Ten to one but he guesses the reason, and that is exactly what I want to avoid, so I shall insist on his keeping his conjecture to himself."

Isabella's opinion of the Tilneys did not influence her friend; she was sure there had been no insolence in the manners either of brother or sister; and she did not credit there being any pride in their hearts. The evening rewarded her confidence; she was met by one with the same kindness, and by the other with the same attention as heretofore: Miss Tilney took pains to be near her, and Henry asked her to dance.

Having heard the day before in Milsom-street, that their elder brother, Captain Tilney, was expected almost every hour, she was at no loss for the name of a very fashionable-looking, handsome young man, whom she had never seen before, and who now evidently belonged to their party. She looked at him with great admiration, and even supposed it possible, that some people might think him handsomer than his brother, though, in her eyes, his air was more assuming, and his countenance less prepossessing. His taste and manners were beyond a doubt decidedly inferior; for, within her hearing, he not only protested against every thought of dancing himself, but even laughed openly at Henry for finding it possible. From the latter circumstance it may be presumed, that, whatever might be our heroine's opinion of him, his admiration of her was not of a very dangerous kind; not likely to produce animosities between the brothers, nor persecutions to the lady. *He* cannot be the instigator of the three villains in horsemen's great coats, by whom she will hereafter be forced into a travelling-chaise and four, which will drive off with incredible speed. Catherine, meanwhile, undisturbed by presentiments of such an evil, or of any evil at all, except that of having but a short set to dance down, enjoyed her usual happiness with Henry Tilney, listening with sparkling eyes to every thing he said; and, in finding him irresistible, becoming so herself.

At the end of the first dance, Captain Tilney came towards them again, and, much to Catherine's dissatisfaction, pulled his brother away. They retired whispering together; and, though her delicate sensibility did not take immediate alarm, and lay it down as fact, that Captain Tilney must have heard some malevolent misrepresentation of her, which he now hastened to communicate to his brother, in the hope of separating them forever, she could not have her partner conveyed from her sight without very uneasy sensations. Her suspense was of full five minutes' duration; and she was beginning to think it a very long quarter of an hour, when they both returned, and an explanation was given, by Henry's requesting to know, if she thought her friend, Miss Thorpe, would have any objection to dancing, as his brother would be most happy to be introduced to her. Catherine, without hesitation, replied that she was very sure Miss Thorpe did not mean to dance at all. The cruel reply was passed on to the other, and he immediately walked away.

"Your brother will not mind it, I know," said she, "because I heard him say before, that he hated dancing; but it was very good-natured in him to think of it. I suppose he saw Isabella sitting down, and fancied she might wish for a partner; but he is quite mistaken, for she would not dance upon any account in the world."

Henry smiled, and said, "How very little trouble it can give you to understand the motive of other people's actions."

"Why? – What do you mean?"

"With you, it is not, How is such a one likely to be influenced, What is the inducement most likely to act upon such a person's feelings, age, situation, and probable habits of life considered? – but, how should *I* be influenced, what would be *my* inducement in acting so and so?"

"I do not understand you."

"Then we are on very unequal terms, for I understand you perfectly well."

"Me? – yes; I cannot speak well enough to be unintelligible."

"Bravo! – an excellent satire on modern language."

"But pray tell me what you mean."

"Shall I indeed? – Do you really desire it? – But you are not aware of the consequences; it will involve you in a very cruel embarrassment, and certainly bring on a disagreement between us."

"No, no; it shall not do either; I am not afraid."

"Well then, I only meant that your attributing my brother's wish of dancing with Miss Thorpe to good-nature alone, convinced me of your being superior in good-nature yourself to all the rest of the world."

Catherine blushed and disclaimed, and the gentleman's predictions were verified. There was a something, however, in his words which repaid her for the pain of confusion; and that something occupied her mind so much, that she drew back for some time, forgetting to speak or to listen, and almost forgetting where she was; till, roused by the voice of Isabella, she looked up and saw her with Captain Tilney preparing to give them hands across.[1]

Isabella shrugged her shoulders and smiled, the only explanation of this extraordinary change which could at that time be given; but as it was not quite enough for Catherine's comprehension, she spoke her astonishment in very plain terms to her partner.

---

[1]   A dance figure with two half-turns, performed by two couples, generally at the top of the set.

"I cannot think how it could happen! Isabella was so determined not to dance."

"And did Isabella never change her mind before?"

"Oh! but, because – and your brother! – After what you told him from me, how could he think of going to ask her?"

"I cannot take surprize to myself on that head. You bid me be surprized on your friend's account, and therefore I am; but as for my brother, his conduct in the business, I must own, has been no more than I believed him perfectly equal to. The fairness of your friend was an open attraction; her firmness, you know, could only be understood by yourself."

"You are laughing; but, I assure you, Isabella is very firm in general."

"It is as much as should be said of any one. To be always firm must be to be often obstinate. When properly to relax is the trial of judgment; and, without reference to my brother, I really think Miss Thorpe has by no means chosen ill in fixing on the present hour."

The friends were not able to get together for any confidential discourse till all the dancing was over; but then, as they walked about the room arm in arm, Isabella thus explained herself: – "I do not wonder at your surprize and I am really fatigued to death. He is such a rattle! – Amusing enough, if my mind had been disengaged; but I would have given the world to sit still."

"Then why did not you?"

"Oh! my dear! it would have looked so particular; and you know how I abhor doing that. I refused him as long as I possibly could, but he would take no denial. You have no idea how he pressed me. I begged him to excuse me, and get some other partner – but no, not he; after aspiring to my hand, there was nobody else in the room he could bear to think of; and it was not that he wanted merely to dance, he wanted to be with *me*. Oh! such nonsense! – I told him he had taken a very unlikely way to prevail upon me; for, of all things in the world, I hated fine speeches and compliments; – and so – and so then I found there would be no peace if I did not stand up. Besides, I thought Mrs Hughes, who introduced him, might take it ill if I did not: and your dear brother, I am sure he would have been miserable if I had sat down the whole evening. I am so glad it is over! My spirits are quite jaded with listening to his nonsense: and then, – being such a smart young fellow, I saw every eye was upon us."

"He is very handsome indeed."

"Handsome! – Yes, I suppose he may. I dare say people would admire him in general; but he is not at all in my style of beauty. I hate a florid complexion and dark eyes in a man. However, he is very well. Amazingly conceited, I am sure. I took him down several times, you know, in my way."

When the young ladies next met, they had a far more interesting subject to discuss. James Morland's second letter was then received, and the kind intentions of his father fully explained. A living, of which Mr Morland was himself patron and incumbent, of about four hundred pounds yearly value, was to be resigned to his son as soon as he should be old enough to take it; no trifling deduction from the family income, no niggardly assignment to one of ten children. An estate of at least equal value, moreover, was assured as his future inheritance.

James expressed himself on the occasion with becoming gratitude; and the necessity of waiting between two and three years before they could marry, being, however unwelcome, no more than he had expected, was borne by him without discontent. Catherine, whose expectations had been as unfixed as her ideas of her father's income, and whose judgment was now entirely led by her brother, felt equally well satisfied, and heartily congratulated Isabella on having every thing so pleasantly settled.

"It is very charming indeed," said Isabella, with a grave face. "Mr Morland has behaved vastly handsome indeed," said the gentle Mrs Thorpe, looking anxiously at her daughter. "I only wish I could do as much. One could not expect more from him, you know. If he finds he *can* do more by and bye, I dare say he will, for I am sure he must be an excellent good hearted man. Four hundred is but a small income to begin on indeed, but your wishes, my dear Isabella, are so moderate, you do not consider how little you ever want, my dear."

"It is not on my own account I wish for more; but I cannot bear to be the means of injuring my dear Morland, making him sit down upon an income hardly enough to find one in the common necessaries of life. For myself, it is nothing; I never think of myself."

"I know you never do, my dear; and you will always find your reward in the affection it makes every body feel for you. There never was a young woman so beloved as you are by every body that knows you; and I dare say when Mr Morland sees you, my dear child – but do not let us distress our dear Catherine by talking of such things. Mr Morland has behaved so very handsome, you know. I always heard he was a most excellent man; and you know, my dear, we are not to suppose but what, if you had had a suitable fortune, he would have come down with something more, for I am sure he must be a most liberal-minded man."

"Nobody can think better of Mr Morland than I do, I am sure. But every body has their failing, you know, and every body has a right to do what they like with their own money." Catherine was hurt by these insinuations. "I am very sure," said she, "that my father has promised to do as much as he can afford."

Isabella recollected herself. "As to that, my sweet Catherine, there cannot be a doubt, and you know me well enough to be sure that a much smaller income would satisfy me. It is not the want of more money that makes me just at present a little out of spirits; I hate money; and if our union could take place now upon only fifty pounds a year, I should not have a wish unsatisfied. Ah! my Catherine, you have found me out. There's the sting. The long, long, endless two years and half that are to pass before your brother can hold the living."

"Yes, yes, my darling Isabella," said Mrs Thorpe, "we perfectly see into your heart. You have no disguise. We perfectly understand the present vexation; and every body must love you the better for such a noble honest affection."

Catherine's uncomfortable feelings began to lessen. She endeavoured to believe that the delay of the marriage was the only source of Isabella's regret; and when she saw her at their next interview as cheerful and amiable as ever, endeavoured to forget that she had for a minute thought otherwise. James soon followed his letter, and was received with the most gratifying kindness.

CHAPTER 17

The Allens had now entered on the sixth week of their stay in Bath; and whether it should be the last, was for some time a question, to which Catherine listened with a beating heart. To have her acquaintance with the Tilneys end so soon, was an evil which nothing could counterbalance. Her whole happiness seemed at stake, while the affair was in suspense, and every thing secured when it was determined that the lodgings should be taken for another fortnight. What this additional fortnight was to produce to her beyond the pleasure of sometimes seeing Henry Tilney, made but a small part of Catherine's speculation. Once or twice indeed, since James's engagement had taught her what *could* be done, she had got so far as to indulge in a secret 'perhaps,' but in general the felicity of being with him for the present bounded her views: the present was now comprised in another three weeks, and her happiness being certain for that period, the rest of her life was at such a distance as to excite but little interest. In the course of the morning which saw this business arranged, she visited Miss Tilney, and poured forth her joyful feelings. It was doomed to be a day of trial. No sooner had she expressed her delight in Mr Allen's lengthened stay, than Miss Tilney told her of her father's having just determined upon quitting Bath by the end of another week. Here was a blow! The past suspense of the morning had been ease and quiet to the present disappointment. Catherine's countenance fell, and in a voice of most sincere concern she echoed Miss Tilney's concluding words, "By the end of another week!"

"Yes, my father can seldom be prevailed on to give the waters what I think a fair trial. He has been disappointed of some friends' arrival whom he expected to meet here, and as he is now pretty well, is in a hurry to get home."

"I am very sorry for it," said Catherine dejectedly, "if I had known this before −"

"Perhaps," said Miss Tilney in an embarrassed manner, "you would be so good − it would make me very happy if −"

The entrance of her father put a stop to the civility, which Catherine was beginning to hope might introduce a desire of their corresponding. After addressing her with his usual politeness, he turned to his daughter and said, "Well, Eleanor, may I congratulate you on being successful in your application to your fair friend?"

"I was just beginning to make the request, sir, as you came in."

"Well, proceed by all means. I know how much your heart is in it. My daughter, Miss Morland," he continued, without leaving his daughter time to speak, "has been forming a very bold wish. We leave Bath, as she has perhaps told you, on Saturday se'nnight.[1] A letter from my steward tells me that my presence is wanted at home; and being disappointed in my hope of seeing the Marquis of Longtown and General Courteney here, some of my very old friends, there is nothing to detain me longer in Bath. And could we carry our selfish point with you, we should leave it without a single regret. Can you, in short, be prevailed on to quit this scene of public triumph and oblige your friend Eleanor with your company in Gloucestershire? I am almost ashamed to make the request, though its presumption would certainly appear greater to every creature in Bath than yourself. Modesty such as your's — but not for the world would I pain it by open praise. If you can be induced to honour us with a visit, you will make us happy beyond expression. 'Tis true, we can offer you nothing like the gaieties of this lively place; we can tempt you neither by amusement nor splendour, for our mode of living, as you see, is plain and unpretending; yet no endeavours shall be wanting on our side to make Northanger Abbey not wholly disagreeable."

Northanger Abbey! — These were thrilling words, and wound up Catherine's feelings to the highest point of extasy. Her grateful and gratified heart could hardly restrain its expressions within the language of tolerable calmness. To receive so flattering an invitation! To have her company so warmly solicited! Every thing honourable and soothing, every present enjoyment, and every future hope was contained in it; and her acceptance, with only the saving clause of papa and mamma's approbation was eagerly given. — "I will write home directly," said she, "and if they do not object, as I dare say they will not" —

General Tilney was not less sanguine, having already waited on her excellent friends in Pulteney-street, and obtained their sanc-

---

1   A week from Saturday.

tion of his wishes. "Since they can consent to part with you," said he, "we may expect philosophy from all the world."

Miss Tilney was earnest, though gentle, in her secondary civilities, and the affair became in a few minutes as nearly settled, as this necessary reference to Fullerton would allow.

The circumstances of the morning had led Catherine's feelings through the varieties of suspense, security, and disappointment; but they were now safely lodged in perfect bliss; and with spirits elated to rapture, with Henry at her heart, and Northanger Abbey on her lips, she hurried home to write her letter. Mr and Mrs Morland, relying on the discretion of the friends to whom they had already entrusted their daughter, felt no doubt of the propriety of an acquaintance which had been formed under their eye, and sent therefore by return of post their ready consent to her visit in Gloucestershire. This indulgence, though not more than Catherine had hoped for, completed her conviction of being favoured beyond every other human creature, in friends and fortune, circumstance and chance. Every thing seemed to cooperate for her advantage. By the kindness of her first friends the Allens, she had been introduced into scenes, where pleasures of every kind had met her. Her feelings, her preferences had each known the happiness of a return. Wherever she felt attachment, she had been able to create it. The affection of Isabella was to be secured to her in a sister. The Tilneys, they, by whom above all, she desired to be favourably thought of, outstripped even her wishes in the flattering measures by which their intimacy was to be continued. She was to be their chosen visitor, she was to be for weeks under the same roof with the person whose society she mostly prized – and, in addition to all the rest, this roof was to be the roof of an abbey! – Her passion for ancient edifices was next in degree to her passion for Henry Tilney – and castles and abbies made usually the charm of those reveries which his image did not fill. To see and explore either the ramparts and keep of the one, or the cloisters of the other, had been for many weeks a darling wish, though to be more than the visitor of an hour, had seemed too nearly impossible for desire. And yet, this was to happen. With all the chances against her of house, hall, place, park, court, and cottage, Northanger turned up an abbey, and she was to be its inhabitant.

Its long, damp passages, its narrow cells and ruined chapel, were to be within her daily reach, and she could not entirely subdue the hope of some traditional legends, some awful memorials of an injured and ill-fated nun.[1]

It was wonderful that her friends should seem so little elated by the possession of such a home; that the consciousness of it should be so meekly born. The power of early habit only could account for it. A distinction to which they had been born gave no pride. Their superiority of abode was no more to them than their superiority of person.

Many were the inquiries she was eager to make of Miss Tilney; but so active were her thoughts, that when these inquiries were answered, she was hardly more assured than before, of Northanger Abbey having been a richly-endowed convent at the time of the Reformation, of its having fallen into the hands of an ancestor of the Tilneys on its dissolution, of a large portion of the ancient building still making a part of the present dwelling although the rest was decayed, or of its standing low in a valley, sheltered from the north and east by rising woods of oak.[2]

CHAPTER 18

With a mind thus full of happiness, Catherine was hardly aware that two or three days had passed away, without her seeing Isabella for more than a few minutes together. She began first to be sensible of this, and to sigh for her conversation, as she walked along the Pump-room one morning, by Mrs Allen's side, without any thing to say or to hear; and scarcely had she felt a five minutes' longing of friendship, before the object of it appeared, and inviting her to a secret conference, led the way to a seat. "This is my favourite place," said she as they sat down on a bench between the doors, which commanded a tolerable view of every body entering at either, "it is so out of the way."

---

1 Cf. Lewis's *Monk* and/or Radcliffe's *Mysteries of Udolpho* and *Sicilian Romance*.
2 Cf. Gilpin's *Observations Relating Chiefly to Picturesque Beauty, on Several Parts of England, particularly the Mountains and Lakes of Cumberland and Westmoreland* (1786). See Appendix C.2.

Catherine, observing that Isabella's eyes were continually bent towards one door or the other, as in eager expectation, and remembering how often she had been falsely accused of being arch, thought the present a fine opportunity for being really so; and therefore gaily said, "Do not be uneasy, Isabella. James will soon be here."

"Psha! my dear creature," she replied, "do not think me such a simpleton as to be always wanting to confine him to my elbow. It would be hideous to be always together; we should be the jest of the place. And so you are going to Northanger! – I am amazingly glad of it. It is one of the finest old places in England, I understand. I shall depend upon a most particular description of it."

"You shall certainly have the best in my power to give. But who are you looking for? Are your sisters coming?"

"I am not looking for any body. One's eyes must be somewhere, and you know what a foolish trick I have of fixing mine, when my thoughts are an hundred miles off. I am amazingly absent; I believe I am the most absent creature in the world. Tilney says it is always the case with minds of a certain stamp."

"But I thought, Isabella, you had something in particular to tell me?"

"Oh! yes, and so I have. But here is a proof of what I was saying. My poor head! I had quite forgot it. Well, the thing is this, I have just had a letter from John; – you can guess the contents."

"No, indeed, I cannot."

"My sweet love, do not be so abominably affected. What can he write about, but yourself? You know he is over head and ears in love with you."

"With *me*, dear Isabella!"

"Nay, my sweetest Catherine, this is being quite absurd! Modesty, and all that, is very well in its way, but really a little common honesty is sometimes quite as becoming. I have no idea of being so overstrained! It is fishing for compliments. His attentions were such as a child must have noticed. And it was but half an hour before he left Bath, that you gave him the most positive encouragement. He says so in this letter, says that he as good as made you an offer, and that you received his advances in the kindest way;

and now he wants me to urge his suit, and say all manner of pretty things to you. So it is in vain to affect ignorance."

Catherine, with all the earnestness of truth, expressed her astonishment at such a charge, protesting her innocence of every thought of Mr Thorpe's being in love with her, and the consequent impossibility of her having ever intended to encourage him. "As to any attentions on his side, I do declare, upon my honour, I never was sensible of them for a moment – except just his asking me to dance the first day of his coming. And as to making me an offer, or any thing like it, there must be some unaccountable mistake. I could not have misunderstood a thing of that kind, you know! – and, as I ever wish to be believed, I solemnly protest that no syllable of such a nature ever passed between us. The last half hour before he went away! – It must be all and completely a mistake – for I did not see him once that whole morning."

"But *that* you certainly did, for you spent the whole morning in Edgar's Buildings – it was the day your father's consent came – and I am pretty sure that you and John were alone in the parlour, some time before you left the house."

"Are you? – Well, if you say it, it was so, I dare say – but for the life of me, I cannot recollect it. – I *do* remember now being with you, and seeing him as well as the rest – but that we were ever alone for five minutes – However, it is not worth arguing about, for whatever might pass on his side, you must be convinced, by my having no recollection of it, that I never thought, nor expected, nor wished for any thing of the kind from him. I am excessively concerned that he should have any regard for me – but indeed it has been quite unintentional on my side, I never had the smallest idea of it. Pray undeceive him as soon as you can, and tell him I beg his pardon – that is – I do not know what I ought to say – but make him understand what I mean, in the properest way. I would not speak disrespectfully of a brother of yours, Isabella, I am sure; but you know very well that if I could think of one man more than another – *he* is not the person."

Isabella was silent. "My dear friend, you must not be angry with me. I cannot suppose your brother cares so very much about me. And, you know, we shall still be sisters."

"Yes, yes," (with a blush), "there are more ways than one of our being sisters. – But where am I wandering to?[1] – Well, my dear Catherine, the case seems to be, that you are determined against poor John – is not it so?"

"I certainly cannot return his affection, and as certainly never meant to encourage it."

"Since that is the case, I am sure I shall not tease you any further. John desired me to speak to you on the subject, and therefore I have. But I confess, as soon as I read his letter, I thought it a very foolish, imprudent business, and not likely to promote the good of either; for what were you to live upon, supposing you came together? You have both of you something to be sure, but it is not a trifle that will support a family now-a-days; and after all that romancers may say, there is no doing without money. I only wonder John could think of it; he could not have received my last."

"You *do* acquit me then of any thing wrong? – You are convinced that I never meant to deceive your brother, never suspected him of liking me till this moment?"

"Oh! as to that," answered Isabella laughingly, "I do not pretend to determine what your thoughts and designs in time past may have been. All that is best known to yourself. A little harmless flirtation or so will occur, and one is often drawn on to give more encouragement than one wishes to stand by. But you may be assured that I am the last person in the world to judge you severely. All those things should be allowed for in youth and high spirits. What one means one day, you know, one may not mean the next. Circumstances change, opinions alter."

"But my opinion of your brother never did alter; it was always the same. You are describing what never happened."

"My dearest Catherine," continued the other without at all listening to her, "I would not for all the world be the means of hurrying you into an engagement before you knew what you were about. I do not think any thing would justify me in wishing you to sacrifice all your happiness merely to oblige my brother, because he is my brother, and who perhaps after all, you know, might be just as happy without you, for people seldom know what they

---

1   Isabella has conceived a third method of she and Catherine becoming sisters – by their marrying the Tilney brothers.

would be at, young men especially, they are so amazingly change-able and inconstant. What I say is, why should a brother's happi-ness be dearer to me than a friend's? You know I carry my notions of friendship pretty high. But, above all things, my dear Catherine, do not be in a hurry. Take my word for it, that if you are in too great a hurry, you will certainly live to repent it. Tilney says there is nothing people are so often deceived in, as the state of their own affections, and I believe he is very right. Ah! here he comes; never mind, he will not see us, I am sure."

Catherine, looking up, perceived Captain Tilney, and Isabella, earnestly fixing her eye on him as she spoke, soon caught his no-tice. He approached immediately, and took the seat to which her movements invited him. His first address made Catherine start. Though spoken low, she could distinguish, "What! always to be watched, in person or by proxy!"

"Psha, nonsense!" was Isabella's answer in the same half whis-per. "Why do you put such things into my head? If I could believe it – my spirit, you know, is pretty independent."

"I wish your heart were independent. That would be enough for me."

"My heart, indeed! What can you have to do with hearts? You men have none of you any hearts."

"If we have not hearts, we have eyes; and they give us torment enough."

"Do they? I am sorry for it; I am sorry they find any thing so disagreeable in me. I will look another way. I hope this pleases you, (turning her back on him,) I hope your eyes are not tor-mented now."

"Never more so; for the edge of a blooming cheek is still in view – at once too much and too little."

Catherine heard all this, and quite out of countenance could listen no longer. Amazed that Isabella could endure it, and jealous for her brother, she rose up, and saying she should join Mrs Allen, proposed their walking. But for this Isabella shewed no inclina-tion. She was so amazingly tired, and it was so odious to parade about the Pump-room; and if she moved from her seat she should miss her sisters, she was expecting her sisters every moment; so that her dearest Catherine must excuse her, and must sit quietly down again. But Catherine could be stubborn too; and Mrs Allen just then coming up to propose their returning home, she joined her and walked out of the Pump-room, leaving Isabella still sitting with Captain Tilney. With much uneasiness did she thus leave them. It seemed to her that Captain Tilney was falling in love with Isabella, and Isabella unconsciously encouraging him; unconsciously it must be, for Isabella's attachment to James was as certain and well acknowledged as her engagement. To doubt her truth or good intentions was impossible; and yet, during the whole of their conversation her manner had been odd. She wished Isabella had talked more like her usual self, and not so much about money; and had not looked so well pleased at the sight of Captain Tilney. How strange that she should not perceive his admiration! Catherine longed to give her a hint of it, to put her on her guard, and prevent all the pain which her too lively behaviour might otherwise create both for him and her brother.

The compliment of John Thorpe's affection did not make amends for this thoughtlessness in his sister. She was almost as far from believing as from wishing it to be sincere; for she had not forgotten that he could mistake, and his assertion of the offer and of her encouragement convinced her that his mistakes could sometimes be very egregious. In vanity therefore she gained but little, her chief profit was in wonder. That he should think it worth his while to fancy himself in love with her, was a matter of lively astonishment. Isabella talked of his attentions; *she* had never been sensible of any; but Isabella had said many things which she hoped had been spoken in haste, and would never be said again; and upon this she was glad to rest altogether for present ease and comfort.

CHAPTER 19

A few days passed away, and Catherine, though not allowing herself to suspect her friend, could not help watching her closely. The result of her observations was not agreeable. Isabella seemed an altered creature. When she saw her, indeed, surrounded only by their immediate friends in Edgar's Buildings or Pulteney-street, her change of manners was so trifling that, had it gone no farther, it might have passed unnoticed. A something of languid indifference, or of that boasted absence of mind which Catherine had never heard of before, would occasionally come across her; but had nothing worse appeared, *that* might only have spread a new grace and inspired a warmer interest. But when Catherine saw her in public, admitting Captain Tilney's attentions as readily as they were offered, and allowing him almost an equal share with James in her notice and smiles, the alteration became too positive to be passed over. What could be meant by such unsteady conduct, what her friend could be at, was beyond her comprehension. Isabella could not be aware of the pain she was inflicting; but it was a degree of wilful thoughtlessness which Catherine could not but resent. James was the sufferer. She saw him grave and uneasy; and however careless of his present comfort the woman might be who had given him her heart, to *her* it was always an object. For poor Captain Tilney too she was greatly concerned. Though his looks did not please her, his name was a passport to her good will, and she thought with sincere compassion of his approaching disappointment; for, in spite of what she had believed herself to overhear in the Pump-room, his behaviour was so incompatible with a knowledge of Isabella's engagement, that she could not, upon reflection, imagine him aware of it. He might be jealous of her brother as a rival, but if more had seemed implied, the fault must have been in her misapprehension. She wished, by a gentle remonstrance, to remind Isabella of her situation, and make her aware of this double unkindness; but for remonstrance, either opportunity or comprehension was always against her. If able to suggest a hint, Isabella could never understand it. In this distress, the intended departure of the Tilney family became her chief consolation; their journey into Gloucestershire was to take place within a few days, and Captain Tilney's removal would at least restore peace to every heart but his own. But Captain Tilney had at present no intention of removing; he was not to be of the party to Northanger, he was to continue at Bath. When Catherine knew this, her resolution was directly made. She spoke to Henry Tilney on the subject, regretting his brother's evident partiality for Miss Thorpe, and entreating him to make known her prior engagement.

"My brother does know it," was Henry's answer.

"Does he? — then why does he stay here?"

He made no reply, and was beginning to talk of something else; but she eagerly continued, "Why do not you persuade him to go away? The longer he stays, the worse it will be for him at last. Pray advise him for his own sake, and for every body's sake, to leave Bath directly. Absence will in time make him comfortable again; but he can have no hope here, and it is only staying to be miserable." Henry smiled and said, "I am sure my brother would not wish to do that."

"Then you will persuade him to go away?"

"Persuasion is not at command; but pardon me, if I cannot even endeavour to persuade him. I have myself told him that Miss Thorpe is engaged. He knows what he is about, and must be his own master."

"No, he does not know what he is about," cried Catherine; "he does not know the pain he is giving my brother. Not that James has ever told me so, but I am sure he is very uncomfortable."

"And are you sure it is my brother's doing?"

"Yes, very sure."

"Is it my brother's attentions to Miss Thorpe, or Miss Thorpe's admission of them, that gives the pain?"

"Is not it the same thing?"

"I think Mr Morland would acknowledge a difference. No man is offended by another man's admiration of the woman he loves; it is the woman only who can make it a torment."

Catherine blushed for her friend, and said, "Isabella is wrong. But I am sure she cannot mean to torment, for she is very much attached to my brother. She has been in love with him ever since they first met, and while my father's consent was uncertain, she fretted herself almost into a fever. You know she must be attached to him."

"I understand: she is in love with James, and flirts with Frederick."

"Oh! no, not flirts. A woman in love with one man cannot flirt with another."

"It is probable that she will neither love so well, nor flirt so well, as she might do either singly. The gentlemen must each give up a little."

After a short pause, Catherine resumed with "Then you do not believe Isabella so very much attached to my brother?"

"I can have no opinion on that subject."

"But what can your brother mean? If he knows her engagement, what can he mean by his behaviour?"

"You are a very close questioner."

"Am I? — I only ask what I want to be told."

"But do you only ask what I can be expected to tell?"

"Yes, I think so; for you must know your brother's heart."

"My brother's heart, as you term it, on the present occasion, I assure you I can only guess at."

"Well?"

"Well! — Nay, if it is to be guess-work, let us all guess for ourselves. To be guided by second-hand conjecture is pitiful. The premises are before you. My brother is a lively, and perhaps sometimes a thoughtless young man; he has had about a week's acquaintance with your friend, and he has known her engagement almost as long as he has known her."

"Well," said Catherine, after some moments' consideration, "*you* may be able to guess at your brother's intentions from all this; but I am sure I cannot. But is not your father uncomfortable about it? — Does not he want Captain Tilney to go away? — Sure, if your father were to speak to him, he would go."

"My dear Miss Morland," said Henry, "in this amiable solicitude for your brother's comfort, may you not be a little mistaken? Are you not carried a little too far? Would he thank you, either on his own account or Miss Thorpe's, for supposing that her affection, or at least her good-behaviour, is only to be secured by her seeing nothing of Captain Tilney? Is he safe only in solitude? — or, is her heart constant to him only when unsolicited by any one else? — He cannot think this — and you may be sure that he would not have you think it. I will not say, 'Do not be uneasy,' because I know that you are so, at this moment; but be as little uneasy as you can. You have no doubt of the mutual attachment of your brother and your friend; depend upon it therefore, that real jealousy never can exist between them; depend upon it that no disagreement between them can be of any duration. Their hearts are open to each other, as neither heart can be to you; they know exactly what is required and what can be borne; and you may be certain, that one will never tease the other beyond what is known to be pleasant."

Perceiving her still to look doubtful and grave, he added, "Though Frederick does not leave Bath with us, he will probably remain but a very short time, perhaps only a few days behind us. His leave of absence will soon expire, and he must return to his regiment. – And what will then be their acquaintance? – The mess-room will drink Isabella Thorpe for a fortnight, and she will laugh with your brother over poor Tilney's passion for a month."

Catherine would contend no longer against comfort. She had resisted its approaches during the whole length of a speech, but it now carried her captive. Henry Tilney must know best. She blamed herself for the extent of her fears, and resolved never to think so seriously on the subject again.

Her resolution was supported by Isabella's behaviour in their parting interview. The Thorpes spent the last evening of Catherine's stay in Pulteney-street, and nothing passed between the lovers to excite her uneasiness, or make her quit them in apprehension. James was in excellent spirits, and Isabella most engagingly placid. Her tenderness for her friend seemed rather the first feeling of her heart; but that at such a moment was allowable; and once she gave her lover a flat contradiction, and once she drew back her hand; but Catherine remembered Henry's instructions, and placed it all to judicious affection. The embraces, tears, and promises of the parting fair ones may be fancied.

CHAPTER 20

Mr and Mrs Allen were sorry to lose their young friend, whose good-humour and cheerfulness had made her a valuable companion, and in the promotion of whose enjoyment their own had been gently increased. Her happiness in going with Miss Tilney, however, prevented their wishing it otherwise; and, as they were to remain only one more week in Bath themselves, her quitting them now would not long be felt. Mr Allen attended her to

Milsom-street, where she was to breakfast, and saw her seated with the kindest welcome among her new friends; but so great was her agitation in finding herself as one of the family, and so fearful was she of not doing exactly what was right, and of not being able to preserve their good opinion, that, in the embarrassment of the first five minutes, she could almost have wished to return with him to Pulteney-street.

Miss Tilney's manners and Henry's smile soon did away some of her unpleasant feelings; but still she was far from being at ease; nor could the incessant attentions of the General himself entirely reassure her. Nay, perverse as it seemed, she doubted whether she might not have felt less, had she been less attended to. His anxiety for her comfort – his continual solicitations that she would eat, and his often-expressed fears of her seeing nothing to her taste – though never in her life before had she beheld half such variety on a breakfast-table – made it impossible for her to forget for a moment that she was a visitor. She felt utterly unworthy of such respect, and knew not how to reply to it. Her tranquillity was not improved by the General's impatience for the appearance of his eldest son, nor by the displeasure he expressed at his laziness when Captain Tilney at last came down. She was quite pained by the severity of his father's reproof, which seemed disproportionate to the offence; and much was her concern increased, when she found herself the principal cause of the lecture; and that his tardiness was chiefly resented from being disrespectful to her. This was placing her in a very uncomfortable situation, and she felt great compassion for Captain Tilney, without being able to hope for his goodwill.

He listened to his father in silence, and attempted not any defence, which confirmed her in fearing, that the inquietude of his mind, on Isabella's account, might, by keeping him long sleepless, have been the real cause of his rising late. – It was the first time of her being decidedly in his company, and she had hoped to be now able to form her opinion of him; but she scarcely heard his voice while his father remained in the room; and even afterwards, so much were his spirits affected, she could distinguish nothing but these words, in a whisper to Eleanor, "How glad I shall be when you are all off."

The bustle of going was not pleasant. – The clock struck ten while the trunks were carrying down, and the General had fixed to be out of Milsom-street by that hour. His great coat, instead of being brought for him to put on directly, was spread out in the curricle in which he was to accompany his son. The middle seat of the chaise was not drawn out, though there were three people to go in it, and his daughter's maid had so crowded it with parcels that Miss Morland would not have room to sit; and, so much was he influenced by this apprehension when he handed her in, that she had some difficulty in saving her own new writing-desk from being thrown out into the street. – At last, however, the door was closed upon the three females, and they set off at the sober pace in which the handsome, highly-fed four horses of a gentleman usually perform a journey of thirty miles: such was the distance of Northanger from Bath, to be now divided into two equal stages. Catherine's spirits revived as they drove from the door; for with Miss Tilney she felt no restraint; and, with the interest of a road entirely new to her, of an abbey before, and a curricle behind, she caught the last view of Bath without any regret, and met with every mile-stone before she expected it. The tediousness of a two hours' bait[1] at Petty-France, in which there was nothing to be done but to eat without being hungry, and loiter about without any thing to see, next followed – and her admiration of the style in which they travelled, of the fashionable chaise and four[2] – postilions handsomely liveried, rising so regularly in their stirrups, and numerous outriders properly mounted, sunk a little under this consequent inconvenience. Had their party been perfectly agreeable, the delay would have been nothing; but General Tilney, though so charming a man, seemed always a check upon his children's spirits, and scarcely any thing was said but by himself; the observation of which, with his discontent at whatever the inn afforded, and his angry impatience at the waiters, made Catherine grow every moment more in awe of him, and appeared to lengthen the two hours into four. – At last, however, the order of release was given; and much was Catherine then surprized by the General's

---

1   A halt to refresh the horses.
2   See Appendix J.1.

proposal of her taking his place in his son's curricle for the rest of the journey: – "the day was fine, and he was anxious for her seeing as much of the country as possible."

The remembrance of Mr Allen's opinion, respecting young men's open carriages, made her blush at the mention of such a plan, and her first thought was to decline it; but her second was of greater deference for General Tilney's judgment; he could not propose any thing improper for her; and, in the course of a few minutes, she found herself with Henry in the curricle, as happy a being as ever existed. A very short trial convinced her that a curricle was the prettiest equipage in the world; the chaise-and-four wheeled off with some grandeur, to be sure, but it was a heavy and troublesome business, and she could not easily forget its having stopped two hours at Petty-France. Half the time would have been enough for the curricle, and so nimbly were the light horses disposed to move, that, had not the General chosen to have his own carriage lead the way, they could have passed it with ease in half a minute. But the merit of the curricle did not all belong to the horses; – Henry drove so well, – so quietly – without making any disturbance, without parading to her, or swearing at them; so different from the only gentleman-coachman whom it was in her power to compare him with! – And then his hat sat so well, and the innumerable capes of his great coat looked so becomingly important! – To be driven by him, next to being dancing with him, was certainly the greatest happiness in the world. In addition to every other delight, she had now that of listening to her own praise; of being thanked at least, on his sister's account, for her kindness in thus becoming her visitor; of hearing it ranked as real friendship, and described as creating real gratitude. His sister, he said, was uncomfortably circumstanced – she had no female companion – and, in the frequent absence of her father, was sometimes without any companion at all.

"But how can that be?" said Catherine, "are not you with her?"

"Northanger is not more than half my home; I have an establishment at my own house in Woodston, which is nearly twenty miles from my father's, and some of my time is necessarily spent there."

"How sorry you must be for that!"

"I am always sorry to leave Eleanor."

"Yes; but besides your affection for her, you must be so fond of the abbey! – After being used to such a home as the abbey, an ordinary parsonage-house must be very disagreeable."

He smiled, and said, "You have formed a very favourable idea of the abbey."

"To be sure I have. Is not it a fine old place, just like what one reads about?"

"And are you prepared to encounter all the horrors that a building such as 'what one reads about' may produce? – Have you a stout heart? – Nerves fit for sliding panels and tapestry?"

"Oh! yes – I do not think I should be easily frightened, because there would be so many people in the house – and besides, it has never been uninhabited and left deserted for years, and then the family come back to it unawares, without giving any notice, as generally happens."

"No, certainly. – We shall not have to explore our way into a hall dimly lighted by the expiring embers of a wood fire – nor be obliged to spread our beds on the floor of a room without windows, doors, or furniture. But you must be aware that when a young lady is (by whatever means) introduced into a dwelling of this kind, she is always lodged apart from the rest of the family. While they snugly repair to their own end of the house, she is formally conducted by Dorothy the ancient housekeeper up a different staircase, and along many gloomy passages, into an apartment never used since some cousin or kin died in it about twenty years before. Can you stand such a ceremony as this? Will not your mind misgive you, when you find yourself in this gloomy chamber – too lofty and extensive for you, with only the feeble rays of a single lamp to take in its size – its walls hung with tapestry exhibiting figures as large as life, and the bed, of dark green stuff or purple velvet, presenting even a funereal appearance? Will not your heart sink within you?"

"Oh! but this will not happen to me, I am sure."

"How fearfully will you examine the furniture of your apartment! – And what will you discern? – Not tables, toilettes, wardrobes, or drawers, but on one side perhaps the remains of a broken lute, on the other a ponderous chest which no efforts can open, and over the fire-place the portrait of some handsome warrior, whose features will so incomprehensibly strike you, that you will not be able to withdraw your eyes from it. Dorothy, meanwhile, no less struck by your appearance, gazes on you in great agitation, and drops a few unintelligible hints. To raise your spirits, moreover, she gives you reason to suppose that the part of the abbey you inhabit is undoubtedly haunted, and informs you that you will not have a single domestic within call. With this parting cordial she curtseys off – you listen to the sound of her receding footsteps as long as the last echo can reach you – and when, with fainting spirits, you attempt to fasten your door, you discover, with increased alarm, that it has no lock."

"Oh! Mr Tilney, how frightful! – This is just like a book! – But it cannot really happen to me. I am sure your housekeeper is not really Dorothy. – Well, what then?"

"Nothing further to alarm perhaps may occur the first night. After surmounting your *unconquerable* horror of the bed, you will retire to rest, and get a few hours' unquiet slumber. But on the second, or at farthest the *third* night after your arrival, you will probably have a violent storm. Peals of thunder so loud as to seem to shake the edifice to its foundation will roll round the neighbouring mountains – and during the frightful gusts of wind which accompany it, you will probably think you discern (for your lamp is not extinguished) one part of the hanging more violently agitated than the rest. Unable of course to repress your curiosity in so favourable a moment for indulging it, you will instantly arise, and throwing your dressing-gown around you, proceed to examine this mystery. After a very short search, you will discover a division in the tapestry so artfully constructed as to defy the minutest inspection, and on opening it, a door will immediately appear – which door being only secured by massy bars and a padlock, you will, after a few efforts, succeed in opening, – and, with your lamp in your hand, will pass through it into a small vaulted room."

"No, indeed; I should be too much frightened to do any such thing."

"What! not when Dorothy has given you to understand that there is a secret subterraneous communication between your apartment and the chapel of St Anthony, scarcely two miles off? –

Could you shrink from so simple an adventure? No, no, you will proceed into this small vaulted room, and through this into several others, without perceiving any thing very remarkable in either. In one perhaps there may be a dagger, in another a few drops of blood, and in a third the remains of some instrument of torture; but there being nothing in all this out of the common way, and your lamp being nearly exhausted, you will return towards your own apartment. In repassing through the small vaulted room, however, your eyes will be attracted towards a large, old-fashioned cabinet of ebony and gold, which, though narrowly examining the furniture before, you had passed unnoticed. Impelled by an irresistible presentiment, you will eagerly advance to it, unlock its folding doors, and search into every drawer; – but for some time without discovering anything of importance – perhaps nothing but a considerable hoard of diamonds. At last, however, by touching a secret spring, an inner compartment will open – a roll of paper appears: you seize it – it contains many sheets of manuscript – you hasten with the precious treasure into your own chamber, but scarcely have you been able to decipher 'Oh! thou – whomsoever thou mayst be, into whose hands these memoirs of the wretched Matilda may fall' – when your lamp suddenly expires in the socket, and leaves you in total darkness."

"Oh! no, no – do not say so. Well, go on."

But Henry was too much amused by the interest he had raised, to be able to carry it farther; he could no longer command solemnity either of subject or voice, and was obliged to entreat her to use her own fancy in the perusal of Matilda's woes. Catherine, recollecting herself, grew ashamed of her eagerness, and began earnestly to assure him that her attention had been fixed without the smallest apprehension of really meeting with what he related. "Miss Tilney, she was sure, would never put her into such a chamber as he had described! – She was not at all afraid."

As they drew near the end of their journey, her impatience for a sight of the abbey – for some time suspended by his conversation on subjects very different – returned in full force, and every bend in the road was expected with solemn awe to afford a glimpse of its massy walls of grey stone, rising amidst a grove of ancient oaks, with the last beams of the sun playing in beautiful splendour on its high Gothic windows. But so low did the building stand, that she found herself passing through the great gates of the lodge into the very grounds of Northanger, without having discerned even an antique chimney.

She knew not that she had any right to be surprized, but there was a something in this mode of approach which she certainly had not expected. To pass between lodges of a modern appearance, to find herself with such ease in the very precincts of the abbey, and driven so rapidly along a smooth, level road of fine gravel, without obstacle, alarm, or solemnity of any kind, struck her as odd and inconsistent. She was not long at leisure however for such considerations. A sudden scud of rain driving full in her face, made it impossible for her to observe anything further, and fixed all her thoughts on the welfare of her new straw bonnet:[1] — and she was actually under the abbey walls, was springing, with Henry's assistance, from the carriage, was beneath the shelter of the old porch, and had even passed on to the hall, where her friend and the General were waiting to welcome her, without feeling one awful foreboding of future misery to herself, or one moment's suspicion of any past scenes of horror being acted within the solemn edifice.[2] The breeze had not seemed to waft the sighs of the murdered to her; it had wafted nothing worse than a thick mizzling rain; and having given a good shake to her habit, she was ready to be shewn into the common drawing-room, and capable of considering where she was.

An abbey! — yes, it was delightful to be really in an abbey! — but she doubted, as she looked round the room, whether any thing within her observation, would have given her the consciousness.

---

1   Cf. *The Mysteries of Udolpho*. When Emily fled Udolpho Castle to escape Montoni her "appearance excited some surprise" among the locals "for she was without a hat, having had time only to throw on her veil before she left the castle." Money is found and "this necessary article of dress" — "a little straw hat, such as was worn by the peasant girls of Tuscany" — is purchased before they continue on their way (444-45).

2   In stark contrast to the Gothic convention in which the approach to the abbey is minutely detailed (Charlotte Smith's *Ethelinde, the Recluse of the Lake* 1789 1.34-35) and/or full of foreboding (Radcliffe's *Romance of the Forest*, 1791 1.2, *The Mysteries of Udolpho*, 1.5).

The furniture was in all the profusion and elegance of modern taste. The fire-place, where she had expected the ample width and ponderous carving of former times, was contracted to a Rumford,[1] with slabs of plain though handsome marble, and ornaments over it of the prettiest English china. The windows, to which she looked with peculiar dependence, from having heard the General talk of his preserving them in their Gothic form with reverential care, were yet less what her fancy had portrayed. To be sure, the pointed arch was preserved — the form of them was Gothic — they might be even casements — but every pane was so large, so clear, so light! To an imagination which had hoped for the smallest divisions, and the heaviest stone-work, for painted glass, dirt, and cobwebs, the difference was very distressing.

The General, perceiving how her eye was employed, began to talk of the smallness of the room and simplicity of the furniture, where every thing being for daily use, pretended only to comfort, &c.; flattering himself however that there were some apartments in the Abbey not unworthy her notice — and was proceeding to mention the costly gilding of one in particular, when taking out his watch, he stopped short to pronounce it with surprize within twenty minutes of five! This seemed the word of separation, and Catherine found herself hurried away by Miss Tilney in such a manner as convinced her that the strictest punctuality to the family hours would be expected at Northanger.

Returning through the large and lofty hall, they ascended a broad staircase of shining oak, which, after many flights and many landing-places, brought them upon a long, wide gallery. On one side it had a range of doors, and it was lighted on the other by windows which Catherine had only time to discover looked into a quadrangle, before Miss Tilney led the way into a chamber, and scarcely staying to hope she would find it comfortable, left her with an anxious entreaty that she would make as little alteration as possible in her dress.

---

1 Benjamin Thompson, Count Rumford (1753-1814), invented a modern fireplace with a sloping back, to conserve heat and prevent smoking.

CHAPTER 21

A moment's glance was enough to satisfy Catherine that her apartment was very unlike the one which Henry had endeavoured to alarm her by the description of. – It was by no means unreasonably large, and contained neither tapestry nor velvet. – The walls were papered, the floor was carpeted; the windows were neither less perfect, nor more dim than those of the drawing-room below; the furniture, though not of the latest fashion, was handsome and comfortable, and the air of the room altogether far from uncheerful. Her heart instantaneously at ease on this point, she resolved to lose no time in particular examination of any thing, as she greatly dreaded disobliging the General by any delay. Her habit therefore was thrown off with all possible haste, and she was preparing to unpin the linen package, which the chaise-seat had conveyed for her immediate accommodation, when her eye suddenly fell on a large high chest, standing back in a deep recess on one side of the fire-place. The sight of it made her start; and, forgetting everything else, she stood gazing on it in motionless wonder, while these thoughts crossed her: –

"This is strange indeed! I did not expect such a sight as this! – An immense heavy chest! – What can it hold? – Why should it be placed here? – Pushed back too, as if meant to be out of sight! – I will look into it – cost me what it may, I will look into it – and directly too – by day-light. – If I stay till evening my candle may go out." She advanced and examined it closely: it was of cedar, curiously inlaid with some darker wood, and raised, about a foot from the ground, on a carved stand of the same. The lock was silver, though tarnished from age; at each end were the imperfect remains of handles also of silver, broken perhaps prematurely by some strange violence; and, on the centre of the lid, was a mysterious cypher, in the same metal. Catherine bent over it intently, but without being able to distinguish any thing with certainty. She could not, in whatever direction she took it, believe the last letter to be a T; and yet that it should be any thing else in that house was a circumstance to raise no common degree of astonishment. If not originally their's, by what strange events could it have fallen into the Tilney family?

Her fearful curiosity was every moment growing greater; and seizing, with trembling hands, the hasp of the lock, she resolved at all hazards to satisfy herself at least as to its contents. With difficulty, for something seemed to resist her efforts, she raised the lid a few inches; but at that moment a sudden knocking at the door of the room made her, starting, quit her hold, and the lid closed with alarming violence. This ill-timed intruder was Miss Tilney's maid, sent by her mistress to be of use to Miss Morland; and though Catherine immediately dismissed her, it recalled her to the sense of what she ought to be doing, and forced her, in spite of her anxious desire to penetrate this mystery, to proceed in her dressing without further delay. Her progress was not quick, for her thoughts and her eyes were still bent on the object so well calculated to interest and alarm; and though she dared not waste a moment upon a second attempt, she could not remain many paces from the chest. At length, however, having slipped one arm into her gown, her toilette seemed so nearly finished, that the impatience of her curiosity might safely be indulged. One moment surely might be spared; and, so desperate should be the exertion of her strength, that, unless secured by supernatural means, the lid in one moment should be thrown back. With this spirit she sprang forward, and her confidence did not deceive her. Her resolute effort threw back the lid, and gave to her astonished eyes the view of a white cotton counterpane, properly folded, reposing at one end of the chest in undisputed possession!

She was gazing on it with the first blush of surprize, when Miss Tilney, anxious for her friend's being ready, entered the room, and to the rising shame of having harboured for some minutes an absurd expectation, was then added the shame of being caught in so idle a search. "That is a curious old chest, is not it?" said Miss Tilney, as Catherine hastily closed it and turned away to the glass. "It is impossible to say how many generations it has been here. How it came to be first put in this room I know not, but I have not had it moved, because I thought it might sometimes be of use in holding hats and bonnets. The worst of it is that its weight makes it difficult to open. In that corner, however, it is at least out of the way."

Catherine had no leisure for speech, being at once blushing, tying her gown, and forming wise resolutions with the most violent dispatch. Miss Tilney gently hinted her fear of being late; and in half a minute they ran down stairs together, in an alarm not wholly unfounded, for General Tilney was pacing the drawing-room, his watch in his hand, and having, on the very instant of their entering, pulled the bell with violence, ordered "Dinner to be on table *directly!*"

Catherine trembled at the emphasis with which he spoke, and sat pale and breathless, in a most humble mood, concerned for his children, and detesting old chests; and the General recovering his politeness. as he looked at her, spent the rest of his time in scolding his daughter for so foolishly hurrying her fair friend, who was absolutely out of breath from haste, when there was not the least occasion for hurry in the world: but Catherine could not at all get over the double distress of having involved her friend in a lecture and been a great simpleton herself, till they were happily seated at the dinner-table, when the General's complacent smiles, and a good appetite of her own, restored her to peace. The dining-parlour was a noble room, suitable in its dimensions to a much larger drawing-room than the one in common use, and fitted up in a style of luxury and expense which was almost lost on the unpractised eye of Catherine, who saw little more than its spaciousness and the number of their attendants. Of the former, she spoke aloud her admiration; and the General, with a very gracious countenance, acknowledged that it was by no means an ill-sized room; and further confessed that, though as careless on such subjects as most people, he did look upon a tolerably large eating-room as one of the necessaries of life; he supposed, however, "that she must have been used to much better sized apartments at Mr Allen's?"

"No, indeed," was Catherine's honest assurance; "Mr Allen's dining-parlour was not more than half as large:" and she had never seen so large a room as this in her life. The General's good humour increased. – Why, as he *had* such rooms, he thought it would be simple not to make use of them; but, upon his honour, he believed there might be more comfort in rooms of only half their size. Mr Allen's house, he was sure, must be exactly of the true size for rational happiness.

The evening passed without any further disturbance, and, in the occasional absence of General Tilney, with much positive cheerfulness. It was only in his presence that Catherine felt the smallest fatigue from her journey; and even then, even in moments of languor or restraint, a sense of general happiness preponderated, and she could think of her friends in Bath without one wish of being with them.

The night was stormy; the wind had been rising at intervals the whole afternoon; and by the time the party broke up, it blew and rained violently. Catherine, as she crossed the hall, listened to the tempest with sensations of awe; and, when she heard it rage round a corner of the ancient building and close with sudden fury a distant door, felt for the first time that she was really in an Abbey. – Yes, these were characteristic sounds; – they brought to her recollection a countless variety of dreadful situations and horrid scenes, which such buildings had witnessed, and such storms ushered in; and most heartily did she rejoice in the happier circumstances attending her entrance within walls so solemn! – *She* had nothing to dread from midnight assassins or drunken gallants. Henry had certainly been only in jest in what he had told her that morning. In a house so furnished, and so guarded, she could have nothing to explore or to suffer; and might go to her bedroom as securely as if it had been her own chamber at Fullerton. Thus wisely fortifying her mind, as she proceeded up stairs, she was enabled, especially on perceiving that Miss Tilney slept only two doors from her, to enter her room with a tolerably stout heart; and her spirits were immediately assisted by the cheerful blaze of a wood fire. "How much better is this," said she, as she walked to the fender – "how much better to find a fire ready lit, than to have to wait shivering in the cold till all the family are in bed, as so many poor girls have been obliged to do, and then to have a faithful old servant frightening one by coming in with a faggot! How glad I am that Northanger is what it is! If it had been like some other places, I do not know that, in such a night as this, I could have answered for my courage: – but now, to be sure, there is nothing to alarm one."

She looked round the room. The window curtains seemed in motion. It could be nothing but the violence of the wind penetrating through the divisions of the shutters; and she stept boldly forward, carelessly humming a tune, to assure herself of its being so, peeped courageously behind each curtain, saw nothing on either low window seat to scare her, and on placing a hand against the shutter, felt the strongest conviction of the wind's force. A glance at the old chest, as she turned away from this examination, was not without its use; she scorned the causeless fears of an idle fancy, and began with a most happy indifference to prepare herself for bed. "She should take her time; she should not hurry herself; she did not care if she were the last person up in the house. But she would not make up her fire; *that* would seem cowardly, as if she wished for the protection of light after she were in bed." The fire therefore died away, and Catherine, having spent the best part of an hour in her arrangements, was beginning to think of stepping into bed, when, on giving a parting glance round the room, she was struck by the appearance of a high, old-fashioned black cabinet, which, though in a situation conspicuous enough, had never caught her notice before. Henry's words, his description of the ebony cabinet which was to escape her observation at first, immediately rushed across her; and though there could be nothing really in it, there was something whimsical, it was certainly a very remarkable coincidence! She took her candle and looked closely at the cabinet. It was not absolutely ebony and gold; but it was Japan,[1] black and yellow Japan of the handsomest kind; and as she held her candle, the yellow had very much the effect of gold. The key was in the door, and she had a strange fancy to look into it; not however with the smallest expectation of finding any thing, but it was so very odd, after what Henry had said. In short, she could not sleep till she had examined it. So, placing the candle with great caution on a chair, she seized the key with a very tremulous hand and tried to turn it; but it resisted her utmost strength. Alarmed, but not discouraged, she tried it another way; a bolt flew, and she believed herself successful; but how strangely mysterious! – the door was still immovable. She paused a moment in breathless wonder. The wind roared down the chimney, the rain

---

1   A fashionable hard varnish imported from the East which produces a blackened, glossy finish on wood.

beat in torrents against the windows, and every thing seemed to speak the awfulness of her situation. To retire to bed, however, unsatisfied on such a point, would be vain, since sleep must be impossible with the consciousness of a cabinet so mysteriously closed in her immediate vicinity. Again therefore she applied herself to the key, and after moving it in every possible way for some instants with the determined celerity of hope's last effort, the door suddenly yielded to her hand: her heart leaped with exultation at such a victory, and having thrown open each folding door, the second being secured only by bolts of less wonderful construction than the lock, though that her eye could not discern any thing unusual, a double range of small drawers appeared in view, with some larger drawers above and below them; and in the centre, a small door, closed also with a lock and key, secured in all probability a cavity of importance.

Catherine's heart beat quick, but her courage did not fail her. With a cheek flushed by hope, and an eye straining with curiosity, her fingers grasped the handle of a drawer and drew it forth. It was entirely empty. With less alarm and greater eagerness she seized a second, a third, a fourth; each was equally empty. Not one was left unsearched, and in not one was any thing found. Well read in the art of concealing a treasure, the possibility of false linings to the drawers did not escape her, and she felt round each with anxious acuteness in vain. The place in the middle alone remained now unexplored; and though she had "never from the first had the smallest idea of finding any thing in any part of the cabinet, and was not in the least disappointed at her ill success thus far, it would be foolish not to examine it thoroughly while she was about it." It was some time however before she could unfasten the door, the same difficulty occurring in the management of this inner lock as of the outer; but at length it did open; and not vain, as hitherto, was her search; her quick eyes directly fell on a roll of paper pushed back into the further part of the cavity, apparently for concealment, and her feelings at that moment were indescribable. Her heart fluttered, her knees trembled, and her cheeks grew pale. She seized, with an unsteady hand, the precious manuscript, for half a glance sufficed to ascertain written characters; and while she acknowledged with awful sensations this striking exemplification of what Henry had fore-told, resolved instantly to peruse every line before she attempted to rest.

The dimness of the light her candle emitted made her turn to it with alarm; but there was no danger of its sudden extinction, it had yet some hours to burn; and that she might not have any greater difficulty in distinguishing the writing than what its ancient date might occasion, she hastily snuffed it. Alas! it was snuffed and extinguished in one. A lamp could not have expired with more awful effect. Catherine, for a few moments, was motionless with horror. It was done completely; not a remnant of light in the wick could give hope to the rekindling breath. Darkness impenetrable and immovable filled the room. A violent gust of wind, rising with sudden fury, added fresh horror to the moment. Catherine trembled from head to foot. In the pause which succeeded, a sound like receding footsteps and the closing of a distant door struck on her affrighted ear. Human nature could support no more. A cold sweat stood on her forehead, the manuscript fell from her hand, and groping her way to the bed, she jumped hastily in, and sought some suspension of agony by creeping far underneath the clothes. To close her eyes in sleep that night, she felt must be entirely out of the question. With a curiosity so justly awakened, and feelings in every way so agitated, repose must be absolutely impossible. The storm too abroad so dreadful! – She had not been used to feel alarm from wind, but now every blast seemed fraught with awful intelligence. The manuscript so wonderfully found, so wonderfully accomplishing the morning's prediction, how was it to be accounted for? – What could it contain? – to whom could it relate? – by what means could it have been so long concealed? – and how singularly strange that it should fall to her lot to discover it! Till she had made herself mistress of its contents, however, she could have neither repose nor comfort; and with the sun's first rays she was determined to peruse it. But many were the tedious hours which must yet intervene. She shuddered, tossed about in her bed, and envied every quiet sleeper. The storm still raged, and various were the noises, more terrific even than the wind, which struck at intervals on her startled ear. The very curtains of her bed seemed at one moment in motion, and at another the lock of her door was agitated, as if by the attempt of somebody to enter. Hollow murmurs seemed to creep along the gallery, and more than once her blood was chilled by the sound of distant moans. Hour after hour passed away, and the wearied Catherine had heard three proclaimed by all the clocks in the house before the tempest subsided, or she unknowingly fell fast asleep.

CHAPTER 22

The housemaid's folding back her window-shutters at eight o'clock the next day, was the sound which first roused Catherine; and she opened her eyes, wondering that they could ever have been closed, on objects of cheerfulness; her fire was already burning, and a bright morning had succeeded the tempest of the night. Instantaneously with the consciousness of existence, returned her recollection of the manuscript; and springing from the bed in the very moment of the maid's going away, she eagerly collected every scattered sheet which had burst from the roll on its falling to the ground, and flew back to enjoy the luxury of their perusal on her pillow. She now plainly saw that she must not expect a manuscript of equal length with the generality of what she had shuddered over in books, for the roll, seeming to consist entirely of small disjointed sheets, was altogether but of trifling size, and much less than she had supposed it to be at first.

Her greedy eye glanced rapidly over a page. She started at its import. Could it be possible, or did not her senses play her false? – An inventory of linen, in coarse and modern characters, seemed all that was before her! If the evidence of sight might be trusted, she held a washing-bill in her hand. She seized another sheet, and saw the same articles with little variation; a third, a fourth, and a fifth presented nothing new. Shirts, stockings, cravats, and waistcoats faced her in each. Two others, penned by the same hand, marked an expenditure scarcely more interesting, in letters, hair-powder, shoe-string and breeches-ball.[1] And the larger sheet, which had enclosed the rest, seemed by its first cramp line, "To

---

1 A kind of soap.

poultice chestnut mare," – a farrier's bill! Such was the collection of papers, (left perhaps, as she could then suppose, by the negligence of a servant in the place whence she had taken them,) which had filled her with expectation and alarm, and robbed her of half her night's rest! She felt humbled to the dust. Could not the adventure of the chest have taught her wisdom? A corner of it catching her eye as she lay, seemed to rise up in judgment against her. Nothing could now be clearer than the absurdity of her recent fancies. To suppose that a manuscript of many generations back could have remained undiscovered in a room such as that, so modern, so habitable! – or that she should be the first to possess the skill of unlocking a cabinet, the key of which was open to all!

How could she have so imposed on herself? – Heaven forbid that Henry Tilney should ever know her folly! And it was in a great measure his own doing, for had not the cabinet appeared so exactly to agree with his description of her adventures, she should never have felt the smallest curiosity about it. This was the only comfort that occurred. Impatient to get rid of those hateful evidences of her folly, those detestable papers then scattered over the bed, she rose directly, and folding them up as nearly as possible in the same shape as before, returned them to the same spot within the cabinet, with a very hearty wish that no untoward accident might ever bring them forward again, to disgrace her even with herself.

Why the locks should have been so difficult to open however, was still something remarkable, for she could now manage them with perfect ease. In this there was surely something mysterious, and she indulged in the flattering suggestion for half a minute, till the possibility of the door's having been at first unlocked, and of being herself its fastener, darted into her head, and cost her another blush.

She got away as soon as she could from a room in which her conduct produced such unpleasant reflections, and found her way with all speed to the breakfast-parlour, as it had been pointed out to her by Miss Tilney the evening before. Henry was alone in it; and his immediate hope of her having been undisturbed by the tempest, with an arch reference to the character of the building they inhabited, was rather distressing. For the world would she not have her weakness suspected; and yet, unequal to an absolute falsehood, was constrained to acknowledge that the wind had kept her awake a little. "But we have a charming morning after it," she added, desiring to get rid of the subject; "and storms and sleeplessness are nothing when they are over. What beautiful hyacinths! – I have just learnt to love a hyacinth."

"And how might you learn? – By accident or argument?"

"Your sister taught me; I cannot tell how. Mrs Allen used to take pains, year after year, to make me like them; but I never could, till I saw them the other day in Milsom-street; I am naturally indifferent about flowers."

"But now you love a hyacinth. So much the better. You have gained a new source of enjoyment, and it is well to have as many holds upon happiness as possible. Besides, a taste for flowers is always desirable in your sex, as a means of getting you out of doors, and tempting you to more frequent exercise than you would otherwise take. And though the love of a hyacinth may be rather domestic, who can tell, the sentiment once raised, but you may in time come to love a rose?"

"But I do not want any such pursuit to get me out of doors. The pleasure of walking and breathing fresh air is enough for me, and in fine weather I am out more than half my time. – Mamma says, I am never within."

"At any rate, however, I am pleased that you have learnt to love a hyacinth. The mere habit of learning to love is the thing; and a teachableness of disposition in a young lady is a great blessing. – Has my sister a pleasant mode of instruction?"

Catherine was saved the embarrassment of attempting an answer by the entrance of the General, whose smiling compliments announced a happy state of mind, but whose gentle hint of sympathetic early rising did not advance her composure.

The elegance of the breakfast set forced itself on Catherine's notice when they were seated at table; and, lucidly, it had been the General's choice. He was enchanted by her approbation of his taste, confessed it to be neat and simple, thought it right to encourage the manufacture of his country; and for his part, to his uncritical palate, the tea was as well flavoured from the clay of

Staffordshire, as from that of Dresden or Sève.[1] But this was quite an old set, purchased two years ago. The manufacture was much improved since that time; he had seen some beautiful specimens when last in town, and had he not been perfectly without vanity of that kind, might have been tempted to order a new set. He trusted, however, that an opportunity might ere long occur of selecting one – though not for himself. Catherine was probably the only one of the party who did not understand him.

Shortly after breakfast Henry left them for Woodston, where business required and would keep him two or three days. They all attended in the hall to see him mount his horse, and immediately on re-entering the breakfast-room, Catherine walked to a window in the hope of catching another glimpse of his figure. "This is a somewhat heavy call upon your brother's fortitude," observed the General to Eleanor. "Woodston will make but a sombre appearance to-day."

"Is it a pretty place?" asked Catherine.

"What say you, Eleanor? – speak your opinion, for ladies can best tell the taste of ladies in regard to places as well as men. I think it would be acknowledged by the most impartial eye to have many recommendations. The house stands among fine meadows facing the south-east, with an excellent kitchen-garden in the same aspect; the walls surrounding which I built and stocked myself about ten years ago, for the benefit of my son. It is a family living, Miss Morland; and the property in the place being chiefly my own, you may believe I take care that it shall not be a bad one. Did Henry's income depend solely on this living, he would not be ill provided for. Perhaps it may seem odd, that with only two younger children, I should think any profession necessary for him; and certainly there are moments when we could all

---

1 Josiah Wedgwood, one of the most astute marketers in the annals of English entrepreneurship, built factories in Stoke-on-Trent, Staffordshire, that produced china. "Wedgewood sold his wares at prices far above his competitors' in elegant showrooms selling nothing else. Here the prices were exhibited with great éclat, and new lines introduced with carefully orchestrated fanfares of publicity, and special viewings by ticket only for the 'nobility and Gentry'" (Monaghan 98-99). General Tilney bemoans his old Wedgwood since it does not carry that year's pattern.

wish him disengaged from every tie of business. But though I may not exactly make converts of you young ladies, I am sure your father, Miss Morland, would agree with me in thinking it expedient to give every young man some employment. The money is nothing, it is not an object, but employment is the thing. Even Frederick, my eldest son, you see, who will perhaps inherit as considerable a landed property as any private man in the county, has his profession."

The imposing effect of this last argument was equal to his wishes. The silence of the lady proved it to be unanswerable.

Something had been said the evening before of her being shown over the house, and he now offered himself as her conductor; and though Catherine had hoped to explore it accompanied only by his daughter, it was a proposal of too much happiness in itself, under any circumstances, not to be gladly accepted; for she had been already eighteen hours in the Abbey, and had seen only a few of its rooms. The netting-box, just leisurely drawn forth, was closed with joyful haste, and she was ready to attend him in a moment. "And when they had gone over the house, he promised himself moreover the pleasure of accompanying her into the shrubberies and garden." She curtsied her acquiescence. "But perhaps it might be more agreeable to her to make those her first object. The weather was at present favourable, and at this time of year the uncertainty was very great of its continuing so. – Which would she prefer? He was equally at her service. – Which did his daughter think would most accord with her fair friend's wishes? – But he thought he could discern. – Yes, he certainly read in Miss Morland's eyes a judicious desire of making use of the present smiling weather. – But when did she judge amiss? – The Abbey would be always safe and dry. – He yielded implicitly, and would fetch his hat and attend them in a moment." He left the room, and Catherine, with a disappointed, anxious face, began to speak of her unwillingness that he should be taking them out of doors against his own inclination, under a mistaken idea of pleasing her; but she was stopt by Miss Tilney's saying, with a little confusion, "I believe it will be wisest to take the morning while it is so fine; and do not be uneasy on my father's account, he always walks out at this time of day."

Catherine did not exactly know how this was to be understood. Why was Miss Tilney embarrassed? Could there be any unwillingness on the General's side to shew her over the Abbey? The proposal was his own. And was not it odd that he should *always* take his walk so early? Neither her father nor Mr Allen did so. It was certainly very provoking. She was all impatience to see the house, and had scarcely any curiosity about the grounds. If Henry had been with them indeed! – but now she should not know what was picturesque when she saw it. Such were her thoughts, but she kept them to herself, and put on her bonnet in patient discontent.

She was struck however, beyond her expectation, by the grandeur of the Abbey, as she saw it for the first time from the lawn. The whole building enclosed a large court; and two sides of the quadrangle, rich in Gothic ornaments, stood forward for admiration. The remainder was shut off by knolls of old trees, or luxuriant plantations, and the steep woody hills rising behind to give it shelter, were beautiful even in the leafless month of March. Catherine had seen nothing to compare with it; and her feelings of delight were so strong, that without waiting for any better authority, she boldly burst forth in wonder and praise. The General listened with assenting gratitude; and it seemed as if his own estimation of Northanger had waited unfixed till that hour.

The kitchen-garden was to be next admired, and he led the way to it across a small portion of the park.

The number of acres contained in this garden was such as Catherine could not listen to without dismay, being more than double the extent of all Mr Allen's, as well her father's, including church-yard and orchard. The walls seemed countless in number, endless in length; a village of hot-houses seemed to arise among them, and a whole parish to be at work within the inclosure. The General was flattered by her looks of surprize, which told him almost as plainly, as he soon forced her to tell him in words, that she had never seen any gardens at all equal to them before; – and he then modestly owned that, "without any ambition of that sort himself – without any solicitude about it, – he did believe them to be unrivalled in the kingdom. If he had a hobby-horse, it was *that*. He loved a garden. Though careless enough in most matters of eating, he loved good fruit – or if he did not, his friends and children did. There were great vexations however attending such a garden as his. The utmost care could not always secure the most valuable fruits. The pinery[1] had yielded only one hundred in the last year. Mr Allen, he supposed, must feel these inconveniences as well as himself."

"No, not at all. Mr Allen did not care about the garden, and never went into it."

With a triumphant smile of self-satisfaction, the General wished he could do the same, for he never entered his, without being vexed in some way or other, by its falling short of his plan.

"How were Mr Allen's succession-houses[2] worked?" describing the nature of his own as they entered them.

"Mr Allen had only one small hot-house, which Mrs Allen had the use of for her plants in winter, and there was a fire in it now and then."

"He is a happy man!" said the General, with a look of very happy contempt.

Having taken her into every division, and led her under every wall, till she was heartily weary of seeing and wondering, he suffered the girls at last to seize the advantage of an outer door, and then expressing his wish to examine the effect of some recent

---

1 Place where pineapples are grown.
2 A series of forcing-houses with graded temperatures through which plants are moved in succession to hardy them for the outside. Richard Bradley in his essay "A Particular Easy Method of Managing Pineapples" (1726) notes that pineapples were the most difficult and exotic hot-house fruit to grow in England requiring "a full three years of growth, an exact temperature, ideal moisture conditions, and correctly constructed stoves" (qtd. in Rousseau 101). General Tilney's penchant for pineapple production attests to both his loyalty to royalty (as does his subscribing to the Loyalist Address Movement), and also to his decadent consumerist tendencies since pineapples historically first appeared in Henry Danckert's (1625-79?) painting of the restored Charles II receiving the first home-grown fruit. While production costs had no doubt fallen significantly from 1726 when Pope's *Epistle to Burlington* (1731) prices them at about half a guinea each – the equivalent today of over a hundred dollars – they were still a luxury item and produced in small numbers by the 1790s. The General's production of one hundred in his pinery – and that in what he describes as a poor year – is an astonishing feat of fruiticulture.

alterations about the tea-house, proposed it as no unpleasant extension of their walk, if Miss Morland were not tired. "But where are you going, Eleanor? – Why do you chuse that cold, damp path to it? Miss Morland will get wet. Our best way is across the park."

"This is so favourite a walk of mine," said Miss Tilney, "that I always think it the best and nearest way. But perhaps it may be damp."

It was a narrow winding path through a thick grove of old Scotch firs; and Catherine, struck by its gloomy aspect, and eager to enter it, could not, even by the General's disapprobation, be kept from stepping forward. He perceived her inclination, and having again urged the plea of health in vain, was too polite to make further opposition. He excused himself, however, from attending them: – "The rays of the sun were not too cheerful for him, and he would meet them by another course." He turned away; and Catherine was shocked to find how much her spirits were relieved by the separation. The shock, however, being less real than the relief, offered it no injury; and she began to talk with easy gaiety of the delightful melancholy which such a grove inspired.

"I am particularly fond of this spot," said her companion, with a sigh. "It was my mother's favourite walk."

Catherine had never heard Mrs Tilney mentioned in the family before, and the interest excited by this tender remembrance, shewed itself directly in her altered countenance, and in the attentive pause with which she waited for something more.

"I used to walk here so often with her!" added Eleanor; "though I never loved it then, as I have loved it since. At that time indeed I used to wonder at her choice. But her memory endears it now."

"And ought it not," reflected Catherine, "to endear it to her husband? Yet the General would not enter it." Miss Tilney continuing silent, she ventured to say, "Her death must have been a great affliction!"

"A great and increasing one," replied the other, in a low voice. "I was only thirteen when it happened; and though I felt my loss perhaps as strongly as one so young could feel it, I did not, I could not then know what a loss it was." She stopped for a moment, and then added, with great firmness, "I have no sister, you know –

and though Henry – though my brothers are very affectionate, and Henry is a great deal here, which I am most thankful for, it is impossible for me not to be often solitary."

"To be sure you must miss him very much."

"A mother would have been always present. A mother would have been a constant friend; her influence would have been beyond all other."

"Was she a very charming woman? Was she handsome? Was there any picture of her in the Abbey? And why had she been so partial to that grove? Was it from dejection of spirits?" –. were questions now eagerly poured forth; – the first three received a ready affirmative, the two others were passed by; and Catherine's interest in the deceased Mrs Tilney augmented with every question, whether answered or not. Of her unhappiness in marriage, she felt persuaded. The General certainly had been an unkind husband. He did not love her walk: – could he therefore have loved her? And besides, handsome as he was, there was a something in the turn of his features which spoke his not having behaved well to her.

"Her picture, I suppose," blushing at the consummate art of her own question, "hangs in your father's room?"

"No; – it was intended for the drawing-room; but my father was dissatisfied with the painting, and for some time it had no place. Soon after her death I obtained it for my own, and hung it in my bed-chamber – where I shall be happy to shew it you; – it is very like." – Here was another proof. A portrait – very like – of a departed wife, not valued by the husband! – He must have been dreadfully cruel to her!

Catherine attempted no longer to hide from herself the nature of the feelings which, in spite of all his attentions, he had previously excited; and what had been terror and dislike before, was now absolute aversion. Yes, aversion! His cruelty to such a charming woman made him odious to her. She had often read of such characters; characters, which Mr Allen had been used to call unnatural and overdrawn; but here was proof positive of the contrary.

She had just settled this point, when the end of the path brought them directly upon the General; and in spite of all her virtuous indignation, she found herself again obliged to walk with him, listen to him, and even to smile when he smiled. Being no longer able however to receive pleasure from the surrounding objects, she soon began to walk with lassitude; the General perceived it, and with a concern for her health, which seemed to reproach her for her opinion of him, was most urgent for returning with his daughter to the house. He would follow them in a quarter of an hour. Again they parted – but Eleanor was called back in half a minute to receive a strict charge against taking her friend round the Abbey till his return. This second instance of his anxiety to delay what she so much wished for, struck Catherine as very remarkable.

CHAPTER 23

An hour passed away before the General came in, spent, on the part of his young guest, in no very favourable consideration of his character. – "This lengthened absence, these solitary rambles, did not speak a mind at ease, or a conscience void of reproach." – At length he appeared; and, whatever might have been the gloom of his meditations, he could still smile with *them*. Miss Tilney, understanding in part her friend's curiosity to see the house, soon revived the subject; and her father being, contrary to Catherine's expectations, unprovided with any pretence for further delay, beyond that of stopping five minutes to order refreshments to be in the room by their return, was at last ready to escort them.

They set forward; and, with a grandeur of air, a dignified step, which caught the eye, but could not shake the doubts of the well-read Catherine, he led the way across the hall, through the common drawing-room and one useless anti-chamber, into a room magnificent both in size and furniture – the real drawing-room, used only with company of consequence. – It was very noble – very grand – very charming! – was all that Catherine had to say, for her indiscriminating eye scarcely discerned the colour of the satin; and all minuteness of praise, all praise that had much meaning, was supplied by the General: the costliness or elegance of any room's fitting-up could be nothing to her; she cared for no furniture of a more modern date than the fifteenth century. When the General had satisfied his own curiosity, in a close examination of every well-known ornament, they proceeded into the library, an apartment, in its way, of equal magnificence, exhibiting a collection of books, on which an humble man might have looked with pride. – Catherine heard, admired, and wondered with more genuine feeling than before – gathered all that she could from this storehouse of knowledge, by running over the titles of half a shelf, and was ready to proceed. But suites of apartments did not spring up with her wishes. – Large as was the building, she had already visited the greatest part; though, on being told that, with the addition of the kitchen, the six or seven rooms she had now seen surrounded three sides of the court, she could scarcely believe it, or overcome the suspicion of there being many chambers secreted. It was some relief, however, that they were to return to the rooms in common use, by passing through a few of less importance, looking into the court, which, with occasional passages, not wholly unintricate, connected the different sides; – and she was further soothed in her progress, by being told, that she was treading what had once been a cloister, having traces of cells pointed out, and observing several doors, that were neither opened nor explained to her; – by finding herself successively in a billiard-room, and in the General's private apartment, without comprehending their connexion, or being able to turn aright when she left them; and lastly, by passing through a dark little room, owning Henry's authority, and strewed with his litter of books, guns, and great coats.

From the dining-room of which, though already seen, and always to be seen at five o'clock, the General could not forego the pleasure of pacing out the length, for the more certain information of Miss Morland, as to what she neither doubted nor cared for, they proceeded by quick communication to the kitchen – the ancient kitchen of the convent, rich in the massy walls and smoke of former days, and in the stoves and hot closets of the present. The General's improving hand had not loitered here: every modern invention to facilitate the labour of the cooks, had been adopted within this, their spacious theatre; and, when the genius of others had failed, his own had often produced the perfection wanted. His endowments of this spot alone might at any time have placed him high among the benefactors of the convent.

With the walls of the kitchen ended all the antiquity of the Abbey; the fourth side of the quadrangle having, on account of its decaying state, been removed by the General's father, and the present erected in its place. All that was venerable ceased here. The new building was not only new, but declared itself to be so; intended only for offices, and enclosed behind by stable-yards, no uniformity of architecture had been thought necessary. Catherine could have raved at the hand which had swept away what must have been beyond the value of all the rest, for the purposes of mere domestic economy; and would willingly have been spared the mortification of a walk through scenes so fallen, had the General allowed it; but if he had a vanity, it was in the arrangement of his offices; and as he was convinced, that, to a mind like Miss Morland's, a view of the accommodations and comforts, by which the labours of her inferiors were softened, must always be gratifying, he should make no apology for leading her on. They took a slight survey of all; and Catherine was impressed, beyond her expectation, by their multiplicity and their convenience. The purposes for which a few shapeless pantries and a comfortless scullery were deemed sufficient at Fullerton, were here carried on in appropriate divisions, commodious and roomy. The number of servants continually appearing did not strike her less than the number of their offices. Wherever they went, some pattened girl stopped to curtsey, or some footman in dishabille sneaked off. Yet this was an Abbey! – How inexpressibly different in these domestic arrangements from such as she had read about – from abbeys and castles, in which, though certainly larger than Northanger, all the dirty work of the house was to be done by two pair of female hands at the utmost. How they could get through it all, had often amazed Mrs Allen; and, when Catherine saw what was necessary here, she began to be amazed herself.

They returned to the hall, that the chief stair-case might be ascended, and the beauty of its wood, and ornaments of rich carving might be pointed out: having gained the top, they turned in an opposite direction from the gallery in which her room lay, and shortly entered one on the same plan, but superior in length and breadth. She was here shewn successively into three large bed-chambers, with their dressing-rooms, most completely and handsomely fitted up; every thing that money and taste could do, to give comfort and elegance to apartments, had been bestowed on these; and, being furnished within the last five years, they were perfect in all that would be generally pleasing, and wanting in all that could give pleasure to Catherine. As they were surveying the last, the General, after slightly naming a few of the distinguished characters, by whom they had at times been honoured, turned with a smiling countenance to Catherine, and ventured to hope, that henceforward some of their earliest tenants might be "our friends from Fullerton." She felt the unexpected compliment, and deeply regretted the impossibility of thinking well of a man so kindly disposed towards herself, and so full of civility to all her family.

The gallery was terminated by folding doors, which Miss Tilney, advancing, had thrown open, and passed through, and seemed on the point of doing the same by the first door to the left, in another long reach of gallery, when the General, coming forwards, called her hastily, and, as Catherine thought, rather angrily back, demanding whither she were going? – And what was there more to be seen? – Had not Miss Morland already seen all that could be worth her notice? – And did she not suppose her friend might be glad of some refreshment after so much exercise? Miss Tilney drew back directly, and the heavy doors were closed upon the mortified Catherine, who, having seen, in a momentary glance beyond them, a narrower passage, more numerous openings, and symptoms of a winding stair-case, believed herself at last within the reach of something worth her notice; and felt, as she unwillingly paced back the gallery, that she would rather be allowed to examine that end of the house, than see all the finery of all the rest. – The General's evident desire of preventing such an examination was an additional stimulant. Something was certainly to be concealed; her fancy, though it had trespassed lately once or twice, could not mislead her here; and what that something was, a short sentence of Miss Tilney's, as they followed the General at some distance down stairs, seemed to point out: – "I was going to take you into what was my mother's room – the room in which she died –" were all her words; but few as they were, they conveyed pages of intelligence to Catherine. It was no wonder that the General should shrink from the sight of such objects as that room must contain; a room in all probability never entered by him since the dreadful scene had passed, which released his suffering wife, and left him to the stings of conscience.

She ventured, when next alone with Eleanor, to express her wish of being permitted to see it, as well as all the rest of that side of the house; and Eleanor promised to attend her there, whenever they should have a convenient hour. Catherine understood her: – the General must be watched from home, before that room could be entered. "It remains as it was, I suppose?" said she, in a tone of feeling.

"Yes, entirely."

"And how long ago may it be that your mother died?"

"She has been dead these nine years." And nine years, Catherine knew, was a trifle of time, compared with what generally elapsed after the death of an injured wife, before her room was put to rights.

"You were with her, I suppose, to the last?"

"No," said Miss Tilney, sighing; "I was unfortunately from home. – Her illness was sudden and short; and, before I arrived it was all over."

Catherine's blood ran cold with the horrid suggestions which naturally sprang from these words. Could it be possible? – Could Henry's father? – And yet how many were the examples to justify even the blackest suspicions! – And, when she saw him in the evening, while she worked[1] with her friend, slowly pacing the drawing-room for an hour together in silent thoughtfulness, with downcast eyes and contracted brow, she felt secure from all possibility of wronging him. It was the air and attitude of a Montoni![2] – What could more plainly speak the gloomy workings of a mind not wholly dead to every sense of humanity, in its fearful review of past scenes of guilt? Unhappy man! – And the anxiousness of her spirits directed her eyes towards his figure so repeatedly, as to catch Miss Tilney's notice. "My father," she whispered, "often walks about the room in this way; it is nothing unusual."

---

1 Needle work

2 The villain of *The Mysteries of Udolpho* who imprisons Emily and her aunt and tries to sell Emily into marriage to obtain her property.

"So much the worse!" thought Catherine; such ill-timed exercise was of a piece with the strange unseasonableness of his morning walks, and boded nothing good.

After an evening, the little variety and seeming length of which made her peculiarly sensible of Henry's importance among them, she was heartily glad to be dismissed; though it was a look from the General not designed for her observation which sent his daughter to the bell. When the butler would have lit his master's candle, however, he was forbidden. The latter was not going to retire. "I have many pamphlets to finish," said he to Catherine, "before I can close my eyes; and perhaps may be poring over the affairs of the nation for hours after you are asleep. Can either of us be more meetly employed? *My* eyes will be blinding for the good of others; and *yours* preparing by rest for future mischief."[1]

But neither the business alleged, nor the magnificent compliment, could win Catherine from thinking, that some very different object must occasion so serious a delay of proper repose. To be kept up for hours, after the family were in bed, by stupid pamphlets, was not very likely. There must be some deeper cause: something was to be done which could be done only while the household slept; and the probability that Mrs Tilney yet lived, shut up for causes unknown, and receiving from the pitiless hands of her husband a nightly supply of coarse food,[2] was the conclusion which necessarily followed. Shocking as was the idea, it was at least better than a death unfairly hastened, as, in the natural course of things, she must ere long be released. The suddenness of her reputed illness; the absence of her daughter, and probably of her other children, at the time – all favoured the supposition of her imprisonment. Its origin – jealousy perhaps, or wanton cruelty – was yet to be unravelled.

In revolving these matters, while she undressed, it suddenly struck her as not unlikely, that she might that morning have passed near the very spot of this unfortunate woman's confinement – might have been within a few paces of the cell in which she

1　Austen suggests that General Tilney is a member of the Loyalist Address Movement who scrutinizes pamphlets at midnight for the public weal. See footnote 1, p. 196 below.

2　Cf. Radcliffe's *A Sicilian Romance* (ch. xiv).

languished out her days; for what part of the Abbey could be more fitted for the purpose than that which yet bore the traces of monastic division? In the high-arched passage, paved with stone, which already she had trodden with peculiar awe, she well remembered the doors of which the General had given no account. To what might not those doors lead? In support of the plausibility of this conjecture, it further occurred to her, that the forbidden gallery, in which lay the apartments of the unfortunate Mrs Tilney, must be, as certainly as her memory could guide her, exactly over this suspected range of cells, and the stair-case by the side of those apartments of which she had caught a transient glimpse, communicating by some secret means with those cells, might well have favoured the barbarous proceedings of her husband. Down that stair-case she had perhaps been conveyed in a state of well-prepared insensibility!

Catherine sometimes started at the boldness of her own surmises, and sometimes hoped or feared that she had gone too far; but they were supported by such appearances as made their dismissal impossible.

The side of the quadrangle, in which she supposed the guilty scene to be acting, being, according to her belief, just opposite her own, it struck her that, if judiciously watched, some rays of light from the General's lamp might glimmer through the lower windows, as he passed to the prison of his wife; and, twice before she stepped into bed, she stole gently from her room to the corresponding window in the gallery, to see if it appeared; but all abroad was dark, and it must yet be too early. The various ascending noises convinced her that the servants must still be up. Till midnight, she supposed it would be in vain to watch; but then, when the clock had struck twelve, and all was quiet, she would, if not quite appalled by darkness, steal out and look once more. The clock struck twelve – and Catherine had been half an hour asleep.

CHAPTER 24

The next day afforded no opportunity for the proposed examination of the mysterious apartments. It was Sunday, and the whole time between morning and afternoon service was required by the

General in exercise abroad or eating cold meat at home; and great as was Catherine's curiosity, her courage was not equal to a wish of exploring them after dinner, either by the fading light of the sky between six and seven o'clock, or by the yet more partial though stronger illumination of a treacherous lamp. The day was unmarked therefore by any thing to interest her imagination beyond the sight of a very elegant monument to the memory of Mrs Tilney, which immediately fronted the family pew. By that her eye was instantly caught and long retained; and the perusal of the highly-strained epitaph, in which every virtue was ascribed to her by the inconsolable husband, who must have been in some way or other her destroyer, affected her even to tears.

That the General, having erected such a monument, should be able to face it, was not perhaps very strange, and yet that he could sit so boldly collected within its view, maintain so elevated an air, look so fearlessly around, nay, that he should even enter the church, seemed wonderful to Catherine. Not however that many instances of beings equally hardened in guilt might not be produced. She could remember dozens who had persevered in every possible vice, going on from crime to crime, murdering whomsoever they chose, without any feeling of humanity or remorse; till a violent death or a religious retirement closed their black career. The erection of the monument itself could not in the smallest degree affect her doubts of Mrs Tilney's actual decease. Were she even to descend into the family vault where her ashes were supposed to slumber, were she to behold the coffin in which they were said to be enclosed — what could it avail in such a case? Catherine had read too much not to be perfectly aware of the ease with which a waxen figure might be introduced, and a supposititious funeral carried on.[1]

The succeeding morning promised something better. The General's early walk, ill-timed as it was in every other view, was

---

[1] Cf. Ann Radcliffe's *Sicilian Romance* (1790) in which the Marquis Mazzini imprisons his first wife in the castle's abandoned south wing for 15 years after a supposed funeral has been held. Provisions are delivered weekly and then monthly by either the servant Vincent or the Marquis himself, who enters the room via a series of passageways and tunnels (ch. 14).

favourable here; and when she knew him to be out of the house, she directly proposed to Miss Tilney the accomplishment of her promise. Eleanor was ready to oblige her; and Catherine reminding her as they went of another promise, their first visit in consequence was to the portrait in her bed-chamber. It represented a very lovely woman, with a mild and pensive countenance, justifying, so far, the expectations of its new observer; but they were not in every respect answered, for Catherine had depended upon meeting with features, air, complexion that should be the very counterpart, the very image, if not of Henry's, of Eleanor's; – the only portraits of which she had been in the habit of thinking, bearing always an equal resemblance of mother and child. A face once taken was taken for generations. But here she was obliged to look and consider and study for a likeness. She contemplated it, however, in spite of this drawback, with much emotion; and, but for a yet stronger interest, would have left it unwillingly.

Her agitation as they entered the great gallery was too much for any endeavour at discourse; she could only look at her companion. Eleanor's countenance was dejected, yet sedate; and its composure spoke her enured to all the gloomy objects to which they were advancing. Again she passed through the folding doors, again her hand was upon the important lock, and Catherine, hardly able to breathe, was turning to close the former with fearful caution, when the figure, the dreaded figure of the General himself at the further end of the gallery, stood before her! The name of "Eleanor" at the same moment, in his loudest tone, resounded through the building, giving to his daughter the first intimation of his presence, and to Catherine terror upon terror. An attempt at concealment had been her first instinctive movement on perceiving him, yet she could scarcely hope to have escaped his eye; and when her friend, who with an apologizing look darted hastily by her, had joined and disappeared with him, she ran for safety to her own room, and, locking herself in, believed that she should never have courage to go down again. She remained there at least an hour, in the greatest agitation, deeply commiserating the state of her poor friend, and expecting a summons herself from the angry General to attend him in his own apartment. No summons however arrived; and at last, on seeing a carriage drive up to the Abbey, she was emboldened to descend and meet him under the protection of visitors. The breakfast-room was gay with company; and she was named to them by the General, as the friend of his daughter, in a complimentary style, which so well concealed his resentful ire, as to make her feel secure at least of life for the present. And Eleanor, with a command of countenance which did honour to her concern for his character, taking an early occasion of saying to her, "My father only wanted me to answer a note," she began to hope that she had either been unseen by the General, or that from some consideration of policy she should be allowed to suppose herself so. Upon this trust she dared still to remain in his presence, after the company left them, and nothing occurred to disturb it.

In the course of this morning's reflections, she came to a resolution of making her next attempt on the forbidden door alone. It would be much better in every respect that Eleanor should know nothing of the matter. To involve her in the danger of a second detection, to court her into an apartment which must wring her heart, could not be the office of a friend. The General's utmost anger could not be to herself what it might be to a daughter; and, besides, she thought the examination itself would be more satisfactory if made without any companion. It would be impossible to explain to Eleanor the suspicions, from which the other had, in all likelihood, been hitherto happily exempt; nor could she therefore, in *her* presence, search for those proofs of the General's cruelty, which however they might yet have escaped discovery, she felt confident of somewhere drawing forth, in the shape of some fragmented journal, continued to the last gasp. Of the way to the apartment she was now perfectly mistress; and as she wished to get it over before Henry's return, who was expected on the morrow, there was no time to be lost. The day was bright, her courage high; at four o'clock, the sun was now two hours above the horizon, and it would be only her retiring to dress half an hour earlier than usual.

It was done; and Catherine found herself alone in the gallery before the clocks had ceased to strike. It was no time for thought; she hurried on, slipped with the least possible noise through the folding doors, and without stopping to look or breathe, rushed forward to the one in question. The lock yielded to her hand, and, luckily, with no sullen sound that could alarm a human being. On tip-toe she entered; the room was before her; but it was some minutes before she could advance another step. She beheld what fixed her to the spot and agitated every feature. – She saw a large, well-proportioned apartment, an handsome dimity bed,[1] arranged as unoccupied with an housemaid's care, a bright Bath stove,[2] mahogany wardrobes and neatly- painted chairs, on which the warm beams of a western sun gaily poured through two sash windows! Catherine had expected to have her feelings worked, and worked they were. Astonishment and doubt first seized them; and a shortly succeeding ray of common sense added some bitter emotions of shame. She could not be mistaken as to the room; but how grossly mistaken in every thing else! – in Miss Tilney's meaning, in her own calculation! This apartment, to which she had given a date so ancient, a position so awful, proved to be one end of what the General's father had built. There were two other doors in the chamber, leading probably into dressing-closets; but she had no inclination to open either. Would the veil in which Mrs Tilney had last walked, or the volume in which she had last read, remain to tell what nothing else was allowed to whisper? No: whatever might have been the General's crimes, he had certainly too much wit to let them sue for detection. She was sick of exploring, and desired but to be safe in her own room, with her own heart only privy to its folly; and she was on the point of retreating as softly as she had entered, when the sound of footsteps, she could hardly tell where, made her pause and tremble. To be found there, even by a servant, would be unpleasant; but by the General, (and he seemed always at hand when least wanted,) much worse! – She listened – the sound had ceased; and resolving not to lose a moment, she passed through and closed the door. At that instant a door underneath was hastily opened; some one seemed with swift steps to ascend the stairs, by

---

1 A bed covered in a stout cotton fabric, woven with raised striped or fancy figures.
2 A fireplace having an iron plate just above the fire with a small opening to produce a draught. This modern appliance indicates that despite Catherine's fears of the General's neglect of his wife his rage for improvements included her apartment and comfort.

the head of which she had yet to pass before she could gain the gallery. She had no power to move. With a feeling of terror not very definable, she fixed her eyes on the staircase, and in a few moments it gave Henry to her view. "Mr Tilney!" she exclaimed in a voice of more than common astonishment. He looked astonished too. "Good God!" she continued, not attending to his address, "how came you here? – how came you up that staircase?"

"How came I up that staircase!" he replied, greatly surprized. "Because it is my nearest way from the stable-yard to my own chamber; and why should I not come up it?"

Catherine recollected herself, blushed deeply, and could say no more. He seemed to be looking in her countenance for that explanation which her lips did not afford. She moved on towards the gallery. "And may I not, in my turn," said he, as he pushed back the folding doors, "ask how *you* came here? – This passage is at least as extraordinary a road from the breakfast-parlour to your apartment, as that staircase can be from the stables to mine."

"I have been," said Catherine, looking down, "to see your mother's room."

"My mother's room! – Is there any thing extraordinary to be seen there?"

"No, nothing at all. – I thought you did not mean to come back till to-morrow."

"I did not expect to be able to return sooner, when I went away; but three hours ago I had the pleasure of finding nothing to detain me. You look pale. I am afraid I alarmed you by running so fast up those stairs. Perhaps you did not know – you were not aware of their leading from the offices in common use?"

"No, I was not. – You have had a very fine day for your ride."

"Very; – and does Eleanor leave you to find your way into all the rooms in the house by yourself?"

"Oh! no; she shewed me over the greatest part on Saturday – and we were coming here to these rooms – but only – (dropping her voice) – your father was with us."

"And that prevented you;" said Henry, earnestly regarding her. – "Have you looked into all the rooms in that passage?"

"No, I only wanted to see – Is not it very late? I must go and dress."

"It is only a quarter past four, (shewing his watch) and you are not now in Bath. No theatre, no rooms to prepare for. Half an hour at Northanger must be enough."

She could not contradict it, and therefore suffered herself to be detained, though her dread of further questions made her, for the first time in their acquaintance, wish to leave him. They walked slowly up the gallery. "Have you had any letter from Bath since I saw you?"

"No, and I am very much surprized. Isabella promised so faithfully to write directly."

"Promised so faithfully! – A faithful promise! – That puzzles me. I have heard of a faithful performance. But a faithful promise – the fidelity of promising! It is a power little worth knowing however, since it can deceive and pain you. My mother's room is very commodious, is it not? Large and cheerful-looking, and the dressing closets so well disposed! It always strikes me as the most comfortable apartment in the house, and I rather wonder that Eleanor should not take it for her own. She sent you to look at it, I suppose?"

"No."

"It has been your own doing entirely?" – Catherine said nothing – After a short silence, during which he had closely observed her, he added, "As there is nothing in the room in itself to raise curiosity, this must have proceeded from a sentiment of respect for my mother's character, as described by Eleanor, which does honour to her memory. The world, I believe, never saw a better woman. But it is not often that virtue can boast an interest such as this. The domestic, unpretending merits of a person never known, do not often create that kind of fervent, venerating tenderness which would prompt a visit like yours. Eleanor, I suppose, has talked of her a great deal?"

"Yes, a great deal. That is – no, not much, but what she did say was very interesting. Her dying so suddenly," (slowly and with hesitation it was spoken,) "and you – none of you being at home – and your father, I thought – perhaps had not been very fond of her."

"And from these circumstances," he replied (his quick eye fixed on her's,) "you infer perhaps the probability of some negligence – some – (involuntarily she shook her head) – or it may be

– of something still less pardonable." She raised her eyes towards him more fully than she had ever done before. "My mother's illness," he continued, "the seizure which ended in her death *was* sudden. The malady itself, one from which she had often suffered, a bilious fever – its cause therefore constitutional. On the third day, in short as soon as she could be prevailed on, a physician attended her, a very respectable man, and one in whom she had always placed great confidence. Upon his opinion of her danger, two others were called in the next day, and remained in almost constant attendance for four-and-twenty hours. On the fifth day she died. During the progress of her disorder, Frederick and I (*we* were both at home) saw her repeatedly; and from our own observation can bear witness to her having received every possible attention which could spring from the affection of those about her, or which her situation in life could command. Poor Eleanor *was* absent, and at such a distance as to return only to see her mother in her coffin."

"But your father," said Catherine, "was *he* afflicted?"

"For a time, greatly so. You have erred in supposing him not attached to her. He loved her, I am persuaded, as well as it was possible for him to – We have not all, you know, the same tenderness of disposition – and I will not pretend to say that while she lived, she might not often have had much to bear, but though his temper injured her, his judgment never did. His value of her was sincere; and, if not permanently, he was truly afflicted by her death."

"I am very glad of it," said Catherine, "it would have been very shocking!" –

"If I understand you rightly, you had formed a surmise of such horror as I have hardly words to – Dear Miss Morland, consider the dreadful nature of the suspicions you have entertained. What have you been judging from? Remember the country and the age in which we live. Remember that we are English, that we are Christians. Consult your own understanding, your own sense of the probable, your own observation of what is passing around you – Does our education prepare us for such atrocities? Do our laws connive at them? Could they be perpetrated without being known, in a country like this, where social and literary intercourse is on such a footing; where every man is surrounded by a neighbour-hood of voluntary spies, and where roads and newspapers lay every thing open?[1] Dearest Miss Morland, what ideas have you been admitting?"

They had reached the end of the gallery; and with tears of shame she ran off to her own room.

CHAPTER 25

The visions of romance were over. Catherine was completely awak-ened. Henry's address, short as it had been, had more thoroughly opened her eyes to the extravagance of her late fancies than all their several disappointments had done. Most grievously was she humbled. Most bitterly did she cry. It was not only with herself that she was sunk − but with Henry. Her folly, which now seemed even criminal, was all exposed to him, and he must despise her for ever. The liberty which her imagination had dared to take with the character of his father, could he ever forgive it? The absurdity of her curiosity and her fears, could they ever be forgotten? She hated herself more than she could express. He had − she thought he had, once or twice before this fatal morning, shewn something like affection for her. − But now − in short, she made herself as miserable as possible for about half an hour, went down when the clock struck five, with a broken heart, and could scarcely give an intelligible answer to Eleanor's inquiry, if she was well. The formi-dable Henry soon followed her into the room, and the only differ-ence in his behaviour to her, was that he paid her rather more attention than usual. Catherine had never wanted comfort more, and he looked as if he was aware of it.

The evening wore away with no abatement of this soothing politeness; and her spirits were gradually raised to a modest tran-

---

1 Reference to the Loyalist Address Movement which arose from King George III's proclamation on 21st May 1792 that "divers wicked and sedi-tious writings" had been circulated throughout the kingdom which might "excite tumult and disorder." The king urged his subjects "to avoid and discourage proceedings, tending to produce riots and tumult and in-structed magistrates to forward any information about seditious activities to the central government" (Dozier, 22).

quillity. She did not learn either to forget or defend the past; but she learned to hope that it would never transpire farther, and that it might not cost her Henry's entire regard. Her thoughts being still chiefly fixed on what she had with such causeless terror felt and done, nothing could shortly be clearer, than that it had been all a voluntary, self-created delusion, each trifling circumstance receiving importance from an imagination resolved on alarm, and every thing forced to bend to one purpose by a mind which, before she entered the Abbey, had been craving to be frightened. She remembered with what feelings she had prepared for a knowledge of Northanger. She saw that the infatuation had been created, the mischief settled long before her quitting Bath, and it seemed as if the whole might be traced to the influence of that sort of reading which she had there indulged.

Charming as were all Mrs Radcliffe's works, and charming even as were the works of all her imitators, it was not in them perhaps that human nature, at least in the midland counties of England, was to be looked for. Of the Alps and Pyrenees, with their pine forests and their vices, they might give a faithful delineation; and Italy, Switzerland, and the South of France, might be as fruitful in horrors as they were there represented. Catherine dared not doubt beyond her own country, and even of that, if hard pressed, would have yielded the northern and western extremities. But in the central part of England there was surely some security for the existence even of a wife not beloved, in the laws of the land, and the manners of the age.[1] Murder was not tolerated, servants were not slaves, and neither poison nor sleeping potions to be procured, like rhubarb, from every druggist. Among the Alps and Pyrenees, perhaps, there were no mixed characters. There, such as were not as spotless as an angel, might have the dispositions of a fiend. But in England it was not so; among the English, she believed, in their hearts and habits, there was a general though unequal mixture of

---

1 Perhaps an ironic reference to Sir William Blackstone's *Commentaries on the Laws in England 1765-9*: "These are the chief legal effects of marriage during the coveture; upon which we may observe, that even the disabilities, which the wife lies under, are for the most part intended for her protection and benefit. So great a favourite is the female sex of the laws of England" (Bk 1, Ch.15).

good and bad. Upon this conviction, she would not be surprized if even in Henry and Eleanor Tilney, some slight imperfection might hereafter appear; and upon this conviction she need not fear to acknowledge some actual specks in the character of their father, who, though cleared from the grossly injurious suspicions which she must ever blush to have entertained, she did believe, upon serious consideration, to be not perfectly amiable.

Her mind made up on these several points, and her resolution formed, of always judging and acting in future with the greatest good sense, she had nothing to do but to forgive herself and be happier than ever; and the lenient hand of time did much for her by insensible gradations in the course of another day. Henry's astonishing generosity and nobleness of conduct, in never alluding in the slightest way to what had passed, was of the greatest assistance to her; and sooner than she could have supposed it possible in the beginning of her distress, her spirits became absolutely comfortable, and capable, as heretofore, of continual improvement by any thing he said. There were still some subjects, indeed, under which she believed they must always tremble; – the mention of a chest or a cabinet, for instance – and she did not love the sight of japan in any shape: but even *she* could allow, that an occasional memento of past folly, however painful, might not be without use.

The anxieties of common life began soon to succeed to the alarms of romance. Her desire of hearing from Isabella grew every day greater. She was quite impatient to know how the Bath world went on, and how the Rooms were attended; and especially was she anxious to be assured of Isabella's having matched some fine netting-cotton, on which she had left her intent; and of her continuing on the best terms with James. Her only dependence for information of any kind was on Isabella. James had protested against writing to her till his return to Oxford; and Mrs Allen had given her no hopes of a letter till she had got back to Fullerton. – But Isabella had promised and promised again; and when she promised a thing, she was so scrupulous in performing it! this made it so particularly strange!

For nine successive mornings, Catherine wondered over the repetition of a disappointment, which each morning became more severe: but, on the tenth, when she entered the breakfast-room, her first object was a letter, held out by Henry's willing hand. She thanked him as heartily as if he had written it himself. "'Tis only from James, however," as she looked at the direction. She opened it; it was from Oxford; and to this purpose: –

"Dear Catherine,

"Though, God knows, with little inclination for writing, I think it my duty to tell you, that every thing is at an end between Miss Thorpe and me. – I left her and Bath yesterday, never to see either again. I shall not enter into particulars, they would only pain you more. You will soon hear enough from another quarter to know where lies the blame; and I hope will acquit your brother of every thing but the folly of too easily thinking his affection returned. Thank God! I am undeceived in time! But it is a heavy blow! – After my father's consent had been so kindly given – but no more of this. She has made me miserable for ever! Let me soon hear from you, dear Catherine; you are my only friend; *your* love I do build upon. I wish your visit at Northanger may be over before Captain Tilney makes his engagement known, or you will be uncomfortably circumstanced. – Poor Thorpe is in town: I dread the sight of him; his honest heart would feel so much. I have written to him and my father. Her duplicity hurts me more than all; till the very last, if I reasoned with her, she declared herself as much attached to me as ever, and laughed at my fears. I am ashamed to think how long I bore with it; but if ever man had reason to believe himself loved, I was that man. I cannot understand even now what she would be at, for there could be no need of my being played off to make her secure of Tilney. We parted at last by mutual consent – happy for me had we never met! I can never expect to know such another woman! Dearest Catherine, beware how you give your heart.

"Believe me," &c.

Catherine had not read three lines before her sudden change of countenance, and short exclamations of sorrowing wonder, declared her to be receiving unpleasant news; and Henry, earnestly watching her through the whole letter, saw plainly that it ended no better than it began. He was prevented, however, from even looking his surprize by his father's entrance. They went to breakfast directly; but Catherine could hardly eat any thing. Tears filled her eyes, and even ran down her cheeks as she sat. The letter was one moment in her hand, then in her lap, and then in her pocket; and she looked as if she knew not what she did. The General, between his cocoa and his newspaper, had luckily no leisure for noticing her; but to the other two her distress was equally visible. As soon as she dared leave the table she hurried away to her own room; but the house-maids were busy in it, and she was obliged to come down again. She turned into the drawing-room for privacy, but Henry and Eleanor had likewise retreated thither, and were at that moment deep in consultation about her. She drew back, trying to beg their pardon, but was, with gentle violence, forced to return; and the others withdrew, after Eleanor had affectionately expressed a wish of being of use or comfort to her.

After half an hour's free indulgence of grief and reflection, Catherine felt equal to encountering her friends; but whether she should make her distress known to them was another consideration. Perhaps, if particularly questioned, she might just give an idea — just distantly hint at it — but not more. To expose a friend, such a friend as Isabella had been to her — and then their own brother so closely concerned in it! — She believed she must wave the subject altogether. Henry and Eleanor were by themselves in the breakfast-room; and each, as she entered it, looked at her anxiously. Catherine took her place at the table, and, after a short silence, Eleanor said, "No bad news from Fullerton, I hope? Mr and Mrs Morland — your brothers and sisters — I hope they are none of them ill?"

"No, I thank you," (sighing as she spoke,) "they are all very well. My letter was from my brother at Oxford."

Nothing further was said for a few minutes; and then speaking through her tears, she added, "I do not think I shall ever wish for a letter again!"

"I am sorry," said Henry, closing the book he had just opened; "if I had suspected the letter of containing any thing unwelcome,

I should have given it with very different feelings."

"It contained something worse than any body could suppose! – Poor James is so unhappy! – You will soon know why."

"To have so kind-hearted, so affectionate a sister," replied Henry warmly, "must be a comfort to him under any distress."

"I have one favour to beg," said Catherine, shortly afterwards, in an agitated manner, "that, if your brother should be coming here, you will give me notice of it, that I may go away."

"Our brother! – Frederick!"

"Yes; I am sure I should be very sorry to leave you so soon, but something has happened that would make it very dreadful for me to be in the same house with Captain Tilney."

Eleanor's work was suspended while she gazed with increasing astonishment; but Henry began to suspect the truth, and something, in which Miss Thorpe's name was included, passed his lips.

"How quick you are!" cried Catherine: "you have guessed it, I declare! – And yet, when we talked about it in Bath, you little thought of its ending so. Isabella – no wonder *now* I have not heard from her – Isabella has deserted my brother, and is to marry your's! Could you have believed there had been such inconstancy and fickleness, and every thing that is bad in the world?"

"I hope, so far as concerns my brother, you are misinformed. I hope he has not had any material share in bringing on Mr Morland's disappointment. His marrying Miss Thorpe is not probable. I think you must be deceived so far. I am very sorry for Mr Morland – sorry that any one you love should be unhappy; but my surprize would be greater at Frederick's marrying her, than at any other part of the story."

"It is very true, however; you shall read James's letter yourself. – Stay – there is one part –" recollecting with a blush the last line.

"Will you take the trouble of reading to us the passages which concern my brother?"

"No, read it yourself," cried Catherine, whose second thoughts were clearer. "I do not know what I was thinking of" (blushing again that she had blushed before,) – "James only means to give me good advice."

He gladly received the letter; and, having read it through, with close attention, returned it saying, "Well, if it is to be so, I can only say that I am sorry for it. Frederick will not be the first man who has chosen a wife with less sense than his family expected. I do not envy his situation, either as a lover or a son."

Miss Tilney, at Catherine's invitation, now read the letter likewise; and, having expressed also her concern and surprize, began to inquire into Miss Thorpe's connexions and fortune.

"Her mother is a very good sort of woman," was Catherine's answer.

"What was her father?"

"A lawyer, I believe. – They live at Putney."

"Are they a wealthy family?"

"No, not very. I do not believe Isabella has any fortune at all: but that will not signify in your family. – Your father is so very liberal! He told me the other day, that he only valued money as it allowed him to promote the happiness of his children." The brother and sister looked at each other. "But," said Eleanor, after a short pause, "would it be to promote his happiness, to enable him to marry such a girl? – She must be an unprincipled one, or she could not have used your brother so. – And how strange an infatuation on Frederick's side! A girl who, before his eyes, is violating an engagement voluntarily entered into with another man! Is not it inconceivable, Henry? Frederick too, who always wore his heart so proudly! who found no woman good enough to be loved!"

"That is the most unpromising circumstance, the strongest presumption against him. When I think of his past declarations, I give him up. – Moreover, I have too good an opinion of Miss Thorpe's prudence, to suppose that she would part with one gentleman before the other was secured. It is all over with Frederick indeed! He is a deceased man – defunct in understanding. Prepare for your sister-in-law, Eleanor, and such a sister-in-law as you must delight in! – Open, candid, artless, guileless, with affections strong but simple, forming no pretensions, and knowing no disguise."

"Such a sister-in-law, Henry, I should delight in," said Eleanor with a smile.

"But perhaps," observed Catherine, "though she has behaved so ill by our family, she may behave better by your's. Now she has really got the man she likes, she may be constant."

"Indeed I am afraid she will," replied Henry; "I am afraid she will be very constant, unless a baronet should come in her way; that is Frederick's only chance. – I will get the Bath paper, and look over the arrivals."

"You think it is all for ambition then? – And, upon my word, there are some things that seem very like it. I cannot forget, that, when she first knew what my father would do for them, she seemed quite disappointed that it was not more. I never was so deceived in anyone's character in my life before."

"Among all the great variety that you have known and studied."

"My own disappointment and loss in her is very great; but, as for poor James, I suppose he will hardly ever recover it."

"Your brother is certainly very much to be pitied at present; but we must not, in our concern for his sufferings, undervalue your's. You feel, I suppose, that in losing Isabella, you lose half yourself: you feel a void in your heart which nothing else can occupy. Society is becoming irksome; and as for the amusements in which you were wont to share at Bath, the very idea of them without her is abhorrent. You would not, for instance, now go to a ball for the world. You feel that you have no longer any friend to whom you can speak with unreserve; on whose regard you can place dependence; or whose counsel, in any difficulty, you could rely on. You feel all this?"

"No," said Catherine, after a few moments' reflection, "I do not – ought I? To say the truth, though I am hurt and grieved, that I cannot still love her, that I am never to hear from her, perhaps never to see her again, I do not feel so very, very much afflicted as one would have thought."

"You feel, as you always do, what is most to the credit of human nature. – Such feelings ought to be investigated, that they may know themselves."

Catherine, by some chance or other, found her spirits so very much relieved by this conversation, that she could not regret her being led on, though so unaccountably, to mention the circumstance which had produced it.

CHAPTER 26

From this time, the subject was frequently canvassed by the three young people; and Catherine found, with some surprise, that her two young friends were perfectly agreed in considering Isabella's want of consequence and fortune as likely to throw great difficulties in the way of her marrying their brother. Their persuasion that the General would, upon this ground alone, independent of the objection that might be raised against her character, oppose the connexion, turned her feelings moreover with some alarm towards herself. She was as insignificant, and perhaps as portionless as Isabella; and if the heir of the Tilney property had not grandeur and wealth enough in himself, at what point of interest were the demands of his younger brother to rest? The very painful reflections to which this thought led, could only be dispersed by a dependence on the effect of that particular partiality, which, as she was given to understand by his words as well as his actions, she had from the first been so fortunate as to excite in the General; and by a recollection of some most generous and disinterested sentiments on the subject of money, which she had more than once heard him utter, and which tempted her to think his disposition in such matters misunderstood by his children.

They were so fully convinced, however, that their brother would not have the courage to apply in person for his father's consent, and so repeatedly assured her that he had never in his life been less likely to come to Northanger than at the present time, that she suffered her mind to be at ease as to the necessity of any sudden removal of her own. But as it was not to be supposed that Captain Tilney, whenever he made his application, would give his father any just idea of Isabella's conduct, it occurred to her as highly expedient that Henry should lay the whole business before him as it really was, enabling the General by that means to form a cool and impartial opinion, and prepare his objections on a fairer ground than inequality of situations. She proposed it to him accordingly; but he did not catch at the measure so eagerly as she had expected. "No," said he, "my father's hands need not be strengthened, and Frederick's confession of folly need not be forestalled. He must tell his own story."

"But he will tell only half of it."

"A quarter would be enough."

A day or two passed away and brought no tidings of Captain Tilney. His brother and sister knew not what to think. Sometimes it appeared to them as if his silence would be the natural result of the suspected engagement, and at others that it was wholly incompatible with it. The General, meanwhile, though offended every morning by Frederick's remissness in writing, was free from any real anxiety about him; and had no more pressing solicitude than that of making Miss Morland's time at Northanger pass pleasantly. He often expressed his uneasiness on this head, feared the sameness of every day's society and employments would disgust her with the place, wished the Lady Frasers had been in the country, talked every now and then of having a large party to dinner, and once or twice began even to calculate the number of young dancing people in the neighbourhood. But then it was such a dead time of year, no wild-fowl, no game, and the Lady Frasers were not in the country. And it all ended, at last, in his telling Henry one morning, that when he next went to Woodston, they would take him by surprize there some day or other, and eat their mutton with him. Henry was greatly honoured and very happy, and Catherine was quite delighted with the scheme. "And when do you think, sir, I may look forward to this pleasure? – I must be at Woodston on Monday to attend the parish meeting, and shall probably be obliged to stay two or three days."

"Well, well, we will take our chance some one of those days. There is no need to fix. You are not to put yourself at all out of your way. Whatever you may happen to have in the house will be enough. I think I can answer for the young ladies making allowance for a bachelor's table. Let me see; Monday will be a busy day with you, we will not come on Monday; and Tuesday will be a busy one with me. I expect my surveyor from Brockham with his report in the morning; and afterwards I cannot in decency fail attending the club. I really could not face my acquaintance if I staid away now; for, as I am known to be in the country, it would be taken exceedingly amiss; and it is a rule with me, Miss Morland, never to give offence to any of my neighbours, if a small sacrifice of time and attention can prevent it. They are a set of very worthy men. They have half a buck from Northanger twice a year; and I dine with them whenever I can. Tuesday, therefore, we may say is out of the question. But on Wednesday, I think, Henry, you may expect us; and we shall be with you early, that we may have time to look about us. Two hours and three quarters will carry us to Woodston, I suppose; we shall be in the carriage by ten; so, about a quarter before one on Wednesday, you may look for us."

A ball itself could not have been more welcome to Catherine than this little excursion, so strong was her desire to be acquainted with Woodston; and her heart was still bounding with joy, when Henry, about an hour afterwards, came booted and great coated into the room where she and Eleanor were sitting, and said, "I am come, young ladies, in a very moralizing strain, to observe that our pleasures in this world are always to be paid for, and that we often purchase them at a great disadvantage, giving ready-monied actual happiness for a draft on the future, that may not be honoured. Witness myself, at this present hour. Because I am to hope for the satisfaction of seeing you at Woodston on Wednesday, which bad weather, or twenty other causes may prevent, I must go away directly, two days before I intended it."

"Go away!" said Catherine, with a very long face; "and why?"

"Why! – How can you ask the question? – Because no time is to be lost in frightening my old housekeeper out of her wits, – because I must go and prepare a dinner for you to be sure."

"Oh! not seriously!"

"Aye, and sadly too – for I had much rather stay."

"But how can you think of such a thing, after what the General said? when he so particularly desired you not to give yourself any trouble, because *any thing* would do."

Henry only smiled. "I am sure it is quite unnecessary upon your sister's account and mine. You must know it to be so; and the General made such a point of your providing nothing extraordinary: – besides, if he had not said half so much as he did, he has always such an excellent dinner at home, that sitting down to a middling one for one day could not signify."

"I wish I could reason like you, for his sake and my own. Good bye. As tomorrow is Sunday, Eleanor, I shall not return."

He went; and, it being at any time a much simpler operation

to Catherine to doubt her own judgment than Henry's, she was very soon obliged to give him credit for being right, however disagreeable to her his going. But the inexplicability of the General's conduct dwelt much on her thoughts. That he was very particular in his eating, she had, by her own unassisted observation, already discovered; but why he should say one thing so positively, and mean another all the while, was most unaccountable! How were people, at that rate, to be understood? Who but Henry could have been aware of what his father was at?

From Saturday to Wednesday, however, they were now to be without Henry. This was the sad finale of every reflection: – and Captain Tilney's letter would certainly come in his absence; and Wednesday she was very sure would be wet. The past, present, and future were all equally in gloom. Her brother so unhappy, and her loss in Isabella so great; and Eleanor's spirits always affected by Henry's absence! What was there to interest or amuse her? She was tired of the woods and the shrubberies – always so smooth and so dry; and the Abbey in itself was no more to her now than any other house. The painful remembrance of the folly it had helped to nourish and perfect, was the only emotion which could spring from a consideration of the building. What a revolution in her ideas! she, who had so longed to be in an abbey! Now, there was nothing so charming to her imagination as the unpretending comfort of a well-connected Parsonage,[1] something like Fullerton, but better: Fullerton had its faults, but Woodston probably had none. – If Wednesday should ever come!

It did come, and exactly when it might be reasonably looked for. It came – it was fine – and Catherine trod on air. By ten o'clock, the chaise-and-four conveyed the trio from the Abbey; and, after an agreeable drive of almost twenty miles, they entered Woodston, a large and populous village, in a situation not unpleasant. Catherine was ashamed to say how pretty she thought it, as the General seemed to think an apology necessary for the flatness

1   A term from landscape gardening and estate management for "a landscape of physical and human variety integrated by and under the authority of a watchful squire" (Daniels 40). Woodston is a well-designed, convenient dwelling with integrated and easily accessible rooms, unlike the General's ostentatious abbey.

of the country, and the size of the village; but in her heart she preferred it to any place she had ever been at, and looked with great
admiration at every neat house above the rank of a cottage, and at
all the little chandler's shops which they passed. At the further
end of the village, and tolerably disengaged from the rest of it,
stood the Parsonage, a new-built substantial stone house, with its
semi-circular sweep and green gates; and, as they drove up to the
door, Henry, with the friends of his solitude, a large Newfound-
land puppy and two or three terriers, was ready to receive and
make much of them.

Catherine's mind was too full, as she entered the house, for her
either to observe or to say a great deal; and, till called on by the
General for her opinion of it, she had very little idea of the room
in which she was sitting. Upon looking round it then, she perceived in a moment that it was the most comfortable room in the
world; but she was too guarded to say so, and the coldness of her
praise disappointed him.

"We are not calling it a good house," said he. – "We are not
comparing it with Fullerton and Northanger – We are considering
it as a mere Parsonage, small and confined, we allow, but decent
perhaps, and habitable; and altogether not inferior to the generality; – or, in other words, I believe there are few country parson-
ages in England half so good. It may admit of improvement,
however. Far be it from me to say otherwise; and any thing in reason – a bow thrown out, perhaps – though, between ourselves, if
there is one thing more than another my aversion, it is a patched-
on bow."

Catherine did not hear enough of this speech to understand or
be pained by it; and other subjects being studiously brought forward and supported by Henry, at the same time that a tray full of
refreshments was introduced by his servant, the General was shortly restored to his complacency, and Catherine to all her usual ease
of spirits.

The room in question was of a commodious, well-proportioned
size, and handsomely fitted up as a dining-parlour; and on their
quitting it to walk round the grounds, she was shewn, first into a
smaller apartment, belonging peculiarly to the master of the house,
and made unusually tidy on the occasion; and afterwards into what

was to be the drawing-room, with the appearance of which, though unfurnished, Catherine was delighted enough even to satisfy the General. It was a prettily shaped room, the windows reaching to the ground, and the view from them pleasant, though only over green meadows; and she expressed her admiration at the moment with all the honest simplicity with which she felt it. "Oh! why do not you fit up this room, Mr Tilney? What a pity not to have it fitted up! It is the prettiest room I ever saw; – it is the prettiest room in the world!"

"I trust," said the General, with a most satisfied smile, "that it will very speedily be furnished: it waits only for a lady's taste!"

"Well, if it was my house, I should never sit any where else. Oh! what a sweet little cottage there is among the trees – apple trees, too! It is the prettiest cottage!"

"You like it – you approve it as an object – it is enough. Henry, remember that Robinson is spoken to about it. The cottage remains."

Such a compliment recalled all Catherine's consciousness, and silenced her directly; and, though pointedly applied to by the General for her choice of the prevailing colour of the paper and hangings, nothing like an opinion on the subject could be drawn from her. The influence of fresh objects and fresh air, however, was of great use in dissipating these embarrassing associations; and, having reached the ornamental part of the premises, consisting of a walk round two sides of a meadow, on which Henry's genius had begun to act about half a year ago, she was sufficiently recovered to think it prettier than any pleasure-ground she had ever been in before, though there was not a shrub in it higher than the green bench in the corner.

A saunter into other meadows, and through part of the village, with a visit to the stables to examine some improvements, and a charming game of play with a litter of puppies just able to roll about, brought them to four o'clock, when Catherine scarcely thought it could be three. At four they were to dine, and at six to set off on their return. Never had any day passed so quickly!

She could not but observe that the abundance of the dinner did not seem to create the smallest astonishment in the General; nay, that he was even looking at the side-table for cold meat which was not there. His son and daughter's observations were of a different kind. They had seldom seen him eat so heartily at any table but his own, and never before known him so little disconcerted by the melted butter's being oiled.

At six o'clock, the General having taken his coffee, the carriage again received them; and so gratifying had been the tenor of his conduct throughout the whole visit, so well assured was her mind on the subject of his expectations, that, could she have felt equally confident of the wishes of his son, Catherine would have quitted Woodston with little anxiety as to the How or the When she might return to it.

CHAPTER 27

The next morning brought the following very unexpected letter from Isabella: –

Bath, April —

My dearest Catherine,

I received your two kind letters with the greatest delight, and have a thousand apologies to make for not answering them sooner. I really am quite ashamed of my idleness; but in this horrid place one can find time for nothing. I have had my pen in my hand to begin a letter to you almost every day since you left Bath, but have always been prevented by some silly trifler or other. Pray write to me soon, and direct to my own home. Thank God! we leave this vile place to-morrow. Since you went away, I have had no pleasure in it – the dust is beyond any thing; and every body one cares for is gone. I believe if I could see you I should not mind the rest, for you are dearer to me than any body can conceive. I am quite uneasy about your dear brother, not having heard from him since he went to Oxford; and am fearful of some misunderstanding. Your kind offices will set all right: – he is the only man I ever did or could love, and I trust you will convince him of it. The spring fashions are partly down; and the hats the most frightful you can imagine. I hope you spend your time pleasantly, but am afraid you never think of me. I will not say all that I could of the family you are with, because I would not be ungenerous, or set you against those you esteem; but it is very difficult to know whom to trust, and young men never know their minds two days together. I rejoice to say, that the young man whom, of all others, I particularly abhor, has left Bath. You will know, from this description, I must mean Captain Tilney, who, as you may remember, was amazingly disposed to follow and tease me, before you went away. Afterwards he got worse, and became quite my shadow. Many girls might have been taken in, for never were such attentions; but I knew the fickle sex too well. He went away to his regiment two days ago, and I trust I shall never be plagued with him again. He is the greatest coxcomb I ever saw, and amazingly disagreeable. The last two days he was always by the side of Charlotte Davis: I pitied his taste, but took no notice of him. The last time we met was in Bath-street, and I turned directly into a shop that he might not speak to me; – I would not even look at him. He went into the Pump-room afterwards; but I would not have followed him for all the world. Such a contrast between him and your brother! – pray send me some news of the latter – I am quite unhappy about him, he seemed so uncomfortable when he went away, with a cold, or something that affected his spirits. I would write to him myself, but have mislaid his direction; and, as I hinted above, am afraid he took something in my conduct amiss. Pray explain every thing to his satisfaction; or, if he still harbours any doubt, a line from himself to me, or a call at Putney when next in town, might set all to rights. I have not been to the Rooms this age, nor to the Play, except going in last night with the Hodges's, for a frolic, at half-price: they teased me into it; and I was determined they should not say I shut myself up because Tilney was gone. We happened to sit by the Mitchells, and they pretended to be quite surprized to see me out. I knew their spite: – at one time they could not be civil to me, but now they are all friendship;

but I am not such a fool as to be taken in by them. You know I have a pretty good spirit of my own. Anne Mitchell had tried to put on a turban like mine, as I wore it the week before at the Concert, but made wretched work of it – it happened to become my odd face, I believe, at least Tilney told me so at the time, and said every eye was upon me; but he is the last man whose word I would take. I wear nothing but purple now: I know I look hideous in it, but no matter – it is your dear brother's favourite colour. Lose no time, my dearest, sweetest Catherine, in writing to him and to me,

Who ever am, &c.

Such a strain of shallow artifice could not impose even upon Catherine. Its inconsistencies, contradictions, and falsehood, struck her from the very first. She was ashamed of Isabella, and ashamed of having ever loved her. Her professions of attachment were now as disgusting as her excuses were empty, and her demands impudent. "Write to James on her behalf! – No, James should never hear Isabella's name mentioned by her again."

On Henry's arrival from Woodston, she made known to him and Eleanor their brother's safety, congratulating them with sincerity on it, and reading aloud the most material passages of her letter with strong indignation. When she had finished it, – "So much for Isabella," she cried, "and for all our intimacy! She must think me an idiot, or she could not have written so; but perhaps this has served to make her character better known to me than mine is to her. I see what she has been about. She is a vain coquette, and her tricks have not answered. I do not believe she had ever any regard either for James or for me, and I wish I had never known her."

"It will soon be as if you never had," said Henry.

"There is but one thing that I cannot understand. I see that she has had designs on Captain Tilney, which have not succeeded; but I do not understand what Captain Tilney has been about all this time. Why should he pay her such attentions as to make her quarrel with my brother, and then fly off himself?"

"I have very little to say for Frederick's motives, such as I believe them to have been. He has his vanities as well as Miss Thorpe, and the chief difference is, that, having a stronger head, they have not yet injured himself. If the *effect* of his behaviour does not justify him with you, we had better not seek after the cause."

"Then you do not suppose he ever really cared about her?"

"I am persuaded that he never did."

"And only made believe to do so for mischief's sake?"

Henry bowed his assent.

"Well, then, I must say that I do not like him at all. Though it has turned out so well for us, I do not like him at all. As it happens, there is no great harm done, because I do not think Isabella has any heart to lose. But, suppose he had made her very much in love with him?"

"But we must first suppose Isabella to have had a heart to lose, – consequently to have been a very different creature; and, in that case, she would have met with very different treatment."

"It is very right that you should stand by your brother."

"And if you would stand by *yours*, you would not be much distressed by the disappointment of Miss Thorpe. But your mind is warped by an innate principle of general integrity, and therefore not accessible to the cool reasonings of family partiality, or a desire of revenge."

Catherine was complimented out of further bitterness. Frederick could not be unpardonably guilty, while Henry made himself so agreeable. She resolved on not answering Isabella's letter; and tried to think no more of it.

CHAPTER 28

Soon after this, the General found himself obliged to go to London for a week; and he left Northanger earnestly regretting that any necessity should rob him even for an hour of Miss Morland's company, and anxiously recommending the study of her comfort and amusement to his children as their chief object in his absence. His departure gave Catherine the first experimental conviction that a loss may be sometimes a gain. The happiness with which their time now passed, every employment voluntary, every laugh indulged, every meal a scene of ease and good-humour, walking where they liked and when they liked, their hours, pleasures and fatigues at their own command, made her thoroughly sensible of the restraint which the General's presence had imposed, and most thankfully feel their present release from it. Such ease and such delights made her love the place and the people more and more every day; and had it not been for a dread of its soon becoming expedient to leave the one, and an apprehension of not being equally beloved by the other, she would at each moment of each day have been perfectly happy; but she was now in the fourth week of her visit; before the General came home, the fourth week would be turned, and perhaps it might seem an intrusion if she staid much longer. This was a painful consideration whenever it occurred; and eager to get rid of such a weight on her mind, she very soon resolved to speak to Eleanor about it at once, propose going away, and be guided in her conduct by the manner in which her proposal might be taken.

Aware that if she gave herself much time, she might feel it difficult to bring forward so unpleasant a subject, she took the first opportunity of being suddenly alone with Eleanor, and of Eleanor's being in the middle of a speech about something very different, to start forth her obligation of going away very soon. Eleanor looked and declared herself much concerned. She had "hoped for the pleasure of her company for a much longer time – had been misled (perhaps by her wishes) to suppose that a much longer visit had been promised – and could not but think that if Mr and Mrs Morland were aware of the pleasure it was to her to have her there, they would be too generous to hasten her return."

– Catherine explained. – "Oh! as to *that*, papa and mamma were in no hurry at all. As long as she was happy, they would always be satisfied."

"Then why, might she ask, in such a hurry herself to leave them?"

"Oh! because she had been there so long."

"Nay, if you can use such a word, I can urge you no farther. If you think it long –"

"Oh! no, I do not indeed. For my own pleasure, I could stay with you as long again." – And it was directly settled that, till she had, her leaving them was not even to be thought of. In having this cause of uneasiness so pleasantly removed, the force of the other was likewise weakened. The kindness, the earnestness of Eleanor's manner in pressing her to stay, and Henry's gratified look on being told that her stay was determined, were such sweet proofs of her importance with them, as left her only just so much solicitude as the human mind can never do comfortably without. She did – almost always – believe that Henry loved her, and quite always that his father and sister loved and even wished her to belong to them; and believing so far, her doubts and anxieties were merely sportive irritations.

Henry was not able to obey his father's injunction of remaining wholly at Northanger in attendance on the ladies, during his absence in London; the engagements of his curate at Woodston obliging him to leave them on Saturday for a couple of nights. His loss was not now what it had been while the General was at home; it lessened their gaiety, but did not ruin their comfort; and the two girls agreeing in occupation, and improving in intimacy, found themselves so well-sufficient for the time to themselves, that it was eleven o'clock, rather a late hour at the Abbey, before they quitted the supper-room on the day of Henry's departure. They had just reached the head of the stairs, when it seemed, as far as the thickness of the walls would allow them to judge, that a carriage was driving up to the door, and the next moment confirmed the idea by the loud noise of the house-bell. After the first perturbation of surprize had passed away, in a "Good heaven! what can be the matter?" it was quickly decided by Eleanor to be her eldest brother, whose arrival was often as sudden, if not quite so unseasonable, and accordingly she hurried down to welcome him.

Catherine walked on to her chamber, making up her mind as well as she could, to a further acquaintance with Captain Tilney, and comforting herself under the unpleasant impression his conduct had given her, and the persuasion of his being by far too fine a gentleman to approve of her, that at least they should not meet under such circumstances as would make their meeting materially painful. She trusted he would never speak of Miss Thorpe; and indeed, as he must by this time be ashamed of the part he had acted, there could be no danger of it; and as long as all mention of Bath scenes were avoided, she thought she could behave to him very civilly. In such considerations time passed away, and it was certainly in his favour that Eleanor should be so glad to see him, and have so much to say, for half an hour was almost gone since his arrival, and Eleanor did not come up.

At that moment Catherine thought she heard her step in the gallery, and listened for its continuance; but all was silent. Scarcely, however, had she convicted her fancy of error, when the noise of something moving close to her door made her start; it seemed as if some one was touching the very doorway – and in another moment a slight motion of the lock proved that some hand must be on it. She trembled a little at the idea of any one's approaching so cautiously; but resolving not to be again overcome by trivial appearances of alarm, or misled by a raised imagination, she stepped quietly forward, and opened the door. Eleanor, and only Eleanor, stood there. Catherine's spirits however were tranquillized but for an instant, for Eleanor's cheeks were pale, and her manner greatly agitated. Though evidently intending to come in, it seemed an effort to enter the room, and a still greater to speak when there. Catherine, supposing some uneasiness on Captain Tilney's account, could only express her concern by silent attention; obliged her to be seated, rubbed her temples with lavender-water, and hung over her with affectionate solicitude. "My dear Catherine, you must not – you must not indeed –" were Eleanor's first connected words. "I am quite well. This kindness distracts me – I cannot bear it – I come to you on such an errand!"

"Errand! – to me!"

"How shall I tell you! – Oh! how shall I tell you!"

A new idea now darted into Catherine's mind, and turning as pale as her friend, she exclaimed, "'Tis a messenger from Woodston!"

"You are mistaken, indeed," returned Eleanor, looking at her most compassionately – "it is no one from Woodston. It is my father himself." Her voice faltered, and her eyes were turned to the ground as she mentioned his name. His unlooked-for return was enough in itself to make Catherine's heart sink, and for a few moments she hardly supposed there were any thing worse to be told. She said nothing; and Eleanor endeavouring to collect herself and speak with firmness, but with eyes still cast down, soon went on. "You are too good, I am sure, to think the worse of me for the part I am obliged to perform. I am indeed a most unwilling messenger. After what has so lately passed, so lately been settled between us – how joyfully, how thankfully on my side! – as to your continuing here as I hoped for many, many weeks longer, how can I tell you that your kindness is not to be accepted – and that the happiness your company has hitherto given us is to be repaid by – but I must not trust myself with words. My dear Catherine, we are to part. My father has recollected an engagement that takes our whole family away on Monday. We are going to Lord Longtown's, near Hereford, for a fortnight. Explanation and apology are equally impossible. I cannot attempt either."

"My dear Eleanor," cried Catherine, suppressing her feelings as well as she could, "do not be so distressed. A second engagement must give way to a first. I am very, very sorry we are to part – so soon, and so suddenly too; but I am not offended, indeed I am not. I can finish my visit here you know at any time; or I hope you will come to me. Can you, when you return from this lord's, come to Fullerton?"

"It will not be in my power, Catherine."

"Come when you can, then." –

Eleanor made no answer; and Catherine's thoughts recurring to something more directly interesting, she added, thinking aloud, "Monday – so soon as Monday; – and you *all* go. Well, I am certain of – I shall be able to take leave however. I need not go till just before you do, you know. Do not be distressed, Eleanor, I can go on Monday very well. My father and mother's having no notice of it is of very little consequence. The General will send a servant with me, I dare say, half the way – and then I shall soon be at Salisbury, and then I am only nine miles from home."

"Ah, Catherine! were it settled so, it would be somewhat less intolerable, though in such common attentions you would have received but half what you ought. But – how can I tell you? – Tomorrow morning is fixed for your leaving us, and not even the hour is left to your choice; the very carriage is ordered, and will be here at seven o'clock, and no servant will be offered you."

Catherine sat down, breathless and speechless. "I could hardly believe my senses, when I heard it; – and no displeasure, no resentment that you can feel at this moment, however justly great, can be more than I myself – but I must not talk of what I felt. Oh! that I could suggest any thing in extenuation! Good God! what will your father and mother say! After courting you from the protection of real friends to this – almost double distance from your home, to have you driven out of the house, without the considerations even of decent civility! Dear, dear Catherine, in being the bearer of such a message, I seem guilty myself of all its insult; yet, I trust you will acquit me, for you must have been long enough in this house to see that I am but a nominal mistress of it, that my real power is nothing."

"Have I offended the General?" said Catherine in a faltering voice.

"Alas! for my feelings as a daughter, all that I know, all that I answer for is, that you can have given him no just cause of offence. He certainly is greatly, very greatly discomposed; I have seldom seen him more so. His temper is not happy, and something has now occurred to ruffle it in an uncommon degree; some disappointment, some vexation, which just at this moment seems important; but which I can hardly suppose you to have any concern in, for how is it possible?"

It was with pain that Catherine could speak at all; and it was only for Eleanor's sake that she attempted it. "I am sure," said she, "I am very sorry if I have offended him. It was the last thing I would willingly have done. But do not be unhappy, Eleanor. An engagement you know must be kept. I am only sorry it was not recollected sooner, that I might have written home. But it is of very little consequence."

"I hope, I earnestly hope that to your real safety it will be of none; but to every thing else it is of the greatest consequence; to comfort, appearance, propriety, to your family, to the world. Were your friends, the Allens, still in Bath, you might go to them with comparative ease; a few hours would take you there; but a journey of seventy miles, to be taken post by you, at your age, alone, unattended!"

"Oh, the journey is nothing. Do not think about that. And if we are to part, a few hours sooner or later, you know, makes no difference. I can be ready by seven. Let me be called in time." Eleanor saw that she wished to be alone; and believing it better for each that they should avoid any further conversation, now left her with "I shall see you in the morning."

Catherine's swelling heart needed relief. In Eleanor's presence friendship and pride had equally restrained her tears, but no sooner was she gone than they burst forth in torrents. Turned from the house, and in such a way! – Without any reason that could justify, any apology that could atone for the abruptness, the rudeness, nay, the insolence of it. Henry at a distance – not able even to bid him farewell. Every hope, every expectation from him suspended, at least, and who could say how long? – Who could say when they might meet again? – And all this by such a man as General Tilney, so polite, so well-bred, and heretofore so particularly fond of her! It was as incomprehensible as it was mortifying and grievous. From what it could arise, and where it would end, were considerations of equal perplexity and alarm. The manner in which it was done so grossly uncivil; hurrying her away without any reference to her own convenience, or allowing her even the appearance of choice as to the time or mode of her travelling; of two days, the earliest fixed on, and of that almost the earliest hour, as if resolved to have her gone before he was stirring in the morning, that he might not be obliged even to see her. What could all this mean but an intentional affront? By some means or other she must have had the misfortune to offend him. Eleanor had wished to spare her from so painful a notion, but Catherine could not believe it possible that any injury or any misfortune could provoke such ill-will against a person not connected, or, at least, not supposed to be connected with it.

Heavily passed the night. Sleep, or repose that deserved the name of sleep, was out of the question. That room, in which her disturbed imagination had tormented her on her first arrival, was again the scene of agitated spirits and unquiet slumbers. Yet how different now the source of her inquietude from what it had been then – how mournfully superior in reality and substance! Her anxiety had foundation in fact, her fears in probability; and with a mind so occupied in the contemplation of actual and natural evil, the solitude of her situation, the darkness of her chamber, the antiquity of the building were felt and considered without the smallest emotion; and though the wind was high, and often produced strange and sudden noises throughout the house, she heard it all as she lay awake, hour after hour, without curiosity or terror.

Soon after six Eleanor entered her room, eager to show attention or give assistance where it was possible; but very little remained to be done. Catherine had not loitered; she was almost dressed, and her packing almost finished. The possibility of some conciliatory message from the General occurred to her as his daughter appeared. What so natural, as that anger should pass away and repentance succeed it? and she only wanted to know how far, after what had passed, an apology might properly be received by her. But the knowledge would have been useless here, it was not called for; neither clemency nor dignity was put to the trial – Eleanor brought no message. Very little passed between them on meeting; each found her greatest safety in silence, and few and trivial were the sentences exchanged while they remained upstairs, Catherine in busy agitation completing her dress, and Eleanor with more good-will than experience intent upon filling the trunk. When every thing was done they left the room, Catherine lingering only half a minute behind her friend to throw a parting glance on every well-known cherished object, and went down to the breakfast-parlour, where breakfast was prepared. She tried to eat, as well to save herself from the pain of being urged, as to make her friend comfortable; but she had no appetite, and could not swallow many mouthfuls. The contrast between this and her last breakfast in that room, gave her fresh misery, and strengthened her distaste for every thing before her.

It was not four-and-twenty hours ago since they had met there to the same repast, but in circumstances how different! With what cheerful ease, what happy, though false security, had she then looked around her, enjoying every thing present, and fearing little in future, beyond Henry's going to Woodston for a day! Happy, happy breakfast! for Henry had been there, Henry had sat by her and helped her. These reflections were long indulged undisturbed by any address from her companion, who sat as deep in thought as herself; and the appearance of the carriage was the first thing to startle and recall them to the present moment. Catherine's colour rose at the sight of it; and the indignity with which she was treated striking at that instant on her mind with peculiar force, made her for a short time sensible only of resentment. Eleanor seemed now impelled into resolution and speech.

"You *must* write to me, Catherine," she cried, "you *must* let me hear from you as soon as possible. Till I know you to be safe at home, I shall not have an hour's comfort. For *one* letter, at all risks, all hazards, I must entreat. Let me have the satisfaction of knowing that you are safe at Fullerton, and have found your family well, and then, till I can ask for your correspondence as I ought to do, I will not expect more. Direct to me at Lord Longtown's, and, I must ask it, under cover to Alice."[1]

"No, Eleanor, if you are not allowed to receive a letter from me, I am sure I had better not write. There can be no doubt of my getting home safe."

Eleanor only replied, "I cannot wonder at your feelings. I will not importune you. I will trust to your own kindness of heart when I am at a distance from you." But this, with the look of sorrow accompanying it, was enough to melt Catherine's pride in a moment, and she instantly said, "Oh, Eleanor, I *will* write to you indeed."

There was yet another point which Miss Tilney was anxious to settle, though somewhat embarrassed in speaking of. It had occurred to her, that after so long an absence from home, Catherine might not be provided with money enough for the expenses of her journey, and, upon suggesting it to her with most affectionate offers of accommodation, it proved to be exactly the case. Catherine had never thought on the subject till that moment; but, upon examining her purse, was convinced that but for this kindness of her friend, she might have been turned from the house without even the means of getting home; and the distress in which she must have been thereby involved filling the minds of both, scarcely another word was said by either during the time of their remaining together. Short, however, was that time. The carriage was soon announced to be ready; and Catherine, instantly rising, a

---

1   Presumably Eleanor Tilneys's maid.

long and affectionate embrace supplied the place of language in bidding each other adieu; and, as they entered the hall, unable to leave the house without some mention of one whose name had not yet been spoken by either, she paused a moment, and with quivering lips just made it intelligible that she left "her kind remembrance for her absent friend." But with this approach to his name ended all possibility of restraining her feelings; and, hiding her face as well as she could with her handkerchief, she darted across the hall, jumped into the chaise, and in a moment was driven from the door.

CHAPTER 29

Catherine was too wretched to be fearful. The journey in itself had no terrors for her; and she began it without either dreading its length, or feeling its solitariness. Leaning back in one corner of the carriage, in a violent burst of tears, she was conveyed some miles beyond the walls of the Abbey before she raised her head; and the highest point of ground within the park was almost closed from her view before she was capable of turning her eyes towards it. Unfortunately, the road she now travelled was the same which only ten days ago she had so happily passed along in going to and from Woodston; and, for fourteen miles, every bitter feeling was rendered more severe by the review of objects on which she had first looked under impressions so different. Every mile, as it brought her nearer Woodston, added to her sufferings, and when within the distance of five, she passed the turning which led to it, and thought of Henry, so near, yet so unconscious, her grief and agitation were excessive.

The day which she had spent at that place had been one of the happiest of her life. It was there, it was on that day, that the General had made use of such expressions with regard to Henry and herself, had so spoken and so looked as to give her the most positive conviction of his actually wishing their marriage. Yes, only ten days ago had he elated her by his pointed regard – had he even confused her by his too significant reference! And now – what had she done, or what had she omitted to do, to merit such a change?

The only offence against him of which she could accuse her-self, had been such as was scarcely possible to reach his knowl-edge. Henry and her own heart only were privy to the shocking suspicions which she had so idly entertained; and equally safe did she believe her secret with each. Designedly, at least, Henry could not have betrayed her. If, indeed, by any strange mischance his father should have gained intelligence of what she had dared to think and look for, of her causeless fancies and injurious examina-tions, she could not wonder at any degree of his indignation. If aware of her having viewed him as a murderer, she could not wonder at his even turning her from his house. But a justification so full of torture to herself, she trusted would not be in his power.

Anxious as were all her conjectures on this point, it was not, however, the one on which she dwelt most. There was a thought yet nearer, a more prevailing, more impetuous concern. How Henry would think, and feel, and look, when he returned on the morrow to Northanger and heard of her being gone, was a ques-tion of force and interest to rise over every other, to be never ceasing, alternately irritating and soothing; it sometimes suggested the dread of his calm acquiescence, and at others was answered by the sweetest confidence in his regret and resentment. To the Gen-eral, of course, he would not dare to speak; but to Eleanor – what might he not say to Eleanor about her?

In this unceasing recurrence of doubts and inquiries, on any one article of which her mind was incapable of more than mo-mentary repose, the hours passed away, and her journey advanced much faster than she looked for. The pressing anxieties of thought, which prevented her from noticing any thing before her, when once beyond the neighbourhood of Woodston, saved her at the same time from watching her progress; and though no object on the road could engage a moment's attention, she found no stage of it tedious. From this, she was preserved too by another cause, by feeling no eagerness for her journey's conclusion; for to return in such a manner to Fullerton was almost to destroy the pleasure of a meeting with those she loved best, even after an ab-sence such as her's – an eleven weeks absence. What had she to say that would not humble herself and pain her family; that would not increase her own grief by the confession of it, extend an useless resentment, and perhaps involve the innocent with the guilty in undistinguishing ill-will? She could never do justice to Henry and Eleanor's merit; she felt it too strongly for expression; and should a dislike be taken against them, should they be thought of unfavourably, on their father's account, it would cut her to the heart.

With these feelings, she rather dreaded than sought for the first view of that well-known spire which would announce her within twenty miles of home. Salisbury she had known to be her point on leaving Northanger; but after the first stage she had been indebted to the post-masters for the names of the places which were then to conduct her to it; so great had been her ignorance of her route. She met with nothing, however, to distress or frighten her. Her youth, civil manners and liberal pay, procured her all the attention that a traveller like herself could require; and stopping only to change horses, she travelled on for about eleven hours without accident or alarm, and between six and seven o'clock in the evening found herself entering Fullerton.

A heroine returning, at the close of her career, to her native village, in all the triumph of recovered reputation, and all the dignity of a countess, with a long train of noble relations in their several phaetons, and three waiting-maids in a travelling chaise and four, behind her, is an event on which the pen of the contriver may well delight to dwell; it gives credit to every conclusion, and the author must share in the glory she so liberally bestows. But my affair is widely different; I bring back my heroine to her home in solitude and disgrace; and no sweet elation of spirits can lead me into minuteness. A heroine in a hack post-chaise, is such a blow upon sentiment, as no attempt at grandeur or pathos can withstand. Swiftly therefore shall her post-boy drive through the village, amid the gaze of Sunday groups, and speedy shall be her descent from it.

But, whatever might be the distress of Catherine's mind, as she thus advanced towards the Parsonage, and whatever the humiliation of her biographer in relating it, she was preparing enjoyment of no every-day nature for those to whom she went; first, in the appearance of her carriage – and secondly, in herself. The chaise of a traveller being a rare sight in Fullerton, the whole family were immediately at the window; and to have it stop at the sweep-gate was a pleasure to brighten every eye and occupy every fancy – a pleasure quite unlooked for by all but the two youngest children, a boy and girl of six and four years old, who expected a brother or sister in every carriage. Happy the glance that first distinguished Catherine! – Happy the voice that proclaimed the discovery! – But whether such happiness were the lawful property of George or Harriet could never be exactly understood.

Her father, mother, Sarah, George, and Harriet, all assembled at the door, to welcome her with affectionate eagerness, was a sight to awaken the best feelings of Catherine's heart; and in the embrace of each, as she stepped from the carriage, she found herself soothed beyond any thing that she had believed possible. So surrounded, so caressed, she was even happy! In the joyfulness of family love every thing for a short time was subdued, and the pleasure of seeing her, leaving them at first little leisure for calm curiosity, they were all seated round the tea-table, which Mrs Morland had hurried for the comfort of the poor traveller, whose pale and jaded looks soon caught her notice, before any inquiry so direct as to demand a positive answer was addressed to her.

Reluctantly, and with much hesitation, did she then begin what might perhaps, at the end of half an hour, be termed by the courtesy of her hearers, an explanation; but scarcely, within that time, could they at all discover the cause, or collect the particulars of her sudden return. They were far from being an irritable race; far from any quickness in catching, or bitterness in resenting affronts: – but here, when the whole was unfolded, was an insult not to be overlooked, nor, for the first half hour, to be easily pardoned. Without suffering any romantic alarm, in the consideration of their daughter's long and lonely journey, Mr and Mrs Morland could not but feel that it might have been productive of much unpleasantness to her; that it was what they could never have voluntarily suffered; and that, in forcing her on such a measure, General Tilney had acted neither honourably nor feelingly – neither as a gentleman nor as a parent. Why he had done it, what could have provoked him to such a breach of hospitality, and so suddenly turned all his partial regard for their daughter into actual ill-will, was a matter which they were at least as far from divining as Catherine herself; but it did not oppress them by any means so long; and, after a due course of useless conjecture, that, "it was a strange business, and that he must be a very strange man," grew enough for all their indignation and wonder; though Sarah indeed still indulged in the sweets of incomprehensibility, exclaiming and conjecturing with youthful ardour. – "My dear, you give yourself a great deal of needless trouble," said her mother at last; "depend upon it, it is something not at all worth understanding."

"I can allow for his wishing Catherine away, when he recollected this engagement," said Sarah, "but why not do it civilly?"

"I am sorry for the young people," returned Mrs Morland; "they must have a sad time of it; but as for any thing else, it is no matter now; Catherine is safe at home, and our comfort does not depend upon General Tilney." Catherine sighed. "Well," continued her philosophic mother, "I am glad I did not know of your journey at the time; but now it is an over perhaps there is no great harm done. It is always good for young people to be put upon exerting themselves; and you know, my dear Catherine, you always were a sad little shatter-brained creature; but now you must have been forced to have your wits about you, with so much changing of chaises and so forth; and I hope it will appear that you have not left any thing behind you in any of the pockets."

Catherine hoped so too, and tried to feel an interest in her own amendment, but her spirits were quite worn down; and, to be silent and alone becoming soon her only wish, she readily agreed to her mother's next counsel of going early to bed. Her parents seeing nothing in her ill-looks and agitation but the natural consequence of mortified feelings, and of the unusual exertion and fatigue of such a journey, parted from her without any doubt of their being soon slept away; and though, when they all met the next morning, her recovery was not equal to their hopes, they were still perfectly unsuspicious of there being any deeper evil. They never once thought of her heart, which, for the parents of a young lady of seventeen, just returned from her first excursion from home, was odd enough!

As soon as breakfast was over, she sat down to fulfil her promise to Miss Tilney, whose trust in the effect of time and distance on her friend's disposition was already justified, for already did Catherine reproach herself with having parted from Eleanor coldly; with having never enough valued her merits or kindness; and never enough commiserated her for what she had been yesterday left to endure. The strength of these feelings, however, was far from assisting her pen; and never had it been harder for her to write than in addressing Eleanor Tilney. To compose a letter which might at once do justice to her sentiments and her situation, convey gratitude without servile regret, be guarded without coldness, and honest without resentment – a letter which Eleanor might not be pained by the perusal of – and, above all, which she might not blush herself, if Henry should chance to see, was an undertaking to frighten away all her powers of performance; and, after long thought and much perplexity, to be very brief was all that she could determine on with any confidence of safety. The money therefore which Eleanor had advanced was inclosed with little more than grateful thanks, and the thousand good wishes of a most affectionate heart.

"This has been a strange acquaintance," observed Mrs Morland, as the letter was finished; "soon made and soon ended. – I am sorry it happens so, for Mrs Allen thought them very pretty kind of young people; and you were sadly out of luck too in your Isabella. Ah! poor James! Well, we must live and learn; and the next new friends you make I hope will be better worth keeping."

Catherine coloured as she warmly answered, "No friend can be better worth keeping than Eleanor."

"If so, my dear, I dare say you will meet again some time or other; do not be uneasy. It is ten to one but you are thrown together again in the course of a few years; and then what a pleasure it will be!"

Mrs Morland was not happy in her attempt at consolation. The hope of meeting again in the course of a few years could only put into Catherine's head what might happen within that time to make a meeting dreadful to her. She could never forget Henry Tilney, or think of him with less tenderness than she did at that moment; but he might forget her; and in that case to meet! – Her eyes filled with tears as she pictured her acquaintance so renewed; and her mother, perceiving her comfortable suggestions to have had no good effect, proposed, as another expedient for restoring her spirits, that they should call on Mrs Allen.

The two houses were only a quarter of a mile apart; and, as they walked, Mrs Morland quickly dispatched all that she felt on the score of James's disappointment. "We are sorry for him," said she; "but otherwise there is no harm done in the match going off; for it could not be a desirable thing to have him engaged to a girl whom we had not the smallest acquaintance with, and who was so entirely without fortune; and now, after such behaviour, we cannot think at all well of her. Just at present it comes hard to poor James; but that will not last for ever; and I dare say he will be a discreeter man all his life, for the foolishness of his first choice."

This was just such a summary view of the affair as Catherine could listen to; another sentence might have endangered her complaisance, and made her reply less rational; for soon were all her thinking powers swallowed up in the reflection of her own change of feelings and spirits since last she had trodden that well-known road. It was not three months ago since, wild with joyful expectation, she had there run backwards and forwards some ten times a-day, with an heart light, gay, and independent; looking forward to pleasures untasted and unalloyed, and free from the apprehension of evil as from the knowledge of it. Three months ago had seen her all this; and now, how altered a being did she return!

She was received by the Allens with all the kindness which her unlooked-for appearance, acting on a steady affection, would naturally call forth; and great was their surprize, and warm their displeasure, on hearing how she had been treated, – though Mrs Morland's account of it was no inflated representation, no studied appeal to their passions. "Catherine took us quite by surprize yesterday evening," said she. "She travelled all the way post by herself, and knew nothing of coming till Saturday night; for General Tilney, from some odd fancy or other, all of a sudden grew tired of having her there, and almost turned her out of the house. Very unfriendly, certainly; and he must be a very odd man; – but we are so glad to have her amongst us again! And it is a great comfort to find that she is not a poor helpless creature, but can shift very well for herself."

Mr Allen expressed himself on the occasion with the reasonable resentment of a sensible friend; and Mrs Allen thought his expressions quite good enough to be immediately made use of again by herself. His wonder, his conjectures, and his explanations, became in succession her's, with the addition of this single remark – "I really have not patience with the General" – to fill up every accidental pause. And, "I really have not patience with the General," was uttered twice after Mr Allen left the room, without any relaxation of anger, or any material digression of thought. A more considerable degree of wandering attended the third repetition: and, after completing the fourth, she immediately added, "Only think, my dear, of my having got that frightful great rent in my best Mechlin[1] so charmingly mended, before I left Bath, that one can hardly see where it was. I must shew it you some day or other. Bath is a nice place, Catherine, after all. I assure you I did not above half like coming away. Mrs Thorpe's being there was such a comfort to us, was not it? You know you and I were quite forlorn at first."

"Yes, but *that* did not last long," said Catherine, her eyes brightening at the recollection of what had first given spirit to her existence there.

"Very true: we soon met with Mrs Thorpe, and then we wanted for nothing. My dear, do not you think these silk gloves wear very well? I put them on new the first time of our going to the Lower Rooms, you know, and I have worn them a great deal since. Do you remember that evening?"

"Do I! Oh! perfectly."

"It was very agreeable, was not it? Mr Tilney drank tea with us, and I always thought him a great addition, he is so very agreeable. I have a notion you danced with him, but am not quite sure. I remember I had my favourite gown on."

Catherine could not answer; and, after a short trial of other subjects, Mrs Allen again returned to – "I really have not patience with the General! Such an agreeable, worthy man as he seemed to be! I do not suppose, Mrs Morland, you ever saw a better-bred man in your life. His lodgings were taken the very day after he left them, Catherine. But no wonder; Milsom-street you know." –

As they walked home again, Mrs Morland endeavoured to impress on her daughter's mind the happiness of having such steady

---

1 Garment made of Mechlin lace.

well-wishers as Mr and Mrs Allen, and the very little consideration which the neglect or unkindness of slight acquaintance like
the Tilneys ought to have with her, while she could preserve the
good opinion and affection of her earliest friends. There was a
great deal of good sense in all this; but there are some situations
of the human mind in which good sense has very little power;
and Catherine's feelings contradicted almost every position her
mother advanced. It was upon the behaviour of these very slight
acquaintance that all her present happiness depended; and while
Mrs Morland was successfully confirming her own opinions by
the justness of her own representations, Catherine was silently
reflecting that *now* Henry must have arrived at Northanger; *now*
he must have heard of her departure; and *now*, perhaps, they were
all setting off for Hereford.

CHAPTER 30

Catherine's disposition was not naturally sedentary, nor had her
habits been ever very industrious; but whatever might hitherto
have been her defects of that sort, her mother could not but perceive them now to be greatly increased. She could neither sit still,
nor employ herself for ten minutes together, walking round the
garden and orchard again and again, as if nothing but motion was
voluntary; and it seemed as if she could even walk about the house
rather than remain fixed for any time in the parlour. Her loss of
spirits was a yet greater alteration. In her rambling and her idleness
she might only be a caricature of herself; but in her silence and
sadness she was the very reverse of all that she had been before.

For two days Mrs Morland allowed it to pass even without a
hint; but when a third night's rest had neither restored her cheerfulness, improved her in useful activity, nor given her a greater
inclination for needle-work, she could no longer refrain from
the gentle reproof of, "My dear Catherine, I am afraid you are
growing quite a fine lady. I do not know when poor Richard's
cravats would be done, if he had no friend but you. Your head
runs too much upon Bath; but there is a time for every thing –
a time for balls and plays, and a time for work. You have had a
long run of amusement, and now you must try to be useful."

Catherine took up her work directly, saying, in a dejected voice, that "her head did not run upon Bath — much."

"Then you are fretting about General Tilney, and that is very simple of you; for ten to one whether you ever see him again. You should never fret about trifles." After a short silence — "I hope, my Catherine, you are not getting out of humour with home because it is not so grand as Northanger. That would be turning your visit into an evil indeed. Wherever you are you should always be contented, but especially at home, because there you must spend the most of your time. I did not quite like, at breakfast, to hear you talk so much about the French-bread at Northanger."

"I am sure I do not care about the bread. It is all the same to me what I eat."

"There is a very clever Essay in one of the books up stairs upon much such a subject, about young girls that have been spoilt for home by great acquaintance — 'The Mirror,'[1] I think. I will look it out for you some day or other, because I am sure it will do you good."

Catherine said no more, and, with an endeavour to do right, applied to her work; but, after a few minutes, sunk again, without knowing it herself, into languor and listlessness, moving herself in her chair, from the irritation of weariness, much oftener than she moved her needle. — Mrs Morland watched the progress of this relapse; and seeing, in her daughter's absent and dissatisfied look, the full proof of that repining spirit to which she had now begun to attribute her want of cheerfulness, hastily left the room to fetch the book in question, anxious to lose no time in attacking so dreadful a malady. It was some time before she could find what she looked for; and other family matters occurring to detain her, a quarter of an hour had elapsed ere she returned down stairs with the volume from which so much was hoped. Her avocations

---

1   Letter in the *Mirror* (No. 12, Sat. 6 March 1779), entitled *Consequence to little folks of intimacy with great ones*, in which John Homespun laments the effects of a recent week-long visit by his two daughters to a wealthy lady. The daughters have learnt to ape fashionable manners, keep late hours, play cards, and use French phrases. Burney's *Camilla* also sees the heroine's mother mistake her daughter's pining for the hero — this time Edgar Mandlebert — as contempt of home-life after a stint in high society.

above having shut out all noise but what she created herself, she knew not that a visitor had arrived within the last few minutes, till, on entering the room, the first object she beheld was a young man whom she had never seen before. With a look of much respect, he immediately rose, and being introduced to her by her conscious daughter as "Mr Henry Tilney," with the embarrassment of real sensibility began to apologize for his appearance there, acknowledging that after what had passed he had little right to expect a welcome at Fullerton, and stating his impatience to be assured of Miss Morland's having reached her home in safety, as the cause of his intrusion. He did not address himself to an uncandid judge or a resentful heart. Far from comprehending him or his sister in their father's misconduct, Mrs Morland had been always kindly disposed towards each, and instantly, pleased by his appearance, received him with the simple professions of unaffected benevolence; thanking him for such an attention to her daughter, assuring him that the friends of her children were always welcome there, and intreating him to say not another word of the past.

He was not ill inclined to obey this request, for, though his heart was greatly relieved by such unlooked-for mildness, it was not just at that moment in his power to say any thing to the purpose. Returning in silence to his seat, therefore, he remained for some minutes most civilly answering all Mrs Morland's common remarks about the weather and roads. Catherine meanwhile – the anxious, agitated, happy, feverish Catherine, – said not a word; but her glowing cheek and brightened eye made her mother trust that this good-natured visit would at least set her heart at ease for a time, and gladly therefore did she lay aside the first volume of the Mirror for a future hour.

Desirous of Mr Morland's assistance, as well in giving encouragement, as in finding conversation for her guest, whose embarrassment on his father's account she earnestly pitied, Mrs Morland had very early dispatched one of the children to summon him; but Mr Morland was from home – and being thus without any support, at the end of a quarter of an hour she had nothing to say. After a couple of minutes' unbroken silence, Henry, turning to Catherine for the first time since her mother's entrance, asked her, with sudden alacrity, if Mr and Mrs Allen were now at Fullerton?

and on developing, from amidst all her perplexity of words in reply, the meaning, which one short syllable would have given, immediately expressed his intention of paying his respects to them, and, with a rising colour, asked her if she would have the goodness to shew him the way. "You may see the house from this window, sir," was information on Sarah's side, which produced only a bow of acknowledgment from the gentleman, and a silencing nod from her mother; for Mrs Morland, thinking it probable, as a secondary consideration in his wish of waiting on their worthy neighbours, that he might have some explanation to give of his father's behaviour, which it must be more pleasant for him to communicate only to Catherine, would not on any account prevent her accompanying him. They began their walk, and Mrs Morland was not entirely mistaken in his object in wishing it. Some explanation on his father's account he had to give; but his first purpose was to explain himself, and before they reached Mr Allen's grounds he had done it so well, that Catherine did not think it could ever be repeated too often. She was assured of his affection; and that heart in return was solicited, which, perhaps, they pretty equally knew was already entirely his own; for, though Henry was now sincerely attached to her, though he felt and delighted in all the excellencies of her character and truly loved her society, I must confess that his affection originated in nothing better than gratitude, or, in other words, that a persuasion of her partiality for him had been the only cause of giving her a serious thought. It is a new circumstance in romance, I acknowledge, and dreadfully derogatory of an heroine's dignity; but if it be as new in common life, the credit of a wild imagination will at least be all my own.

A very short visit to Mrs Allen, in which Henry talked at random, without sense or connection, and Catherine, wrapt in the contemplation of her own unutterable happiness, scarcely opened her lips, dismissed them to the extasies of another tête-à-tête; and before it was suffered to close, she was enabled to judge how far he was sanctioned by parental authority in his present application. On his return from Woodston, two days before, he had been met near the Abbey by his impatient father, hastily informed in angry terms of Miss Morland's departure, and ordered to think of her no more.

Such was the permission upon which he had now offered her his hand. The affrighted Catherine, amidst all the terrors of expectation, as she listened to this account, could not but rejoice in the kind caution with which Henry had saved her from the necessity of a conscientious rejection, by engaging her faith before he mentioned the subject; and as he proceeded to give the particulars, and explain the motives of his father's conduct, her feelings soon hardened into even a triumphant delight. The General had had nothing to accuse her of, nothing to lay to her charge, but her being the involuntary, unconscious object of a deception which his pride could not pardon, and which a better pride would have been ashamed to own. She was guilty only of being less rich than he had supposed her to be. Under a mistaken persuasion of her possessions and claims, he had courted her acquaintance in Bath, solicited her company at Northanger, and designed her for his daughter in law. On discovering his error, to turn her from the house seemed the best, though to his feelings an inadequate proof of his resentment towards herself, and his contempt of her family.

John Thorpe had first misled him. The General, perceiving his son one night at the theatre to be paying considerable attention to Miss Morland, had accidentally inquired of Thorpe if he knew more of her than her name. Thorpe, most happy to be on speaking terms with a man of General Tilney's importance, had been joyfully and proudly communicative; – and being at that time not only in daily expectation of Morland's engaging Isabella, but likewise pretty well resolved upon marrying Catherine himself, his vanity induced him to represent the family as yet more wealthy than his vanity and avarice had made him believe them. With whomsoever he was, or was likely to be connected, his own consequence always required that theirs should be great, and as his intimacy with any acquaintance grew, so regularly grew their fortune. The expectations of his friend Morland, therefore, from the first over-rated, had ever since his introduction to Isabella, been gradually increasing; and by merely adding twice as much for the grandeur of the moment, by doubling what he chose to think the amount of Mr Morland's preferment, trebling his private fortune, bestowing a rich aunt, and sinking half the children, he was able to represent the whole family to the General in a most respectable light. For Catherine, however, the peculiar object of the General's curiosity, and his own speculations, he had yet something more in reserve, and the ten or fifteen thousand pounds which her father could give her, would be a pretty addition to Mr Allen's estate. Her intimacy there had made him seriously determine on her being handsomely legacied hereafter; and to speak of her therefore as the almost acknowledged future heiress of Fullerton naturally followed. Upon such intelligence the General had proceeded; for never had it occurred to him to doubt its authority. Thorpe's interest in the family, by his sister's approaching connection with one of its members, and his own views on another, (circumstances of which he boasted with almost equal openness,) seemed sufficient vouchers for his truth; and to these were added the absolute facts of the Allens being wealthy and childless, of Miss Morland's being under their care, and – as soon as his acquaintance allowed him to judge – of their treating her with parental kindness. His resolution was soon formed. Already had he discerned a liking towards Miss Morland in the countenance of his son; and thankful for Mr Thorpe's communication, he almost instantly determined to spare no pains in weakening his boasted interest and ruining his dearest hopes. Catherine herself could not be more ignorant at the time of all this, than his own children. Henry and Eleanor, perceiving nothing in her situation likely to engage their father's particular respect, had seen with astonishment the suddenness, continuance and extent of his attention; and though latterly, from some hints which had accompanied an almost positive command to his son of doing every thing in his power to attach her, Henry was convinced of his father's believing it to be an advantageous connection, it was not till the late explanation at Northanger that they had the smallest idea of the false calculations which had hurried him on. That they were false, the General had learnt from the very person who had suggested them, from Thorpe himself, whom he had chanced to meet again in town, and who, under the influence of exactly opposite feelings, irritated by Catherine's refusal, and yet more by the failure of a very recent endeavour to accomplish a reconciliation between Morland and Isabella, convinced that they were separated for ever, and spurning a friendship which could be no longer serviceable, hastened to contradict all that he had said before to the advantage of the Morlands; – confessed himself to have been totally mistaken in his opinion of their circumstances and character, misled by the rhodomontade of his friend to believe his father a man of substance and credit, whereas the transactions of the two or three last weeks proved him to be neither; for after coming eagerly forward on the first overture of a marriage between the families, with the most liberal proposals, he had, on being brought to the point by the shrewdness of the relator, been constrained to acknowledge himself incapable of giving the young people even a decent support. They were, in fact, a necessitous family; numerous too almost beyond example; by no means respected in their own neighbourhood, as he had lately had particular opportunities of discovering; aiming at a style of life which their fortune could not warrant; seeking to better themselves by wealthy connexions; a forward, bragging, scheming race.

The terrified General pronounced the name of Allen with an inquiring look; and here too Thorpe had learnt his error. The Allens, he believed, had lived near them too long, and he knew the young man on whom the Fullerton estate must devolve. The General needed no more. Enraged with almost every body in the world but himself, he set out the next day for the Abbey, where his performances have been seen.

I leave it to my readers' sagacity to determine how much of all this it was possible for Henry to communicate at this time to Catherine, how much of it he could have learnt from his father, in what points his own conjectures might assist him, and what portion must yet remain to be told in a letter from James. I have united for their ease what they must divide for mine. Catherine, at any rate, heard enough to feel, that in suspecting General Tilney of either murdering or shutting up his wife, she had scarcely sinned against his character, or magnified his cruelty.

Henry, in having such things to relate of his father, was almost as pitiable as in their first avowal to himself. He blushed for the narrow-minded counsel which he was obliged to expose. The conversation between them at Northanger had been of the most unfriendly kind. Henry's indignation on hearing how Catherine had been treated, on comprehending his father's views, and being ordered to acquiesce in them, had been open and bold. The General, accustomed on every ordinary occasion to give the law in his family, prepared for no reluctance but of feeling, no opposing desire that should dare to clothe itself in words, could ill brook the opposition of his son, steady as the sanction of reason and the dictate of conscience could make it. But, in such a cause, his anger, though it must shock, could not intimidate Henry, who was sustained in his purpose by a conviction of its justice. He felt himself bound as much in honour as in affection to Miss Morland, and believing that heart to be his own which he had been directed to gain, no unworthy retraction of a tacit consent, no reversing decree of unjustifiable anger, could shake his fidelity, or influence the resolutions it prompted.

He steadily refused to accompany his father into Herefordshire, an engagement formed almost at the moment, to promote the dismissal of Catherine, and as steadily declared his intention of offering her his hand. The General was furious in his anger, and they parted in dreadful disagreement. Henry, in an agitation of mind which many solitary hours were required to compose, had returned almost instantly to Woodston; and, on the afternoon of the following day, had begun his journey to Fullerton.

CHAPTER 31

Mr and Mrs Morland's surprize on being applied to by Mr Tilney for their consent to his marrying their daughter, was, for a few minutes, considerable; it having never entered their heads to suspect an attachment on either side; but as nothing, after all, could be more natural than Catherine's being beloved, they soon learnt to consider it with only the happy agitation of gratified pride, and, as far as they alone were concerned, had not a single objection to start. His pleasing manners and good sense were self-evident recommendations; and having never heard evil of him, it was not their way to suppose any evil could be told. Good-will supplying the place of experience, his character needed no attestation. "Catherine would make a sad, heedless young house-keeper to be sure," was her mother's foreboding remark; but quick was the consolation of there being nothing like practice.

There was but one obstacle, in short, to be mentioned; but till that one was removed, it must be impossible for them to sanction the engagement. Their tempers were mild, but their principles were steady, and while his parent so expressly forbad the connexion, they could not allow themselves to encourage it. That the General should come forward to solicit the alliance, or that he should even very heartily approve it, they were not refined enough to make any parading stipulation; but the decent appearance of consent must be yielded, and that once obtained – and their own hearts made them trust that it could not be very long denied – their willing approbation was instantly to follow. His *consent* was all that they wished for. They were no more inclined than entitled to demand his *money*. Of a very considerable fortune, his son was, by marriage settlements, eventually secure; his present income was an income of independence and comfort, and under every pecuniary view, it was a match beyond the claims of their daughter.

The young people could not be surprized at a decision like this. They felt and they deplored – but they could not resent it; and they parted, endeavouring to hope that such a change in the General, as each believed almost impossible, might speedily take place, to unite them again in the fullness of privileged affection. Henry returned to what was now his only home, to watch over his young plantations, and extend his improvements for her sake, to whose share in them he looked anxiously forward; and Catherine remained at Fullerton to cry. Whether the torments of absence were softened by a clandestine correspondence, let us not inquire. Mr and Mrs Morland never did – they had been too kind to exact any promise; and whenever Catherine received a letter, as, at that time, happened pretty often, they always looked another way.

The anxiety, which in this state of their attachment must be the portion of Henry and Catherine, and of all who loved either, as to its final event, can hardly extend, I fear, to the bosom of my readers, who will see in the tell-tale compression of the pages before them, that we are all hastening together to perfect felicity. The means by which their early marriage was effected can be the only doubt: what probable circumstance could work upon a temper like the General's? The circumstance which chiefly availed was the marriage of his daughter with a man of fortune and consequence, which took place in the course of the summer – an accession of dignity that threw him into a fit of good-humour, from which he did not recover till after Eleanor had obtained his forgiveness of Henry, and his permission for him "to be a fool if he liked it!"

The marriage of Eleanor Tilney, her removal from all the evils of such a home as Northanger had been made by Henry's banishment, to the home of her choice and the man of her choice, is an event which I expect to give general satisfaction among all her acquaintance. My own joy on the occasion is very sincere. I know no one more entitled, by unpretending merit, or better prepared by habitual suffering, to receive and enjoy felicity. Her partiality for this gentleman was not of recent origin; and he had been long withheld only by inferiority of situation from addressing her. His unexpected accession to title and fortune had removed all his difficulties; and never had the General loved his daughter so well in all her hours of companionship, utility, and patient endurance, as when he first hailed her, "Your Ladyship!" Her husband was really deserving of her; independent of his peerage, his wealth, and his attachment, being to a precision the most charming young man in the world. Any further definition of his merits must be unnecessary; the most charming young man in the world is instantly before the imagination of us all. Concerning the one in question therefore I have only to add – (aware that the rules of composition forbid the introduction of a character not connected with my fable) – that this was the very gentleman whose negligent servant left behind him that collection of washing-bills, resulting from a long visit at Northanger, by which my heroine was involved in one of her most alarming adventures.

The influence of the Viscount and Viscountess in their brother's behalf was assisted by that right understanding of Mr Morland's circumstances which, as soon as the General would allow himself to be informed, they were qualified to give. It taught him that he had been scarcely more misled by Thorpe's first boast of the family wealth, than by his subsequent malicious overthrow of it; that in no sense of the word were they necessitous or poor, and that Catherine would have three thousand pounds. This was so material an amendment of his late expectations, that it greatly contributed to smooth the descent of his pride; and by no means without its effect was the private intelligence, which he was at some pains to procure, that the Fullerton estate, being entirely at the disposal of its present proprietor, was consequently open to every greedy speculation.

On the strength of this, the General, soon after Eleanor's marriage, permitted his son to return to Northanger, and thence made him the bearer of his consent, very courteously worded in a page full of empty professions to Mr Morland. The event which it authorized soon followed: Henry and Catherine were married, the bells rang, and every body smiled; and, as this took place within a twelvemonth from the first day of their meeting, it will not appear, after all the dreadful delays occasioned by the General's cruelty, that they were essentially hurt by it. To begin perfect happiness at the respective ages of twenty-six and eighteen, is to do pretty well; and professing myself moreover convinced, that the General's unjust interference, so far from being really injurious to their felicity, was perhaps rather conducive to it, by improving their knowledge of each other, and adding strength to their attachment, I leave it to be settled by whomsoever it may concern, whether the tendency of this work be altogether to recommend parental tyranny, or reward filial disobedience.

Appendix A: Jane Austen's Correspondence with Crosby Publishing House

[Jane Austen, under the pseudonym Mrs. Ashton Dennis, wrote to Crosby in April 5, 1809 to enquire about her MS. novel *Susan*.]

Gentleman, – In the spring of the year 1803 a MS. novel in two vols. entitled *Susan*, was sold to you by a gentleman of the name of Seymour, and the purchase money £10 recd. at the same time. Six years have passed, and the work, of which I am myself the Authoress, has never to the best of my knowledge appeared in print, tho' an early publication was stipulated for at the time of sale. I can only account for such a extraordinary circumstance by supposing that the MS. by some carelessness to have been lost, and if that was the case am willing to supply you with another copy, if you are disposed to avail yourselves of it, and will engage for no further delay when it comes into your hands. It will not be in my power from particular circumstances to command this copy before the month of August, but then if you accept my proposal you may depend on receiving it. Be so good as to send me a line in answer as soon as possible as my stay in this place will not exceed a few days. Should no notice be taken of this address, I shall feel myself at liberty to secure the publication of my work by applying elsewhere.

> I am, Gentlemen, etc, etc.,
>
> M.A.D.

[Austen received the following abrupt reply.]

Madam, – We have to acknowledge the receipt of your letter of the 5th. inst. It is true that at the time mentioned we purchased of Mr. Seymour a MS. novel entitled *Susan*, and paid him for it the sum of £10, for which we have his stamped receipt, as a full consideration, but there was not any time stipulated for its publication, neither are we bound to publish it. Should you or any one else we shall take proceedings to stop the sale. The MS. shall be yours for the same as we paid for it.

> For Crosby & Co.
> I am yours, etc.
> Richard Crosby.

Appendix B: Jane Austen's Private Family Correspondence

[The following letter from Eliza de Feuillide to Philadelphia Walter provides a factual source for Henry Tilney's fictionalized account on page 127.

Eliza de Feuillide (1761–1813) (née Hancock), "Betsy", was the daughter of Philadelphia Austen (1730-92), Jane Austen's paternal aunt, and Tysoe Saul Hancock (d. 1775).

Eliza married Jean-François Capot de Feuillide in France 1781, but he was guillotined on 22 February, 1794. Their son, Hastings de Feuillide, born in 1786, was sickly and died in autumn 1801. Eliza later married her cousin, Jane's brother, Henry Austen on the 31 December 1797. After the summer of 1796, and especially after her brother Henry's marriage to Eliza in 1797, Jane was in repeated contact with this favourite cousin. It was Jane who was called to London in April 1813 to attend Eliza on her deathbed.

The recipient of the letter, Philadelphia Walter, Eliza's half cousin, was one of six children by William Hampson Walter and Susanna Weaver. Philadelphia married George Whitaker and died in 1834.]

Eliza de Feuillide to Philadelphia Walter.
7th June 1792

My dear Friend,

... I believe it is since I last wrote that my journey to Bath has taken place, from which I derived little amusement, perhaps more owing to the state of my spirits, than anything else. After about a fortnight's stay we returned to London & M. de F. proposed remaining here some time, but he soon received accounts from France which informed him that already having exceeded his leave of absence, if he still continued in England he would be considered as one of the Emigrants, & consequently his whole property forfeited to the nation. Such advices were not to be neglected & M. de F. was obliged to depart for Paris, but not however without giving me hopes of his return in some months, that is to say when the state of affairs will let him, for at present it is a very difficult business, for a military man especially to obtain leave to absent himself. ...

I think of quitting town about the 15th or 16th of this month and paying two visits in Surrey, one to my very old acquaintance *Mrs. Farhill* who has got, as I am told, a very pretty place near Bagshot; the remainder of the summer I believe I shall spend with our good friends at Steventon, & hope the quiet and good air will be of great service to my health which indeed stands much in need of some such restorative. I have really been very ill for some days past, but that has been chiefly owing to a sudden alarm which I experienced; I suppose you have heard of the commotions we have of late had in this metropolis, & Tuesday last going thro' Mount Street in my carriage I most unexpectedly found myself in the midst of an immense mob who were contending with a large party of Guards on horseback, because these latter endeavored to disperse them & prevent their demolishing some houses which they were determined, & had begun, to pull down. The noise of the populace, the drawn swords & pointed bayonets of the guards, the fragments of bricks & mortar thrown on every side, one of which had nearly killed my coachman, the firing at one end of the street which was already begun, altogether in short alarmed me so much that I really have never been well since. The confusion continued all that day & night & the following day, & for these eight & forty hours, I have seen nothing but large parties of soldiers parading up & down in this street to which Mount Street is very near, their being only Grosvenor Square between. My apprehensions have been that they would set fire to these houses they were so bent on demolishing, & think that if that was the case how soon in such a city as this a fire very trifling in its beginning might be productive of the most serious consequences. ...

Believe me most truly your affectionate & faithful friend

Eliza.

Richard Austen-Leigh notes that "the disturbances in Mount Street took place on June 5 and 6, 1792, and arose from the arrest of a party of servants who had been too freely celebrating the King's birthday on June 4" (*Austen Papers 1704-1856* 145).

Appendix C: Examples of Jane Austen's Reading

1. Ann Radcliffe, *Romance of the Forest* (1791)

As she sat musing, her eyes fixed on the opposite wall, she perceived the arras, with which the room was hung, wave backwards and forwards; she continued to observe it for some minutes, and then rose to examine it farther. It was moved by the wind, and she blushed at the momentary fear it had excited: but she observed that the tapestry was more strongly agitated in one particular place than elsewhere, and a noise that seemed something more than that of the wind, issued thence. ... She felt about the tapestry, and perceiving the wall behind shake under her hand, she lifted the arras, and discovered a small door, whose loosened hinges admitted the wind, and occasioned the noise she had heard.

The door was held by only a bolt, having undrawn which, and brought the light, she descended by a few steps into another chamber: she instantly remembered her dreams. The chamber was not much like that in which she had seen the dying Chevalier, and afterwards the bier; but it gave her a confused remembrance of one through which she had passed. Holding up the light to examine it more fully, she was convinced by its structure that it was part of the ancient foundation. A shattered casement, placed high from the floor, seemed to be the only opening to admit light. She observed a door on the opposite side of the apartment; and after some moments of hesitation, gained courage, and determined to pursue the inquiry. 'A mystery seems to hang over these chambers,' she said, 'which it is, perhaps, my lot to develope; [sic] I will, at least, see to what that door leads.'

She stepped forward, and having unclosed it, proceeded with faltering steps along a suite of apartments, resembling the first in style and condition, and terminating in one exactly like that where her dream had represented the dying person. The remembrance struck so forcibly upon her imagination, that she was in danger of fainting; and looking round the room, almost expected to see the phantom of her dream.

Unable to quit the place, she sat down on some old lumber to recover herself, while her spirits were nearly overcome by a superstitious dread, such as she had never felt before. She wondered to what part of the abbey these chambers belonged, and that they had so long escaped detection. The casements were all too high to afford any information from without. When she was sufficiently composed to consider the direction of the rooms, and the situation of the abbey, there appeared not a doubt that they formed an interior part of the original building.

As these reflections passed over her mind, a sudden gleam of moonlight fell upon some object without the casement. Being now sufficiently composed to wish to pursue the inquiry, and believing this object might afford her some means of learning the situation of these rooms, she combatted her remaining terrors, and, in order to distinguish it more clearly, removed the light to an outer chamber; but before she could return, a heavy cloud was driven over the face of the moon, and all without was perfectly dark: she stood for some moments waiting a returning gleam, but the obscurity continued. As she went softly back for the light, her foot stumbled over something on the floor, and while she stooped to examine it, the moon again shone, so that she could distinguish, through the casement, the eastern towers of the abbey. This discovery conformed her former conjectures concerning the interior situation of these apartments. The obscurity of the place prevented her discovering what it was that had impeded her steps, but having brought the light forward, she perceived on the floor an old dagger: with a trembling hand she took it up, and upon a closer view perceived that it was spotted and stained with rust.

Shocked and surprised, she looked round the room for some object that might confirm or destroy the dreadful suspicion which now rushed upon her mind; but she saw only a great chair, with broken arms, that stood in one corner of the room, and a table in a condition equally shattered, except that in another part lay a confused heap of things, which appeared to be old lumber. She went up to it, and perceived a broken bedstead, with some decayed remnants of furniture, covered with dust and cobwebs, and which seemed, indeed, as if they had not been moved for many years. Desirous, however, of examining further, she attempted to raise what appeared to have been part of the bedstead, but it slipped from her hand, and rolling to the floor, brought with it some of the remaining lumber. Adeline started aside, and saved herself; and when the noise it made had ceased, she heard a small rustling sound, and as she was about to leave the chamber, saw something falling gently among the lumber.

It was a small roll of paper, tied with a string and covered with dust. Adeline took it up, and on opening it perceived an hand-writing. She attempted to read it, but the part of the manuscript she looked at was so much obliterated, that she found this difficult, though what few words were legible impressed her with curiosity and terror, and induced her to return with it immediately to her chamber.

Having reached her own room, she fastened the private door, and let the arras fall over it as before. It was now midnight. The stillness of the hour, interrupted only at intervals by the hollow sighings of the blast, heightened the solemnity of Adeline's feelings. She wished she was not alone, and before she proceeded to look at the manuscript, listened whether Madame La Motte was yet in her chamber: not the least sound was heard, and she gently opened the great door.

[The following night Adeline has an opportunity to read the manuscript.]

She now took [the manuscript] from the drawer in which it had been deposited, and intending only to look cursorily over the first few pages, sat down with it by her bed side.

She opened it with an eagerness of inquiry, which the discoloured and almost obliterated ink but slowly gratified. The first words on the page were entirely lost; but those that appeared to commence the narrative were as follows.

—

"Oh! ye, whoever ye are, whom chance or misfortune may hereafter conduct to this spot – to ye I speak – to ye reveal the story of my wrongs, and ask you to avenge them. Vain hope! yet it imparts some comfort to believe it possible, that what I now write may one day meet the eye of a fellow creature; that the words, which tell my sufferings, may one day draw pity from the feeling heart.

"Yet stay your tears – your pity now is useless: long since have the pangs of misery ceased; the voice of complaining is passed away. It is weakness to wish for compassion which cannot be excited till I shall sink in the repose of death; and tasted, I hope, the happiness of eternity.

"Know then, that on the night of the twelfth of October, in the year 1642, I was arrested on the road to Caux, and on the very spot where a collumn [sic] is erected to the memory of the immortal Henry, by four ruffians, who, after disabling my servant, bore me through wilds and woods to this abbey. Their demeanour was not that of common banditti and I soon perceived they were employed by a superior power to perpetrate some dreadful purpose. Entreaties and bribes were vainly offered them to discover their employer, and abandon their design: they would not reveal even the least circumstance of their intentions.

But when, after a long journey, they arrived at this edifice, their base employer was at once revealed, and his horrid scheme but too well understood. What a moment was that! All the thunders of Heaven seemed launched at this defenceless head! O Fortitude! nerve my heart to –"

Adeline's light was now expiring in the socket, and the paleness of the ink so feebly shone upon, baffled her effort to discriminate the letters; it was impossible to procure a light from below, without discovering that she was yet up, a circumstance which would excite surprise, and lead to explanations such as she did not wish to enter upon. Thus compelled to suspend the inquiry, which so many attendant circumstances had rendered awfully interesting, she retired to her humble bed.

What she had read of the M.S. awakened a dreadful interest in the fate of the writer, and called up terrific images to her mind. "In these apartments!" – said she, and she shuddered and closed her eyes (Vol 2, Ch 8 and 9).

2. William Gilpin, *Observations, Relative to Picturesque Beauty on the Mountains and Lakes of Cumberland and Westmoreland* (1786)

Ruins are commonly divided into two kinds; castles, and abbeys. Of the former few countries perhaps can produce so many, as this island; for which various causes may be assigned. ... In the ruins of castles however, other countries may compare with ours. But in the remains of abbeys no country certainly can. ... But it is the mode of architecture, which gives such excellence to these ruins. The Gothic style, in which they are generally composed, is, I apprehend, unrivalled among foreign nations; and may be called a peculiar feature in English landscape....

The English architect however began, by degrees, to strike out a new mode of architecture for himself; without searching the continent for models. This is called the Gothic; but for what reason, it is hard to say: for the Goths, who were never in England, had been even forgotten, when it was reinvented; which was about the reign of Henry II. It is besides found no where, I believe, but in England; except in such parts of France, as were in possession of the English.

In this beautiful species of architecture the antiquarian points out three periods.

When it first appeared, the round Saxon arch began to change into the pointed one; and the short, clumsy pillar began to clutter: but still the Saxon heaviness in part prevailed. Salisbury-Cathedral, which was finished about the year 1250, is generally considered as a very pure Specimen of the Gothic, in its first, and ruder form.

By degrees improvements in architecture were introduced. The east-window being inlarged [sic], was trailed over with beautiful scraw-work; while the cluttered-pillar began to increase in height, and elegance; and to arch, and ramify along the roof. In short, an intire [sic] new mode of architecture, purely British, was introduced. The grandeur of the Roman – the heaviness of the Saxon – and the grotesque ornament of the Saracenic, were all equally replenished. An airy lightness pervaded the whole; and ornaments of a new invention took place. The cathedral of York, and part of Canterbury, among many others, are beautiful examples of this period of Gothic architecture.

About the time of the latter Henries, the last period began to obtain; in the architecture of which the flat, stone roof, and a variety of different ornaments were the chief characteristics. Of this inriched [sic] style King's college chapel in Cambridge, and Henry VIII's at Westminster, are two of the most elegant examples. The flat, stone roof is generally, even at this day, considered, as a wonderful effort of art. It is said, that Sir Christopher Wren himself could not conceive it. He would say, "Tell me where to place the first stone; and I will follow it with a second."

This style is generally considered as the perfection of Gothic architecture. I own, it rather appears to me the decline of the art. The ornaments, so affectedly introduced, and patched on; as the rose, and portcullis in King's college chapel, have not, in my eyes, the beauty of the middle style; in which every ornament rises naturally from the several members of the building; and makes a part of the pile itself. Nor has the flat roof, with all it's ornaments, in my opinion, the simplicity and beauty of the ribbed, and pointed one.

Abbeys formerly abounded so much in England, that a delicious valley could scarce be found, in which one of them was not stationed. The very states of many of these ancient edifices are now obliterated by the plough; yet still so many elegant ruins of this kind are left; that they may be called, not only one of the peculiar features of English landscape; but may be ranked also among it's most picturesque beauties (1.1.13-17).

Language, like light, is a medium; and the true philosophic stile, like light from a northern window, exhibits objects clearly, and distinctly, without soliciting attention to itself.

Some artists, when they give their imagination play, let it loose among uncommon scenes – such as perhaps never existed: whereas the nearer they approach the simple standard of nature in its beautiful forms, the more admirable their fictions will appear. It is thus in writing romances. The correct taste cannot bear those unnatural situations in which heroes and heroines are often placed, whereas a story *naturally* and, of course, affectingly told, either with pen or pencil, though known to be a fiction, is considered a transcript from nature; and takes possession of the heart. The *marvellous* disgusts the sober imagination: which is gratified only with the pure characters of nature.

3. Sentimental Heroines

[The following excerpts from contemporaneous fictional works indicate traditional literary representations of the sentimental heroine's musical, artistic and pet loving talents.]

a. Elizabeth Hervey *Louisa* (1790)

Musical accomplishments
Louisa modestly took Miss Bensley's place at the harpsichord; and after a prelude, which occasioned the tonnoesscurs to cast upon each other very significant looks, she executed the piece with such taste and justness, as astonished the rest of the performers. The room echoed with brava! brava! Everybody was delighted with the composition. ... Upon which she played a rondeaux, which enchanted them all; and everyone was desirous of knowing who composed it – but nothing further could be learned, than that it was the composition of a friend; and by a faint blush that over-spread her

cheek as she spoke, Mr. Melcomb suspected it was her own, which indeed was the case (1.82-83).

b. Charlotte Smith *Emmeline* (1788)

[*Emmeline* features repeatedly in Austen's *Juvenilia* as a favourite and suggests interesting links between those early writings and *Northanger Abbey*.]

Artistic skills
[The hero Delamere] "sat in unsupportable anxiety 'till she should summons the maid.

Her music book lay open on a *piano forte* in the breakfast parlour. A song which he had a few days before desired her to learn, as being one which particularly charmed him, seemed to have been just copied into it, and he fancied the notes and the writing were executed with more than her usual elegance. Under it was a little *porte feuille* of red morocco. Delamere took it up. It was untied; and two or three small tinted drawings fell out. He saw the likeness of Mrs. Stafford, done from memory; one yet more striking of his sister Augusta; and two or three unfinished resemblances of persons he did not know, touched with less spirit than the other two. A piece of silver paper doubled together enclosed another; he opened it – it was a drawing of himself, done with a pencil, and slightly tinged with a crayon; strikingly like; but it seemed unfinished, and somewhat effaced.

Though among so many other portraits, this could not be considered as a very flattering distinction, Delamere, on seeing it, was not master of his transports. He now believed Emmeline (whom he could never induce to own that her partiality for him exceeded the bounds of friendship) yet cherished in her heart a passion she would not avow" (115).

c. Helen Maria Williams *Julia* (1790)

Care for small creatures
Julia had "frequently been engaged in the very same business of rescuing flies from destruction; and, when she saw a worm lying in her path, had often conveyed it to a place of safety among the untrodden grass, to prevent its being crushed by some foot less careful than her own" (1.104-05).
. . .
"In her way she saw a young bird that was unable to fly, hopping on the pavement. A boy seized it, whom she bribed with a shilling to relinquish his prize, which she was taking home, when it escaped from her hand, and fell down the area of a house. She desired the servant, who attended her, to knock at the door; and a search was made for the little fugitive, but it could no where be found. Julia wrote the following lines on this incident."

Mistaken bird, ah, whither hast thou stray'd?
My friendly grasp, why eager to elude?
This hand was on thy pinion lightly laid,
And fear'd to hurt thee by a touch too rude.

Is there no foresight in a Thrush's breast,
That thou down yonder gulph from me would'st go?
That gloomy area lurking cats infest,
And there the dog may rove, alike thy foe.

I would with lavish crumbs my Bird have fed,
And bought a crystal cup to wet thy bill;
I would have made of down and moss thy bed,
Soft, though not fashion'd with a Thrush's skill.

Soon as thy strengthen'd wing could mount the sky,
My willing hand had set my captive free:
Ah, not for her, who loves the muse, to buy
A selfish pleasure, bought with pain to thee!

The vital air, and liberty, and light,
Had all been thine: and love and rapt'rous song,
And sweet parental joys, in rapid flight,
Had led the circle of thy life along.

Securely to my window hads't thou flown,
And ever thy accustom'd morsel found;
Nor should thy trusting breast the wants have known,
Which other Thrushes knew, when winter frown'd.

Fram'd with the wisdom Nature lent to thee,
Thy house of straw had brav'd the tempest's rage;
And thou, thro' many a spring, hadst liv'd to see
The utmost limit of a Thrush's age.

Ill-fated Bird! And does the Thrush's race,
Like Man's, mistake the path that leads to bliss:
Or, when his eye that tranquil path can trace,
The good he well discerns, thro' folly miss? (2.26-29).

Appendix D: Catherine Morland's Reading Material

1. Ann Radcliffe, *The Mysteries of Udolpho* (1794)

While imprisoned in her uncle Montoni's Castle of Udolpho Emily misses the way to her chamber. She and Annette, her Aunt's nervous and talkative maid, vainly search through a variety of room and passageways until they come upon a large gallery.

'How cold these rooms are, ma'amselle!' said Annette: 'nobody has lived in them for many, many years, they say. Do let us go.'

'They may open upon the great stair-case, perhaps,' said Emily, passing on till she came to a chamber, hung with pictures, and took the light to examine that of a soldier on horseback in a field of battle. – He was darting his spear upon a man, who lay under the feet of the horse, and who held up one hand in a supplicating attitude. The soldier, whose beaver was up, regarded him with a look of vengeance, and the countenance, with that expression, struck Emily as resembling Montoni. She shuddered, and turned from it. Passing the light hastily over several other pictures, she came to one concealed by a veil of black silk. The singularity of the circumstance struck her, and she stopped before it, wishing to remove the veil, and examine what could thus be carefully concealed, but somewhat wanting courage. 'Holy Virgin! what can this mean?' exclaimed Annette. 'This is surely the picture they told me of at Venice.'

'What picture?' said Emily. 'Why a picture – a picture,' replied Annette, hesitatingly – 'but I never could make out exactly what it was about, either.'

'Remove the veil, Annette.'

'What! I, ma'amselle! – I! not for the world!' Emily, turning round, saw Annette's countenance grow pale. 'And pray, what have you heard of this picture, to terrify you so, my good girl?' said she. 'Nothing, ma'amselle: I have heard nothing, only let us find our way out.'

'Certainly: but I wish first to examine the picture; take the light, Annette, while I lift the veil.' Annette took the light, and immediately walked away with it, disregarding Emily's calls to stay, who, not choosing to be left alone in the dark chamber, at length followed her. 'What is the reason of this Annette?' said Emily, when she overtook her, 'what have you heard concerning that picture, which makes you so unwilling to stay when I bid you?'

'I don't know what is the reason, ma'amselle,' replied Annette, 'nor any thing about the picture, only I have heard there is something very dreadful belonging to it – and that it has been covered up in black *ever since* and that nobody has looked at it for a great many years – and it somehow has to do with the owner of this castle before Signor Montoni came to the possession of it – and' –

'Well Annette,' said Emily, smiling, 'I perceive it is as you say – that you know nothing about the picture.'

'No, nothing, indeed, ma'amselle, for they made me promise never to tell: but' – (Vol 2, Ch 5, 232-33)

It may be remembered, that, in a chamber of Udolpho, hung a black veil, whose singular situation had excited Emily's curiosity, and which afterwards disclosed an object, that had overwhelmed her with horror; for, on lifting it, there appeared, instead of the picture she had expected, within a recess of the wall, a [waxen] human figure of ghastly paleness, stretched at its length, and dressed in the habiliments of the grave. What added to the horror of the spectacle, was, that the face appeared partly decayed and disfigured by worms, which were visible on the features and the hands (Vol 4, Ch 17).

Appendix E: Reviews of Northanger Abbey

1. *British Critic* n.s. 9 (March 1818): 293-301

In order to impart some degree of variety to our journal, and select matter suited to all tastes, we have generally made it a point to notice one or two of the better sort of novels; but, did our fair readers know, what a vast quantity of useful spirits and patience, we are for this purpose generally forced to exhaust, before we are able to stumble upon any thing that we can at all recommend to their approbation; what innumerable letters we are compelled to read from the witty Lady Harriet F— to the pathetic Miss Lucretia G—; through what an endless series of gloomy caverns, long and winding passages, secret trap doors, we are forced to pass – now in the Inquisition, now in a gay modern assembly – this moment in the east wing of an old castle in the Pyrenees; in the next, among banditti; and so on, through all the changes and chances of this transitory life, acquiescing in every thing, with an imperturbable confidence, that he or she, who has brought us into all these difficulties, will, in their own good time, release us from them: sure we are, that even the most resolute foes to all the solid parts of learning, will agree with us in admitting, that the sound and orthodox divinity with which so considerable a portion of our pages is usually filled, and of which we have so often had the mortification to hear many sensible young ladies complain, is nevertheless very far from being quite so dull and exhausting, as are their own favourite studies, when indiscriminately pursued. In return for this concession on their part, we on our's will frankly allow, that a good novel, such, for example, as that present before us, is, perhaps, among the most fascinating productions of modern literature, though we cannot say, that it is quite so improving as others.

Northanger Abbey and *Persuasion*, are the productions of a pen, from which our readers have already received several admired productions; and it is with most unfeigned regret, that we are forced to add, they will be the last. ...

With respect to the talents of Jane Austen, they need no other voucher, than the works which she has left behind her; which in some of the best qualities of the best sort of novels, display a degree of excellence that has not often been surpassed. In imagination, of all kinds, she appears to have been extremely deficient; not only her stories are utterly and entirely devoid of invention, but her characters, her incidents, her sentiments, are obviously all drawn exclusively from experience. The sentiments which she puts into the mouths of her actors, are the sentiments, which we are every day in the habit of hearing; and as to her actors themselves, we are persuaded that fancy, strictly so called, has had much less to do with them, than with the characters of Julius Caesar, Hannibal, or Alexander, as represented to us by historians. At description she seldom aims; at that vivid and poetical sort of description, which we have of late been accustomed to, (in the novels of a celebrated anonymous writer) never; she seems to have no other object in view, than simply to paint some of those scenes which she has herself seen, and which every one, indeed, may witness daily. Not only her characters are all of them belonging to the middle size, and with a tendency, in fact, rather to fall below, than to rise above the common standard, but even the incidents of her novels, are of the same description. Her heroes and heroines, make love and are married, just as her readers make love, and were or will be, married; no unexpected ill fortune occurs to prevent, nor any unexpected good fortune, to bring about the events on which her novels hinge. She seems to be describing such people as meet together every night, in every respectable house in London; and to relate such incidents as have probably happened, one time or another, to half the families in the United Kingdom. And yet, by a singular good judgment, almost every individual represents a class; not a class of humourists, or of any of the rarer specimens in our species, but one of those classes to which we ourselves, and every acquaintance we have, in all probability belong. The fidelity with which these are distinguished is often admirable. It would have been impossible to discriminate the characters of the common-place people, whom she employs as the instruments of her novels, by any set and formal descriptions; for the greater part of them, are such as we generally describe by saying that they are persons of 'no characters at all.' Accordingly our authoress gives no definitions; but she makes her *dramatis personæ* talk; and the sentiments which she places in their mouths, the little phrases which she makes them use, strike so familiarly upon our memory as soon as we hear them repeated, that we instantly recognize among some of our acquaintance, the sort of persons she intends to signify, as accurately as if we had heard their voices. This is the forte of our authoress; as soon as ever she leaves the shore of her own experience, and attempts to delineate fancy characters, or such as she may perhaps have often heard of, but possibly never seen, she falls at once to the level of the mere ordinary novellists [sic]. Her merit consists altogether in her remarkable talent for observation; no ridiculous phrase, no affected sentiment, no foolish pretension seems to escape her notice. It is scarcely possible to read her novels, without meeting with some of one's own absurdities reflected back upon one's conscience; and this, just in the light in which they ought to appear. For in recording the customs and manners of common-place people in the commonplace intercourse of life, our authoress never dips her pen in satire; the follies which she holds up to us, are, for the most part, mere follies, or else natural imperfections; and she treats them, as such, with good-humoured pleasantry; mimicking them so exactly, that we always laugh at the ridiculous truth of the imitation, but without ever being incited to indulge in feelings, that might tend to render us ill-natured, and intolerant in society. This is the result of that good sense which seems ever to keep complete possession over all the other qualities of the mind of our authoress; she sees every thing just as it is; even her want of imagination (which is the principal defect of her writings) is useful to her in this respect, that it enables her to keep clear of all exaggeration, in a mode of writing where the least exaggeration would be fatal; for if the people and the scenes which she has chosen, as the subjects of her composition, be not painted with perfect truth, with exact and striking resemblance, the whole effect ceases; her characters have no merit in themselves, and whatever interest they excite in the mind of the reader, results almost entirely, from the unaccountable pleasure, which, by a peculiarity in our nature, we derive from a simple imitation of any object, without any reference to the abstract value or importance of the object itself. This fact is notorious in painting; and the novels of Miss Austen alone, would be sufficient to prove, were proof required, that the same is true in the department of literature, which she has adorned. For our readers will perceive (from the instance which we are now about to present, in the case of the novels before us,) that be their merit what it may, it is not founded upon the interest of a narrative. In fact, so little narrative is there in either of the two novels of which the publication before us consists, that it is difficult to give any thing like an abstract of their contents. *Northanger Abbey*, which is the name of the first novel, is simply, the history of a young girl, the daughter of a country clergyman of respectability, educated at home, under the care of her parents; good kind of people, who taught their large family all that it was necessary for them to know, without apparently troubling themselves about accomplishments in learning of any kind, beyond what our fathers and mothers were instructed in. Our heroine is just such a person, as an education under such circumstances, would lead us to expect; with respect to the hero of the tale, (for every heroine must have a hero) that which fortunately threw one in the way of Catherine, was a journey to Bath which she happily made, in company with the lady of the manor, who was ordered to that place of fashionable resort, for the benefit of her health[1]. The first evening of Catherine's acquaintance with the gaiety of the Bath balls, was unpromising, from the circumstance that neither she, nor Mrs. Allen, her chaperon, had any knowledge of a single individual in the room; and the manner in which our authoress paints the effects of this circumstance upon the feelings and conversation of both, is sufficiently entertaining; but our heroine's second visit, was more favourable; for she was then introduced to a young clergyman, who is the other wheel upon which the interest of the narrative is made to run. The young clergyman's name was Tilney.

The description of our heroine's residence at Bath, is chiefly taken up with an account of her intimacy with a family of the name of Thorpe, consisting of a foolish mother, a foolish son, and four or five foolish daughters; the eldest of whom is a fine handsome girl, thinking of nothing but finery and flirting, and an exact representation of that large class of young women,

---

1   It is actually Mr Allen's poor health that prompts the trip to Bath.

in the form they assume among the gayer part of the middling ranks of society; for flirts, like all other parts of the animal kingdom, may be divided into two or three species. The character is pourtrayed with admirable spirit and humour; but the impression conveyed by it, is the result of so many touches, that it would be difficult to place it before our readers by means of extracts. During the time of our heroine's intimacy with this family, the acquaintance with Mr. Tilney goes on; he proves to be the son of a General Tilney, a proud rich man; but who, in consequence of misinformation respecting the circumstances and family of Catherine, acquiesces in Miss Tilney's request of inviting Catherine to pass a few weeks with them, at their family seat of Northanger Abbey. This visit forms the next and only remaining incident in the novel; the result of it was the marriage of Catherine with the son. The circumstance which principally renders the history of our heroine's residence at Northanger Abbey amusing, arises from the mistakes which she makes, in consequence of her imagination, (which had just come fresh from the *Mysteries of Udolpho*,) leading her to anticipate, that the Abbey which she was on the point of adorning by her presence, was to be of the same class and character, as those which Mrs. Radcliffe paints. On her arrival, she was, as may be supposed, a little disappointed, by the unexpected elegance, convenience, and other advantages of General Tilney's abode; but her prepossession was incurable.

Catherine, in a few days, was forced to resign all her hopes of discovering subterraneous passages, mysterious pictures, or old parchments; but, however, she still hoped to be able to detect a hidden secret, in the instance of the General, who having been an unkind husband to his late wife, and being, moreover, of a haughty and supercilious temper, she naturally concluded must have the weight of his wife's untimely end upon his conscience. A thousand little circumstances combined to give strength to her suspicions. But we have no room for extracts; if our readers wish to be entertained with the whole history of our heroine's mistakes in this way, we can safely recommend the work to their perusal. *Northanger Abbey*, is one of the very best of Miss Austen's productions, and will every way repay the time and trouble of perusing it. Some of the incidents in it are rather improbable, and the character of General Tilney seems to have been drawn from imagination, for it is not a very probable character, and is not pourtrayed with our authoress's usual taste and judgment.[1] There is also a considerable want of delicacy in all the circumstances of Catherine's visit to the Abbey; but it is useless to point them out;

---

1 Maria Edgeworth makes a similar comment in a private letter to Mrs Ruxton (21 Feb 1818): "The behaviour of the General in *Northanger Abbey*, packing off the young lady without a servant or the common civilities which any bear of a man, not to say gentleman, would have shown, is quite outrageously out of drawing and out of nature" (*Letters from England 1813-1844*.)

the interest of the novel, is so little founded upon the ingenuity or probability of the story, that any criticism upon the management of it, falls with no weight upon that which constitutes its appropriate praise, considered as a literary product. ...

2. "*Northanger Abbey* and *Persuasion*," *Blackwood's Edinburgh Magazine* n.s.2 (May 1818): 453-55

We are happy to receive two other novels from the pen of this amiable and agreeable authoress, though our satisfaction is much alloyed, from the feeling, that they must be the last. We have always regarded her works as possessing a higher claim to public estimation than perhaps they have yet attained. They have fallen, indeed, upon an age whose taste can only be gratified with the highest seasoned food. This, as we have already hinted, may be partly owing to the wonderful realities which it has been our lot to witness. We have been spoiled for the tranquil enjoyment of common interests, and nothing now will satisfy us in fiction, any more than in real life, but grand movements and striking characters. A singular union has, accordingly, been attempted between history, and poetry. The periods of great events have been seized on as a ground work for the display of powerful or fantastic characters: correct and instructive pictures of national peculiarities have been exhibited; and even in those fictions which are altogether wild and monstrous, some insight has been given into the passions and theories which have convulsed and bewildered this our 'age of Reason'. In the poetry of Mr Scott and Lord Byron, in the novels of Miss Edgeworth, Mr Godwin, and the author of *Waverley*, we see exemplified in different forms this influence of the spirit of the times, – the prevailing love of historical, and at the same time romantic incident, – dark and high-wrought passions, – the delineations, chiefly of national character, – the pursuit of some substance, in short, yet of an existence more fanciful often than absolute fiction, – the dislike of a cloud, yet the form which is embraced, nothing short of a Juno. In this raised state of our imaginations, we cannot, it may be supposed, all at once descend to the simple representations of common life, to incidents which have no truth, except that of universal nature, and have nothing of fiction except in not having really happened, – yet the time, probably, will return, when we shall take a more permanent delight in those familiar cabinet pictures, than even in the great historical pieces of our more eminent modern masters; when our sons and daughters will deign once more to laugh over the Partridges and the Trullibers, and to weep over the Clementinas and Clarissas of past times, as we have some distant recollection of having been able to do ourselves, before we were so entirely engrossed with the Napoleons of real life, or the Corsairs of poetry; and while we could enjoy a work that was all written in pure English, without ever dreaming how great would be the embellishment to have at least one half of it in the dialect of Scotland or of Ireland.

When this period arrives, we have no hesitation in saying, that the delightful writer of the works now before us, will be one of the most popular of English novelists, and if, indeed, we could point out the individual who, within a certain limited range, has attained the highest perfection of the art of novel writing, we should have little scruple in fixing upon her. She has confined herself, no doubt, to a narrow walk. She never operates among deep interests, uncommon characters, or vehement passions. The singular merit of her writings is, that we could conceive, without the slightest strain of imagination, any one of her fictions to be realised in any town or village in England, (for it is only English manners that she paints,) that we think we are reading the history of people whom we have seen thousands of times, and that with all this perfect commonness, both of incident and character, perhaps not one of her characters is to be found in any other book, portrayed at least in so lively and interesting a manner. She has much observation, – much fine sense, – much delicate humour, – many pathetic touches, – and throughout all her works, a most charitable view of human nature, and a tone of gentleness and purity that are almost unequalled. It is unnecessary to give a particular account of the stories here presented to us. They have quite the same kind of merit with the preceding works of their author. As stories they are nothing in themselves, though beautiful and simple in their combination with the characters. The first is the more lively, and the second the more pathetic; but such is the facility and the seemingly exhaustless invention of this lady, that, we think, like a complete mistress of a musical instrument, she could have gone on in the same strain forever, and her happy talent of seeing something to interest in the most common scenes of life, could evidently never have been without a field to work upon. But death has deprived us of this most fascinating companion, and the few prefatory pages which contain a sketch of her life, almost come upon us like the melancholy invitation to the funeral of one whom we had long known and loved....

Such was this admirable person, the character of whose life fully corresponds with that of her writings. There is the same good sense, happiness, and purity in both. Yet they will appear very defective to that class of readers who are constantly hunting after the broad display of religious sentiments and opinions. It has been left for this age to discover that Mr Addison himself was scarcely a Christian: but we are very certain, that neither the temper of his writings, nor even that of Miss Austen's, (novels as they are, and filled with accounts of balls and plays, and such abominations,) could well have been formed without a feeling of the spirit of Christianity.

3. *Gentleman's Magazine* 1,38 (July 1818): 52-53

The two novels now published have no connexion with each other. The characters in both are principally taken from the middle ranks of life, and are well supported. *Northanger Abbey*, however is decidedly preferable to the second Novel, not only in the incidents, but even in its moral tendency.

4. [Archbishop Richard Whately],[1] "*Northanger Abbey* and *Persuasion*," *Quarterly Review* 24 (January 1821): 352-76

The time seems to be past when an apology was requisite from reviewers for condescending to notice a novel; when they felt themselves bound in dignity to deprecate the suspicion of paying much regard to such trifles, and pleaded the necessity of occasionally stooping to humour the taste of their fair readers. The delights of fiction, if not more keenly or more generally relished, are at least more readily acknowledge by men of sense and taste; and we have lived to hear the merits of the best of this class of writings earnestly discussed by some of the ablest scholars and soundest reasoners of the present day.

We are inclined to attribute this change, not so much to an alteration in the public taste, as in the character of the productions in question. Novels may not, perhaps, display more genius than formerly, but they contain more solid sense; they may not afford higher gratification, but it is of a nature which men are less disposed to be ashamed of avowing. We remarked, in a former Number, in reviewing a work of the author now before us, that 'a new style of novel has arisen, within the last fifteen or twenty years, differing from the former in the points upon which the interest hinges; neither alarming our credulity nor amusing our imagination by wild variety of incident, or by those pictures of romantic affection and sensibility, which were formerly as certain attributes of fictitious characters as they are of rare occurrence among those who actually live and die. The substitute for these excitements, which had lost much of their poignancy by the repeated and injudicious use of them, was the art of copying from nature as she really exists in the common walks of life, and presenting to the reader, instead of the splendid scenes of an imaginary world, a correct and striking representation of that which is daily taking place around him.'[2]

Now, though the origin of this new school of fiction may probably be traced, as we there suggested, to the exhaustion of the mines from which materials for entertainment had been hitherto extracted, and the necessity of gratifying the natural craving of the reader for variety, by striking into an

---

1   This review is ascribed to Richard Whately (1787-1863), Archbishop of Dublin.

2   Cf. Unsigned review of *Emma* by Walter Scott in the *Quarterly Review* October 1815, issued March 1816, xiv, 188-201.

untrodden path; the consequences resulting from this change have been far greater than the mere supply of this demand. When this Flemish painting, as it were, is introduced – this accurate and unexaggerated delineation of events and characters – it necessarily follows, that a novel, which makes good its pretensions of giving a perfectly correct picture of common life, becomes a far more *instructive* work than one of equal or superior merit of the other class; it guides the judgment, and supplies a kind of artificial experience. It is a remark of the great father of criticism, that poetry (i.e. narrative, and dramatic poetry) is of a more philosophical character than history; inasmuch as the latter details what has actually happened, of which many parts may chance to be exceptions to the general rules of probability, and consequently illustrate no general principles; whereas the former shews us what must naturally, or would probably, happen under given circumstances; and thus displays to us a comprehensive view of human nature, and furnishes general rules of practical wisdom. It is evident, that this will apply only to such fictions as are quite *perfect* in respect of the probability of their story; and that he, therefore, who resorts to the fabulist rather than the historian, for instruction in human character and conduct, must throw himself entirely on the judgment and skill of his teacher, and give him credit for talents much more rare than the accuracy and veracity which are the chief requisites in history. We fear, therefore, that the exultation which we can conceive some of our gentle readers to feel, at having Aristotle's warrant for (what probably they have never dreamed of) the *philosophical character* of their studies, must, in practice, be somewhat qualified, by those sundry little violations of probability which are to be met with in most novels; and which so far lower their value, as models of real life, that a person who had no other preparation for the world than is afforded by them, would form, probably, a less accurate idea of things as they are, than he would of a lion from studying merely the representations on China tea-pots.

Accordingly, a heavy complaint has long lain against works of fiction, as giving a false picture of what they profess to imitate, and disqualifying their readers for the ordinary scenes and everyday duties of life. And this charge applies, we apprehend, to the generality of what are strictly called novels, with even more justice than to romances. When all the characters and events are very far removed from what we see round us, – when, perhaps, even supernatural agents are introduced, the reader may indulge, indeed, in occasional day-dreams, but will be so little reminded of what he has been reading, by any thing that occurs in actual life, that though he may perhaps feel some disrelish for the tameness of the scene before him, compared with the fairy-land he has been visiting, yet at least his judgment will not be depraved, nor his expectations misled; he will not apprehend a meeting with Algerine banditti on English shores, nor regard the old woman who shews him about an antique country seat, as either an enchantress or the keeper of an imprisoned damsel. But it is otherwise with those fictions which differ from common life in little or nothing but the improbability of the occurrences: the reader is insensibly led to calculate upon some of those lucky incidents and opportune coincidences of which he has been so much accustomed to read, and which, it is undeniable, *may* take place in real life; and to feel a sort of confidence, that however romantic his conduct may be, and in whatever difficulties it may involve him, all will be sure to come right at last, as is invariably the case with the hero of a novel. ...

The change, however, which we have already noticed, as having taken place in the character of several modern novels, has operated in a considerable degree to do away this prejudice: and has elevated this species of composition, in some respects at least, into a much higher class. For most of that instruction which used to be presented to the world in the shape of formal dissertations, or shorter and more desultory moral essays, such as those of the Spectator and Rambler, we may now resort to the pages of the acute and judicious, but not less amusing, novelists who have lately appeared. If their views of men and manners are no less just than those of the essayists who preceded them, they are to be rated lower because they present to us these views, not in the language of general description, but in the form of well-constructed fictitious narrative? If the practical lessons they inculcate are no less sound and useful, it is surely no diminution of their merit that they are conveyed by example instead of precept: nor, if their remarks are neither less wise nor less important, are they the less valuable for being represented as thrown out in the course of conversations suggested by the circumstances of the speakers, and perfectly in character. The praise and blame of the moralist are surely not the less effectual for being bestowed, not in general declamation, on classes of men, but on individuals representing those classes, who are so clearly delineated and brought into action before us, that we seem to be acquainted with them, and feel an interest in their fate.

Biography is allowed, on all hands, to be one of the most attractive and profitable kinds of reading: now such novels as we have been speaking of, being a kind of fictitious biography, bear the same relation to the real, that epic and tragic poetry, according to Aristotle, bear to history: they present us (supposing, of course, each perfect in its kind) with the general, instead of the particular, – the probable, instead of the true; and, by leaving out those accidental irregularities, and exceptions to general rules, which constitute the many improbabilities of real narrative, present us with a clear and *abstracted* view of the general rules themselves; and thus concentrate, as it were, into a small compass, the net result of wide experience.

Among the authors of this school there is no one superior, if equal, to the lady whose last production is now before us, and whom we have much regret in finally taking leave of: her death (in the prime of life, considered as a writer) being announced in this the first publication to which her name is prefixed. We regret the failure not only of a source of innocent amusement, but also of that supply of practical good sense and instructive example, which she would probably have continued to furnish better than any of her contemporaries: – Miss Edgeworth, indeed, draws characters and details conversations, such as they occur in real life, with a spirit and fidelity not to be surpassed; but her stories are most romantically improbable, (in the sense above explained,) almost all the important events of them being brought about by most *providential* coincidences; and this, as we have already remarked, is not merely faulty, inasmuch as it evinces a want of skill in the writer, and gives an air of clumsiness to the fiction, but is a very considerable drawback on its practical utility: the personages either of fiction or history being then only profitable examples, when their good or ill conduct meets its appropriate reward, not from a sort of independent machinery of accidents, but as a necessary or probable result, according to the ordinary course of affairs. Miss Edgeworth also is somewhat too avowedly didactic: that seems to be true of her, which the French critics, in the extravagance of their conceits, attributed to Homer and Virgil; viz. that they first thought of a moral, and then framed a fable to illustrate it; she would, we think, instruct more successfully, and she would, we are sure, please more frequently, if she kept the design of teaching more out of sight, and did not so glaringly press every circumstance of her story, principal or subordinate, into the service of a principle to be inculcated, or information to be given. A certain portion of moral instruction must accompany every well-invented narrative. Virtue must be represented as producing, at the long run, happiness; and vice, misery; and the accidental events, that in real life interrupt this tendency, are anomalies which, though true individually, are as false generally as the accidental deformities which vary the average outline of the human figure. They would be as much out of place in a fictitious narrative, as a wen[1] in an academic model. But any *direct* attempt at moral teaching, and any attempt whatever to give scientific information, will, we fear, unless managed with the utmost discretion, interfere with what, after all, is the immediate and peculiar object of the novelist, as of the poet, *to please*. If instruction do not join as a volunteer, she will do no good service. ...

Miss Austin has the merit (in our judgment most essential) of being evidently a Christian writer: a merit which is much enhanced, both on the score of good taste, and of practical utility, by her religion being not at all obtrusive. She might defy the most fastidious critic to call any of her novels, (as Cœlebs was designated, we will not say altogether without reason,) a 'dramatic sermon.' The subject is rather alluded to, and that incidentally, than studiously brought forward and dwelt upon. In fact she is more sparing of it than would be thought desirable by some persons; perhaps even by herself, had she consulted merely her own sentiments; but she probably introduced it as far as she thought would be generally acceptable and profitable: for when the purpose of inculcating a religious principle is made too palpably prominent, many readers, if they do not throw aside the book with disgust,

---

[1] A blemish, ulcer, or spot. Imperfection of classical form or line.

are apt to fortify themselves with that respectful sort of apathy with which they undergo a regular sermon, and prepare themselves as they do to swallow a dose of medicine, endeavouring to *get it down* in large gulps, without tasting it more than is necessary.

The moral lessons also of this lady's novels, though clearly and impressively conveyed, are not offensively put forward, but spring incidentally from the circumstances of the story; they are not forced upon the reader, but he is left to collect them (though without any difficulty) for himself: her's is that unpretending kind of instruction which is furnished by real life; and certainly no author has ever conformed more closely to real life, as well in the incidents, as in the characters and descriptions. Her fables appear to us to be, in their own way, nearly faultless; they do not consist (like those of some of the writers who have attempted this kind of common-life novel writing) of a string of unconnected events which have little or no bearing on one main plot, and are introduced evidently for the sole purpose of bringing in characters and conversations; but have all that compactness of plan and unity of action which is generally produced by a sacrifice of probability: yet they have little or nothing that is not probable; the story proceeds without the aid of extraordinary accidents; the events which take place are the necessary or natural consequences of what has preceded; and yet (which is a very rare merit indeed) the final catastrophe is scarcely ever clearly foreseen from the beginning, and very often comes, upon the generality of readers at least, quite unexpected. We know not whether Miss Austin ever had access to the precepts of Aristotle; but there are few, if any, writers of fiction who have illustrated them more successfully.

The vivid distinctness of description, the minute fidelity of detail, and air of unstudied ease in the scenes represented, which are no less necessary than probability of incident, to carry the reader's imagination along with the story, and give fiction the perfect appearance of reality, she possesses in a high degree; and the object is accomplished without resorting to those deviations from the ordinary plan of narrative in the third person, which have been patronized by some eminent masters. We allude to the two other methods of conducting a fictitious story, viz. either by narrative in the first person, when the hero is made to tell his own tale, or by a series of letters; both of which we conceive have been adopted with a view of heightening the resemblance of the fiction to reality. At first sight, indeed, there might appear no reason why a story told in the first person should have more the air of a real history than in the third; especially as the majority of real histories actually are in the third person; nevertheless, experience seems to show that such is the case: provided there be no want of skill in the writer, the resemblance to real life, of a fiction thus conducted, will approach much the nearest (other points being equal) to a deception, and the interest felt in it, to that which we feel in real transactions. ...

Miss Austin, though she has in a few places introduced letters with great effect, has on the whole conducted her novels on the ordinary plan, describing, without scruple, private conversations and uncommunicated feelings: but she has not been forgetful of the important maxim, so long ago illustrated by Homer, and afterwards enforced by Aristotle, of saying as little as possible in her own person, and giving a dramatic air to the narrative, by introducing frequent conversations; which she conducts with a regard to character hardly exceeded even by Shakspeare [sic] himself. Like him, she shows as admirable a discrimination in the characters of fools as of people of sense; a merit which is far from common. To invent, indeed, a conversation full of wisdom or of wit, requires that the writer should himself possess ability; but the converse does not hold good: it is no fool that can describe fools well; and many who have succeeded pretty well in painting superior characters, have failed in giving individuality to those weaker ones, which it is necessary to introduce in order to give a faithful representation of real life: they exhibit to us mere folly in the abstract, forgetting that to the eye of a skilful naturalist the insects on a leaf present as wide differences as exist between the elephant and the lion. Slender, and Shallow, and Aguecheek, as Shakspeare has painted them, though equally fools, resemble one another no more than Richard and Macbeth, and Julius Cæsar; and Miss Austin's Mrs. Bennett, Mr. Rushworth, and Miss Bates, are no more alike than her Darcy, Knightley, and Edmund Bertram. Some have complained, indeed, of finding her fools too much like nature, and consequently tiresome; there is no disputing about tastes; all we can say is, that such critics must (whatever deference they may outwardly pay to received opinions) find the *Merry Wives of Windsor* and *Twelfth Night* very tiresome; and that those who look with pleasure at Wilkie's pictures, or those of the Dutch school, must admit that excellence of imitation may confer attraction on that which would be insipid or disagreeable in the reality.

Her minuteness of detail has also been found fault with; but even where it produces, at the time, a degree of tediousness, we know not whether that can justly be reckoned a blemish, which is absolutely essential to a very high excellence. Now, it is absolutely impossible, without this, to produce that thorough acquaintance with the characters, which is necessary to make the reader heartily interested in them. Let any one cut out from the Iliad or from Shakspeare's plays every thing (we are far from saying that either might not lose some parts with advantage, but let him reject every thing) which is absolutely devoid of importance and of interest *in itself*; and he will find what is left will have lost more than half its charms. We are convinced that some writers have diminished the effect of their works by being scrupulous to admit nothing into them which had not some absolute, intrinsic, and independent merit. They have acted like those who strip off the leaves of a fruit tree, as being of themselves good for nothing, with the view of securing more nourishment to the fruit, which in fact cannot attain its full maturity and flavour without them. ...

To say the truth, we suspect one of Miss Austin's great merits in our eyes to be, the insight she gives us into the peculiarities of female character. Authoresses can scarcely ever forget the esprit de corps – can scarcely ever forget that they *are authoresses.* They seem to feel a sympathetic shudder at exposing naked a female mind. Elles se peignent en buste, and leave the mysteries of womanhood to be described by some interloping male, like Richardson or Marivaux, who is turned out before he has seen half the rites, and is forced to spin from his own conjectures the rest. Now from this fault Miss Austin is free. Her heroines are what one knows women must be, though one never can get them to acknowledge it. As liable to 'fall in love first,' as anxious to attract the attention of agreeable men, as much taken with a striking manner, or a handsome face, as unequally gifted with constancy and firmness, as liable to have their affections biassed by convenience or fashion, as we, on our part, will admit men to be. ...

But we must proceed to the publication of which the title is prefixed to this article. It contains, it seems, the earliest and the latest productions of the author; the first of them having been purchased, we are told, many years back by a bookseller, who, for some reason unexplained, thought proper to alter his mind and withhold it. We do not much applaud his taste; for though it is decidedly inferior to her other works, having less plot, and what there is, less artificially wrought up, and also less exquisite nicety of moral painting; yet the same kind of excellences which characterise the other novels may be perceived in this, in a degree which would have been highly creditable to most other writers of the same school, and which would have entitled the author to considerable praise, had she written nothing better.

We already begin to fear, that we have indulged too much in extracts, and we must save some room for *Persuasion,* or we could not resist giving a specimen of John Thorpe, with his horse that *cannot* go less than 10 miles an hour, his refusal to drive his sister 'because she has such thick ankles,' and his sober consumption of five pints of port a day; altogether the best portrait of a species, which, though almost extinct cannot yet be quite classed among the Palæotheria, the Bang-up Oxonian. Miss Thorpe, the jilt of middling life, is, in her way, quite as good, though she has not the advantage of being the representative of a rare or a diminishing species. We fear few of our readers, however they may admire the naiveté, will admit the truth of poor John Morland's[1] postscript, 'I can never expect to know such another woman.'...

On the whole, Miss Austin's works may safely be recommended, not only as among the most unexceptional of their class, but as combining, in an eminent degree, instruction with amusement, though without the direct effort at the former, of which we have complained, as sometimes defeating its object. For those who cannot, or will not, *learn* any thing from productions of

1   Should read James Morland.

this kind, she has provided entertainment which entitles her to thanks; for mere innocent amusement is in itself a good, when it interferes with no greater; especially as it may occupy the place of some other that may *not* be innocent. The Eastern monarch who proclaimed a reward to him who should discover a new pleasure, would have deserved well of mankind had he stipulated that it should be blameless. Those, again, who delight in the study of human nature, may improve in the knowledge of it, and in the profitable application of that knowledge, by the perusal of such fictions as those before us.

Appendix F: Map of Bath, circa 1800.

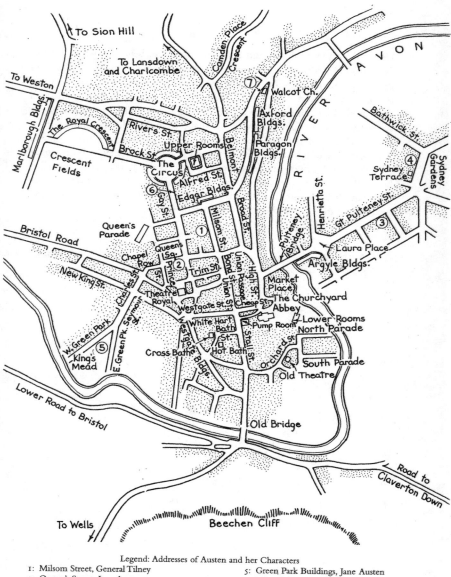

Legend: Addresses of Austen and her Characters

1: Milsom Street, General Tilney
2: Queen's Street, Jane Austen
3: Pulteney Street, the Allens and Catherine Morland
4: Sydney Terrace, Jane Austen
5: Green Park Buildings, Jane Austen
6: Edgar Buildings, the Thorpes
7: Walcot Church

Appendix G: Day Trips from Bath

[Austen's accurate information about the distances between destinations in *Northanger Abbey* provides further clues about individual characters. The astute reader understands that the Tilneys' projected day trip from Bath to Wick Rocks or Claverton Downs is far more sensible and practical than Thorpe's own overly long trip to Blaise Castle and Kingsweston. Thorpe not only exaggerates his horse's physical prowess but also misjudges the time required for each outing such that the desired destination is seldom reached. General Tilney, on the other hand, micromanages the return journey to Northanger Abbey to suit his own gustatory appetite. Catherine complains that the party had a three-hour refreshment break at Petty France, some fourteen miles north of Bath, despite a substantial breakfast in Bath, before resuming the final fifteen-mile leg of the trip to Northanger Abbey.]

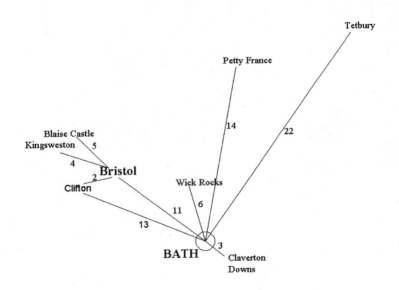

Appendix H: Map of South West England, circa 1856

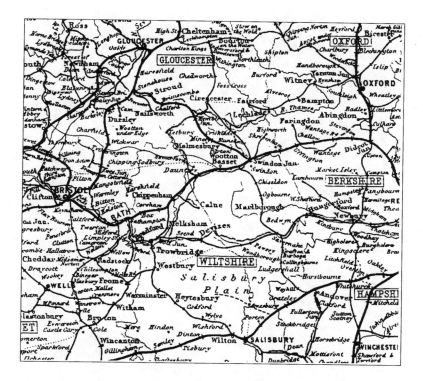

Ordnance Survey Map of South-West England showing major journeys in *Northanger Abbey*

Distance in miles:

Fullerton Junction – Salisbury	19	Oxford – Tetbury	41
– Oxford	50	– Walcot Church	62
– Bath	57	– Bath	63
– Northanger Abbey	70	Bath – Petty France	14
		– Northanger Abbey	30

Appendix I: Frontispiece to the 1833 edition of Northanger Abbey

Appendix J: Horse-Drawn Transportation

[William Felton's *Treatise on Carriages* (1794) was an immediate success and testifies to the "increasing coach production" of the late 18th century as a "profitable branch of British commerce well into the mid-19th century" (1.i). He notes "that many more gentlemen amused themselves in getting carriages built than in building houses" (1.iv) and it is easy to picture the consumerist General Tilney delightedly perusing the two-volumes which provide extensive details about the design, the cost and possible accoutrements of the various carriages.

Much like automobiles today, carriages acted as status symbols and indicated much about the owner. Although John Thorpe lies to Catherine about seeing Henry Tilney in a "Phaeton with bright chestnuts" he accurately imagines the appropriate mode of transportation for the Tilneys while in town. When boasting to an uncomprehending Catherine about his own second-hand gig – "curricle-hung you see; seat, trunk, sword case, splashing board, lamps, silver moulding" – he actually reveals his limited business acumen since Felton's *Treatise* indicates he paid the going rate.]

1. **Chaise and Four:** "A Post-Chaise, for travelling with on the continent, requires, like the coach, to be built strong, and furnished with conveniences suitable for the journey" (2. 60). Felton indicates that prices begin around £177.10.6. for the Travelling Post-Chaise and £201.1.6. for the Travelling Coach. He further notes that "nothing contributes more to fashion or grandeur, than a good display of ornaments about a carriage, of which there are a great variety of patterns; but, in this, neatness with elegance is to be regarded, as the expence which may be added above the former description increases the price to almost double that of a plain coach" (2. 35).

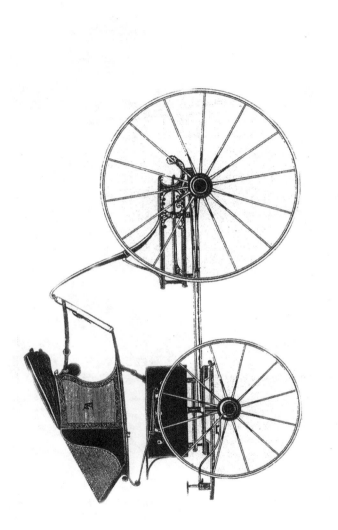

2. **Phaeton:** Described "as the most pleasant sort of carriage in use, as they contribute, more than any other, to health, amusement, and fashion, with the superior advantage of lightness, over every other sort of four-wheeled carriages, and are much safer, and more easy to ride in, than those of two wheels (2.68). Felton lists Phaeton prices ranging from £174.10.0. to £92.19.0.

3. Curricle: The Curricle is "a superior kind of two-wheeled carriage" normally drawn by two horses abreast and listed at £103.5.0. (Felton 2.94, 101).

4. Gig: "Gigs are one-horse chaises, of various patterns, devised according to the fancy of the occupier" and listed at £57.5.6 (Felton 2. 107, 109).

Works Cited/Recommended Reading

Anderson, Walter E. "From Northanger to Woodston: Catherine's Education to Common Life." *Philological Quarterly* 63:4 (Fall 1984):493-509.

Austen, Jane. *Minor Works.* Ed. R.W. Chapman. Oxford: Oxford UP, 1954.

———. *Jane Austen's Letters to Her Sister Cassandra and Others.* Ed. R.W. Chapman. 2 vols. Oxford: Clarendon Press, 1932.

———. *Selected Letters, 1796-1817.* Ed. R.W. Chapman. Oxford: Oxford UP, 1955.

———. *The Novels of Jane Austen: The Text based on Collation of the Early Editions.* Ed. R.W. Chapman. 5 vols. London: Oxford UP, 1952.

———. *Shorter Works.* London: The Folio Society, 1975.

———. *Northanger Abbey, Lady Susan, The Watsons, and Sanditon.* Ed. John Davie. Oxford: Oxford UP, 1988.

———. *Northanger Abbey.* Intro. Margaret Drabble. London: Virago, 1989.

Austen-Leigh, James Edward. *A Memoir of Jane Austen.* London: Bentley, 1871.

———. *A Memoir of Jane Austen.* Ed. R.W. Chapman. Oxford UP: Oxford, 1926 rep. 1951.

Austen-Leigh, Richard A. *Austen Papers 1704-1856.* London, 1870-71.

———. *Austen Papers, 1704-1856.* Colchester: Spottiswoode, Ballantyne, 1942.

Austen-Leigh, William, Richard Austen-Leigh and Deirdre Le Faye. *Jane Austen: A Family Record.* London: The British Library, 1989.

Axelrad, Arthur M. "Jane Austen's 'Susan' Restored." *Persuasions: Journal of the Jane Austen Society of North America* 15:1 (Dec 1993): 44-45.

Bander, Elaine. "*Sanditon, Northanger Abbey,* and *Camilla*: Back to the Future?" *Persuasions: Journal of the Jane Austen Society of North America.* 19 (Dec 1997): 195-204.

Barbauld, Anna Laetitia. *The British Novelists; with an Essay and Prefaces, Biographical and Critical.* London: F.C. and J. Rivington, 1810.

Barrett, Eaton Stannard. *The Heroine.* London: Henry Colburn, 1813.

Bennett, John. *Letters to a Young Lady.* Warrington: The Author, 1789.

Brook, Christopher. *Jane Austen: Illusion and Reality.* Cambridge: Brewer, 1999.

Brownstein, Rachel M. "*Northanger Abbey, Sense and Sensibility, Pride and Prejudice.*" *The Cambridge Companion to Jane Austen.* Ed. Edward Copeland and Juliet McMaster. Cambridge: Cambridge UP, 1997. 32-57.

———. *Becoming a Heroine: Reading about Women in Novels.* New York: Viking Press, 1982.

Burlin, Katrin R. "At the Crossroads: Sister Authors and Sister Arts." *Fetter'd or Free: British Women Novelists 1670-1815.* Ed. Mary Anne Schofield and Cecilia Macheski. Athens, Ohio: Ohio UP, 1986. 60-84.

Butler, Marilyn. *Romantics, Rebels and Reactionaries: English Literature and its Background 1760-1830.* Oxford: Oxford UP, 1981.

———. *Jane Austen and the War of Ideas*. Oxford: Clarendon Press, 1987.

Casal, Elvira. "Motherhood and Reality in *Northanger Abbey*." *Persuasions: Journal of the Jane Austen Society of North America*. 20 (1998): 147–53.

Castellanos, Gabriela. *Laughter, War and Feminism: Elements of Carnival in Three of Jane Austen's Novels*. New York: Peter Lang, 1994.

Cohen, Paula Marantz. "Jane Austen's Rejection of Rousseau: A Novelistic and Feminist Initiation". *Papers on Language and Literature*. Edwardsville, IL. 30:3 (Summer 1994): 215–34.

Collins, Irene. "The Rev. Henry Tilney, Rector of Woodston." *Persuasions: Journal of the Jane Austen Society of North America*. 20 (1998): 154–64.

Conger, Syndy McMillen. "Austen's Sense and Radcliffe's Sensibility." *Gothic* 2 (1987):16–24.

Daniels, Stephen and Charles Watkins. *The Picturesque Landscape: Visions of Georgian Herefordshire*. Nottingham: University of Nottingham and Hereford City Art Gallery, 1994.

Dozier, Robert. *For King, Constitution and Country: the English Loyalists and the French Revolution*. Lexington: University Press of Kentucky, 1983.

Dussinger, John A. "Parents Against Children: General Tilney as Gothic Monster." *Persuasions: Journal of the Jane Austen Society of North America*. 20 (1998): 165–74.

Dwyer, June. *Jane Austen*. New York: Continuum, 1989.

Edgeworth, Maria. *Letters from England 1813-1844*. Ed. Christina Colvin. Oxford: Clarendon Press, 1971.

Erickson, Lee. "The Economy of Novel Reading: Jane Austen and the Circulating Library." *Studies in English Literature-1500-1900* 30:4 (Autumn 1990): 573–90.

Evans, Mary. *Jane Austen and the State*. London: Tavistock, 1987.

Felton, William. *Treatise on Carriages: Supplement Comprehending all the Necessary Repairs; with Instructions how to Preserve and Purchase all Kinds of Carriages and Harness, with the Price Annexed*. London, 1794.

Fergus, Jan. *Jane Austen: A Literary Life*. New York: St. Martin's, 1991.

Fordyce, James. *Sermons to Young Women*. London: Millar, Cadell, Dodsley and Payne, 1766.

Gay, John. *Fables*. London, 1727.

Gilbert, Sandra M., and Susan Gubar. *The Madwoman in the Attic: The Woman Writer and the Nineteenth-Century Literary Imagination*. New Haven: Yale UP, 1979.

Graham, Kenneth W. "The Case of the Petulant Patriarch." *Persuasions: Journal of the Jane Austen Society of North America*. 20 (1998): 119–34.

Halperin, John, ed. *Jane Austen: Bicentenary Essays*. Cambridge: Cambridge UP, 1975.

———. *Jane Austen: Her Life*. London: Macmillan, 1984.

Handley, Graham. *Jane Austen*. London: Bristol Classical Press, 1992.

Hardy, Barbara. *A Reading of Jane Austen*. London: Owen, 1975.

Harding, D. W. *Regulated Hatred and Other Essays on Jane Austen*. Ed. Monica

Lawlor. London: Athlone Press, 1998.

Hays, Mary. *Memoirs of Emma Courtney*. Ed. Eleanor Ty. Oxford: Oxford UP, 1996.

———. *Letters and Essays, Moral and Miscellaneous*. London, 1793.

Hervey, Elizabeth. *Louisa*. Dublin: P. Wogan, 1790.

Hoeveler, Diane. "Vindicating *Northanger Abbey*: Mary Wollstonecraft, Jane Austen, and Gothic Feminism." *Jane Austen and Discourses of Feminism*. Ed. Devoney Looser. New York: St. Martin's, 1995. 117-35.

Honan, Park. *Jane Austen: Her Life*. New York: St. Martin's, 1987.

Horwitz, J. Barbara. *Jane Austen and the Question of Women's Education*. New York: Peter Lang, 1991.

Hunt, Linda C. "A Woman's Portion: Jane Austen and the Female Character." *Fetter'd or Free? British Women Novelists 1670-1815*. Ed. Mary Anne Schofield and Cecilia Macheski. Athens, Ohio: Ohio UP, 1986. 8-28.

Jerinic, Maria. "In Defense of the Gothic: Rereading *Northanger Abbey*." *Jane Austen and Discourses of Feminism*. Ed. Devoney Looser. New York: St. Martin's, 1995. 137-49.

Johnson, Claudia L. *Jane Austen: Women, Politics, and the Novel*. Chicago: University of Chicago Press, 1988.

Justice, George. "*Northanger Abbey* as Anti-Courtship Novel." *Persuasions: Journal of the Jane Austen Society of North America*. 20 (1998): 185-195.

Kelly, Gary. "Jane Austen and the English Novel of the 1790's." *Fetter'd or Free: British Women Novelists 1670-1815*. Ed. Mary Anne Schofield and Cecilia Macheski. Athens, Ohio: Ohio UP, 1986. 285-306.

Kern, Jean B. "The Old Maid, or 'to grow old, and be poor, and laughed at'." *Fetter'd or Free: British Women Novelists 1670-1815*. Ed. Mary Anne Schofield and Cecilia Macheski. Athens, Ohio: Ohio UP, 1986. 201-214.

Kindred, Sheila. "From Puppet to Person: The Development of Catherine's Character in the Bath Chapters of *Northanger Abbey*." *Persuasions: Journal of the Jane Austen Society of North America*. 20 (1998): 196-206.

Kirkham, Margaret. *Jane Austen, Feminism and Fiction*. Sussex: Harvester Press, 1983.

Knox Shaw, Peter. "*Northanger Abbey* and the Liberal Historians." *Essays in Criticism*. 49:4 (Oct 1999): 319-43.

Lamont, Claire. "Jane Austen's Gothic Architecture." *Exhibited by Candlelight: Sources and Developments in the Gothic Tradition*. Ed. Valeria Tinkler-Villani, Peter Davidson and Jane Stevenson. Amsterdam: Rodopi, 1995. 107-15

Lane, Maggie. "The French Bread at Northanger." *Persuasions: Journal of the Jane Austen Society of North America*. 20 (1998): 135-45.

———. *Jane Austen Society Collected Reports 1976-1985*. Jane Austen Society: London, 1989.

———. *Jane Austen's Family: Through Five Generations*. London: Robert Hale, 1984.

Lang, Susan. "Converging (or Colliding) Traditions: Integrating Hypertext into Literary Studies." *Texts and Textuality: Textual Instability, Theory, and*

Interpretation. Ed. Philip Cohen. New York: Garland, 1997. 291-312

Lau, Beth. "Madeline at *Northanger Abbey*: Keats's Anti-Romances and Gothic Satire." *Journal of English and Germanic Philology.* 84:1 (Jan 1985): 30-50.

Le Faye, Deirdre, ed. *Jane Austen's Letters.* Oxford: Oxford UP, 1997.

Litvak, Joseph. "Charming Men, Charming History." *On Your Left: The New Historical Materialism.* Ed. Ann Kibbey, Thomas Foster, Carol Siegel and Ellen E. Berry. New York: New York UP, 1996. 248-74.

Lodge, David. *Small World: An Academic Romance.* New York: Macmillan, 1984.

Looser, Devoney. "Reading Jane Austen and Rewriting 'Herstory'." *British Women Writers and the Writing of History, 1670-1820.* Baltimore: Johns Hopkins UP, 2000. 178-203.

———. "(Re)Making History and Philosophy: Austen's *Northanger Abbey*." *European Romantic Review* 4:1 (Summer 1993): 34-56.

Loveridge, Mark. "Northanger Abbey: Or, Nature and Probability." *Nineteenth Century Literature.* Berkeley: U of California Press 56:1 (June 1991): 1-29

Malina, Debra. "Rereading the Patriarchal Text: *The Female Quixote, Northanger Abbey*, and the Trace of the Absent Mother." *Eighteenth-Century Fiction.* 8:2 (Jan 1996): 271-92.

McMaster, Juliet. "Clothing the Thought in the Word: The Speakers of *Northanger Abbey*." *Persuasions: Journal of the Jane Austen Society of North America.* 20 (1998): 207-21.

Merrett, Robert. "Consuming Modes in *Northanger Abbey*: Jane Austen's Economic View of Literary Nationalism." *Persuasions: Journal of the Jane Austen Society of North America.* 20 (1998): 222-35.

Minma, Shinobu "General Tilney and Tyranny: *Northanger Abbey*." *Eighteenth-Century Fiction.* 8:4 (July 1996): 503-18.

Moers, Ellen. *Literary Women.* Garden City, New York: Doubleday, 1976.

Monaghan, David. Ed. "'Real Solemn History' and Social History" *Jane Austen in a Social Context.* New Jersey: Barnes and Noble, 1981. 86-104.

More, Hannah. *Strictures on the Modern System of Female Education.* London,: T. Cadell and W. Davies, 1799.

Morris, Eileen. "Jane Austen's Hidden Message to a Publisher." *Persuasions: Journal of the Jane Austen Society of North America* 16, 4 (Dec 1982): 16-17.

Morrison, Paul. "Enclosed in Openness: Northanger Abbey and the Domestic Carceral." *Texas Studies in Literature and Language* 33:1 (Spring 1991): 1-23.

Moss, Thomas. *Poems on Several Occasions.* Wolverhampton, 1769.

Mudrick, Marvin. *Jane Austen: Irony as Defense and Discovery.* Princeton and London: Princeton UP, 1952

Nardin, Jane. "Children and their Families in Jane Austen's Novels." *Jane Austen: New Perspectives, Women and Literature.* Ed. Janet M. Todd. New York: Holmes and Meier, 1983. 73-87.

Neill, Edward. "The Secret of *Northanger Abbey*." *Essays in Criticism.* 47:1 (Jan 1997): 13-32.

Noizet, Pascale. "L'Amour moderne: De tradition en transgression ou ... la féminité en question." *Tangence.* 47 (Mar 1995): 8-20.

Nollen, Elizabeth Mahn. "Female Detective Figures in British Fiction: Coping with Madness and Imprisonment." *Clues: A Journal of Detection* 15:2 (Fall-Winter 1994): 39-49

Oh, Jung hwa. "Catherine Morland and Henry Tilney: Two Readers in *Northanger Abbey*." *The Journal of English Language and Literature*. Seoul, Korea. 40:4 (Winter 1994): 657-74.

Opie, Amelia. *Adeline Mowbray*. Ed. Shelley King and John Pierce. Oxford; Oxford UP, 1999.

Paulson, Ronald. "Gothic Fiction and the French Revolution." *ELH*. 48:3 (Fall 1981): 532-54.

Perez Gallego, Candido. "Dos dimensiones estilisticas de Jane Austen." *Revista Canaria de Estudios Ingleses*. 22-23 (Apr-Nov 1991): 9-21.

Poovey, Mary. *The Proper Lady and the Woman Writer: Ideology as Style in the Works of Mary Wollstonecraft, Mary Shelley and Jane Austen*. Chicago: U of Chicago Press, 1984.

Radcliffe, Ann. *The Mysteries of Udolpho*. Ed. Bonamy Dobrée. Oxford; Oxford UP, 1980.

——. *The Romance of the Forest*. Ed. Chloe Chard. Oxford: Oxford UP, 1986.

Ray, Joan Klingel. "Austen's *Northanger Abbey*." *Explicator*. 54:3 (Spring 1996): 142-44.

Reid-Walsh, Jacqueline. "'Entering the World' of Regency Society: the Ballroom Scenes in *Northanger Abbey, The Watsons* and *Mansfield Park*." *Persuasions: Journal of the Jane Austen Society of North America*. 16 (Dec 1994): 115-24.

Richardson, Samuel. *Sir Charles Grandison*. Ed. Joselyn Harris. London: Oxford UP, 1972.

Roberts, Bette B. "The Horrid Novels: *The Mysteries of Udolpho* and *Northanger Abbey*." *Gothic Fictions: Prohibition/Transgression*. Ed. Kenneth W. Graham. New York: AMS, 1989. 89-III.

Roberts, Marilyn. "Adapting Jane Austen's *Northanger Abbey*: Catherine Morland as Gothic Heroine." *Nineteenth-Century Women at the Movies: Adapting Classic Women's Fiction to Film*. Ed. Barbara Tepa Lupack. Bowling Green, OH: Popular, 1999. 129-39.

Roberts, Warren. *Jane Austen and the French Revolution*. New York: St. Martin's Press, 1979.

Rousseau, G.S. "Pineapples, Pregnancy, Pica and *Peregrine Pickle Tobias Smollett: Bicentennial Essays*. Ed. G. S. Rousseau and P.G. Boucé. New York: Oxford UP, 1971. 79-110.

Sato, Megumi. "Women's Reading and Creation in *Northanger Abbey*." *Shiron* 33 (July 1999): 55-68.

Sellei, Nora. "Self-Reflexive Literariness in Jane Austen's *Northanger Abbey*: Or, How a Book Reveals Itself as a Book." *British and American Studies/Revista de Studii Britanice si Americane*. 1:1 (1996): 17-23.

Selwyn, David. *Jane Austen and Leisure*. London: Hambledon Press, 1999.

Shaw, Narelle. "Free Indirect Speech and Jane Austen's 1816 Revision of Northanger Abbey." *Studies in English Literature, 1500-1900* 30:4 (Autumn

1990): 591–601.

Smith, Amy. "Julia's and Louisa's: Austen's *Northanger Abbey* and the Sentimental Novel" *English Language Notes* 30 (Sept 1992): 33–43.

Smith, Charlotte. *Emmeline: The Orphan of the Castle*. Ed. Anne H. Ehrenpreis. London: Oxford UP, 1971.

———. *Letters of A Solitary Wanderer*. Dublin: Burnet, Wogan, Brown, 1799.

Southam, B.C. *Jane Austen*. Ed. Ian Scott-Kilvert. Essex: Longman, 1975.

Spencer, Jane. *The Rise of the Woman Novelist from Aphra Behn to Jane Austen*. Oxford: Blackwell, 1986.

Spring, David. "Interpreters of Jane Austen's Social World." *Jane Austen: New Perspectives*. Ed. Janet M. Todd. New York: Holmes and Meier, 1983. 53–72.

Stovel, Bruce. *"Northanger Abbey* at the Movies." *Persuasions: Journal of the Jane Austen Society of North America*. 20 (1998): 236–247.

Sulloway, Alison G. *Jane Austen and the Province of Womanhood*. Philadelphia: University of Pennsylvannia Press, 1989.

Tandrup, Birthe. "Free Indirect Style and the Critique of the Gothic in 'Northanger Abbey'." *The Romantic Heritage: A Collection of Critical Essays*. Ed. Karsten Engelberg. Copenhagen: Univ. of Copenhagen, 1983. 81–92.

Tayler, Irene. "Jane Austen Looks Ahead." *Fetter'd or Free: British Women Novelists 1670-1815*. Ed. Mary Anne Schofield and Cecilia Macheski. Athens, Ohio: Ohio UP, 1986. 426–33.

Teachman, Debra. *Student Companion to Jane Austen*. Westport, Connecticut: Greenwood Press, 2000.

Todd, Janet M. *Jane Austen: New Perspectives*. New York: Holmes and Meier, 1983.

———. *Feminist Literary History*. New York: Routledge, 1988.

———. "Sensibility: An Introduction." *British Journal for Eighteenth Century Studies* 12 (Spring 1989): 108–09.

Ty, Eleanor. "Catherine's Real and Imagined Fears: What Happens to Female Bodies in Gothic Castles." *Persuasions: Journal of the Jane Austen Society of North America*. 20 (1998): 248–260.

Uphaus, Robert W. "Jane Austen and Female Reading." *Studies in the Novel* 19 (1987): 334–45.

Vredenburgh, Joan R. "General Tilney and the Milsom Street Merchants – Brothers Under the Skin?" *Persuasions: Journal of the Jane Austen Society of North America*. 18 (1996): 42–45.

Wallace, Tara Ghoshal. *"Northanger Abbey* and the Limits of Parody." *Studies in the Novel* 20:3 (Fall 1988): 262–73.

Williams, Carolyn O. "General Tilney and the Maidens All Forlorn: Typecasting in *Northanger Abbey*." *Women's-Writing* 5:1 (1998): 41–59.

Williams, Helen Maria. *Julia: A Novel*. Ed. Gina Luria. New York: Garland, 1974.

Wollstonecraft, Mary. *The Wrongs of Woman*. Ed. Gary Kelly. Oxford: Oxford UP, 1976.

———. *A Vindication of the Rights of Woman: with Strictures on Political and Moral Subjects*. London: J. Johnson, 1792.